DARKFELL

Also by Mary Corran

Imperial Light
Fate

Mary Corran

DARKFELL

MILLENNIUM
An Orion Book
LONDON

First published in Great Britain in 1996 by
Orion Books Ltd
Orion House, 5 Upper St Martin's Lane,
London WC2H 9EA

A CIP catalogue record for this book
is available from the British Library

ISBN 1 85798 455 2 (cased)
ISBN 1 85798 456 0 (trade paperback)

Typeset at The Spartan Press Ltd,
Lymington, Hants
Printed in Great Britain by
Clays Ltd, St Ives plc

TO TOM

The Lure

Reign of the Emperor Amestatis V, Year 50

It was Kerron who disturbed the snake.

The path was littered with loose chippings of stone and his lead foot slipped on some, sending them trickling down the slope to strike what the travellers thought was a round grey boulder. Except that the sound of the impact was not at all like that of stone on stone.

Kerron was in front because he always had to be first, whether from insecurity, or conceit, or whatever other spur pricked his pride.

Ninian, walking behind him and her cousin Ran, but ahead of Affer and Quest, at first saw only Kerron taking a startled step back, not the cause. She peered ahead, only belatedly realising the full horror of Kerron's situation as the round grey boulder in the shadow of the hilly incline stirred into life and motion. A huge oval head snapped up with lightning speed from a curved shape which was not stone but close-packed coils, animate, not petrified, not grey but silver once out of the shade. With appalling rapidity the head whipped up and back, rising from a trunk thicker than a man's thigh, only to halt and sway sinuously at a level just above Kerron's head. From this posture a pair of unblinking oval red eyes gazed down from the depths of a great silver hood, whence a narrow serpent's tongue flickered evilly in and out of open jaws.

'Don't move,' came a staccato instruction.

It was Ran's voice, the command entirely superfluous. The only creature daring to move on the open hillside was the serpent, which swayed gently back and forth with a graceful, circular motion. Ninian, frozen in place by horror, tore her eyes away from the snake with an immense effort, too frightened to bear to watch.

On the eastern horizon a wide band of gold cloud appeared with the dawn, fading to pale yellow, then at last to grey-white as Ninian dared raise her head slowly skyward. Lower down the

1

slope, beyond Kerron's perilous stand, mists still clung to the hillside and valley below with seeming malignancy, an impenetrable sea of dense grey fog from which, at odd intervals, small islands rose to the surface to break the monotony.

To the north and further east lay mountain ranges, still snow-capped even in mid-summer. To the west lay the scrubby terrain which led, in due course, to the *Uquair*, the great desert of the south. The distances were too big for Ninian to contemplate with any sense of reality.

Over the eastern mountains lay the Plains, the granary of all the peoples of the Empire, and beyond them the great city of Ammon of the Nine Levels. Further south stood the city of Enapolis, capital of the Empire, home to the Emperor who was the unity of his disparate peoples, and of Lord Quorden, High Priest of the Order of Light which held administrative and executive authority in the Empire. The city was said to be larger than Lake Avardale itself. Ninian had never seen any of the places, knowing them only by name and repute. To her, as to her four travelling companions, the totality of the Empire was less real than the Wetlands where the *akhal* lived, the lake people; one of the nine peoples who made up the Empire.

'The rest of you stay back; if you come closer the snake may strike Kerron.' Ran was stooping to the earth as she spoke, with a slow, fluid movement.

Sweat beaded Ninian's forehead as she watched her cousin, a year the younger but far more in command of herself. Ran was graceful and controlled, making no awkward or sudden moves to startle the serpent hovering menacingly over Kerron.

He was taller than the others, a Thelian of the people of the cities, not *akhal*, but dressed like them in loose white overshirt and trousers in token of their pilgrimage; unlike his fair companions his hair was black and his eyes green. His skin was normally a pale pink, but now his face was predominantly white, his expression rigid as he strove to stay completely still, displaying a courage Ninian would not have believed him to possess.

She knew she could never have stayed so still, not with that swaying silver head so close to her own. It could strike him easily, if it chose to, but did not, almost as if it dared him to move.

'Ran –'

Affer's high, boyish voice came from behind in a strangled protest, but his sister did not heed the anguished remonstrance. Ran's long, broad fingers were busy seeking and gathering two flat, heavy stones, while her sharp eyes never left the swaying serpent. The segment of the hill where they stood was sheltered, covered in the hot summer months by a blanket of dry, gold-brown grasses; Ninian wondered unhappily what else they hid, and how many more of the grey boulders littering the slope were not what they seemed.

Yet she had thought the place wonderfully peaceful when they set out before dawn that morning. There had been no breeze, only a few melancholy bird calls to disturb the silence. She had felt no forewarning of menace, of this danger lying in wait for them, for all her pride in her instinct for trouble, which so rarely led her astray.

'Kerron! Gods, help him!'

Quest's painful whisper came as Ran finally straightened. Ninian could only watch, terrified that all Ran would accomplish would be to place herself in Kerron's peril, and an irrational anger humbled her. She knew she would never have the same blind courage Ran possessed, and at the same time knew with ungenerous certainty she would rather have Ran alive than Kerron; Kerron, the cuckoo so carelessly deposited in Arcady's nest.

Why had the snake not struck? What was it waiting for, swaying with that dizzying motion, barring the way? Ninian held her breath as Ran slowly drew back her arm.

'Kerron, *run*! Now!'

As she was speaking, Ran threw her first stone, launching it with perfect accuracy at its target. As Kerron flung himself desperately back, Ran leaped forward, second stone in hand, and as the first struck the serpent's head full between the eyes, the second was already on its way, and Ran was stooping for more, all caution gone. The serpent drew itself back and up with jaws wide, ready to strike, double fangs bared, but the second stone struck hard on the first, and then Ran threw again, and a third stone, too, struck home.

Affer screamed. Kerron lay sprawled on the grass, utterly helpless as the serpent's bright red gaze flickered from him to Ran. Ninian caught her breath.

Then, with astonishing speed, the silver serpent lowered its hood, and with a contorted movement seemed to fling itself down flat on the ground, stretching out and slithering a retreat of its great length. There was a warning rustle as it writhed over the dry grasses, loose coils shifting from side to side to give momentum to its flight. Ran threw two more stones, but the snake was out of even her range. The rising sun lit on the moving silver body, a glistening stream rippling across the hillside, in departing no longer menacing but oddly beautiful.

3

Ran walked to where Kerron lay on the grass, reaching out a hand to help him up. 'Are you all right?'

Green eyes blazed in the white oval of his face as Kerron visibly fought with himself, until he could stretch out a hand to her that did not shake.

'Thanks,' he said shortly. Ran grinned, not offended by the lack of gratitude. They had been brought up as brother and sister on the same lake estate, ever since the day seventeen years before when Bellene, present Steward, had found the basket that held the infant Kerron floating on the lake by Arcady's pier. Ninian knew it had never mattered to Ran that Kerron was Thelian, not *akhal*; she had accepted him as just another cousin. Ninian never understood why she could not do the same; what difference she sensed in Kerron that repelled her. As heir to Arcady, it was her duty to accept him without reservation. But, looking at him, she knew she could not.

'Ran? Kerron? Are you hurt at all? Did it bite either of you?' Quest's voice was sharp with anxiety.

Ran shook her head. 'No, although it makes no sense. The snake could have bitten Kerron easily.'

'Thanks.' Kerron was regaining his composure if not his colour.

With an inarticulate cry, Affer ran to his sister, the green tinge to his skin more pronounced than usual from fear and fatigue. His eyes, the same blue as their home lake of Avardale, were blurred with angry tears as he clung to Ran's waist, burying his face in her loose white overshirt.

'Hush, Affer; it's all over. Don't be frightened.' Ran put her hand on her brother's fair head and stroked the feathery hair, her expression softening. Standing together, her sturdy body served to emphasise her brother's frailty, the thin limbs and ungainly body. At seventeen, she was two years the elder and much the taller of the pair, broader in the shoulder; her square features and clear blue eyes were about the same as his, but in some fashion she seemed more finished, he an imperfect imitation.

'I'm glad you're safe, Kerron,' Ninian managed at last, aware of the inadequacy of the sentiment.

'Are you?' Her sympathy for the Thelian's white face evaporated at the sneer in his voice.

'Don't sound so cross, Ninian; no one was hurt,' Ran observed over Affer's muffled head.

'You could have been killed!' Ninian was still feeling shaky and unlike herself, a lingering sense of guilt and shame at her own inadequacy making her speak more sharply than she intended.

4

Ran shrugged. 'But we weren't.'

'You're my responsibility, in my care – '

But before Ninian could say more the weight and warmth of Quest's arm was around her shoulders, and she was silenced. The comfort of his presence, the acute awareness of his touch, were almost more than she could bear. After today . . .

Angry tears came into her eyes as she let herself surrender to the agony of contact, certain, with bitterness in her heart, that to him the clasp which made her blood race was friendly, no more. Then she caught sight of Kerron, standing alone, still pale-faced, and the pain eased. Ran and Affer had one another, as close as brother and sister could ever be. For the moment she had Quest; but who was there to love Kerron, or be loved by him? Even in the midst of her misery she was sure it was better to nurse her hopeless love for Quest than to be incapable of loving. Pity for Kerron stirred.

'I wonder what it was doing; the snake, I mean.' Quest was looking at Kerron. 'Unless it was defending itself. I saw no venom sac; perhaps it wasn't even poisonous.'

The familiar deep resonance of his voice stabbed at her, and the warmth of his breath came against her neck; Ninian closed her eyes, willing her body not to make a fool of her by any betraying gesture. She loved Quest, not for his beauty – although he was beautiful, if it was fitting to use such a word – but simply because she had always loved him, ever since she could remember. They had known one another all their lives, born and bred on neighbouring estates, she at Arcady, he at Kandria. Her love for him, his for her, had always seemed a natural extension of themselves, and now she was older she longed for physical expression of her feeling.

But Quest had betrayed them both, denying her as well as himself, ever since he had announced his intention to enter the priesthood and leave her behind.

Priests of the Order of the Lords of Light were forbidden to marry; such was the command of the gods themselves, given to the first High Priest. Although Quest loved her, Ninian was aware his vocation mattered more to him than she did, which was why he had sworn himself to celibacy, even though he had not as yet taken any official vows. He was to donate his life as a sacrificial offering to the gods, giving them, too, whatever there was of his love for her, but without her consent. Her sacrifice, as well as his.

'Bellene once told us that in the old days there was a goddess who was depicted sometimes as a silver serpent,' Ran remarked, still stroking Affer's hair. 'Perhaps this snake came as a warning not to go on.'

Quest's head snapped back on his long neck; he released Ninian almost absent-mindedly and she steeled herself against resentment.

'Don't talk such nonsense; you know better than to say such things,' he said coldly. 'Or not where I can hear you, if you must.'

'It was only a joke!' Ran cast up her eyes in mock despair, and Quest smiled.

Ninian watched him covertly, contrasting the open innocence and vulnerability in the narrow oval of his face with Kerron's air of cynicism. The fair aureole of hair that curled around Quest's sculpted features, the startling amber eyes, were softer, more spiritual than Kerron's starker colouring. The Thelian's green eyes and mass of thick, black hair made him a dark and brooding figure, secretive. Ninian's heart ached, knowing the amber eyes were fixed not on her but on some inner vision she could not share; even had she wanted to.

'Well? Are we staying here all day, or are we going to move on? I thought the reason we started so early this morning was to reach the Barren Lands before the midday heat; you *akhal* have such sensitive skins!' Kerron's voice taunted them all; Ninian wondered how much of the sarcasm was intended, how much only a defence. The Thelian stood a head taller than even Ran or Quest; at nineteen, both men were destined for the priesthood. Ninian thought it incredible two such different characters should have chosen – or been chosen for – the same path.

'Of course we're going on.' Ninian thought Quest sounded irritable, unusually for him. For a brief instant, Kerron's green eyes met hers, and she knew a stab of guilt, aware he had read her distrust of him; they had never been friends. For a second time, she knew a stab of pity for him as her heart reproached her for being unkind.

'We've still plenty of time,' Ran put in as her brother raised his head, eyes dark with remembered fear. 'Are you tired, Affer? If so, we can stay here and rest for a bit, then catch up with the others later.'

'Here?' He shuddered, his thin face displaying horror at the suggestion. 'I can manage, Ran.'

'Then give Quest a push, Ninian,' Ran suggested with a grin. 'From that dreamy expression, I think he's gone to sleep standing up.'

Despite herself, Ninian giggled. She gave Quest's arm a gentle shake, blushing as she did so. He started at the touch, drawing away from her. 'Lead on then, Ran,' he said coolly, adding in an acid voice: 'Unless Kerron wants to go first.'

Kerron looked amused. 'Do you know, Quest,' he said with a half-smile, 'I believe you may be almost human after all?'

'It's only at the base of this hill, or so the pedlar said,' Ninian intervened hastily. 'Let's get on. It's going to be very hot later.'

Unnoticed, the mists had lifted from the valley floor. Far below Ninian had her first sight of their real destination, the Barren Lands where, more than sixty years before, the Lords of Light themselves had appeared to the first Quorden, Founder of the Order. They had revealed to him the means to preserve the Empire from the coming of the second great drought, which would mean the second end of the world, and in that time of revelation had altered all their lives forever. As Ninian understood it, before that time the Emperor was sole authority in the Empire; but afterwards, dominion had passed by necessity to Lord Quorden and his successors, to whom alone the gods chose to speak.

Ninian tried to see ahead, but could make out no detail except a solid mass of colour, orange-red, a blood-coloured ocean of dust.

'Are you coming?'

She shook herself; Kerron and Quest had already begun their descent, leaving her in the rear with Ran and Affer. It was now a fine summer's day, with a welcome light easterly breeze, for she was already uncomfortably warm. The *akhal* were a cool-blooded people, not like Thelians and Plainsfolk and sandmen. Ninian wondered what it was like to live in the heat of the desert as the sand people did, to feel the burning sun always overhead, even in winter.

Dull misery sapped the energy in her legs, and Ninian would have given almost anything to be home at Arcady, the lake lapping at her feet. Glancing aside, she caught sight of Ran gazing north, an entranced smile on her face.

'I wish I understood,' she said with a sigh. 'I don't see how you can yearn so strongly to get away from the Wetlands in exchange for hills and cold snow.' She shuddered. 'Let alone climb those mountains.'

'This may be my only chance,' Ran said fiercely. 'Bellene will never let me leave Arcady again as long as she's Steward; she always said if I went without her consent I could never come back, never see Affer again. And I can hardly take him with me.' She gave a mirthless laugh as she cast a glance at his frail figure. 'When Quest mentioned this pilgrimage, he must have been surprised how quickly I said I'd come.'

'But this journey *is* your dream,' Ninian responded with sudden bitterness. 'To me, it only brings the end of mine. After today, we're accounted of age, and Quest is free to enter the priesthood.'

'Of age, yes! I think the *akhal* custom of a coming-of-age journey is just a sop, because our forebears knew this was the only chance we'd ever have to get away from the lakes and the endless round of work.'

'Quest says this is a pilgrimage.'

'He would.' Ran scowled, watching Affer ahead. 'Is it that for you, Ninian? Would you have chosen to come *here*, if it hadn't been Quest who suggested it?'

'No. And I'm very grateful, Ran; I know you'd rather have gone north to the mountains, but you came with me because Bellene wouldn't let me come alone with just Kerron and Quest.' Ninian sighed. 'The gods, too, must know why I came: for me, because this is the last time I'll ever have Quest to myself.'

'Will I get a reward for my unselfishness, do you think?' But Ran plainly did not mean her question to be taken seriously.

'You saved Kerron's life. Aren't you angry he doesn't seem to care?'

Ran shrugged. 'You don't like him, Ninian, so you don't try to understand him,' she said, truthfully, but without tact. 'You're so busy thirsting for Quest that you don't see that Kerron *was* grateful; he just hates having to be. And so should I, in his place; what other choice has he always had?'

'I know.' Ninian sighed again, aware of being ungenerous. 'It's just he always rubs me up the wrong way. I wish we could go home.'

Ran frowned, staring north to the white-topped mountain range, where the peak of Mount Hylar in the distance rose highest of all. The longing in her face told Ninian where she would rather be; Ninian shook her head, acknowledging the restless energy, the impatience of restraint, which made up a large part of Ran's character.

Further down the trail Kerron was in front, walking rapidly, his longer legs eating up the distance. Behind him, Quest followed more sedately, his slender figure pacing elegantly, as if his mind was somewhere quite different. Ninian regarded his back with a new surge of self-pity. The sun was growing steadily hotter, but neither the two men, nor Ran, seemed aware of discomfort, although sweat was already trickling down Ninian's face and back. She stripped off her loose overshirt and put it in her pack, leaving on only the sleeveless knitted vest and tight leggings that *akhal* wore for swimming.

'They say you get out of the Barren Lands only a measure of what you take in with you,' she murmured, more to herself than to her cousin. 'That the gods perceive our true selves and deal with each of us as is our due. Do you think it's true?'

But Ran was not listening; she quickened her pace, and even Affer moved faster, as if he, too, was eager to reach their destination. Ninian bit her lip and went on, struggling with an ignoble desire to go back, to retreat to the safety of the familiar.

As she descended to the lowest section of the slope, she noticed all traces of vegetation had died away, leaving the stones bare. Even the insects which had troubled them on the higher gradients did not seem to have followed them down.

It was not an auspicious omen.

The others were waiting for her at the base of the hill, with various degrees of impatience, but Ninian did not notice. As she looked, she stood stock still, stunned at the sight of a burning orange-red expanse of desert, seemingly without bounds.

She stepped forward.

One moment, Ninian had been walking along the trail, her feet kicking up clouds of dust at every step. Then, in the instant she took one further step, there was a profound alteration in her surroundings, and Ninian had the sense that she had, unbeknown to herself, crossed over some invisible boundary and now found herself in a land which it seemed to her could not possibly exist within the physical confines of the Empire.

A misshapen terrain of fragmented rock formed into fantastic shapes and massive standing stones, all in a land floored by dark dust, stretched away as far as she could see. Ninian blinked. The uniform bright orange-red of the rock, of the dust at her feet, assaulted her vision, burning her eyes until they watered. Wherever she looked the brightness was all about her, pressing down on her from cloudless skies overhead.

There was only brightness and shadow, no real shade, even beneath the standing stones which stretched up vertiginously, making her dizzy. Were they natural, or had some creature or deity had a hand in placing them there, scattering them across the wide and barren vale with a careless cast? Ninian could not even begin to guess. She swallowed, her throat dry and tight.

What troubled her most was the silence. There was no breeze in the valley to stir the dust, where she could observe no footprints, neither human nor animal. There were no insects, no birds, no small creatures living among the barren stones. Nothing flew in the air or moved along the ground. The stillness and silence were absolute.

'Just think. This is where the Lords of Light appeared to our Lord Quorden,' Quest whispered. His voice sounded unearthly, and Affer started nervously. 'More than sixty years ago, when the rains began to fail. Imagine how he must have felt, how terrified and yet how exalted he must have been, to be so honoured that the gods should entrust him with our salvation.'

'I wonder what it was like. If they spoke to him in words, I mean, or if Lord Quorden just received the revelation in an instant,' Ran murmured. 'And how he managed to remember everything they said.'

'*Ran!*'

Quest's shocked voice did not disturb her. 'There's nothing irreverent in curiosity.'

'They say these lands have always been barren, even before the time of the first drought, however long ago that was,' Kerron observed softly in his turn. 'No one ever lived here. I could believe that.'

'Perhaps the gods themselves do.' Quest's expression was distant, as if he was thinking, not seeing. 'Here, where they gave us the true faith and drew us away from worship of the false goddess who was leading us to destruction, so that we might be saved from the end of the world. It seems right, doesn't it, that in this barren place the Lords of Light should save us from the coming of the drought? As if these lands are a lesson of what may come to pass if we fail them, showing us how our world once was and would become again without rain.'

'I heard one of the desert pedlars, a sandman from Arten, say Emperor Amestatis doesn't believe in the gods,' Ran commented, looking about her more with curiosity than awe. Ninian admired her courage. 'They say he and Lord Quorden are bitter enemies, and that Lord Quorden would depose him, if he could.' She stooped and picked up a small piece of the orange-red rock and crushed it easily in the palm of her broad hand; tiny fragments of stone trickled out from between her fingers, falling to the ground in a shower of dust.

'You shouldn't listen to rebel gossip, Ran. Arcady has a name for unconventionality as it is, and you, Affer, and Ninian, and even Kerron, by association, should be especially careful of what you say. Hush.' Quest held up a hand in reproof, his expression still distant. 'Don't you feel the gods themselves may be listening to you? Who knows how they might punish you for such heresy.'

'I didn't say I believed it; only that I'd heard it said.' Ran's blue eyes sparked with irritation. 'That's hardly a crime, and anyway it might be true; why not? Imagine if a priest tried to tell Bellene how to run Arcady! I shouldn't be surprised if the Emperor was no great lover of Lord Quorden. And you're not a priest yet, Quest, to question my loyalty or my faith.'

'Have you forgotten why we came here?' he challenged. 'This is a pilgrimage, an offering to the gods.'

'That was why *you* came, not me!' Ran glanced at Ninian, still irritated. 'Don't presume you know more about this place than we do; your so-called vocation doesn't convince or impress me. I don't pretend to understand you, or your reasons for wanting to be a priest; it always seems to me you believe it's a sort of competition to gain their favour.'

Kerron was watching her with an amused smile, but Ninian could find nothing humorous in the situation. The same question had occurred to her.

'The call to serve isn't so easily explained – ' Quest began.

Ran snorted. 'I imagine not, or I might understand why they chose you. What sort of gods would demand you give up Ninian for their sake, after all these years it's been plain you should be together? I don't mean to offend you, Quest,' she went on, not caring in the least, 'but it seems to me simple nonsense. We *akhal* exist as part of all life in the Wetlands, no more and no less, as we've always been; that's what really matters.'

Quest shook his head, his face clouded. 'If only it were so easy, Ran. You know I love Ninian.' The simple admission stung the listening Ninian to the heart, reminding her of what might have been. 'I never wanted to hurt her, but when the call came I could no more resist than I could stop breathing. I must lose Ninian, as she must run Arcady as Steward after Bellene, as my brother Jerom rules Kandria, but I – only those the gods summon may be priests. It's a command, no matter my own wishes.' His look invited Kerron to concur with his statement, but the other man only scowled.

'And in order to show how much more you love the gods than we do, you love Ninian and the rest of us less?' Ran demanded cynically. 'What strange gods! It sounds as if they would rather we feared than worshipped them.'

'You mustn't say such things – ' Quest began angrily. But before he could say any more Affer interrupted, giving him a violent push on the chest that almost knocked him flat.

'Stop it! Stop it, both of you!'

Ran reached for him, but Affer flinched, standing with his

hands over his ears, his narrow features pinched in pain, and there were tears in his eyes.

'You always argue, both of you, and I hate it!' His voice had not yet broken, and was still high and uncertain.

'Affer – ' Ran tried, but when she would have touched him he stepped back, out of her reach.

'No. Leave me alone!' He was shouting, holding them all at bay with the force of his emotion. 'I wish I hadn't come!'

His voice echoed in the stillness, startling them all, even Affer himself. With a wordless cry, he turned on his heels and fled, leaving behind a trail of dust hanging in the air, the only movement in the valley.

'Leave him, Ran,' Kerron advised, when she would have followed. 'He needs to be by himself for a while; you know what he's like. And you'll be able to find him easily enough.' He smiled, pointing at the ground. 'Just follow his footsteps.'

Ran hesitated, then shrugged. It struck Ninian, forcefully and unwillingly, that her cousin and Kerron were in some ways very alike, which perhaps explained their friendship. Both were essentially solitary creatures, strong-willed, careless of opinion. It always surprised her how well they seemed to understand one another, when she sometimes thought she understood neither.

'I suppose you're right.' Ran sighed. 'Poor Affer! I wish he didn't feel everything so deeply.'

'Amazing he should be your brother,' Kerron agreed dryly, and Ran laughed.

'How true. Well, Kerron? As a man with a priestly vocation,' and she shot Quest a mocking smile, which he studiously ignored, 'will you come with me and explore this place, or would you rather be left alone to ponder the great mysteries?'

'Oh, I leave that to these dreamers.' Kerron smiled unpleasantly, but an uncertainty in his expression made Ninian wonder suddenly if it was really himself he mocked. Quest shook his head, refusing the provocation.

'If we're going to separate, I think we should agree to meet here again by mid-afternoon. It's not quite midday now. Is that long enough for you?'

'After a mere seven days' walk to get here?' Kerron arched an elegant black eyebrow; his chill smile took in Quest's red face, flushed by the heat and the beginnings of sunburn. 'No, that's quite long enough for me. Coming, Ran?'

She nodded, turning as they walked away to wink at Ninian to let her know she planned for her to be left alone with Quest.

'Then we'll see you later,' Ninian commented through stiff lips, terrified Quest would notice, but he seemed quite unaware of anything beyond his surroundings.

'Enjoy yourselves!' Ran called back with a wave of her hand; Kerron sent Ninian a wicked grin to show her he understood what was happening, even if Quest did not. Furious, Ninian felt herself blush.

Silence fell once more as the pair moved out of earshot, soon out of sight, hidden by a series of standing stones.

Ninian swallowed, reminding herself that she had Quest alone for what would probably be the very last time in her life. Determination returned to her, and her spirits lifted.

She turned to face him, catching a look of wonderment on his face as he surveyed their setting, wishing she could read his mind as easily and know what he was thinking.

'It was here, Ninian; here where it all began,' Quest said breathily; it was obvious he was not seeing her at all, except as an audience. 'What do you think? If I promise to offer them the service of my life, do you think it possible the Lords of Light might read my heart and speak to me, too, as they did to Lord Quorden? Or is it too great an arrogance even to presume to think it possible?'

The sun caught his hair in a golden aureole around his well-shaped head, and Ninian was suddenly overwhelmed by awareness of his startling beauty. She drew in a deep breath. The exultation in his expression took him beyond her, far away from her. She knew a savage desire to fight the unseen gods, to bring him down and pull him back, anchoring him to earth.

'How should I know, Quest?' she said sharply. 'Perhaps they might even choose to speak to me?'

Quest's eyes snapped back into focus. For the first time on their shared journey, Ninian enjoyed the satisfaction of knowing herself the full centre of Quest's shocked attention.

Affer could hardly see for the tears streaming down his cheeks. He wiped his eyes with a grubby hand and ran on, not caring where he was going. All he wanted was to get away, away from Ninian's pain and Quest's inner turmoil, from Ran's angry impatience and Kerron's bitter tongue.

Why he had given way to his feelings he was not sure. The incident with the snake had upset him, but it was over. Yet, somehow, he felt as if something inside him, some tight part of him, had suddenly broken.

The heat bore down on him and Affer's steps began to falter. He wished again, as he had every day since they set out, that he had not come, that he had told Ran he would stay at Arcady, where even now he could be swimming in the lake, cool and safe, instead of burning in an arid desolation where he did not feel the presence of any friendly deity, no matter what Quest might say. The blazing sun overhead frightened him. He told himself not to be a fool, for everything frightened him; he was a dreadful coward. Ran always told him his fears were without cause, but that did not make them untrue, or not to him. He had no courage, only an excess of imagination, which constantly dreamed up terrors where none existed.

At long last, his tears ceased to flow, not least because he was very thirsty and dry inside, although dripping with sweat from the heat and exertion. Affer stopped, looking about for some shade where he could drink the water from the flask in his pack and wait for Ran to come and find him.

He knew she would come; she always did.

He had paid no heed to his surroundings as he ran, but now he realised he had no idea in which direction he had come, for the sun was high overhead, centred in cloudless skies. Only his footsteps in the otherwise undisturbed dust gave him any sense of security; Ran could follow them and find him, unless a wind came to blow them away. Affer thought he did not believe any breeze ever ventured to cross the Barren Lands.

He could see no sign of Ran, nor any of the others; he must have come quite a long way. He turned to face one of the odd circles of tall standing stones of the same orange-red rock and dust all around him. There was little shade to be had, even from them, now it was almost noon, but there was no other choice.

In his headlong need for escape he had not had time to comprehend the extent of his solitude, and in any case to be alone was a rare pleasure at any time, especially at Arcady, where there were two hundred other *akhal* of his kindred living on the estate. Here, however, the aloneness felt different; he did not seem to be by himself by choice, but, rather, deliberately isolated from his friends. Affer's eyes hurt from the powerful glare of the sun, and he wished he could shut it out.

Deeply disquieted, Affer crouched down in the shadow of the widest of the standing stones, trying to shrink into the narrow breadth of shade, fighting a rising panic. The absolute absence of sound now felt like a roaring in his ears, and the heaviness of the dry, hot air terrified him, making it hard to breathe.

He began to feel a rhythm to the pulsing of the sun as it beat down on him and on the land, burning them both. Affer shrank lower, kneeling in the dust, burying his head in his thin hands as he cowered away from the heat pressurising his skull, searing his fine hair and pale skin. The Wetlands were cool most of the year, and Affer had never before thought of the sun as an enemy, but now he knew it was. It was too bright, too strong.

'Oh Ran, I'm so afraid,' he moaned, lips and throat as dry as the dust on which he knelt. He wished that he could hear her familiar voice; all his passionate emotions directed to her in his terror and loneliness. Because of Ran, he had never thought himself lonely, for she was always with him, looking after him. But now she was somewhere in the arid vastness of the Barren Lands, and he could not find her, and without her he was nothing. Terror filled his mind.

It seemed to Affer that he knelt there for endless days, although it could only have been for a short time. In his despair, he reached out in his imagination, calling on Ran, on Ninian, even Kerron, willing them to come to his rescue; but there was only silence, which went on until he believed he would have given the whole part of his soul to hear a human voice.

At his lowest ebb, he thought he heard someone – not Ran, nor any voice he recognised, but a voice nonetheless, speaking to him.

'Who's there?' he whispered, lifting his head joyfully. 'Kerron, is that you?'

There was no direct answer, but still Affer welcomed the sound, until its very unfamiliarity, and uncertainty that it was not simply the product of his imagination, made him wonder if what he was hearing was really a ghost voice, or, rather, voices, since there were more than one. What were they? The residue of people or creatures who had once lived in the land before it died and became this barren nothingness? If anything had ever lived there.

'Ran, *please*,' he whispered, trusting her as he had trusted her all his life. But instead of her familiar presence the ghost voices came again, this time louder, more distinct, repeating themselves again and again in his mind:

'Mine, mine –' came a shout of triumph.

'I will be with you.'

'Mine to surrender –' spoken with fierce hunger.

'A prisoner; never free!'

As the sun continued to beat down on him, Affer found he wished the silence back instead of these angry, ugly voices, whose owners were concerned with dark emotions, with greed and bitterness, with selfish desire and deception. He put his hands over his ears, but that did not shut them out, for they spoke directly into his mind. As he crouched in the dust, moaning, it came to Affer that the voices he heard did not belong to ghosts, but to people he knew and loved, that they belonged to Ninian, and Kerron, and Quest, and Ran; not as he knew them but in other, unknown guises. These were their secret selves, their private selves, and he wanted to shut them out, the knowledge painful.

The voices in his mind ebbed and flowed. Affer knelt, trembling, while the sun hovered high over him, burning him, watching him, as if it was a giant eye that spied on his very thoughts, with only contempt for his thin, white-clad body, now liberally smeared with dust. He prayed for relief, but no gods answered him, and soon he no longer believed there were any gods in the forsaken lands.

'Do you really loathe Quest as much as all that?' Ran asked.

In profile, Kerron's angular face was easy to read; he stiffened. 'He's a fool,' he said shortly. 'Listen to him, in rhapsodies because he believes the gods will speak to him and confirm his view of his own importance! Does he think being a priest is all about such nonsense?' Green eyes glowed with secret amusement; Ran wondered what piece of knowledge he found so entertaining. 'He talks loftily of the gods, but when we reach Enapolis it is I the priests will choose for – ' He stopped abruptly, glowering at Ran, as if the disclosure were her fault. 'And if you tell anyone I said that,' he snapped, 'I'll make sure you're sorry!'

'Don't threaten me, Kerron,' Ran said, her own quick temper firing in ready response. 'Of course I won't say anything, if you don't want me to; but don't try to bully me. I'm not Affer.' She was furious, more so than the offence warranted; she fought her temper down, ignoring the nudge of anger tempting her to retaliate. 'I don't care if you outdo Quest.'

'Oh, I shall; I shall enter the political section of the service.' A quick smile escaped Kerron, against his will. 'At Arcady Bellene favours the Emperor; this will upset her.'

'You'd not use that against her?' Ran frowned, not really believing him capable of such treachery.

He shrugged. 'I shall owe the Order my first loyalty.'

'I don't understand why you mean to be a priest, and I'm sure it has nothing to do with being summoned by the gods.' She gave a hard laugh. 'I wish I were as free as you to choose my own way, but Bellene will never let me; sometimes I think she hates me.'

But Kerron seemed not to have heard her comment. 'Quest cares too much about people to rise high in the Order,' he said, speaking mostly to himself. 'He's a conventional man, with too many ties to the *akhal*; he'll stay in the Wetlands and never see the world, and never know what passed him by, but I – I know the priesthood is a route to power.' He lifted his face to the skies, to the blazing sun overhead, and there was something strange in his expression. He looked happy for once, the habitual discontent absent from his eyes. 'Do you know,' he added more conversationally, 'I think Quest may have been right, for once? There's something unusual about this place. I feel at home.'

'I wish I did.' Ran wiped her sweating forehead, wishing for shade and a breeze. 'I wonder where Affer is. Should we go after him now?'

But again, Kerron seemed not to be listening. 'I shall succeed,' he said softly. 'High Priest Borland won't last forever, and I'll be the only priest in the Wetlands with no ties of family, an outsider willing to put the Order first. Quest doesn't understand about power, about politics, which is the heart of the Order.' He broke off, suddenly hostile. 'In Enapolis, Thelians rule Order and Empire, not *akhal*,' he said fiercely. 'There, Quest will be the outsider.'

'Kerron,' Ran interrupted impatiently, 'I asked you about Affer. Can't you listen for a moment?'

'He'll be all right.'

'How would you know?' Ran found her temper rising dangerously high. Kerron's egocentric view of the world, his constant need to affirm some superiority was worse than an irritant in her anxiety. 'Is it possible for you to think of someone other than yourself?' she asked sourly. 'How nice it must be, to be so sure you're the centre of the universe, the rest of us mere satellites!'

'When that's the position you assign yourself?' Unexpectedly, Kerron laughed, although usually he was quick to take offence. 'You're just jealous, Ran. Because you couldn't be a priest because you're a woman. After all, the gods are masculine.'

'What rubbish!' Ran rounded on him, furious. 'Tell me, Kerron; why are you being so vile today? You sound as if you hate all of us, and want revenge for some deep wrong, forgetting it was Bellene who took you in when she found you on the lake. Your own people did much less for you than that!'

The reminder of his parents' desertion of him when he was an infant was unfortunate; Kerron's expression grew icy. 'What should I care for a man who spent a few moments giving himself pleasure, or for a woman who took nine months in bearing me, only to throw me away without a second thought, as if I were an unwanted kitten? Bellene and the rest of you took me in, true;

but I often wonder why. Perhaps to give you someone to whom you could feel superior, just because I can't swim so deep, or so fast!'

Ran struggled again to rein in her temper, momentarily sorry for him. 'Is that why you resent us all so? You know it's not true. You've been a brother to me and Affer, a friend. You've everything you want – from the sound of it more than Quest has, if I hear you right. You've a future with the priests, a family with us at Arcady. Isn't that enough for you?'

'You want me to be grateful to you, but for what?' Kerron's lips twisted in a bitter expression. 'Do you think I don't know Bellene wishes she'd never found me, that Ninian always disliked me? Gratitude makes poor fodder, year after year.'

He turned his head away abruptly, and in the movement Ran caught a glimpse of something shiny at his throat.

'What's that?' She reached up a hand to his neck and tugged at the thin gold chain that met her searching fingers; a small turquoise stone depending from it. Kerron pulled away, but not in time; Ran fixed him with an accusing eye. 'That's Affer's amulet,' she said coldly. 'He said he'd lost it.'

'I found it by the lake. I was going to give it back to him.'

Ran stared at Kerron incredulously. His expression was sullen, resentful and defensive at the same time. She suddenly wanted to hit him, very hard indeed. 'You took it?'

Kerron shrugged carelessly. 'I borrowed it; Affer won't mind.'

'I thought he was your friend.'

'Then he'd lend it to me, wouldn't he?' Kerron said with a smirk.

New rage built in her, rising in force until she no longer cared to contain it. Ran lashed out, slapping Kerron's face with all the strength of her right arm behind the blow; the motion was intoxicating. 'How dare you?' she hissed. 'That amulet belonged to our mother, and she gave it to Affer before she died. It's all he has of her. How dare you take it? You're always talking about how other people hurt your feelings, but you never care who you hurt.' An evil impulse compelled her to add, not meaning it: 'Perhaps Bellene was right, and she should have left you on the lake –'

She stopped, knowing she had just dealt him an inexcusable blow. Kerron's left cheek flared in scarlet lines, tracking the marks of her fingers. Ran felt a moment of remorse as Kerron touched his face with long fingers, green eyes sparking with anger, and something more.

'It's good to know what you really think of me,' he said in a voice that shook, his face the colour of milk. 'I used to think we were friends. Which would have been an error of judgment, wouldn't it?'

She was torn. Her temper, although it flared rapidly, was also quick to cool, and Ran was already ashamed of herself; but for once it was a relief not to control her anger, to say whatever came into her mind.

'You don't make it easy for anyone to like you, Kerron,' she retorted. 'You have to be a friend to have one, which means being able to consider someone other than yourself.' Righteous anger suffused her, an oddly pleasurable and physical sensation, as if she was letting go of all the rage and resentment which had festered in her mind for years: her fury at Bellene, for keeping her close to Arcady: at her parents for dying and leaving Affer in her care: even at Affer himself, for needing her and tying her down. 'When have you ever done anything for anyone but yourself?'

'A fine accusation, coming from you!' Kerron's anger was better controlled but he, too, seemed to obtain a measure of relief from unrestrained speech. 'You talk of freedom, saying how desperate you are to leave Arcady, making Affer feel guilty for being alive, because he knows you blame him for keeping you there! You're quite as selfish as I am, strutting around, thinking yourself hard done by because Bellene won't let you go, when all you're good for is gutting fish and spinning flax!'

For one frozen moment, Ran was too hurt to respond, but the moment did not last. 'A fine priest you'll be,' she struck back. 'Preaching sacrifice and restraint for the common good, that the gods care for us, when you don't believe in any gods, and you don't care for anyone except yourself! You're a hypocrite of the worst kind, Kerron, and if they let you become a priest it says something strange about the gods and their choice of ministers.'

At that, he slapped her back, as hard as she had struck him, and she was glad of it, glad to have proven him no better than herself. Her face stung, but Ran managed a triumphant smile. It was a mistake.

'All you *akhal* are less than human,' Kerron whispered, his voice trembling with rage and bitterness. 'You used to laugh at me, because you could do things I couldn't, but wait and see! When I rule the Wetlands as High Priest you'll get a taste of your own medicine.' His face was half red and half white beneath the mass of black hair; Ran had never thought him quite so alien. She let out a laugh to hide her unease, and Kerron flushed scarlet from the neck up.

'Dream your little dreams, Kerron,' she said unpleasantly. 'If they make you feel important, what harm can they do?'

A shutter came down over his features. Ran was made unwillingly aware that something in their relationship had shattered, that they were both guilty of speaking unforgivable truths. Ran knew herself in the wrong, quite as much as he.

'Kerron, I won't say I'm sorry. But I shouldn't have said what I did.'

He looked at her, evidently waiting for something more. Ran nearly swallowed her pride, but remembrance that he, too, had said hurtful things held her back. She stood stiff-backed under his surveillance.

'So be it, then.'

Kerron turned away, a deliberate rebuff. He did not look back as he strode away, heading further into the Barren Lands, a tall, lonely, white-clad figure against the orange-red of the landscape.

Ran felt a chill of misgiving as she watched him go. It was only Kerron, and he deserved what she had said, but nevertheless her impatience had led her into cruelty. She had hurt him, more than he had hurt her because he was more vulnerable. She waited, but he did not come back.

Ran started to retrace her steps to where they had left Quest and Ninian. The others were long gone, but once she found the spot she sought out Affer's trail, her breathing coming rather fast as she kept her eyes lowered to the dust, following the scuffed footprints leading east.

She did not want to, would not, think about Kerron.

Kerron strode out, his step lengthening in time with the rapid pulsing of his heart as he crossed the burning ground, the rhythm of mind and body pressing him on. He was blind to thought, aware only of sensations of rage and loneliness and hunger for revenge for all the unspecified injuries life had dealt him.

As he walked on, all the dark feelings inside himself rose to the surface, and it seemed to Kerron that they were welcomed in the barren landscape surrounding him, filling up the open spaces where there had been only stone and dust and empty sky. He had never imagined that feelings could have so much power, nor understood them so plainly as echoes from and to himself; he revelled in sensations, supported by their force, his hungry loneliness briefly sated by a self-righteous justification he could believe, at that moment, raised him above his companions in some moral or rational sense.

His pace slowed, then finally ceased. Kerron tried to believe he was coldly happy to be free from any lingering sense of obligation to the *akhal*; even to Ran. He knew, now, what she really thought of him: alien, outcast, a cuckoo set down unwanted in Arcady's nest. The pain of knowing it would pass.

'*The akhal are an unnatural race, a perversion of what is right and pure, made so by unwholesome magic. They are less than the dust beneath your feet, Thelian.*'

Kerron whirled round, wondering where the voice came from; he wanted to see the person who had spoken aloud what was so close to his own thoughts. But there was no one visible in the empty landscape, no rocks nearby large enough to provide shelter.

'Who's there?' he called softly. 'Who are you?'

'*Listen to me, and I will help you, Thelian. I am your friend,*' came the voice, reassuring. Kerron looked again, blinking in the glare of the sun, but still could see no one. He was quite alone, yet he no longer experienced his familiar isolation. He shivered, smelling the heat and dust of the day.

'I'm listening,' he whispered, licking dry lips. 'Where are you? Let me see you.'

'*You cannot see me, yet I see you, and have chosen you. You are to be a priest in the Order of the Lords of Light, and you will be favoured, and rise high,*' returned the voice, and Kerron shook his head, puzzled, for it seemed to him that the voice was speaking directly into his mind, and that he did not hear it at all in the conventional sense. '*Be patient,*' consoled the voice. '*The akhal will fall to the darkness, when it comes. I promise you so much, Thelian. And you shall rule them.*'

'Is it true?' Kerron's own voice sounded breathless in his ears. 'Do you mean it?' His anger fell away, and in his mind he knew a sharp exultation that he had been right in what he said to Ran. Here, in this place where the gods had spoken to the first Quorden, something had spoken to him, too, had welcomed him and chosen him. 'Then I shall hear you,' he murmured. 'Just tell me what I must do.'

'*You will know, when the time comes. Farewell, Thelian.*'

There was no sound, no movement, but all the same he knew that the owner of the voice had departed on the final word.

All his life, Kerron had believed himself destined for greatness; now he knew it to be true. This journey to the Barren Lands had done far more than mark him as adult, the old *akhal* custom serving only to reinforce his conviction that he had been born for a reason. And he was no longer alone.

'Thank you,' he said, with heartfelt gratitude.

It was perhaps the first time in his life he had known real thankfulness, without bitterness or resentment, for a favour freely given. Kerron's lips creased in a wide smile as he looked up into the brightness of the sky, staring straight at the sun without blinking, and he laughed aloud, and heard the sound of his own voice echoing back from the vast, empty spaces all around him.

Ninian matched her pace to Quest's, wishing he would emerge from his thoughts and talk to her. The silence made her profoundly uneasy, although she could not have explained why it was disturbing. It seemed to her that there was something about the place that defied the apparent emptiness, making her feel she was being observed.

'Don't you wish you could see something alive? Apart from us,' she ventured at last, daring Quest's discouraging expression.

'Why? Don't you see? These lands serve as a warning of the dangers of the first great drought, and the second to come, unless we obey the will of the gods,' he said shortly. 'No wonder the Lords of Light appeared in this place; there's something here.'

'I know. I feel it too.' Ninian wished she did not also feel the sweat trickling down her back and between her breasts.

Quest glanced at her. 'You're not very suitably dressed,' he observed, apparently indifferent to the curve of her breasts in the close-fitting vest; he did not look as if the heat was troubling him, still wearing his long linen overshirt with its full sleeves.

'I don't believe the gods care what I am, or am not, wearing,' she said, beginning to be annoyed, not least by his lack of interest in her anatomy. The heat stirred her blood, sensitising her skin to the soft material, making her aware of the contact. 'After all, they watch over us all the time, or so the priests say!'

'Don't be so irreverent, and do be quiet. I want to think.'

Quest strode on, not seeming to care whether she kept up with him or not. Ninian sighed and blinked back tears, lengthening her stride, glad her legs were only a little shorter than his. She and Quest were built to a similar scale, taller and slighter than average for *akhal*, with long, slender limbs, but his hair, though fair like her own, curled thickly about his head, where hers was as straight as reeds. And, too, there was something about Quest that Ninian thought would have identified him even in a multitude of their people; not his beauty, which she did not envy, her own looks only moderate, but those qualities of dreamer and idealist. He possessed, too, the attendant selfishness of those attributes, but in her heart she knew he was kind, generous and thoughtful, when his attentions were not engaged by perceptions of the gods.

Watching him, it tore at her to know that in so short a time he would be lost to her. It was such a *waste*.

'Can you explain to me, Quest, why you must be a priest?' she asked suddenly. 'Please?'

She thought he had not heard, for he was silent for a long time and she hesitated to repeat the question; but at last his face relaxed, and he smiled. 'Shall we stop here?' he asked, pausing, much to her relief. 'I'll try, Ninian; but it's hard to express what the call feels like.'

'Please.'

'I suppose I first felt it when I was only fifteen: Affer's age. But I fought it, because it seemed to me it would mean the end of all the things I was brought up to expect – love; a family.' The meaningful look he gave her, so plainly encompassing his feelings for her, made her momentarily furious. 'It isn't so much that I hear the gods calling me, Ninian, but more a *sureness* that this is what I have to do. Not what I want, but what I must. If life has meaning, if death is not something to fear, this is right.'

Wounded, Ninian bit her lip. 'How can you know?' she argued irritably. 'It sounds like *wanting* to me. What if I *wanted* to be a priest? But of course, you'd say I couldn't be, because I'm a woman; even though the vocation might be mine, as much as yours. Is there really so much difference between us?'

'Oh, Ninian! Why do you always make things so personal?' Quest sounded exasperated. 'You don't understand. Just be satisfied to be Steward of Arcady in time. You'll have the care of two hundred people in your hands; that's not so very different from what my duties will be as priest.'

She knew perfectly well that he did not believe what he was saying for a moment, and she gritted her teeth.

'Don't patronise me. It seems odd to think of you as a priest, standing between all of us and the gods, as if we weren't good enough for them to hear,' she observed unpleasantly. 'Bellene said that in the old days there were no priests; each of us would say our own prayers, as we liked. You say the gods prefer some kind of hierarchical order – '

'That was hardly the same thing. And it isn't a question of precedence,' Quest interrupted irritably.

'But that's how it sounds,' Ninian retorted. 'Because my view is different from yours doesn't make it less valid.'

'You've no authority for your *view*, as you call it,' he said calmly. 'The Lords of Light communicate directly with the High Priest of the Order himself; that is his authority, and ours – that is, the authority of the priests – comes from him. Your opinions are formed subjectively, influenced by your wishes and ties of family and friendship, and opinions are all they are. That's why the priests of the Order must be celibate, so that they objectively minister equally to all those in their care, after their first duty, which is to the gods themselves.'

'And you call that objective? As if love detracts from duty?' Ninian asked bitterly.

'But spiritual love is different.'

'Only in your eyes!' Ninian was surprised at the depth of her irritation. 'Is a parent's sacrifice for a child any less than the sacrifices we make in temple? One may be bound up in human love, the other in faith, but they seem the same to me, born of duty and affection.'

'That's exactly why you don't understand it when I speak of my calling,' Quest said, sounding equally annoyed. 'You reduce everything to a personal level! You know nothing of dreams of what might be, of a perfect communion with the gods themselves.'

'How useful!'

He ignored the jibe. 'The gods have given us a warning, not least in the existence of these lands here, as well as their promise that if we submit to their rule and give up our false worship, then our empire will survive; but if we don't, if our faith fails, then our world will wither and die in a second drought worse than the one history claims came before. If we don't keep faith with the gods, our world will all be like this.' He made a gesture with both hands, encompassing the barrenness around them. 'And we will all die a dry death!'

At the description of *akhal* hell, Ninian bit back the retort that sprang to her mind, and soon she found it was forgotten from another cause. Quest's voice faded as she stared at him, taking in his familiar, loved figure as if she were really seeing him for the first time. A sudden wave of intense physical desire for him spread through her, and she arched her back in response, aware of a warmth growing in her stomach.

Quest must have sensed her change of mood, for he asked suddenly, in a voice grown unexpectedly husky: 'Why are you looking at me like that?'

'Like what?' Ninian was shocked at the invitation in her own voice. What was she doing? Surely she had too much pride to throw herself, unwanted, at this man, no matter what she was feeling. Was she trying to make Quest break his vow? *But he hasn't made it yet*, she told herself, shivering despite the heat.

He took a step towards her, until their bodies were almost

touching. His skin was smooth, soft. 'Ninian – ' he said, sounding hoarse. 'Don't. Don't look at me like that.'

'Why not? You're not a priest yet,' she whispered. She lifted a hand tentatively to his chest, feeling the burning heat of his skin through the thin shirt. With incredulous joy, she saw in his eyes that his desire for her matched her own need for him. A lingering remnant of common sense warned her to stop while she still could, to step back, away from danger, but she had held herself in check for so long that she simply swept sense aside, her breathing coming more rapidly.

'Ninian – ' Quest's voice trembled, then hardened. 'Why not? Why not? Perhaps the gods have given you to me.' Then his hands were at her waist, and his eyes darkened to a deep gold as he pulled her roughly to him, their bodies crushed together in mutual passion, and Ninian did not hear his last observation, lost in sensation as he bent his head and kissed her, hard; his violence found an answering spark in herself.

The sun blazed down on them, but neither Ninian nor Quest remembered where they were, or why.

She was bound up in sensation, every nerve-ending responsive to Quest's lightest touch, every moment ecstasy. Even as he whispered, 'Why shouldn't I have what all men have, just this once? Perhaps the gods approve?' she heard nothing, knew only the feeling of rapture of a hunger soon to be satisfied. By the time they at last lay naked on the hard ground, dust-covered bodies entwined, she was heedless of everything but Quest's physical presence, unaware of discomfort, of the burning sun overhead.

Their lovemaking was more the resolution of a long-fought battle between them than any act of love, both fighting to take what they wanted from the other, rendered conscienceless by the strength of desire, yet both surrendering to it with an equal willingness. There was no guilt, no clumsiness, yet the act was somehow innocent, as if it was meant to be. Ninian had never been so aware of her own body, as if she was able, in some fashion, to observe the internal workings of her physical self. She was both *there*, and at the same time absent, a mere observer.

For a brief moment, her pleasure checked, and she was in herself again.

'*I shall have a child from this,*' she said in a half-whisper, her head thrown back. She felt as if the words were forced from her, although Quest did not hear them, and Ninian was seized with an absolute conviction that what she had said was true; this was no mere intuition. She had no doubt at all that from their actions would come a daughter, born of this moment in the dust.

'Sarai. I shall call her Sarai, after my mother,' she gasped softly, distracted as her body moved in time with Quest's, the future, or so she thought, not yet irrevocable. She cried out, wondering as she did so which of the many moments of pleasure was the one which sealed her child's existence, bringing Sarai from the realms of the possible to the real.

Afterwards, as she lay with her head on Quest's smooth chest, Ninian wondered why she was so sure that what she had said was true, that Sarai was no dream but real, and it occurred to her she should say something to Quest. She stirred, almost speaking the words aloud, but something made her hesitate, and, greedily, she hugged her secret to herself, not admitting the dishonesty. This was hers, this knowledge, just as this other life was growing in her body, not his, and she would not share it yet, while it still was new and precious.

Quest was almost asleep. Ninian lay still, becoming aware of discomfort, of her skin burning in the unfamiliar heat of the sun, of the hardness of the ground and the hot stickiness of her body; she reached for her vest, lying in the dust where Quest had discarded it.

'What's the matter? Where are you going?' Quest asked drowsily, as her weight left him. He sounded frightened. Ninian slipped the vest over her head, and he closed his eyes again. She sat back on her heels, looking down at the man she had always loved.

Love for him was still there, but not in the form she had believed. Not as, so the legends had it, Sythera and Columb, first of the *akhal*, had loved one another, nor as their daughter Arkata had loved her chosen Adamon, for whom she had mourned lifelong after his death. She loved Quest as a friend, no more than that.

Ninian felt her face flame as she realised that what she had thought of as a passionate, romantic love had been nothing more than self-deception; she had been more in love with the idea of loving Quest than the reality. She had been, as Bellene had told her often enough as she was growing up, a spoiled child crying: '*I want*' for what she could not have.

Unshaded by sexual infatuation, she could look at Quest with new eyes, her mind and body now uncoupled, and Ninian saw a very young and innocent man, far younger than herself in maturity, one for whom the world still held its illusions. With his remarkable eyes closed in sleep, exposing the vulnerability in his face, Ninian felt a fierce protectiveness, wondering how hard the fall would be when Quest's illusions finally shattered.

'What have I done to you?' she whispered softly.

His body was well-formed, muscled impressively about the chest, legs and shoulders, as were most *akhal* from constant swimming in the lakes. Quest's skin was hairless, unlike Kerron's, which was covered with fine, dark hairs on his arms, legs and chest, and even on his face, where no *akhal* grew hair; a difference between Thelian and *akhal*. Legend had it that all nine peoples of the Empire were ultimately descended from the same Thelian stock, but Ninian was not sure she believed it.

Quest's body was as familiar to her as her own. They had swum together since they were children. Ninian was ashamed, not at their lovemaking, which was natural and fine, but at her self-deception, and not a little at her part in making Quest break his self-imposed vow of celibacy.

'I'm sorry,' she began. 'I shouldn't – '

He stirred and interrupted her, sitting up abruptly. 'Don't be. Do you know, I used to lie awake at night dreaming of loving you, Ninian? Even though I knew I shouldn't even be thinking about you.' He smiled in lazy fashion. 'But here, in this place, I felt the Lords of Light themselves smile on me, and give you to me.'

'Oh?' She froze, suddenly furious. 'I'm not theirs to give, I think.' But she knew he had not meant to offend her. 'Then you're not angry that I seduced you?'

'Did you? I thought it was I who tempted you. But no.' He looked at her, his expression open and trusting. 'How else could I know exactly what I shall be giving up when I become a priest? I'll always be grateful for this gift.' He gave her a searching look. 'And you? How do you feel? This must be the only time, Ninian.'

She nodded. 'It was a mistake, Quest; my mistake.' She lifted her head, surprising a look of shocked hurt on his face. Confused, she hurried on: 'I've been making a fool of myself over you for years, and you put up with it. I do love you, Quest, but as a friend. I was infatuated with the idea of you. But thanks to you this has been a true rite to adulthood today.'

She would not tell him what they had done, that they were to have a daughter. Ninian hugged the secret to herself, not sure whether she was silent from some obscure need for reprisal, or whether it was simply that she did not want to share the knowledge yet. On their return to the Wetlands, Quest and Kerron would go immediately to Enapolis for instruction; it was no time to tell him. Bellene would welcome a child, for the resources of Arcady were not overstretched at present; there was food in plenty, and space.

'We should go and find the others; it's getting late.' She got to her feet, stretching. 'Ouch! I think the sun's burned parts of me it shouldn't.'

Quest stayed where he was, frowning. 'I dreamed,' he said abruptly. 'I dreamed just now that you hated me, that you wanted to hurt me.'

'Me?' Ninian stepped into her leggings.

'Now you say this was all a mistake.' He stared coldly into the dust, not looking at her.

A chill ran up Ninian's spine. 'Nonsense, it's your imagination,' she said quickly, suppressing an upsurge of guilt; he could not possibly know.

'Perhaps. This place is enough to give anyone dreams.' But it was not an answer. Without any trace of embarrassment, Quest rose to his feet and bent to retrieve his own clothes, frowning over their dusty condition. Ninian noticed his hair was saturated with red dust.

When they were both ready, Quest gestured north. He did not hold out his hand to her, and Ninian was made uncomfortably aware the omission was deliberate. Were they, then, no longer even friends? Had she destroyed even that?

Yet when she looked at Quest, she could see from his expression he was once more in thrall to the atmosphere of the Barren Lands, dreaming of his gods and not of her. In the distance, as she shaded her eyes, Ninian could make out three figures grouped severally by a large boulder, each standing separate, as if there had been a quarrel.

'I wonder, did something happen to them here? Did this strangeness come to them, too?' she asked aloud. There was something about the place, something that felt wrong. Would she ever know or understand why she and Quest had succumbed on impulse?

'We'll never be the same, none of us, because we came here today,' she said quietly, again with the frightening sensation that the words were being forced out of her, that she had no knowledge of intent to speak them.

Quest turned to her. 'What was that?'

'Nothing.' Ninian sighed, knowing she lied, unwillingly aware she had spoken only the truth, even if she had not known it until then. 'I wish we hadn't come.'

But Quest did not hear her as he bent his head to one side, listening intently in the silence.

Ninian wondered, uneasily and unhappily, whose voice he thought he heard.

Chapter One

Reign of the Emperor Amestatis V, Year 60

1

Ninian stood up, knuckling her aching back. Two bearded sandmen from the south, dark-skinned men clad in robes once white but now an indeterminate grey, heads covered by the green and yellow skull-caps of the Denib tribe, waited as she beckoned two *akhal* men to bring forward the crates they had agreed in exchange.

'Twenty lengths of linens, and a dozen vials of fever medicine,' she said, making it not quite a question.

'That is so, lady.' The taller of the two men bowed low, golden eyes watching intently as the crates were loaded onto the raft. 'And in return you have received fifty man-weight of our finest salt.'

'Then we're both satisfied. Are we your final call?'

'Indeed, lady; now we return home to Arten.'

'Have you come from Ismon?' Ninian named the most northerly of the quartet of lakes that made up the Wetlands.

The sandman shook his head. 'No, lady; we were not given leave by the Order to go so far, although we made submission, of course. We have been east to Weyn only, and here. We do not go to Harfort; strangers are not welcome there these days.'

Ninian frowned. 'I've heard of no trouble in the north.'

The two sandmen exchanged looks; the elder glanced about, then spoke in low tones. 'No trouble here in the Wetlands, no, lady; but the rebels are active in Ammon, and elsewhere, too, and thus travel is frowned on now. They say rebels may even have escaped here, to the Wetlands, to hide, waiting for the signal to rise. They are against the rule of the priests; fighting to restore the Emperor to what he once was.'

Ninian stiffened, not liking the direction the conversation was taking in so public a place, even within the bounds of Arcady; the sandmen could, after all, be testing her. Such things did occur; the widespread unrest throughout the Empire encouraged such suspicions. 'There are always tales,' she said coolly. 'But thank you, friends, for this news, for it explains why we've had few travellers here lately, and know little of what goes on in the world outside.'

'Then we must be on our way, lady.' The man inclined his head.

Ninian did not try to detain him, waiting politely as the *akhal* helped the sandmen launch their raft into deeper water, from where they began to pole expertly east, to the river that led away south from the lake. By the pier, men and women were gathering up the bags of salt to carry to the curing houses, for use in preserving the fish which composed the staple diet of the *akhal*. Once salted, the fish would be smoked in the cone-shaped smoking houses before finally being stored in cool caverns dug into the hillside behind the houses. Ninian watched, momentarily idle in the late afternoon. It was late spring, her favourite season, when the skies seemed widest and the lake at its most clear.

Away to the western boundary with the Wellwater estate where the reeds grew thickest she could see Sarai, her nine-year-old daughter, in the company of several friends, all busy twisting the sweet-smelling reeds into the plaits used for fuel. Sarai stood waist-deep in water, her long, supple figure enough to make any mother proud; she was laughing, looking happy for once, and Ninian smiled.

'*Oh!*'

The startled exclamation came from a woman on the shore, pointing agitatedly east. Ninian turned in response.

'Gods, what is it?' she breathed.

Far away, beyond the mountains, perhaps as far off as the Plains of Ashtar, a solid-seeming column of pale green light soared upward to the skies. Ninian shaded her eyes, thinking she could make out another flash of colour in the column, a deep blue, just before the light suddenly vanished and she heard a crash of thunder as the eastern skies grew dark.

'There's a storm coming,' someone remarked. Sounds of thunder carried over the mountains in the clear air, and at once lightning, too, crackled in the distance, forking down from dark grey clouds.

From somewhere west and north a bell began to sound, beginning with three staccato clangs. Ninian listened, identifying both sender and question. Jerom from Kandria, the estate neighbouring Arcady's eastern border, was sending a message to the priests at Wellwater, demanding an explanation of the green light. He was quick off the mark, but then he was Quest's elder brother.

A lighter bell rang overhead, only once. Ninian returned to look up at the tower of the great house of Arcady, raising and waving an arm in answer to the summons: one bell was her call. The shadowy figure standing by the window withdrew, and Ninian sighed; Bellene grew more imperious with each passing year.

She trotted along the path linking pier and house, recently paved at her own suggestion, since whenever it rained the track became a muddy slide. Ran, who had evidently also heard the bell, emerged from the western side of the house, Affer as ever at her side. Both followed Ninian as she made her way along the broad façade of Arcady.

'What do you think she wants this time?' Ran inquired irritably.

'Probably to talk about that light. Did you see it?' Ninian opened the door to the tower, a rounded protrusion built onto the original house at the front eastern corner, dark stone covered with creeper. It was dimly lit inside by tall slits up the length of the narrow stairway, although it was bright enough at the top.

'We did.' Ran held the door open for Affer, then let it slam. Ninian held her tongue, guessing her cousin's mood to be as stormy as the eastern clouds.

As they emerged into the octagonal tower room, Ninian thought she would account it a good day if, just for once, she did not have to arbitrate an argument between Ran and Bellene. However, the offended expression of the Steward of Arcady at finding her heir accompanied by other young relatives did not encourage Ninian to hope that today would be anything above the commonplace.

The sun had set, slipping behind the western horizon, and it was the time of evening when there was usually a pause in the activities of those who lived in the Wetlands. Even the wind and the birds seemed to be still, to hold their collective breaths in hushed expectancy; nothing disturbed the surface of the lakes, no fish came up to feed.

Ninian observed the nightly spectacle from one of the northern windows of Bellene's tower, the highest point in Arcady, momentarily forgetful of her companions, who sat in an ominous and accusatory silence. Ran and Bellene were both in fine form.

She stared out into the cool, damp air of twilight. West, on the far side of Lake Avardale, lay the distant lights, coming on now as lamps were lit, of the Wellwater estate. None of the old *akhal* family lived there now. It was owned by the Order, home to the priests and their guard and administrative centre of the Wetlands, supported by tithes and day-labour from *akhal* estates around the lake. The white dome of the temple in the grounds glowed in the moonlight, and Ninian wondered momentarily what Quest was doing, whether he, too, was looking at the lake. Did he still observe this nightly custom, or had his steady rise in the priesthood forbidden him such a simple pleasure?

On the eastern shore, nearer to Arcady, on the far side of the river lay the boundary of the Kandria estate where Quest had been born and where his elder brother, Jerom, held the reins. The main house and many of the outbuildings were already lit up. Smoke rose from drying sheds at the rear, drifting up to darkening skies; further back and east the sails of the mill which ground nuts into flour – for the soil was too poor for grain crops – moved only stiltedly in the absence of any real breeze. The lights on the estate marked out a plan of the buildings, similar in design to Arcady, although Arcady had no mill, specialising instead in febrifuges, trading medicines and nursing skills for other staples.

There was no storm in the east, now; it had passed over while Ran and Bellene were arguing, a fitting commentary, Ninian had thought at the time. She felt oddly restless. Quest had remarked how often the rains failed on the Plains lately, a disaster for the grainfields of the Empire, but this storm seemed to give the lie to his observation.

It was almost time. The moon was rising over the lake, lighting dark shapes of tiny islets that dotted the waters, distinguishing the one true land amongst them, Sheer Island, which stood at a point equidistant between Arcady, Wellwater and Kandria. The stark shape of the high cliff, known at Arcady as Arkata's cliff after the foundress of the estate, marked the north of the island, rising to the night sky in shadow form; a sharp pillar of rock Ninian, who did not care much for heights, had never climbed, although she knew Ran had done so for a dare. Legend said Arkata had climbed it, too.

'Has it started yet?'

Ran came to join her at the window, peering out and down without any of the nervousness Ninian felt; she longed to take hold of Ran's shirt and pull her back.

'Not yet.' She frowned in disapproval at her cousin's appearance; Ran's short hair was a tangled mess, her blue shirt and loose trousers muddy; she looked as if she had been digging the garden in them, and probably had.

32

Ran glanced down. 'Don't say it, Ninian!' She shrugged her solid shoulders impatiently. 'It seems such a waste of time to worry about clothes.'

'You're too old to be so careless.' Bellene's acerbic voice enunciated the words distinctly, as if she was eager to continue their earlier argument. The Steward of Arcady was at her most formal, white hair carefully coaxed into a high topknot; only the old among the *akhal* wore their hair long, since it was a nuisance when wet, even feather-fine *akhal* hair which dried in an instant. This evening, Bellene had chosen to wear a full robe of dark green with a high collar and a belt of silver links for her middle, since she had abandoned her waist a decade before at a mere seventy-five years of age. Her formal attire was matched by an expression of rigid disapproval, one Bellene wore more often than most of late.

'Does it really matter?' Ran muttered, her face set and angry.

Ninian glanced back. Bellene was frowning, lips pursed and grey eyes only half-open. She was still, despite her age, a tall woman, only a little bent by her years, although her once powerful muscles were wasted, and her hands and fingers were stiff, with inflamed joints. The last winter seemed to have added to the collection of wrinkles on her long face, which had a more noticeable tinge of green in it than most *akhal*, and Ninian was surprised to observe an air of frailty in the old woman. The coming of spring had not worked its usual rejuvenating effect.

'It's beginning. Look. Look there!' Ran pointed towards Sheer Island.

A wide pebbled strand was all that stood between the main house of Arcady and the lake front to the north, where the water was shallowest. West, it deepened sharply, beyond the jetty where the boats and rafts were drawn up for the night.

Out on the lake, rays of moonlight caught a flicker of some darker gleam beneath the water. Sparks of blue-green light seemed suddenly to fan out from around the island in all directions, setting the whole lake on fire with colour, lights weaving from side to side as if each point were alive and in motion. Some *akhal* told their children the lights were the monster, Avar, that lived in the deepest reaches of Lake Avardale, from where it swam to the surface when the moon rose, drawn by its shining, to swim and dance in the shallower waters and eat naughty *akhal* children. Certainly, if she did not look too closely, Ninian thought she could imagine the outline of a creature, with wings and a long tail.

She shook her head; she was too old to believe such stories.

'I wish they would stay,' Affer said softly, startling Ninian, who had forgotten he was there. His serious face was very pale.

Ran looked up sharply. 'Why?'

Affer shook his head. At twenty-five he was little changed from the boy who had been an unwilling pilgrim a decade before. He was still too thin, his narrow face still distressingly expressive. Ninian wished he had been able to learn at least a measure of self-protection, but feared he never would.

'The lights frighten me,' he said nervously, his eyes darting from Ran to the window. 'They're so beautiful. But sometimes I think they call me.'

'Rubbish.' Ran scowled.

'I know.' Affer turned away, face set. Ninian thought Ran looked worried, and wondered why, then forgot Affer as words forced themselves on her, and she found herself saying:

'The lights are more than they seem. They matter to us, to all *akhal*, and to Avardale most of all.'

'Is that one of your future truths?' Ran asked irritably. 'And if so, is that it?'

'Calloran, your rudeness is outrageous!' Bellene sounded more than usually peevish. 'Well, Ninian?'

'It was, and no, I don't know any more.' Ninian sighed. Since their return from the Barren Lands all those years ago, she had found herself plagued at intervals with a faculty for speaking prophecies at moments over which she had absolutely no control. She could recognise the sayings were true, but no more. Looking at Affer, she thought perhaps she was fortunate that was all she had to endure; he, poor boy, was far worse off than she. She wondered again what Quest and Kerron had gained from their pilgrimage, but the subject seemed taboo between them, and they had never discussed it.

'It's not very helpful, is it?' Ran commented.

Ninian smiled ruefully. 'Not much. Are you coming down to the hall? The gong should sound for supper any moment now.'

'I don't think so. I'm not hungry; I think I'll go for a swim. I'll see you later.' With that, Ran walked to the stairs and jumped down three at a time, making more noise than was necessary.

'Poor child,' Bellene observed detachedly. 'So much energy, and so little patience! Her namesake, Arkata's daughter, was much the same, or so they said. She takes after my youngest sister, her grandmother, just as you, Ninian, are like my brother; your grandfather was a reliable young man.'

Ninian thought of protesting on Ran's behalf, but knew it would do no good; Affer simply hung his head, a gesture guaranteed to irritate his grand-aunt.

34

'Come along, then, both of you! Help me up.' Bellene beckoned imperiously. She held out her arms. 'Calloran may not be hungry, but I've an appetite this evening.'

'What do you really think?' Ninian asked curiously. 'About that column of green light we saw, I mean.'

'I did realise what you were talking about.' Bellene snorted. 'When I was a girl, they would have said it was to do with the old gods whose temple once stood on Sheer Island; there were always lights in the old Empire, before the coming of the priests. I can recall a great lightstone there, from the eastern islands; it was called the Tearstone, and they said Arkata placed it there herself. Was it blue or green?' She frowned, trying to remember. 'I'm not sure; it was so long ago that the priests came and tore down the temple and broke up the stone. It was a great pity.'

'Do you really think the light over the mountains might be connected, Bellene?' Affer asked nervously. 'What does it mean?'

'There was a temple on the Plains, too, in the old days,' Bellene mused; then her mood changed. 'How should I know?' she snapped, something in her expression warning Ninian she knew more than she would say. 'No doubt High Priest Borland will tell us what we should believe, as is his wont!'

Ninian blew out one of the lamps on the table and picked up the second. 'Shall we go down? I just heard the gong,' she observed neutrally.

'Then go ahead of me. I like to have something soft in front, in case I fall,' Bellene remarked grandly. Ninian looked down at her small breasts and flat stomach, and wondered if Bellene had been trying to make a joke. The fact that the Steward of Arcady had no sense of humour did not prevent her making spasmodic attempts to disguise its absence.

As Ninian took a first step down the narrow stairway the lamp she held tilted, and drops of burning fish-oil spilled on to her left hand. She let out an involuntary cry of pain as a wide red mark scored her skin and began to throb. Ninian sighed.

She had known from the moment she woke that it was going to be one of those days. The only comfort she could offer herself was that it would soon be over.

Quest stood on the parapet surrounding the white dome of the temple at Wellwater, waiting for the moon to rise over the lake. A light breeze moulded the skirts of the dark blue soutane to his long body, tugging at the gold cuffs which indicated his religious rank. His hair, still thick and long, hung to below his shoulders, and the curls billowed out around his head, framing his intense face, where fire glowed in the depths of amber eyes.

Quest looked across to the lights of Kandria, his old home, then to Arcady; he found himself thinking again about Ninian and Sarai, and frowned.

Sarai was his acknowledged daughter; it was wrong for her to be brought up at Arcady, away from the members of his family. She should be with his brother Jerom and his wife, Cassia, as was Kandria's custom, not under Bellene's baleful eye. But Ninian went her own way, whatever he said, and so far he had enjoyed no success in persuading her of the error of her position.

He wondered why he always let her do what she wanted, when he possessed the authority to enforce his will. Was it guilt?

The cool air soothed his momentary irritation, which was in any case of less immediate importance than the midnight service at which he was to preach. The prospect was pure pleasure to Quest, who found deep satisfaction in answering the call of the Lords of Light to their service in the priesthood. Had it not been for the unexpected existence of Sarai, with the consequent reminder of the physical pleasures he had renounced, he thought he would have been wholly content.

Suddenly, lights began to spring up all over the lake, and Quest followed their movement with his eyes, still finding pleasure in the nightly spectacle. There was beauty, and colour, and motion, all combining to encourage him in the notion that the lights were, in some real fashion, alive; not the monster Avar his mother had warned him about in childhood, but some mystic spirit of the lake.

Quest frowned again, remembering an uneasy dream, one of the dreams that had plagued him ever since his return from the Barren Lands ten years before. The last one had shown him a dark image of himself looking on as the waters of the lake rose to subsume him and all the land around Avardale. He shook himself, disliking the memory of past terror; all his instincts shied his thoughts away from the idea of death.

His gaze returned to the flickering lights on the expanse of lake: to north and south, east and west. And what, Quest wondered suddenly, was he supposed to make of that other light, that green-white column which had appeared in the east between the land and the stars? Had it been gods-sent?

Perhaps Lord Jiva and Lord Antior are pleased with our sacrifice, as Lord Quorden has given us to hope for the coming harvest on the Plains, and will reward us with rain, and the drought will ease, Quest thought dreamily, the possibility firming into reality in his mind. He threw back his head, revelling in the darkness, gazing up at the night sky in ecstatic contemplation as he felt himself joined in spirit and service to his gods, no longer *I* but *we*. Omigon, the dark star of the north, had blotted out white Annoin, or Arkata's star, blazing more brightly than Pharus, the Emperor's star in the east. He remembered idly that such a conjunction was supposed to portend a great event.

Quest remained in the same rapt posture until the bell inside the temple began to toll, calling him to evening worship.

'Send these two to Enapolis, tonight; they should reach the High Priest by tomorrow evening.' Kerron handed two metal capsules to the bird-man, and received three in return, to decode when he was alone; that rule was the first he had learned when he entered the political service of the Order. 'For the eyes of Lord Quorden alone,' he added firmly.

'Of course, reverence.' Jordan, bird-man to the Order in the Wetlands for more than twenty years, ducked his head and accepted two small capsules before busying himself with the pair of message-birds he had chosen from the dozen in the mews. To the uninformed, there was little to distinguish one from another; all ugly creatures, half hawk, half carrion-eater, with the worst points of both, except for the secret hawk eyes and the wide band of turquoise covering backs and wings – an Imperial colour that marked them as the *Emperor's Birds*, as they were known. Jordan had been scandalised to hear it said that the Emperor himself, Amestatis V, had a nose not unlike the beaks of his nestlings, but he refused to believe it. When the Lord Hilarion, the Imperial Heir, had visited the Wetlands the previous year, Jordan had observed the young man to possess a very modest protuberance.

'Have you done yet?' Kerron asked impatiently.

'Nearly, reverence.' Jordan fitted the capsule with its coded message into the container on the second bird's scrawny leg, then stood back and held out his arm, waiting for the creature to hop from its perch inside the cage onto his thick leather gauntlet, steadying himself to take the weight. The birds were large and heavy.

'Get on with it!' Kerron took a hurried step back, for message-birds were notorious for their ill-temper and this one had a baleful eye.

With an upward sweep of the bird-man's powerful arm, the first messenger was launched skywards, followed soon after by its fellow, and as Kerron watched they soared high, to be lost in the night skies, winging their way east and south to Enapolis at a pace which would allow them to cross the distance in a night and a day, where a man would take fifteen days or more on foot to reach the capital.

Without a word of thanks to Jordan, who knew better than to expect one, Kerron left the mews and headed for the temple where evening service was due to begin. Quest was to preach later, at the midnight ritual. Kerron still detested his *akhal* rival, but was too intelligent to deny that Quest owned capacities that made him a gifted preacher. Kerron smiled to himself, knowing he had the ear of Quorden, High Priest of all the Order, shrewd enough to be aware that his political value held a far greater prospect of advancement through the ranks than Quest's priestly talents. He himself was spy rather than priest, his rank equal to Quest's, the soutane bearing the same gold insignia at the cuffs. His future depended on his wits, not on spurious dogma or faith; those were only tools of the Order, a moral force backed by military might.

Lord Quorden had spies in every place, in every camp; knowledge was power. Kerron understood that lesson well.

It irked him that the distance of Lake Avardale from Enapolis was so great. The news of the green light in the east would have reached Lord Quorden long before his own birds arrived. He sent word because his duty was to report any oddity, any piece of news from the Wetlands which might prove useful to the Order. Which was little enough at present, he thought with a yawn.

He followed the path from the mews to the temple, which stood on high ground, brooding until he came to the pier. It was time for the evening lights, and he paused, casting a cold eye south in the direction of Arcady. He had no gratitude to Bellene for rescuing his infant self from a watery grave and bringing him up among the *akhal*, but only remembered bitterness. They had never lost an opportunity to make him feel an outsider, inferior. He was always the alien among them who could not swim well, or long, who could not bear the cold, nor hold his breath for more than a count of fifty. He was a Thelian, of the Emperor's race, as were many of the Order, but they had made him feel subordinate, isolated, as if he were the one who was unnatural.

'The akhal are dependent for their lives on the waters of the lakes. If anything were to happen to those waters, they would die. The lakes are their source of food and drink, their life blood,' the now familiar voice whispered consolingly in his mind.

Kerron nodded; the voice had never led him astray, not in the ten years of its companionship. Although he did not believe in any gods, he believed in the voice. Sometimes, it seemed to him that it was actually a part of himself, an extra unconscious sense, which warned and advised him. With the help of the voice, as it had promised, Kerron had risen high in the Order.

The lights out on the lake began to sparkle. Kerron was not at a sufficiently high point to receive the full effect, but he had observed the spectacle for most of the nights of his life, barring the two years he had spent in Enapolis, and he paused, listening to the stillness in a rare moment of doubt.

'The lights are a danger, and must be put out, just as the lights in the temples of old were crushed and darkened,' whispered the voice. 'They stand in your way, in the way of the rule of the Order.'

Kerron wished he could find a means to hide his more private thoughts from the voice, for on this occasion he did not want to believe what it told him. It might have been his upbringing among the lake people, but he had a sentimental affection for the lights, and in any case it was hard to see how the phenomenon could be dangerous.

The lights and the voice reminded him of a problem which remained unresolved, from Lake Ismon in the north. Kerron frowned, looking down at the capsules in his hand. He took the one bearing Lord Quorden's private seal and opened it, withdrawing the message it contained and deciphering it as he read:

To: Kerron, Priest

Month Five, day nineteen

We continue to await word that you have captured the rebel Plainsman who has taken refuge with those of like mind around Lake Ismon, and are much displeased at the delay. We believe him to own information of value in rooting out other traitors who threaten the stability of our rule. You say there is a sickness around the lake which has affected the people, but your request to offer aid is denied; unless the Plainsman is surrendered to us, there is to be no communication between Ismon and outside. The disease the rebels spread is more infectious than any other ailment, their opposition to our teachings and our authority a threat more potent than any fever.

Maintain the isolation until such time as the Plainsman is surrendered or taken. Should it prove the latter, you will have proof of a rebel cell within your own boundaries, and will deal with its members accordingly.

Quorden, High Priest of the Order of Light,
Mouthpiece of the gods, Guardian of the Empire

A part of Kerron was pleased at the prospect of delivering *akhal* rebels to the capital, a deed which would certainly advance his own status within the Order, although it would make his remaining in the Wetlands more problematic. He was alien enough, for all his upbringing at Arcady; this would merely be the final proof. The *akhal* were clannish in their loyalties, firm in their sense of their own superiority.

Yet it disturbed him that the sickness he had reported was to run its course unassuaged; there had been deaths, or so the last message had informed him two days previously. How should he protect his own position, claiming ignorance of the full state of affairs should the news from Ismon come out, or the situation grow worse? He could foresee danger in ignoring such potential disaster.

'The rebels are the enemy, those who would destroy the Order and bring back the old ways, leaving you with nothing. For, after all, who are you but a foundling, unwanted, without influence, without family. What chance is there for you to share power outside the Order?'

The power of the old Administrative families had been seized by the priesthood, but not without a struggle, and Kerron wanted no return to those ways, where he would have no opportunity to earn authority.

Opposing forces in his mind urged contrary solutions to the problem of Ismon, pragmatism and malice.

'Leave them be and do as Lord Quorden commands; think about the lights in the lake. The lights must be put out.' There was a viciousness in the voice's pronouncement that Kerron had never heard before.

'I'll see what can be done,' he murmured. The lights were still sparkling across the lake, and Kerron's agreement faltered as he watched. What would it be like if they were gone and the waters of the lake were dead, without light? He shivered.

The ordinary lights of Arcady winked at him, reminding Kerron quite how much he had hated Bellene as a child. He could think of only Ran, and perhaps Affer, with any remembered pleasure. In many ways, he and Ran were too much alike for comfort, although she would not have thanked him for saying so. Only the existence of Affer saved her from being quite as egocentric as Kerron himself.

He wondered if she knew that the true power of Wellwater lay with him, not with High Priest Borland, an *akhal* weakling who drank too much and indulged his other senses, too. It would please Kerron to know that Ran knew him as the real authority in the Wetlands, as far Quest's superior in influence as he knew himself to excel the *akhal* in all other ways. He alone knew the mind of Lord Quorden, which was the mind of the gods.

It was a foolish consideration; he was alone, and would always be alone. That was the only safety.

Kerron laughed.

*

Ran exited the tower and turned left across the pebbles to the lake. Her feet were bare, and as she stood in the shallows she felt the cold mud squelch between her toes as water lapped around her ankles in gentle ripples.

Behind her, the great house of Arcady stood out starkly from the landscape, a large, dark building, old as time, shaped from vast blocks of stone that made Ran wonder how anyone had ever managed to move them. There was no regularity to the building's frame; over hundreds of years sections had been added or torn down, depending on the numbers of *akhal* the estate supported, and there were extensions on the western side that housed the youngest and the old, or anyone incapable of climbing stairs.

Arcady, *Arkata's House*, so Bellene said was the origin of the estate's title. The *akhal*, too, were named for their legendary ancestress, whose daughter Calloran had bequeathed Ran, over the generations, her own name. It was said to have been Arkata who petitioned the old gods for her people to take their present form as *akhal*, so that they could swim and dive deep. It was she who had ordered the construction of the now ruined temple on Sheer Island, and she who had first climbed the cliff and stared down at the deep water.

Ninian would inherit all that tradition. Ran glanced back at the house with momentary guilt, aware she made Ninian's life more difficult than was necessary.

Arcady's roof was flat, with a high parapet; immense chimneys east and south-west marked the hearths of the great hall and kitchens respectively. To the fore stood the frame that held the message bell and a shelter for the drums. The mass of windows breaking the façade on five floors all owned wooden shutters, most standing open to the night, for the *akhal* disliked enclosed spaces and made use of them on only the coldest nights. Bellene's tower, private sanctum of the Stewards of Arcady, loomed high over the house and land like a giant eye from the east; the eight windows in the tower room gave access over the entire estate, as many learned to their cost. Bellene was a vigilant Steward, missing little; or at least that had been the case until recently.

At present, two hundred *akhal* made their home at Arcady. The number could vary from twenty fewer to fifty more; it was a well-run estate and could support up to two hundred and fifty, but Bellene wanted no increase, and her word was law. Any woman or man born at Arcady had the right to live there; a woman bequeathed that right to her children, but a man did not, for Arcady, alone among the *akhal* and rare in the Empire, followed descent through the maternal line in memory of Arkata,

41

the estate passing from woman to woman without regard – in theory at least – to degree of kinship. Ran's mother, Bellene's niece, had been the original heir, but after her death when Ran was fifteen, Bellene had chosen Ninian to replace her, and Ran had never really regretted it. To live at Arcady as its Steward would suffocate her. But, for the moment, she had the worst of both worlds, neither heir nor free to leave.

Ninian would let her go. That was the hope Ran clung to when frustration rose so strongly that she had to be alone for fear of striking out physically at restraint. Even at Affer, whom she loved, but who was the most immediate cause of her confinement.

She had no interest in the tasks she was set; there was no job at Arcady she had not undertaken, from looking after the babies to herding the touchy hill-cattle they bred for hides. She was even handy in the still-room, though lacking Ninian's special skill for the tedious process of making their stores of medicines. All Ran had ever wanted was to leave Arcady, to travel far away and find the world beyond the Wetlands before it was too late; to discover her physical limits and exceed even those. The pilgrimage to the Barren Lands had not lessened but rather increased her hunger for freedom.

She shivered, but not from cold. Slipping off her loose overshirt and trousers, leaving only the white tight-fitting vest and leggings she wore for swimming, Ran waded out into the lake. The water crept up to her thighs, and she felt the cold strike the pit of her stomach. Laughing, she gave in to the temptation to plunge in head first and spare herself the torture of slow immersion.

By the time she surfaced she was some way out. Ran turned on her back and floated, looking broodingly back at the shore, although the worst of her tension had eased. She could see on the shore a long-furred white cat, one of a colony that inhabited Arcady's grounds and stole its fish. Lake-cats were supposedly feral, but living side by side with the *akhal* had evidently removed fear of their human companions, and the swimming cats were as close to being pets as Bellene would allow.

Ran resumed her swim, heading north for Sheer Island, and to her surprise, she spied a light flickering inland, away from the shore. Her curiosity was instantly aroused. As far as she knew no one but herself ever visited the island; it was forbidden territory by reason of the ruins of the old temple, a taboo enforced by the Order in the past with some strictness, but now there was no need, for the ban had become habit.

The water was cool, not cold, and while some might not enjoy swimming at night, there was no creature in the lake Ran feared, not the vicious snapping-fish nor the long rock-eels. She enjoyed the sensation of absolute control over her body, revelling in her strength. All *akhal* were excellent swimmers, lake water their natural second element, but Ran was good even by their highest standards.

The moon shone on the surface of the lake, but no blue-green lights moved beneath the water, and her imagination was too limited to allow her to be frightened of notional monsters. Ran drew in a deep breath and ducked down, swimming under the surface for quite a long way before coming up for air. She surfaced at last to find the southern shore of Sheer Island before her, where the water grew shallow as the bottom shelved steeply.

It was cold out of the water; Ran shivered, noticing the wind had sprung up. Shaking herself to get the water from her fine hair, she saw again a flicker of light inland, to the west.

The southern section of the island was relatively flat, in contrast with the steep cliff on the northern side. Ran stepped onto land covered by a layer of prickly bushes and littered with broken stones, many from the ruined temple. The few times she had visited Sheer Island in daylight Ran had been able to identify small pieces of decoratively carved rock, including one fragment depicting a swimming cat, but for the most part the destruction of the temple had been thorough. It had taken the form of a low stone circle, at its centre a tall statue of a naked woman standing, hands held out at shoulder height, palms cupped together, and in them she had held the Tearstone. Bellene said the stone was half an orb in shape, a lightstone mined in the Eastern Isles of the Empire by another of the peoples, men and women who each bore a small lightstone embedded in the palm of their right hand. The stone had shone with its own light over the lake in honour of deities the Order claimed were not gods but evil spirits, intent on destruction.

Ran made little noise as she trod inland, stubbing her bare toes only once as she brushed aside the heavy undergrowth. The flicker of flames ahead showed her she was not alone; a fire had been built in the shelter of the cliff, which rose a sheer three hundred feet or more next to the part of the lake where the water was deepest and no one ever swam. Ran had climbed the cliff once, in response to a dare from Kerron, and she could remember looking down from the peak into the dark waters, terrified of falling, although she would never have admitted to fear.

How had the old *akhal* song gone?

> *'As we looked down*
> *From the high cliff,*
> *Afraid of the dark.'*

Ran remembered she had been afraid.

She was close enough to hear the crackle of the fire and smell its smoke, which was dry, as if it burned leaves as well as wood. Ran crouched in the shadows, making out the shape of a seated figure beside the flames inclining head and shoulders to the fire.

She stood up; momentarily careless, her foot came down on a dry twig, which cracked noisily.

The narrow figure leaped instantly to its feet, peering out into the darkness. 'Who's there?'

Ran stood up. 'Only me. Ran, from Arcady,' she added helpfully as she moved to stand within the compass of the flames. The man by the fire stepped warily back, almost tripping over the block of stone on which he had been sitting.

'What're you doing here?' he demanded, flourishing a branch in her direction. He was young, with hair so pale as to be almost white, and now she recognised him, an *akhal* from the northern Lake; Ran saw too that he was hurt, supporting his right arm, where a dark red stained the sleeve of his white shirt.

'I saw the light from your fire and came to see who was here. No one but me ever comes here,' Ran explained, dropping down to kneel by the fire and holding out her hands to the flames. 'I could ask you the same question. You're a long way from home, Maryon.'

He relaxed, dropping the branch and slumping down onto the stone seat. 'I thought you'd know me,' he said, in a hoarse voice. 'Did you come because of the light?'

'No; I just came for a swim. What's the matter with your arm?'

Firelight showed Ran a long gash from shoulder to half-way down Maryon's upper arm, which still bled. She made to touch it, but the young man drew back.

'It's not too bad – leave it. It's not important.'

'What are you doing here? How did you get here? I don't see a boat, or a raft. And how did you get that cut?' The injury looked like a knife wound, and Ran wondered if he had been in a fight. 'Are you hiding from trouble?'

Maryon's head jerked up, and Ran was struck by an extreme tension in his thin face. He was Affer's age, and she knew him by sight rather than intimately, for he belonged to Carne, a northern estate at Lake Ismon; his family travelled as pedlars, bartering goods or services for medicines and nut-flour since ingredients for neither grew well so far north. There had been rumours that his family favoured the rebel cause, but as far as she knew it was all talk, no proof. Arcady, after all, also had a reputation for dissent and difference. Maryon was a fair, slight young man, with a roving eye and a cheerful grin, or that was how she remembered him. Now, however, he looked as wary as Affer, constantly on the point of flight.

'Can I trust you?' he whispered.

'In what? Have you hurt anyone?'

'*No!*' Maryon shook his head convulsively. 'Ran, is there anyone sick at Arcady?'

She shook her head, puzzled. 'No, or no one with more than the usual spring fevers. Why?'

'I don't know how much to tell you.' Maryon clutched his arm; dark blood oozed between the fingers of his left hand as he bit his lip. 'I must tell someone; that's why I came south. It might as well be you.'

'Tell me what?'

'About the sickness.' The young man shook his head despairingly. 'All around the lake the plants are dying, and the fish, and everything else. The water smells rotten, and the lake's being clogged by a green weed with purple flowers that spreads everywhere, too fast to clear.' He paused, and Ran, with rare tact, busied herself feeding pieces of wood to the fire while Maryon recovered himself. 'And all of us, too,' he went on in muffled tones. 'We can't swim any more, or drink the water, although it's too late now, anyway. Most of us were taken ill days ago; it was all so quick. We thought the priests would let us get help from you at Arcady, but they refused, and set the guard to watch us. And now my brother and sisters are dead, and my father, too – ' He broke off with a sob.

'What sort of illness, Maryon?' No word of any sickness had reached Lake Avardale.

'You don't understand.' He thumped his good fist on his thigh. 'We need your help with medicines and nursing; that's one of the reasons I'm telling you this, but you must listen! We sent word south to Wellwater for help, but no one came, and it's much worse than that. The Order commanded their guard to seal off the lake and land estates, and refused to let us ask for help. That's how I got this.' He indicated the wound on his arm. 'One of them shot at me as I came through the pass south; they'd have killed me if they'd caught me. I swam down the river and across the lake, and I've been hiding here since last night.'

Ran gave him a troubled look. 'Why did they seal off the lake, Maryon?'

He turned his face away from her. 'They said we were harbouring an escaped rebel, a Plainsman, and they would only let us leave if we gave him up.'

'I see.' She saw in his expression it was pointless to question him further on that score. 'Has this illness spread? It's not just at Carne?'

'You think I'm making this up?' Maryon jumped to his feet in passion. 'Of all my kin, of a hundred and eleven of us at Carne, there was only me fit enough to come away. There were green warning flags flying from other houses around the lake, too.' He subsided wearily onto the stone seat, sinking his head into his hands.

'You don't look any too well yourself,' Ran observed, realising her remark tactless when he flinched. 'Sorry. You must come to Arcady, where Ninian can see to you. Can you swim?'

'We can't risk a boat; someone might see. I'll swim.' His voice was bitter. 'Your lake is still clear.'

'And then?' Ran eyed him uneasily. 'Maryon, if we're to get help through to your family we need a permit from Wellwater; no one travels beyond Avardale without licence. Will you let us ask Quest? If the situation is really so serious, I'm sure he would help. Would you trust him?'

'Quest?' Maryon seized on the name. 'Yes, I'd trust him; I remember him. But not the Thelian.' He did not notice Ran's expression at the mention of Kerron, and she sighed inwardly, aware of the dislike and distrust in which he was generally held by the *akhal*. She decided it was not the time to argue.

'We should go; it's late.'

Maryon staggered as he rose to his feet. Ran glanced down at the stone he had been using as a seat, which she now saw was part of a carved head, with a crown of hair and wide-set eyes, and the bridge of a nose.

'This must have been part of the statue from the old temple,' she observed in an aside. 'I suppose no one bothered to break it up completely. I wonder what happened to the Tearstone?'

'What does it matter?' Maryon asked angrily, stamping out the fire.

'You're still bleeding; let me bind your arm.' Ran tore the bottom section of her vest into strips with strong fingers, winding them round the jagged cut. 'That's better. Does it hurt much?'

'No.' Maryon tested the arm, wincing as he raised it to shoulder height.

The fire was out. Ran helped him down to the shore, stumbling from time to time as she set her feet down on sharp fragments of stone. The lights of Arcady gleamed south as their guide.

'You can't imagine how foul the water smells at home,' Maryon said softly. 'This is so different; you can feel it's alive.'

'Where did the sickness come from? I thought Lake Ismon was fed by pure mountain water?'

'It is, but a few days ago the river from the mountains began to flow with bad water. We could see and smell it, and the weeds that came down with it. The filth seemed to spread like a plague.' Maryon shook his head wearily.

'What about the other lakes? About Weyn, and Harfort?' A dreadful thought suddenly occurred to her. 'Harfort is fed by Ismon and that same river, just as we are, and it also leads into Weyn.'

'I don't know,' Maryon said hopelessly. 'I hadn't thought about it.'

'We must find out. And I don't understand why we've heard nothing about this plague. The priests must know it may spread if it's water-borne.'

'Why should priests make sense? Why should they care, least of all that Thelian who runs Wellwater as a spy for Lord Quorden? What are we to him?' Maryon asked bitterly. 'My sisters were just children, and yet they died.'

'And were you sheltering this rebel they wanted so badly?' But Maryon only shook his head and said nothing, and Ran reminded herself of the urgency of his errand. 'Come on.' She waded out into the lake, finding it warm in comparison with the chill of the night air.

Maryon followed, less eagerly. He sank to his shoulders in the water and pushed away, swimming side-stroke to save his injured arm. Ran followed, struck by a sudden doubt about her course of action. If Maryon was the carrier of a contagious fever, she should not take him to Arcady without warning Ninian first. Yet from what he said the disease was spread by contact with water, and not from person to person.

What was the importance of the rebel Plainsman, if Maryon and his family had chosen to refuse to hand him over to the priests, despite their predicament? Could any one man be so valuable? Or had they refused simply because Carne was not sheltering him? Although, remembering Maryon's guilty expression, that seemed unlikely; Ran wished she knew more about the world beyond the Wetlands. But her thoughts returned to the more pressing problem.

If Ismon was diseased, how long would it be before its waters dispersed to corrupt the other lakes to which it was linked? All four were joined by rivers, Ismon to Harfort and Avardale, Harfort to Weyn, Weyn to Avardale. Would the plague spread to them all? The prospect appalled her.

For the first time since she had stood on top of Arkata's cliff on Sheer Island and dared to look down, a dozen years before, Ran understood what it must feel like to be like Affer, and to be constantly afraid of the intangible.

2

The Talfor estate lay on the northernmost shore of Lake Avardale, its boundaries defined by south-flowing rivers to the west and the east. To the north, steep hills led away over the pass to Lake Ismon; further west, marshy ground gave way to swamp proper, an uninhabitable region for creatures other than reptiles and amphibians and insects. Poisonous gases, low lying, sometimes crept eastwards from the swamp, but never reached the shores of the lake.

No one noticed the first few flowers which flowed south from Ismon, free-floating plants with blossoms of purple and white-striped leaves. They floated with the current, bobbing on the surface of the water, waxen leaves massed protectively about each single bloom.

Other contagions spread by river from Ismon, invisible pollutants which scented the water, not with the healthy odour of decomposing leaves but with whiffs of something dry and sour, rebarbative. These organisms, like the flowers, came singly at first, scouts in the vanguard of a massive army, testing the waters before launching the full invasion.

Around Lake Ismon free-floating plants already clogged the north-western quarter of the lake, and the pollutants from the mountains had spread their putrescence through the water and in the air, until there was no place left it had not made its presence known.

As day dwindled into night, so Lake Avardale came to life. In its depths, blue-green lights glittered, flashing here and there, everywhere. Where the lights touched, the plants with purple flowers and white-striped leaves shrivelled and died. The evil odour of pollution was swept away by gusts of cleaner, purer air.

Chapter Two

1

Sarai sat on the end of the pier, legs dangling over the side. Most of the boats and rafts were gone, taking medicines north to the other estates around the lake, but this particular boat had gone west to Wellwater, and she was waiting for its return.

A cool breeze ruffled her short hair, which curled in a way her mother's never had: Ninian's was as straight as the water plantain that grew around the edges of the lake. Overhead the skies were banded pale blue and white with the promise of a fine spring day. A low mist hovered over the surface of the lake, giving it an air of mystery.

Landward, the slopes of the hills to the south were greening after the long winter, leaves emerging to cover the starkness of thick branches waving awkwardly from ivy-clad trunks; the soil was poor, good only for grazing, but the nut trees provided timber enough for Arcady, and flour through the medium of Kandria's mill. Sarai glanced up at the great house and thought Bellene's tower, its eight windows alive and watchful, was glowering down on her, and all the other inhabitants of Arcady, looking to find fault. As if they felt it too, most people walked with hurried steps as they went about their work.

Everyone was always busy at this time of year; Sarai, too, had her ordained tasks, but had decided to forget about them for one morning.

She liked spring by the lake. Already there was colour from the marsh flowers along the banks, the golden margills and pink barflowers. Small fish swam around the wooden struts of the pier, prey for the blue-winged fisher-birds, and, closer to land, for members of the cat colony, equally expert anglers. If she bent over, Sarai could see her own reflection in the still waters of the lake, rather enjoying the image thus presented; she was slight, but with strong, straight limbs and the promise of being taller than her mother in due course. She did not consider she looked very much like either Ninian or Quest, but was, rather, herself; at nine she had a powerful sense of her own individuality, which struggled with a keen insecurity about the worth of that personal identity.

She jumped to her feet at the sight of a small rowing boat drawing closer to the pier, waving her arms energetically over her head at one of the three seated figures.

'Mother, Mother, they're coming,' Sarai shouted excitedly, dancing along the pier. 'They're almost here!'

Fortunately for her peace of mind, Ninian, too, had been keeping a look-out for their visitors, and was already half-way to the pier when the summons came. She took Sarai's hand as she joined her and both stood waiting for their visitors to land.

Ninian frowned at her daughter. 'What are you doing here, Sarai? I thought I told you to go and help Affer in the drying sheds?'

'But not when Father was coming,' Sarai pleaded, fixing amber eyes – very like her father's, Ninian reflected – on her mother's face. 'You don't really mind, do you?'

'Not this time.' Ninian allowed herself to smile. 'I suppose you don't see him very often, it's true. When was the last time you went to temple, except for festivals, Sarai?'

The girl wriggled uncomfortably. 'But that's different; he can't see me then, not with everyone else there. In temple he's not Father, only a priest.'

Ninian could not deny the statement, impressed at the accuracy with which Sarai had identified her own difficulty. 'He's here officially today, too, Sarai; don't forget that. And see – Kerron's come with him. You must be polite and make him welcome, not just your father. This was once his home, too.'

'But he doesn't like us,' Sarai objected sulkily, her expressive face clouding.

Ninian set her face in a smile of welcome as the boat reached the end of the pier and Farse, one of the Arcady boatmen, edged his way along to the bank, guiding the boat with his arms as he clung to the timbers between the struts. He was close to sixty and nearly bald, his left hand missing the middle two fingers, the legacy of an encounter with a snapper-fish. Facing him in the stern sat the two priests, identically robed with marks of equal rank; neither made a move to help the boatman, but Quest looked up and smiled into the excited face of his daughter, peering down at him at a precarious angle.

'Will you help me out, Sarai?' he asked, with a laugh, as the boat glided to a stop. Farse held it steady. 'Give me your hand.' The girl did so, reaching down a long arm. Quest climbed agilely up onto the pier; Kerron followed with equal agility but less enthusiasm.

'I could manage this interview alone, if you would rather remain here,' he observed to Quest in a neutral voice. 'It falls more to my domain than yours, in any event.'

Quest let his arm fall from Sarai's shoulders, responding to the not very oblique criticism with a defensiveness Ninian thought foolish. 'I shall come,' he said stiffly.

Kerron favoured Ninian with a chill smile. 'Well, Ninian? Where is this man you brought us here to see?'

'In the infirmary.' Ninian could never bring herself to use 'Reverence', the correct form of address, to either Quest or Kerron; she could not offer respect to a man she had known since boyhood simply by reason of his cloth. The dark blue soutane was merely a uniform, not a mark of divine favour. The errant thought crossed her mind that it would be a strange god who would choose Kerron, the arch-pragmatist, as servant, and she lowered her eyes to hide their spark of amusement.

'Well?' Kerron gave his companions an irritated look. 'Shall we go?'

'Don't begrudge me a few moments to greet my daughter,' Quest said with a smile. 'I doubt the gods do, and they have the greatest claim on me. Surely young Maryon can wait a little while.' But already he had loosened his hand from Sarai's determined grip, not noticing how her face instantly fell. Ninian's expression hardened. There were times when she felt murderous towards Quest for his insensitivity, no matter how often she tried to tell herself his carelessness stemmed from ignorance, not intention. She found it hard to forgive him, not least because he always walked away and left her with the problems he had caused. Not for the first time, she wondered if she should ever have told him he was Sarai's father; it would have been much simpler for her, perhaps even for him.

'So you remember Maryon, from Carne?' she said hastily. 'He's very ill, but rational enough.'

'And what story is this he's spreading?' Kerron looked down his nose in a way Ninian found disconcerting. 'Plague, in the north? I've heard nothing so dramatic.'

She gave him a weary look. 'I'd rather let you hear him for yourself.'

'It's all nonsense.' Kerron brushed past her, not waiting for her to lead the way. He strode ahead in the direction of the infirmary, back stiff with disapproval.

'We'll see.' Quest followed, pausing to allow Ninian to walk alongside him; he looked worried. 'I hope that this young man brought no infection with him.'

Ninian's mouth tightened; was this another excuse to take Sarai away from Arcady and install her in his brother's household? He had tried so many over the years.

'So do I,' she replied coolly. 'In case you've forgotten, there are nearly two hundred people living here; the last thing we need is an epidemic!'

Quest looked annoyed, but, although he opened his mouth to speak, evidently thought better of it. Sarai trailed unhappily in their wake as they followed Kerron along the west side of the house, passing kitchens and store rooms and traversing the herb garden at the rear to reach a long, low, whitewashed building with a thatched roof, its situation comparatively isolated. Smoke rose from a narrow chimney at one end, and one of a dozen sets of plain shutters stood open.

'I see you took some precautions, Ninian,' Quest observed, turning to face her. 'I was worried you'd put him in the main house. At least you had the sense to keep him separate.'

'I had him brought here as soon as Ran told me what was the matter with him; in any case, I thought it might be better if he didn't spread this story and cause panic. She found him on Sheer Island, you know.'

'And what was she doing there?' Kerron inquired, turning back, but he looked merely interested, not disapproving. 'It's forbidden territory.'

'She saw a light and went to see what it was,' Ninian explained untruthfully.

'At night?'

'You know Ran. She always liked to swim in the dark.' Ninian waited for Kerron's quick nod of agreement; which came more naturally than she had expected. 'Are you both coming in?'

'Certainly. You can confirm the fever isn't contagious?' Ninian nodded, opening the door at the end of the infirmary building, trying to keep a tight hold on her temper. Kerron was only being his usual self.

She paused in the narrow passage that ran the length of the building as the priests joined her, but when Sarai would have followed, Ninian shook her head.

'You mustn't come in, Sarai, not unless I say so. Your father wouldn't like it any more than I do.'

Sarai's lips firmed in a stubborn expression. 'You said what Maryon had wasn't catching.'

'That's beside the point. Go and wait outside – you'll see your father again before he leaves, I promise.'

The girl paused, just long enough to make certain anyone watching would understand she was making up her own mind; then, to Ninian's relief, did as she was told. Quest's irritable gaze followed the small figure as she retreated.

'You allow her far too much freedom,' he remarked.

'And you're so knowledgeable about how to bring up a child?' But Ninian flushed, remembering Kerron's presence; it was hardly the most appropriate time or place for a domestic argument. Yet she could not resist adding: 'If you spent more time with her, you'd know it never does a lot of good just telling Sarai to do something without saying *why*.'

Testy silence greeted her remark. Unworthily satisfied, Ninian knocked softly, then opened a door on her left, holding it for the others to precede her.

Ran sat on a stool on the far side of the bed beside the open window, bathing Maryon's forehead with a cool cloth. He was awake, eyes open as they turned first to Ninian, then to the priests.

Kerron took up a position at the end of the bed, followed by Maryon's resigned gaze; Quest moved to the side of the sick man, leaving room for Ninian to stand beside him.

'You've come at last!' Ran looked up, ceasing her ministrations. 'You certainly took your time.'

'You look as well as ever, Ran,' Quest murmured. Ran and Kerron exchanged a mute and mutual friendly acknowledgement. 'How is your patient?'

Ninian thought Maryon looked much worse than on the previous night; his skin was a pale shade of greenish-white, and his face was very drawn. The bandage on his arm, fresh that morning, was newly stained with blood, a deep, dark red, not a healthy colour.

'Maryon, are you up to talking?' she asked quietly. Although the window shutters were open there was a sour smell of sickness in the room.

'I can manage.' Maryon struggled to sit up, and Ran bent to help him; pale eyes glittered angrily in his thin face as he turned to Quest. 'What have they told you?' he demanded hoarsely. 'What I said – '

'I gather you came here with some tale of a plague in the north,' Kerron interrupted. 'Is this correct?'

'Yes.' Maryon was breathing too rapidly, Ninian thought, but he could answer for himself. 'You – your Order sent priests to Carne, to spy on us, for us to feed and lodge, just as you did to other estates in the north, because you hoped to prove us rebels. Because we're loyal first to the Emperor, and only then to you.' He forced a laugh. 'I hope they were bored!' Then his voice sank. 'Did you think they'd be immune to this plague?'

'Plague? What plague?' Kerron was dismissive. 'The word I have from Ismon is that an infectious complaint has spread around the lake, a sickness brought from the east by a rebel escaped from the riots in Ammon, whom you at Carne are hiding from us.' He paused, looking perfectly collected. 'Lord Quorden gave the order to contain the lake until the man was taken, and to prevent this complaint from spreading. But you take it on yourself to break his restriction, bringing the risk of fever with you.'

Ninian recalled the sandmen the previous afternoon saying they had been refused licence to travel north, but nothing in Kerron's expression suggested any emotion stronger than annoyance. Surely, if there were plague in the north he would show at least some anxiety?

'Tell us what happened, from the beginning, and why you came.' Quest frowned Kerron into silence. Their eyes met; Kerron shrugged and looked away.

'If you'll listen.' Maryon lay back, weary; Ninian was seized with the uncomfortable conviction that he no longer cared what happened to him.

'Go on, Maryon,' she urged.

'It started perhaps seven or eight days ago, maybe more.' He began slowly, words coming more rapidly as he went on. 'The river was in spring spate from the mountains, as usual, no matter what they say about drought in the rest of the Empire. It was then we noticed some sort of weed flowing down to us, and the water itself began to smell rank, foul.' He turned his head feverishly from side to side as if he could still smell the infection. 'It was dirty water, but we couldn't stop it reaching the lake. It was all so quick. The foulness seemed to contaminate whatever it touched, and within a couple of days the waters around Carne were polluted. And, of course, all of us had swum in the lake, or drunk from it, or eaten fish.' He gave a bitter laugh. 'But that was only the beginning.'

'You sent messages to Wellwater, asking for help?' Quest inquired, frowning. 'What reply did you receive?' The door opened silently to admit Affer; he slipped inside and went over to the window. Ran gave her brother a quick look; as Ninian watched, Affer swallowed and nodded his head.

'Of course, we sent to Wellwater as soon as we realised we had an epidemic on our hands, asking for medicines and help from Arcady.' Maryon's gaze flicked to Kerron, his white face impassive. 'But the guard said that unless we handed over the rebel they claimed we were hiding at Carne no one could leave or come to Ismon. And all the time there were more green warning flags flying at each house, and I could smell the foul smell of the water!'

'We were aware of this illness, as I said,' Kerron remarked coldly. 'But the messages we received were far less alarmist than this. And you omit to mention that you refused to give us the rebel Plainsman you shelter.'

'How dare you?' Maryon struggled to sit up straight, his expression outraged. 'For the sake of one man who did you no harm you let my family die, and your own people with them? But of course.' Flushed, he lifted an accusing finger. 'We're none of us *your* people!'

Pale colour stained Kerron's cheeks. 'If you made such an accusation when you were well, Maryon, you might find yourself in serious trouble. I am a priest, and make no distinction between *akhal* and Thelian, between sandman and Plainsman. All the peoples of the Empire lie in the care of the Lords of Light, and you would do well to remember it.'

Ninian saw Affer shudder and reach out a hand to Ran. 'But Kerron,' she interrupted, seeing Maryon had no more to say, 'why didn't you ask us for medicines? We would willingly have sent them.'

'There was, and is, no need.' He was at his most distant, emotions bound tightly in a cocoon. 'And my orders from Lord Quorden are to seal off Ismon until the rebel Plainsman has been taken. The decision is his, not mine.'

'But if so many have died – '

'You say many are dead from this disease, Maryon,' Quest asked, interrupting. 'What is the illness, and how do you know it came from the lake?'

'The sickness starts with a headache and fever,' Maryon whispered wearily. 'We tried all the usual remedies, but none of them worked, and soon we had no medicines left; that was one of the reasons I came south, to beg for more. But the guard watch all the exits, by river or by land, and even when I pleaded with them they wouldn't let me come.'

Quest turned to Kerron. 'Did you set this guard to such a close watch?'

'Certainly. It was necessary; the Plainsman is still in hiding somewhere. Lord Quorden believes he has information of great value about the rebels' plans.' Kerron gave Maryon a look of contempt. 'He's trying to hide his own guilt, because he and his kin would rather hide a Plains rebel who fought against our Order in Ammon, who stole grain being distributed to the poor, than do their duty to their own people. Perhaps Maryon really came south with a message from this man, hoping to escape attention by spreading stories of a plague.'

'But there remains the fact that Maryon is ill,' Ran commented dryly. Kerron stiffened.

'I might take your comment amiss, Ran, if I didn't know you so well; I remember that Maryon chose to come here.'

'Are you trying to suggest I, or all Arcady, might be in league with him, and thus the rebels?' Ran seemed amused, though Affer shrank away from the ice in Kerron's tone. 'You know better than that.'

'Don't be a fool, Ran,' Quest interjected testily. 'Kerron, I am concerned about this. If sickness has spread as Maryon says, it may come here, too.' Ninian nodded her agreement.

'You are allowing this man to infect you with panic, for whatever reasons he owns, if not with his illness, which I have done my best to isolate.'

Quest frowned. 'I don't like this.'

'Are you doubting my judgment, or suggesting I disobey direct commands from Enapolis?' Kerron demanded. 'Lord Quorden has his reasons for hunting this Plainsman; our only duty is to seek him out and take him, which Maryon and his kin are doing their utmost to prevent. I will not have his lies spread through Avardale!'

Ninian shook her head. 'We don't want to start a panic, I agree. No one at Arcady outside this room, apart from Bellene, is aware of anything except that Maryon is sick.'

Kerron scowled. 'How ill is he?'

'Without knowing how the fever progresses, it's hard to say.' Ninian glanced at her patient, who seemed unconscious. 'So far, nothing I've given him has helped; his fever is worse, if anything, and his blood seems tainted. Look at its colour. I'd say, if I had to, that the sickness was one of the blood itself.'

'I see.'

'And if Maryon's story is true, then we should do something now, not take the risk that pollution from Ismon won't infect Avardale,' Ran observed to Kerron, looking angry.

'I see no point in discussing it.' Kerron turned to Quest. 'Are you ready to return to Wellwater?'

Quest looked down at Maryon, then shrugged. 'There's nothing more to be gained here, I think.'

'I'd be grateful if you would find time to talk to Sarai,' Ninian said stiffly. 'She's been looking forward to seeing you.'

'How difficult it must be for you, Ninian,' Kerron remarked; the spark of malice in his green eyes made her wonder why he felt the need to goad her.

'If you're going to snipe, children, go outside!' Ran grinned at Kerron, and Ninian caught the answering gleam in his expression, a sight seen only rarely. What had they done to him, to cause him to grow into a cold man who wound himself in bitterness and protective isolation?

Ran's smile faded as Kerron departed. 'I'll stay for the moment, Ninian, but I'd like to talk to you later this morning.' Ninian nodded.

Quest, about to follow Kerron, paused to survey Maryon's exhausted features. He was thoughtful as he left the room, waiting only until Ninian closed the door before launching into speech.

'I hope you're right about this illness, Ninian. I think in any case you should send Sarai to my brother, Jerom, at Kandria. He and Cassia would keep her safe while there's any question of infection.'

'I knew you'd try this.' Ninian had been waiting for the attempt since Quest set foot on Arcady soil, and she spoke angrily. 'I'm not sending her to your family just to relieve your feelings of guilt at having a child at all. I am not going to carry your burden for you.'

'How dare you – ' But Ninian would not let him continue.

'Sarai is my daughter. I carried her. I have looked after her since she was born while you were in Enapolis, training for the priesthood. That was your choice. I watched over her while you fulfilled what you said was your vocation, which precludes your being a father to her in any real sense. That she loves you is your good fortune, not what you deserve, and gives you no right to tell me what to do with her.'

'She's my child, and will be my only child! You gave me no chance, no choice.' Quest had never sounded so angry.

'At Arcady our custom is for women to bear their children among their own people, not to be sent among strangers when they're most vulnerable,' Ninian retorted. 'She's my daughter, and will grow up among my family.'

Quest's eyes narrowed to slits of gold. 'Take care, Ninian; because if you endanger Sarai, then I will take her away from you, whatever you may say or try to do. And I have every moral and legal right to do so.'

'Your daughter? Is that what the Order preaches, to take

children from their mothers and give them to strangers?' Ninian demanded with scorn. 'Does it never occur to you, Quest, that you might be wrong, that the gods you believe you serve might not be the calculating deities of your imagination, might not weigh every prayer and thought and sacrifice on some great moral scales?'

'I warn you again, Ninian.' There was no vestige of affection in the way he looked at her; it was how he had been when he first returned from Enapolis and learned of Sarai's existence. He had hated her, then, making her wish she had kept silence, but they had come to better terms since, or so she had believed. 'You understand nothing about the nature of the gods. I advise you to keep your opinions to yourself, or face the penalties of the law. Arcady and its unnatural customs would bear little weight before the courts.'

'Your courts, you mean. Before you went to Enapolis you didn't think Arcady *unnatural*,' Ninian said angrily. 'Is that what they taught you there? Conformity to one man's view of the world? And if you think so little of women, why should you care for a mere daughter?'

'Enough!' Quest looked as if he would have liked to hit her; it was hard to believe they had once enjoyed mutual passion. Ninian remembered his smooth body lying naked in the orange-red dust of the Barren Lands, the innocence she had observed in his face, the tenderness she had felt, which was one sort of love, and shook her head.

His gaze flicked past her to Sarai, watching them both with an uncertain expression. 'She's my daughter too, Ninian, and you'd do well to remember it! If any harm comes to her because of Maryon, you'll lose her. Is that clear?'

'I thank you for your concern for the rest of us here.' But Ninian, recalled to Sarai's presence, also spoke softly.

They left the infirmary in silence. Sarai waited until sure she had her mother's full attention, then reached out and took her father's hand. Quest smiled down at her, and Ninian sighed, aware that Sarai knew her power to wound, and was using it now to avenge her own pain, never quite sure which parent to blame. Sarai saw her mother every day, her father rarely; it was hardly surprising she chose him now. Quest's satisfied expression told Ninian he thought he had won their debate with Sarai's preference, but Ninian could have disillusioned him.

'Did Bellene have anything to say about the green light in the east yesterday?' Kerron asked casually, catching her unawares. 'She always had strong opinions on everything.'

'I'm sorry. The light?' Ninian nearly tripped over a stone. 'No, she said she thought it might be some freak weather conditions, because of the storm that came afterwards, but we were waiting to hear what you had to tell us.' She omitted Bellene's other observations.

'It's not my place to guess at the meanings of omens; Lord Quorden will inform us of their significance in due course. It merely occurred to me you might still mistakenly hold onto some of those superstitions from the old days; I remember Bellene's stories when we were children, about the Tearstone and the island and the foundress of Arcady.'

'They were only stories,' Ninian said neutrally, surprised at any reference to their shared past. 'But I'll be glad to know more about the light.'

He would not believe her; the inhabitants of Arcady had never been strong adherents of the organised tenets of the Order, preferring to hold to mystical convictions of a tie between land and lake and *akhal*. But he only said: 'Come to morning service in two days at Wellwater. We should have news from the capital by then.'

'Thank you.' She hesitated. 'Kerron, are you sure we can't do anything about the situation in the north?'

'As I said, I have my orders. But if they should change, or if the situation should warrant it, I'll come to you for medicines.' He sounded as if he meant it, increasing her doubts about Maryon's story. 'You've no reason to worry.'

They walked on in silence, Kerron ignoring greetings from people he had once lived among; he had been too angry and too selfish to make many friends at Arcady.

Quest and Sarai were waiting at the end of the pier, boat and Farse already in position. All the mist had cleared from the lake, which sparkled in the sunlight, waters calm and clear and tempting. Ninian smiled at Quest.

'Don't you ever think how much more pleasant it would be to shed your dignity and swim back to Wellwater?'

'There are always sacrifices to be made; this is one of ours,' he observed with a sigh as he looked regretfully at the clear water. 'But it is hard on a day like this.'

'Father, why does being a priest mean you can't?' Sarai tugged at his sleeve for attention, a scowl on her face. 'Is it wrong to swim, then?'

'No, of course not, not for you.' Quest put a hand on his daughter's feathery curls and ruffled her hair. 'But we in the Order learn to be obedient to the will of the gods, and to observe restraint in such pleasures, in respect of their dignity if not our own.'

'Then I never want to be a priest!' Sarai's promise sounded heartfelt, and Ninian hid a smile.

'We must go. Ninian, let me know how Maryon goes on.' With an abrupt change of mood Quest turned away from Sarai and let himself down into the waiting boat. Kerron saw him safely seated before joining him to take his own place.

On the pier, hurt by the rejection, Sarai did not wave as the boat moved away; nor, after the first time, did Quest look back.

'What did I say?' Sarai asked Ninian, misery raw in her high voice. 'Did I do something wrong? Why did he go like that, without even saying goodbye?'

Ninian knelt down and put her arms around the stiff body of her daughter. For one furious moment she knew she would have enjoyed telling Sarai exactly what she thought of her father; but the girl was trembling, needing reassurance, not revenge.

'You didn't do anything wrong, Sarai,' she said gently. 'His duty made him go; he didn't mean to hurt your feelings.'

'I don't understand.' It came out as a childish wail. 'Why? Why does being a priest matter more to him than I do?'

'It isn't like that.' Ninian wiped a tear from Sarai's cheek, trying to find the right words; it would be all too easy to turn her daughter against Quest, if she chose, but to do so would be to destroy a mutual affection which, even if it excluded herself, brought pleasure to both father and child. She sighed, struggling with her temper. 'When your father became a priest he had to promise to put the gods first in everything, ahead even of you. You wouldn't want him to break his sworn word, would you?'

'Yes, I would!' Sarai broke away from Ninian's embrace and blinked back more angry tears. 'It isn't *fair*!'

Understanding the real depths of her misery, Ninian forbore to point out that in life very little, if anything, was fair. In any case, she had the conviction that in this, at least, Sarai was right. She and Quest had created Sarai, she was their responsibility. Surely, if their duty lay anywhere, it was first to their child, and only then, in her own case, to the other inhabitants of Arcady in her care, and in his to his gods? Was her life not lived well and to a purpose if she hurt no one and broke no moral injunction, even if she paid only lip service to his creed? Where was the value of Quest's faith, if it was not supported by generous action and an acceptance of duty?

But her own belief in what constituted duty did not seem to accord with the teachings of the Order. For them, a failure of faith was a moral defect to be punished, whereas Ninian regarded the issue as a purely personal dilemma; to cause harm, deliberately and with malice, was to her the greatest evil.

'Would you like to swim out to the fish-pens and see if any of the nets need mending?' Ninian asked Sarai, who was still staring out at the lake with eyes blurred by misery.

'Oh, all right.' Sarai sniffed and looked suspicious, but the prospect of so popular a task seemed to give her pleasure; she gave Ninian a quick hug. 'Can I go now?'

'You *may*.' Ninian grinned as Sarai made a face. 'Off with you, then. But be back in time for the noon meal.'

'I will.' Sarai was already slipping off her sandals and outer clothes. In the tight-fitting vest and leggings she looked very small and slight, but as she slipped into the water by the pier, letting herself down with practised ease, Ninian was impressed by her strength and the agility with which the child sped away from shore, swimming arm over arm in a burst of angry energy.

The fish-pens were some way from shore, netted areas where each estate nurtured breeding stock of fish as a precautionary measure to ensure an adequate food supply in poor years. There was constant rivalry among the children of Arcady to be chosen to give the fish their daily feed or check the nets for damage. Ninian thought she could accurately be accused of nepotism on this occasion and sighed, wishing it were easier to separate the roles of mother and heir.

A whiff of pungent smoke drifted towards the pier, and Ninian sniffed, wrinkling her nose in sudden disgust. Whoever was in charge of the drying sheds that morning had failed to notice some of the fish were not merely smoking but burning. With a last look out at the lake and Sarai, Ninian turned back resolutely to the great house and her other duties; she would have to find time to inform Bellene what Kerron and Quest had said.

Ninian glanced up at the sun to find the morning already half-gone. She lengthened her step, and as she rounded the corner of the house a thick grey cloud blew across the sun, and suddenly she was no longer warm but cold, all the day's spring heat gone in an instant. She shivered, and inside her grew the unwelcome conviction that what she felt at that moment meant more than it seemed.

'Something is going to happen, something will darken all our lives,' she whispered, with chill awareness that she was speaking future truth; what before the long-ago pilgrimage she would have called intuition, now transmuted somehow into certainty. 'The dark will come to Avardale, and our lights will fade, and unless we remember the old truths they will die.'

But as she finished speaking she had no knowledge what the words meant, nor how important they might prove, nor if there were any way to prevent the advent of her envisioned shadows.

'So, Kerron says there is no danger in this disease in Ismon, nor from the pollution Maryon mentions,' Bellene observed with detachment. 'But you – what do you think?'

There were four of them in the tower room: Bellene, Ninian, Ran and Affer. Ninian, to whom the question was addressed, frowned into her lap.

'I can only speak of what I've seen,' she said briefly. 'Maryon is sick, no question of it; but I am unfamiliar with his form of illness. But, equally, Kerron seemed quite sure of his facts.'

'And you, Ran? You found the man on Sheer Island – and I shall *not* ask what you were doing there! What do you say?' Bellene's gaze was keen as it fixed first on Ran, then, with speculation, on Affer. The fingers of her left hand toyed with the green carnelian thumb ring she wore on the right, inscribed with the shape of a giant fish with fins, the symbol of the Stewardship of Arcady. 'Would you say our guest was a truthful man?'

'Certainly.' Ran's reply was as straightforward as everything else about her. 'Why should he lie? Maryon and his folk are probably hiding this Plainsman that Lord Quorden seems so eager to find, but what difference does that make to what he said about the pollution? And in any case . . . '

'And in any case Affer knows better.' Bellene nodded, her brooding gaze switching to his slighter figure. 'Tell us, then, Affer. What truth did you hear in Kerron's thoughts?'

Silence descended as three of the quartet waited for Affer to speak. Ninian saw him shoot his sister a haunted look, and it struck her, as it had many times, how much all their lives had been altered by the pilgrimage to the Barren Lands. She knew a deep sympathy for Affer. What kind of gods would grant anyone so thin-skinned the ability to hear other people's private thoughts? Affer had taken his fears with him, and had returned with them magnified a hundred times.

The tower room walls were bare-plastered and the floor polished wood covered with rush mats. A reed fire burned in the hearth, giving out a little heat, but the room was never warm since there were no shutters at the windows and there was always a through breeze. It had been the private domain of the Stewards of Arcady since anyone could remember, perhaps even from Arkata's day.

The room lacked any obvious interior design, the walls decorated with implements of a long-bygone age. Coloured fishing flies and hooks clung to the plaster, the skull of a large long-toothed fish sat on a narrow ledge, and a short plain hunting horn carved from bone, yellowed with age but the only item not covered in dust or enveloped by spiders' webs, lay within Bellene's reach. A few dried rushes and leaves added to the collection of unidentifiable oddities the Stewards of Arcady had gathered over the generations. Like all other Arcady-bred children, Ninian found the tower fascinating as well as intimidating; no one ever knew when Bellene might be watching them from its many windows. It was a powerful incentive to work hard, for the Steward was a severe taskmistress, quite capable of ordering meals missed or extra work given to those she saw shirking their duties.

'Well, Affer?' Bellene's look was not encouraging; a streak of the same impatience so evident in Ran underlay her mood, and Affer swallowed.

'It was this morning, Bellene, in Maryon's room in the infirmary. I couldn't help it; I didn't want to hear him, but I couldn't shut him out.' Sweat beaded his brow, and Ran put a hand on his shoulder.

'He hates it,' she said stiffly.

'But he must tell us.' Under Bellene's gaze, perhaps from long habit, Ran subsided. 'Go on, Affer.'

'It was Kerron's thoughts; I can always tell it's him. He sounds quite different from Quest.' Affer shook his head blindly: 'It was when he was talking about the illness in the north, and the lake. He was lying, Bellene; he knew it was all true, but he didn't want to believe it or think about it. He felt confused and angry, wishing the problem would go away.'

'And why does this knowledge upset you so much?' Bellene's voice was acid. 'Speak more slowly, Affer, so we can all hear what you say.'

'I'm sorry.' In the abjectness of his misery, he reminded Ninian of no one more than Sarai. 'His mind was open to me; I didn't like it, his thoughts – I think he hates us, the *akhal*,' he continued dismally. 'I think if something happened to us, he'd be glad, but he wouldn't actively do us harm, just not lift a hand to help. It's hard to explain, he sounds so lonely, but at the same time not alone.'

'Nonsense!'

Ran was furious in her brother's defence. 'It's not nonsense! Affer never makes things up.' She glared at her elderly relative.

'You will not interrupt me when I am speaking.' Bellene sat stiffly upright, head erect; she did not raise her voice, but at once there were no other sounds in the room. 'While I am Steward of Arcady, my word is your command. Is that plain, Ran, or must I send you to work in the smoking sheds for a month?'

Ninian saw her cousin struggle with her temper and held her own breath, but sense won out, and she mumbled an inaudible apology. Ninian could have told her that the older Bellene grew, the less tolerant she became. As more of the details of life at Arcady slipped from her memory, so Bellene fought to affirm her own authority with a more than imperious hand.

'Affer, I was not doubting your word; you were always an excessively truthful boy.' Affer managed a doubtful smile at the tepid compliment. 'However, I think you may be reading too much into what you heard; you said yourself it was confused, and this ability of yours, like Ninian's, is unpredictable.'

Unwillingly, Affer nodded, although it was obvious to Ninian he believed he had spoken no more than the exact truth. She wondered what it must be like to hear the true thoughts in someone else's mind, to sense their real feelings. She thought it would be an extremely uncomfortable experience, even for someone less sensitive, with better barriers, than Affer. And how did you separate a momentary impulse from a deeper thought? What would she have heard in Quest's mind that morning, if she had been able to listen?

'I feel we must wait before we take any action of our own, not least to see whether young Maryon recovers,' Bellene observed. 'This is hardly the time to go against the orders of Kerron, let alone Lord Quorden. These are uneasy times, and we at Arcady are more vulnerable than most, since our existence alone irks the priests' sense of what is fitting. If there is a chance this is rebel business, we should abstain until we know more.'

'But don't you want to know the truth?' Ran half-rose to her feet. 'Shouldn't you send someone north to see if Maryon is right?'

'You, I suppose? You were always so transparent, Calloran.' Bellene's tone was dry; Ran stiffened at the use of her full name, which she detested. 'You expect me to send you to Ismon to indulge your travel-lust; well, you will be sadly disappointed!' Ran bit her lip; Ninian saw her eyes blaze with sudden fury. 'If,' Bellene continued scathingly, 'and I stress the word, *if*, I send anyone north in due course, I shall consider sending you, since your work is so unwilling as to be almost worthless!'

Hope leaped into Ran's hungry face. 'Thank you.'

'You've nothing yet to thank me for, Calloran. You know my edict; if you leave Arcady without my express permission, you don't come back! Not even to see your brother.' To Ninian's relief, Ran listened in silence; they had all heard Bellene say much the same before, and even Affer was not really afraid Ran would desert him.

The old lady's good humour seemed to have been restored by her outburst, or perhaps the assertion of control. She rapped her thumb ring on the table for attention, then leaned back in the heavy chair with a self-satisfied expression.

'Poor Ran; you think me very cruel to keep you here, but I would be worse than cruel to let you go outside the Wetlands,' she went on, half-pitying. 'Here, we have water and enough to eat, and our family and friends all around us. But beyond the Wetlands there is the Order and their guard and the drought: league upon league of dusty lands, where starving men prey upon each other and on women for enough to eat and drink, or for their other hungers! Outside the lakes, life is very different. The overfull cities breed rebellion in these dry days, and the priests stand by and watch while their flocks starve, and even the Emperor, Amestatis himself, has no power to intervene, for his father, Amestatis IV, gave away the rule to the High Priest of the Order, to the first Quorden.' Bellene gave a cackle of laughter. 'And if young Maryon and his rebel kin think they can change the world, perhaps they need a lesson in common sense!'

'I should like to see for myself.' Ran managed to speak calmly, despite the fire in her core; Ninian listened with relieved admiration. 'I should like to go over the mountains and see where that green light came from, the one we saw yesterday.'

'Kerron said that if we went to service in temple two days from now he would have had word from Enapolis about the light,' Ninian observed, sensing from long experience that Bellene was about to crush her cousin's hopes. 'I thought I would go then, and take Sarai.'

'Sensible, and it will please her father.' Bellene transferred her unfriendly attentions to her heir; she could never resist a dig at her relations with Quest. 'Did he say anything more?'

'He seemed interested to know what you thought about the light, and whether you were saying it had anything to do with the old tales you used to tell us when we were children. I said you weren't.'

'I see.' Bellene turned the words over in her mind, nodding. 'Yes, I think it would be a good plan for you to take Sarai, and Ran and Affer too, to this service. It may prove illuminating.'

'Do you remember what I said yesterday? That the lights in the lake were important to us,' Ninian said hesitantly, ignoring the attempt at a pun. 'Do you think this other light, too, matters?'

Bellene shrugged. 'How should I know? If it came from the eastern temple of the Plains, perhaps; perhaps it signifies some survival from the old times, before the Order. There have always been tales of such things, legends of power. Here at Arcady, where we are guardians of – ' But instead of concluding her sentence she broke off, looking cross. Ninian's curiosity was aroused; for more than once Bellene had hinted at some secret that lay with the Stewards of Arcady, and it seemed they had just come very close to it. But she was not to be enlightened. 'Never mind,' the Steward added shortly. 'Ninian, where is your daughter? I told her to come to me for instruction this morning, and she failed.'

'I sent her to take a look at the fish-nets; she was upset.' Ninian shrugged away the lack of sympathy from the old woman who had no interest in nor capacity for understanding how anyone except herself might feel.

'Then send her to me after the noon meal; her handwriting is a disgrace for a girl of her age. If you want to train her as your heir, she must have a legible hand at the very least!'

'I haven't thought that far ahead.' Ninian rose to her feet, glad the gathering could be brought to an end. 'If you'll excuse me, I've work that must be seen to.'

This reminder earned her an icy look. 'And I've some thinking to do! Out, then; all of you. You've already wasted too much of my time.'

Dismissed, the trio carefully refrained from speech until they reached the base of the stairway, aware that sound travelled all too clearly up to the tower.

'She's in a bitter mood today,' Ran muttered, once safely outside.

'This business has shaken her more than she shows, and she's aware there's nothing she can do about it,' Ninian said, trying to be fair to both sides; Ran, too, could be irritating. 'She's too old to do much more than supervise the estate nowadays, and resents it deeply.'

'Is that why she won't let me go? Because she's too old to keep hold of Arcady any more?'

'There's some truth in that.' More disturbed than usual by something in her cousin's face, Ninian put a hand on her arm. 'Be patient, Ran; you know I'll let you leave, when the time comes.'

Ran turned her face away. 'But how long will that be? Bellene could live for years; she's as tough as flint.'

'Don't.' Ninian lifted her hand away. 'Don't wish her dead.'

'I didn't mean that, not really.' Ran flushed guiltily. 'If only she'd let me go.'

'Just be patient.' Ninian saw Affer was upset. 'It's still possible you may have a chance to go north; Maryon is very ill.'

'And if he dies, I get away. It seems those are the only choices – Bellene's or Maryon's death and I can leave, or they live and I must stay.' Ran let out a bitter laugh. 'It makes it hard to hope for the right thing!'

And it seemed that not all her thoughts were directed the way she would have liked, for Affer turned a despairing face to her, as if he had captured an errant and unwelcome idea.

'You're my conscience, Affer,' Ran said, managing to smile; and she gave him a hug. 'Don't worry. I'll try to be good.'

His face brightened as he heard the truth in her voice. Ninian, watching them, thought she had rarely admired Ran more, for fighting so hard against her own desperate longings in order to ease her brother's anxiety.

People, she reflected as she left them, were never as they seemed, but a far more complex blend of moods and thoughts and personalities. She wondered what it would be like to be born to no family, no ties at all of affection or duty, like Kerron. Would it be easier, then, to do as you pleased, without the need to consider the results of your actions? Or would such an existence be unbearably lonely? Love and even liking were reciprocal bonds, needing response. Was that what Kerron lacked? A friend? Or was it that he had never seemed to want anyone, unless it was Ran?

What would Ran have been like without Affer? Or herself without Sarai, and without the burden of being heir to Arcady? Would she, Ninian, be truly free, or only a selfish and self-centred woman without a gift for affection? Was it human bonds of love and liking that made society, or was it possible to live an estimable existence without such ties, as the priests claimed? And if it was, what was the purpose of such a life?

Ninian sighed, relieved in the main that she did not have the opportunity to discover what might have been. If he had been reading her thoughts, she feared neither Affer nor herself would have liked what they might uncover in the deeper recesses of her mind.

2

Kerron took the message-capsules from Jordan, the bird-man, but one glance at their markings told him what he needed to know. He walked away from the mews, away from prying eyes.

Had the sickness really spread so far, and in so short a time? He was not certain whether or not he believed it, yet it was true there was no news from the north.

'Well, voice?' he asked aloud. 'Have you nothing to say about this? Is this a part of what you want me to understand?'

'*It is a part of the whole. The lake is life to the* akhal; *the lights are life to the lake. That is all you need to know.*'

Kerron's thoughts were confused. A part of him was not unhappy at the illness spreading around Lake Ismon; the area was filled with trouble-makers, hot-headed *akhal* rebels. Yet, for all that, he was oddly unwilling to be responsible for their deaths. He wished he knew nothing about the situation, could know nothing until it was too late. It might be a cowardly ideal, but Kerron was too intelligent to be unaware that to be the cause of so much death would alter him infinitely beyond his present understanding.

'What do you want me to do?' he said to the air. 'Does this pollution have anything to do with the lights in the lake?'

Silence answered him. Kerron took out the other capsules and looked at them, wanting distraction.

The messages came from a wide area. There were none from Enapolis, and Kerron pondered the question of what, precisely, the Plainsman Lord Quorden was so eager to question could possibly know. The antipathy between Emperor and High Priest of the Order was hardly a secret, nor, given the transfer of power from one to the other, could it be otherwise. Yet could anyone, even a rebel, be of sufficient value to the Order to be worth the death of hundreds, if what Maryon said was true? And the man was still secreted somewhere; there had been no news of him.

Word of riots in the Plains city of Ammon had reached Kerron many days before, but the Wetlands had no over-populated cities, no starving people. If any rebels had fled to the Wetlands seeking sanctuary they would be discovered in due course, no matter if they found allies around Ismon. Outsiders were too noticeable among the *akhal* to stay hidden forever.

It was plain to Kerron that Lord Quorden had some deep-laid scheme in mind for his rule of the Empire which did not include Emperor Amestatis; he had sought means to discredit the old man for as long as Kerron had been aware of the battle between them, and Kerron was willing enough to help, if only to advance his own ambitions.

He would do nothing; he would obey the orders of Lord Quorden. That was his duty, and his future.

The deaths of *akhal* from Ismon were none of his doing and not his concern. He blotted out the thoughts from his mind, exerting his will to consign them to oblivion.

Chapter Three

1

It was only the third morning after the sighting of the green light from the eastern Plains, but even so attendance at the temple at Wellwater might still have been sparse had it not been for two message-birds the previous evening, seen winging their way home from the south-east to their mews. As it was, the place was crowded with *akhal* dressed in their smartest clothes, mostly pale blues and greens.

'Standing room only,' Ran murmured to Ninian as they found a place for themselves and Sarai on the right, facing the altar. Affer, looking miserable, stood reluctantly on the left with the men and older boys from Arcady.

'Well, everyone wants to know the news from Enapolis.' But Ninian spoke in a low voice, noticing who had just managed to find a place beside her and Sarai; her heart sank. Cassia, wife to Quest's brother Jerom, was no favourite of hers. Tall, handsome, and cool of manner, Cassia always seemed to Ninian devoid of any emotion warmer than tolerance.

Attendance at services was always erratic at Wellwater. *Akhal* wandered in and out of the temple as they saw fit, staying for as long as they felt necessary, with a great deal of coming and going by the pier as rafts and boats were drawn up and launched; it was not respectful to swim to service.

There was less noise than usual inside the temple, for Quest had stood up to preach. His aureole of bright hair crowned a face which no one could deny was lit from within. His expression was rapt, as if he were truly lost in contemplation of the Lords of Light, and as he began to speak his voice took on new depth and richness. The *akhal* normally hung on his words, drawn by his obvious sincerity and gift for oratory.

'For as we are to the land in which we live, so are we to the gods, that we possess both that same capacity for great good as well as great evil,' he proclaimed, and he seemed no longer only Quest, as if his self were dissolved into some mystic union. 'And that is how we shall be judged, in our duality. In sacrifice, we give up those things we cherish most dearly: our wives and our husbands, our children and our friends. In doing so, we begin to comprehend the greatness of their value at that very moment of our loss, to make the sting sharper still and our offering more precious.

'Fear not. The gods know well the measure of each offering, as well as those we withhold, and so they judge each one of us according to our merits . . .'

Kerron, listening with only half an ear since he had heard Quest preach a similar sermon before, wondered cynically how his fellow priest could possibly believe the nonsense he was spouting. The concept of deities who sounded no more than petty clerks, spending their days recording credits and debits in thousands upon thousands of columns as they judged the hearts of the faithful, struck Kerron as both mercenary and ridiculous. If he had chosen to believe in any deities, they would not be so mean-minded.

Unlike Quest, Kerron knew the real function of the Order and its creed, which was to legitimise the seizure of power by Lord Quorden from the Emperor. The present High Priest might pay lip-service to his religious function, but his piety was entirely political in nature. The old gods had served that purpose for the Emperor, the new for his own Order; it was a war between the two factions with rule of the peoples as its prize.

'The light you saw in the east on the Plains of Ashtar is a sign from the gods themselves that they have found us worthy of favour,' Quest continued. 'We have been sent word by Lord Quorden himself that the portents for the harvest this year are favourable. There will be food once more for all the hungry peoples of the Empire, and the rains will come again and free us from the fear of the drought and a dry death.'

Kerron gave a snort, aware that since the *akhal* were almost entirely self-sufficient, needing to buy little grain from the Plains farmers, the promise was less than impressive. The lake people rarely travelled outside the Wetlands, even if the Order permitted such licence, and had little knowledge of hardships elsewhere, of the starvation of the Plains people and those in the cities as once-fertile soil became dust as the rains failed. Was Quest really so naïve that he believed what he was saying? The Order controlled all trade in grain and could pretend harvest yields were whatever figure they chose. But he noted that the explanation for the Plains light seemed to be well received.

When the voice told him he must destroy the lights in the lake, was there any link to this light also? It had possessed some of the same qualities of brightness and intensity.

'Yet we must not presume on the favour of the gods, and must continue in our worship and our sacrifice, each man striving towards the absolute obedience the gods require from us, and which is our first duty . . . '

Kerron saw Ran lean to Ninian, her lips forming the words: '*And women too, I presume?*' and saw Ninian shake her head with a smile. He wondered what the priests of Enapolis would make of the *akhal* form of service, which was so very different from the austere and authoritatively strict ritual observed in the capital.

Growing up at Arcady among a group of strong-minded girls and women, Kerron was conscious that the Order's teaching on the spiritual inferiority of women was just a trick, a device to elevate the status of the priesthood, ordaining women's gendered incapacity for the role to encourage their subjection; making use of religious fervour to order and to authorise commonplace misogyny. He believed in it no more than in the Lords of Light, nor any of the texts the first Lord Quorden had written down as the fruits of his supposed communication with his deities.

Other religious cults had grown up in the early days of the Order, before they were suppressed, and Kerron, who had studied their histories during his time in Enapolis with some interest, had been intrigued to discover that most of them found some means to reduce the status of women, rendering them less valuable, less capable of perfection, ordaining their servitude. Only one had not, an egalitarian cult which had originated among the fisher people; its members had been quashed with greater ferocity than any of the others, such views not only heretical but threatening to social order.

Kerron noticed Sarai scowl and glance up at her father, then down at her lap, where she began to tap her fingers on her thigh, obviously bored. It pleased him to think that Quest's own daughter, an intelligent child, should be less than impressed with his preaching. He watched her surreptitiously. There were times he knew bitter envy of her, who could enjoy the solace of knowing herself wanted, but at others, more rarely, he felt pity for her, torn so obviously between the contrasting forces of her parents.

His own had not remained long enough to cause him any such conflict of loyalty. He, at least, was free from such bonds.

The main structure of the temple conformed in style to the Enapolis model where its ritual did not, being a high, domed building, the dome itself of white stone. The interior possessed a complex geometric pattern in dark blue and gold, the colours of the Order, gilding the stone floor, the design repeated in the dome high overhead. Elsewhere, however, the *akhal* horror of a dry death was evidenced behind the altar, where the smiling image of Jiva, the beneficent Lord of Light, opposed his malevolent twin, Antior, whose hands held fire, ready to rain it down on the unsuspecting *akhal*. It amused Kerron to note that the piles of offerings on the altar, the dried fish and wine and ells of cloth, were higher in front of Antior than they were in front of his gentle brother. Pragmatism dictated that force called for greater appeasement than did softness.

'Why have you done nothing about the lights in the lake, when you have been commanded to seek out their source and destroy it?'

Kerron stiffened in surprise. The voice had never before spoken during a service, and rarely as if it were his master.

'You are dilatory. Why do you delay? Have you not listened when you were told that only darkness will bring you what you most desire?'

'But why?' Kerron whispered. 'And how?'

What was he supposed to do if the origin of the lights lay fathoms deep in the lake? He was at best a poor swimmer in comparison with the *akhal*, unable to hold his breath underwater for more than a fifty-count, and he could not go deep: the pressure was agony to his ears.

'Do you seek to break the bargain made between us?'

'Never that.'

The voice must have been satisfied by the response, for Kerron felt the odd sense of pressure that accompanied its presence withdraw, leaving him disturbed in mind. The bargain between them had not, surely, suggested he must do as the voice bade him? It was his helpmeet, not his owner.

He wished again it would advise him on the situation in the north. He had received no word of any kind from Ismon since his visit to Arcady. Perhaps Maryon had been telling the truth.

A sharp cry drew him from his uneasy abstractions. Kerron looked up to see Affer fighting his way out of the throng of worshippers in a panic. With a word to Ninian, Ran, too, began to make her way back to the doors at the rear of the temple. Ninian looked as if she would have liked to join them, but Cassia had a proprietary hand on Sarai's shoulder.

An uneasy sensation trickled down Kerron's spine as he watched Ran catch up with her brother and draw him outside. Others might suggest that Affer was mentally unstable, but they had been boys together and Kerron knew it was not so. Affer was excessively sensitive, not retarded. It was an odd coincidence that he should have cried out just at that moment, and not for the first time Kerron wondered if anything out of the ordinary had happened to his fellow pilgrims in the Barren Lands. If he had found the voice there, or been found by it, what had Ran and the others discovered? What had they taken in with them which had been returned to them, as he had been given back more than himself? He had never asked Ran, almost afraid to learn the answer, but now he wished he had.

What would he do if the voice ever chose to leave him? The thought chilled him, despite its recent peremptory tones. He shivered at the contemplation of so great a loneliness.

Affer knew the thoughts were Kerron's; no one else's mind set held the same mingling of hard certainty and unexpected confusion. That awareness did nothing to prevent him experiencing the full horror of the unwanted knowledge that flowed from Kerron. Affer cried out in protest, desperate for it to stop but unable to shut it out except by physically distancing himself.

Ran caught up with him by the doors, but one look at his face must have convinced her to let him be, for instead of drawing him back she followed him out into the fresh air and down to the pier, where their raft was waiting. There was no one else about, and she waited patiently for him to recover, struggling with his sense of shame and revulsion.

'Are you better now?' she asked eventually.

'I – yes.' But Affer shuddered, though the thoughts he had heard were now only in his memory.

'What was it? What did you hear?'

He found it hard to speak. 'Kerron,' he managed to croak. 'His mind.'

Ran was frowning. 'Was it so horrible?'

'Yes. No. Horrible, but tormented, too.' Affer shuddered again. 'Ran, you can't imagine.'

'No.' She took his arm and drew him down to sit on the shingle. 'What was he thinking?'

'It was about the sickness at Carne, and around Lake Ismon.' Affer swallowed bile, knowing he could never put into words the pictures Kerron's thoughts had conjured in his brain. 'He was thinking about them, and there was such hate in his mind, but fear, too, and terror of being alone.'

'Hush.' She put a hand over his mouth, and he knew he must have been babbling. He wanted to be sick, but there was nothing in his stomach, and after a time the feeling subsided.

'So it was all true.' Ran released him and sat back, leaning on her hands.

'You're thinking we can get away from Arcady now, aren't you?' Affer asked, suddenly hearing the thought as clearly as his own.

'Yes. Do you mind?'

'No.' He wondered if he meant it. 'It's easier when there's no one else near.'

'I know. Bellene must say yes now.' Despite his own lingering sense of horror, Ran's eyes shone. 'Don't be upset, Affer; I don't mean to hurt you, but I've waited so long.'

'You sound glad.'

'Sorry.' But she was not repentant. 'Just think: I might even be able to go as far as the Plains, to see where that light came from!'

Affer said nothing, relieved at the intense excitement coming from his sister, a welcome overlay to his own thoughts.

He knew he was weak; he knew he should be as strong and capable as Ran, but there was no point in self-deception. His excess of sensibility drained him, for he seemed to have no means to defend or protect himself from the unwelcome floods of feeling that threatened at times to overwhelm him, exhausting him. There was peace only in solitude, where he did not have to fear the infringement of other minds on his.

When he was alone, at least he knew the fears were his own.

Whatever had happened to him in the Barren Lands a decade before, Affer knew that in some fashion he would never understand it had stunted his development. Ran still treated him as if he was a child, and so did Bellene, and in a sense they were right: the ability others seemed to possess, the knowledge of what was important and what was not, had passed him by. He often wondered why the ability sometimes to hear thoughts had been given to *him*, what quality of his had earned him such a torture? Had the gods given him what they thought he deserved? But why?

He only half-listened while Ran enthusiastically outlined a route for their proposed journey. A school of pink fish was swimming in the shallows of the lake with jerky movements, changing direction in a perfect arc at some unseen alarm. Their scales glittered in the sunlight, and Affer concentrated on their motion, wishing not to think.

He had learned over the years to identify the minds of those he heard most often. Ran's was tempestuous, fiery and disturbing, as if she were in constant argument with herself. He knew she loved him, but could not avoid hearing the undertones of frustration which sometimes made her wish him strong and capable.

Ninian was easier. He liked her thoughts, which were usually clear and warm. She had none of Ran's confusion, but strong, positive feelings, seeking ways to resolve problems rather than brooding over them. Sarai, however, was more like Ran. Affer could hear, oddly enough, echoes of both Quest and Ninian in the tone of her mind, for she had some of Ninian's strength as well as Quest's stubborn dreaminess, a difficult combination.

Quest himself was hard to understand, and sometimes Affer was puzzled by his thoughts; it was as if Quest was capable of believing directly contradictory ideas at the same time. If Affer understood him right, his priestly calling was one of submersion of his self in the service of the gods; but Affer had never sensed such submission in Quest's mind. The priest had a very strong sense of self, although apparently unaware of it. It was as if there was a background and a foreground to his mind, separate, as if the latter actively reinforced the former, each unknown to the other. Quest preached of the riches promised by the gods after death, but he was terrified of dying, an empty space in his mind at the prospect of not existing.

And there was Kerron.

On the surface his thought processes came over as arrogant and insensitive; yet hiding below that superficial layer Kerron's mind, more than any other Affer heard, seethed with a confusion of hot anger and pain and resentment and deep loneliness. Affer thought the reason he had never understood Kerron was because the priest had never understood himself.

'Are you listening, sleepyhead?'

Affer gave a start. 'I'm sorry; I was thinking.'

'Never mind.' Ran was staring into the lake. 'I expect you think me a fool, Affer, but I feel, just now, as if I'd been tied up tight for years, and suddenly someone has come along and cut me free.' There was a catch in her voice. 'I can't tell you how much it means to me to get away from Arcady.'

'I do know.' It was true; he did. Affer thought he was probably the only person able to understand the depths of his sister's need to escape what to her was the prison of Arcady. Just as the legacy of their pilgrimage had altered him, so it had changed Ran, too, taking her brave spirit and twisting her longing for adventure into need, so that her passion to explore the world beyond the Wetlands was transformed into a desperate hunger which remained unsatisfied, stifling her. No one else, least of all Bellene, understood that.

'Aren't you afraid, Ran?' he asked.

'Afraid?' She frowned. 'Of what?'

'Of what we may find.'

He caught a flash of guilty acknowledgement in her mind, then heard the impatience that overshadowed it.

'Knowing is better than imagining, Affer,' she said at last. 'There's no point in being afraid of something before it happens.'

But Affer, as he sat on the shingle, feeling the light caress of the wind on his face and breathing in long gulps of lake-scented air, was suddenly assaulted by a sensation of suffocation, of decaying matter, of drowning in a river of decomposing flesh and rotting vegetation. The sour smell was strong in his nostrils, making him gag, and he only barely stopped himself retching. Then the air was fresh and clean again, and he knew none of his imaginings had been real, but only the stuff of his own fears.

It was at that moment that the drums began to sound at Arcady, and the great bell tolled from the roof with its identifying single tone.

Bellene sat waiting in the main hall at Arcady, ignoring the boys and girls bustling about importantly as they laid the long tables for the noon meal.

There was no fire in the wide hearth, since it was well on into spring, and Bellene would have thought it a weakness to display how strongly she felt the cold as she aged. A fire during the day was at best wasteful, at worst shameful. She would not admit that cold was her reason for choosing to await Quest in the hall rather than the tower.

She could no longer swim, even on the warmest days of summer, nor enjoy her old solitude. Her blood had thinned, her breathing was shallow and rapid, as if her lungs were too worn and tired to draw in proper breaths. Bellene despised this weakness in herself, this evidence that she was losing control over her own body as well as of the daily concerns at Arcady.

Yet she was alive, and young Maryon was dead.

Morning was an unusual time to die. It was more usual for death to visit the sick in the hours between midnight and dawn, when the spirit and body were at their most separate. Maryon's had been no easy dying, no simple slipping away, but a struggle as he fought to stay alive, as if the illness that drained him was a physical opponent which could be beaten.

The drums and bell would bring them; Ninian, and Sarai, and Ran, and Quest.

Bellene did not mourn the passing of one man, even a young one; there had been so many changes in her long life that she was beyond mourning and loss. She had reached an age where she spent more time considering what was to come than what had been, and while she paid lip-service to the Order's creed, she had little time in reality for so austere and wrathful a religion, which offered little consolation to the old, and in which suffering and sacrifice seemed the most substantial components.

What were the priests' assurances of an eternity of service to the gods but an attempt to disguise the reality of death? There were moments she could even look forward to a cessation to existence, even while she feared it.

She was better able to believe the lakes themselves were alive, that all the creatures dependent on their water for existence, *akhal* included, were a part of the same single animating spirit. Quest would have condemned her views as heretical, had she been so foolish as to voice them, but they comforted her. There was great consolation in perceiving her own term as a part of the whole, a cycle in which nothing was wasted and where there was no ending.

Few *akhal* were old enough, as she was, to remember a time when there had been no Order, no priests. Bellene could recall the conversion of the *akhal*, an event which took place rather later than in the cities of the Empire. It had been when Bellene herself was fifteen years old, five years after the Foundation of the Order, a desperate choice for the *akhal* made in a bad year when there had been no rains and no torrents from the mountains in the spring. What were the words of the old song?

> 'With the spring came the sun,
> But the snow did not melt,
> Nor the rivers run,
> And shadow lay thick
> On Ismon's bed,
> Where only the weed grew,
> Living, among the dead.
> And the sun hid its face
> In the mists – '

The land had been parched, lake levels lower than since the first end of the world, and the *akhal* had believed the old prophecy come true, that the second end of the world was coming; for it was said that when the spring torrents failed, so too would the Empire.

The priests had come from the east and the south and spread their message of sacrifice and salvation of the land, of redemption and the promise of life if the *akhal* would only shed their false beliefs and accept the truths of the Lords of Light. And later, by the time water flowed again from the mountains the year following, the Order was established with priestly and temporal authority at Wellwater.

Arcady, oldest of all the estates, home of the heirs of Arkata and Adamon, had been converted with the rest. What choice had they, when the priests proclaimed that unbelief angered the gods, and in that anger they would withhold the rains and condemn the *akhal* to the dry death? Only Ival and Isma of Wellwater, along with one hundred and fifty of their kindred, had held out against the priests; they had died. It was said, privately, that their drinking water, the well after which the estate was named, had been poisoned, but no one knew how it had happened. That they all died had been used by the Order as proof of the anger and vengeance of the Lords of Light, and the priests took the estate for their own.

There was no more resistance. Soon after, the priests and their soldiers – and what need should men of gods have for soldiers? Bellene wondered – had rowed over to Sheer Island and destroyed the old statue and the great Tearstone which had been its heart, shattering them to pieces, claiming the light was evil. But even at fifteen Bellene had not believed the Tearstone could be malign, Arkata's light, for it was she who had caused the temple to be built, and more, if the old tales were true.

Light.

The lights in the lake were the same she recalled from her childhood, but the Tearstone had been fixed. A gift of light lay at the heart of the secret trust of Arcady, the charge she had not yet passed on to Ninian, which must be done soon. It would be unforgivable to die while she alone held the secret, even if part of her rebelled at sharing the burden she had carried for so many years. Dark days were coming to Avardale.

It was hard to let go.

Bellene sighed, startling a boy engaged in putting out round wooden plates on the table behind her, making him jump and drop his load; the plates landed on the table with a crash.

It was while she was still engaged in telling the boy, in precise terms, exactly what the future held for careless children at Arcady, that Bellene was made aware of Quest, Ninian, Ran, Affer and Sarai, waiting patiently inside the hall, listening to her fluent diatribe with rapt attention.

The main hall at Arcady occupied almost half the space of the original ground floor, the remainder taken up by kitchens, scullery and storerooms. It should have been light, since it had three outside walls and a profusion of windows, but perhaps because the stone from which the original house had been built was so dark and so solid, or perhaps because the whitewash had not yet been renewed after the smoky winter fires, the hall was dim. Bellene's tower, reached from the north-east corner where a second door led into its base, seemed to cast its gloom over the place, in spirit if not in reality.

All the furniture was heavy, massive, built for longevity not for beauty, to last for generations of *akhal*. It was a pride of Arcady that it was rare to waste precious wood on new chairs or tables or bedsteads; if something was broken or damaged, wherever possible it was repaired, not replaced. Every piece in the hall bore the patina of extreme age.

'Come over here,' Bellene summoned imperiously. She clapped her hands at the remaining children, who disappeared at once.

'So Maryon is dead,' Quest observed, standing over her. 'I heard the drums.' Drums were for death; three times three rolls for a woman, three times two for a man at Arcady, the reverse of custom elsewhere.

'Where's Kerron? Why isn't he with you?' Bellene's eyes snapped with annoyance.

'He had other duties.'

'Sit down.' The old woman scowled, indicating a heavy chair opposite her own, ignoring her own kin. 'How can I talk to you when you stand towering over me, like Mount Elas!'

'Very well.' Quest took the proffered seat.

'Sarai, fetch your father some wine,' Ninian whispered. 'You know the kind he likes.' Sarai nodded and skipped away.

'Maryon died, but I don't know why,' Bellene said coolly. 'Except that nothing we could give him had any effect.'

'I see.' Quest frowned. 'And you're still certain this sickness isn't contagious?'

'Ran, Ninian and I have shared the nursing, and none of us is the worse for it, not even I, for all my years.' Bellene met his gaze. 'The young man's dead, Quest, so what about the tale he told? Are we still to do nothing, and wait for this pollution to come to Avardale?'

'Are you suggesting Kerron lied when he assured us there was no plague, and no pollution?'

'Perhaps.'

'Can you give me any reason why he should, or why I should believe he should?'

'Don't be more of a fool than you must,' Bellene snapped. 'Of course I can, and so can you. If I were being generous, I could say he kept the news to himself to prevent panic spreading around the lakes. He might simply have underestimated the dangers of the disease.'

'I brought your wine, Father.'

Sarai returned, holding out a long-stemmed cup, carved from horn and filled to the brim. She avoided her mother's gaze and stood leaning against Quest's chair, not quite touching him.

'Thank you, Sarai.' As he smiled at her, the resemblance between them was marked. Ninian felt a stab of pain, as if Quest had somehow stolen a part of her child away from her. He went on: 'Did you enjoy the service today?'

'I suppose so.' She looked down and scuffed her feet on the wooden floor. 'It went on such a long time.'

Ninian caught surprise and hurt on Quest's face, and thought grimly that if he spent more time with Sarai he would have expected her response. He might understand how much she resented his impersonality in temple, and how deeply she objected to the gulf the Order placed between him and his daughter.

'Away with you, child,' Bellene interrupted. 'You may talk to your father when we've finished here.'

'But – ' But Sarai, looking sullenly at her elderly kinswoman, realised the futility of protest. She waited a moment, as if hoping her father would ask her to stay, then turned on her heel and stalked off, back rigid.

'I want her away from here.' Quest turned to Ninian. 'You nursed Maryon here, with all the possibility of infection, and now he's dead. If you couldn't cure him, it seems to me you can't honestly claim to know much about the course of the illness.'

The direction of his thoughts was obvious. 'We're sure Maryon brought no infection,' Ninian answered calmly. 'We've a great deal of experience with fevers here at Arcady; I wouldn't risk Sarai to a mere opinion.'

'But that's precisely what you are doing. I'll take her to Kandria myself and leave her with Jerom, where she should have been sent the instant Maryon was given shelter here.' Quest's eyes darkened. 'If you had paid the slightest heed to my wishes, there need never have been any risk to my daughter.'

'And there's none now.'

'We're here to discuss Maryon and the dangers of pollution, not Sarai,' Bellene interjected crossly. 'In any case, that is not an issue. The child is Arcady born, and remains here.'

Quest got to his feet. 'I have a right to place her where I think she'll be safe!'

'Here, no, you have no such right.' The quarrel seemed to give Bellene pleasure; her eyes brightened. 'At Arcady, we count the mother, not the father. Sarai is Ninian's daughter, witnessed as such by me and others present at the birth.'

'The law rules descent through the male line,' Quest said angrily. 'Your custom is counter to the rule. Unless I take my daughter with me, now, I will do my best to see the inheritance customs of Arcady annulled for all time.'

'You can't.' Bellene gave him an evil smile. 'We at Arcady are the heirs to Arkata, first of all the *akhal*; our law is hers. I hold letters from the Emperor himself, from Amestatis, acknowledging Arcady's right to follow its customs, with an endorsement from the Lord Hilarion, the Imperial Heir, which I obtained during his visit to the Wetlands last year.'

'He's not yet acknowledged heir – ' Quest began.

'Priest you may be, but the Order has existed a mere five and seventy years, whereas from time immemorial Arcady has passed from woman to woman,' Bellene remarked grandly, ignoring the interruption. 'Our customs have at least as much force as yours.'

'The gods ordained the hierarchy of man and woman in the Empire, revealing themselves to a man, not a woman. That tells us, even if they had not, that there is some quality which exists in man and not in woman, or that there is some lack in her. The existence of your customs are an offence, to the Order and to the gods themselves.'

'What nonsense!' Bellene pronounced with deep scorn. 'We in the Empire all spring from common roots, *akhal* and sand people and Plains people, men and women. Do we look at the fish in the lake and say the males are in some fashion superior to the females, when it takes more than a keen eye to tell the difference between them? Why should I believe it when the gods tell me I am less than a person by reason of my sex? And now, because we choose not to follow your pattern, you make our objection not merely difficult, but conveniently heretical! Take yourself off, priest! I have nothing more to say to you.' She turned away with an angry sniff.

Quest's gaze sought Ninian.

'Sarai stays with me,' she said quickly. 'If you were going to take her yourself, I should accept you had the right; but you have none to send her away from us both.'

'None of you understands that the gods do indeed do as they will, not as you want,' Quest retorted. 'The custom of Arcady will fail if it goes against the will of the Lords of Light.'

'Or yours?' Ran observed contemptuously.

'Why must you make our daughter a battlefield between us?' Ninian asked bitterly. 'You put your own selfish feelings before Sarai's welfare.'

'And what of you? Are you so certain she will come to no harm here? Have you bothered to consider what may happen when you're proven wrong and I right?'

'Sarai doesn't want to go away; she's told me so.' Ninian felt troubled, trying to understand his continued hostility. 'Why are you always so sure you're right? Won't you ever accept what I say?'

'If you go against the will of the gods, how can you be other than mistaken?'

'But who is to say what the gods will – why you, rather than me?' Ninian asked, close to unexpected despair.

'Because I am a priest of the Order, ordained by Lord Quorden in Enapolis, servant to the gods. Their authority in me is what makes me your superior, no quality of mine. It is to that authority you should give way, not my own.'

'But how can I tell? Even here you might claim divine authority, when it's only a mask for your own wishes. You're saying that as a priest you must always be right, always have the upper hand in any dispute.'

'Not me, but the priest who is myself, yes,' Quest agreed seriously.

'No.' But Ninian said no more. Not only was the argument pointless, it also veered dangerously close to a statement of heresy, and she would not give him that weapon to use against her. 'No, Quest,' she continued carefully. 'Our customs are different. We must agree to disagree.'

'This argument isn't over, Ninian. Think about what I've said, and you'll come to understand what you must do.'

'Must?'

'*Enough!*' Bellene raised her voice to an uncomfortable level. Silenced, Quest stood and took his leave with a curt bow.

'We're still left with the mystery of Maryon's death,' the Steward continued, once he had gone. 'Ran, you have my leave to journey north and report on what you find.'

'May Affer come with me?'

Bellene inclined her head. 'Well, Affer?' she asked. 'Do you want to go? And did you hear anything useful in Quest's mind?'

'Only that he meant and believed what he said, Bellene.'

'You may depart in the morning; there is some urgency, I think.

I enjoin you to be careful, since you have no permit other than mine; you will have to take the long road, avoiding the passes.'

'I thought we would go to Weyn first, then on to Harfort and Ismon.'

Ninian heard a new animation in Ran's voice, and felt a sudden bitter resentment. 'Is that all you can think of? That all this trouble gives you an excuse to get your own way at last?' But she was instantly ashamed at her outburst, remembering for how many years Ran had been patient, in her fashion.

'Ninian.' Ran was about to apologise, but Ninian shook her head.

'I'm sorry. Quest catches me on the raw just now.'

'He does seem to have changed recently, doesn't he?' Ran looked more pensive. 'Perhaps he thinks having a daughter at unconventional Arcady stands in the way of his upward progress in the Order.'

Ninian shrugged, unconvinced. 'Perhaps.'

A steady drift of people into the hall signified the arrival of the noon meal. The older children busied themselves fetching trays and dishes and jugs from the kitchens. Ninian, escorting Bellene to the high table, looked for Sarai and found her scowling into a basket of unleavened bread.

'Has *he* gone?' Sarai asked as she took her place. Her face had a closed look, and her hair was wet.

'Didn't you go to the pier to watch him leave?' Ninian asked in surprise.

'No. We had a race in the lake. I won.' Sarai turned away and Ninian sighed inwardly. In the wrong with both father and daughter! Watching, her heart ached for Sarai, so obviously fighting back the tears.

It was impossible to blame Quest entirely for the quarrel between them, much as she would have liked to. She had known Quest was intended for the priesthood before she had lain with him; he had not lied to her, nor tried to evade his duty to their child. Sarai's existence had come as a shock to him when he returned from the capital, but he had accepted her and done his best, in his own way, to ensure she knew he cared for her.

The custom of Arcady, the custom of Kandria – what did either one of them matter? Ninian thought impatiently. Sarai was herself. It was nonsense to claim maternal or paternal descent as a fixed or finite rule when the child was there to give the lie to both.

'Food, my dear Ninian, has a way of improving most tempers. Eat, and between mouthfuls tell me about the sermon Quest preached this morning.' Bellene's voice broke into Ninian's thoughts, and she pulled herself together.

'Of course.'

The hall was full, and there was a low buzz of chatter and the smells of spicy fish, fresh bread, and acid wine, diluted half and half with water from the lake, but as Ninian glanced out of the unshuttered window she thought she caught a whiff of corruption, of something long dead and overlooked. When she breathed in again there was nothing more than the familiar, slightly metallic, scent of the lake.

The first person Quest encountered on his return to Wellwater was Kerron, and he wondered if the other man had been waiting for him.

'Is there news from Ismon?' Quest asked, somewhat anxiously.

Kerron turned his head. 'No. Should there be?'

'You know Maryon died this morning?'

The other raised a quizzical eyebrow. 'Certainly.'

'Have others died?'

'Not that I heard.' He seemed uninterested, his gaze fixed at a point on the lake.

'Tell me,' Quest asked suddenly, unable to resist. 'You don't seem to mind, Kerron. I've never seen you look at a woman as if you wanted her physically – nor a man, either, for that matter. No offence,' he added quickly, although the Order was not opposed to same-sex pairings among its male adherents. 'But does it never trouble you, this celibacy the Order requires of us?'

Kerron's green eyes held genuine amusement as he considered the question. 'I?' he said at last. 'No, I don't find it troublesome; I have no need of companionship, physical or otherwise. Do you find it difficult?'

'I can hardly claim sexual innocence, can I, with a daughter alive at Arcady?' Quest said bitterly. 'When she was younger, I managed well enough, but now she's growing older and every time I look at her I find I remember every detail of how she was conceived.' He gave a sigh. 'Be grateful to be spared such temptation!'

'Believe me, I am. But at least you're an honest man, Quest, unlike our High Priest. Since you've been so frank, I shall return the compliment, and say I despise Borland's habit of adopting the prettiest young acolyte for his minion. Everyone knows what the boy's service includes.'

'I agree.' There was a rare moment of empathy between the two men, enduring long enough for Quest to wonder why Kerron made himself so unapproachable. 'I know some among the priesthood believe celibacy means only that we should hold aloof from women, but to my mind the interdict is strict on the physical act of sex itself; the prohibion is absolute, not gendered.'

'The purpose, after all, is to keep our affections for the gods alone.'

Quest wondered if Kerron was mocking him; there was a sly smile on the long face, and the green eyes were hooded. 'Perhaps they are testing me,' he said, slowly. 'It might be so.'

'Indeed.' Again, Kerron's smile was sly. 'As you once said to me, to each of us within the Order the call to priesthood is different. Perhaps you should doubt the strength of your vocation.'

The brief moment of truce was over. Quest wondered at his stupidity in speaking of so personal a matter to Kerron, making himself vulnerable for no benefit. He gave a curt nod and moved away from the pier, leaving Kerron standing alone.

Uneasy thoughts accompanied his steps. Quest had never doubted his vocation, never questioned the sacrifices it entailed. If he had difficulties, they were of his own making. If he had not succumbed to physical desire when he was alone with Ninian, this weakness in his body would not now return to plague him. He had been tested then, of that he was certain, and he was being tested now.

He must prove his will capable of sustaining any trial the gods might send. He might have failed them once, but he would not fail a second time.

2

There was no need to attend the midnight ritual, but Quest went nonetheless, and listened to Kerron's voice speaking the familiar words. The man's austere appearance should have distinguished him before the altar, his tall figure and strong profile strikingly alien to the *akhal*. Yet Quest thought there was something almost theatrical about him, as if Kerron was always conscious of being observed.

Quest hurried out once service was over, striding out of the temple into the night. There were few lights from the estates closest to Wellwater, and none from the lake. In the stillness Quest heard murmurings from the lake shore, probably night creatures swimming or fishing along the banks. It was too late for any birds except owls, and cats were nocturnal, although he had never seen one hunting at night.

The land inclined sharply on the western side of the lake, so the great house of Wellwater had been built backing into the hill itself, a dark presence intentionally of a similar design to Arcady, using the same massive blocks of stone. The sight made Quest wonder briefly what life had been like for the early settlers in the Wetlands, who had come after the end of the first great drought. His own ancestors.

Originally arranged for a large *akhal* extended family, the great house had long since been refitted to the requirements of the Order. The attics housed the acolytes who performed many of the menial tasks required by the priests, since female servants were forbidden and in any case the *akhal* had no custom of domestic service. The estates around the lakes were tithed for goods and day labour, for work on the buildings and the land, but not for duties inside the house.

On the floor below lived the most recently ordained priests, at present only a dozen; Wellwater was headquarters of the Order in the Wetlands, an administrative and religious centre, and several served as clerks rather than clerics, under Borland's rule in theory, Kerron's in practice. Borland's idleness was proverbial at Wellwater.

Borland himself occupied half the second floor, with a small separate chamber for the acolyte who served him. Quest was quartered on the first floor, on the south side, the remainder of the space used for offices, or to store the mass of tax and legal records generated by the administration of the district. Kerron was housed below, in the north wing, close to the mews and the Guard encampment north of the temple.

Quest had three rooms to himself, furnished in minimal fashion, but although they were dark the rooms were restful, their proportions pleasing and the furniture well matched. He had brought with him a few pieces from Kandria, at his brother Jerom's insistence, and so there was a large, well-used and polished oak table at which he wrote his sermons, the high-backed chair his father had always used at table, and a heavy oak chest, dark with age, which had belonged to his mother.

Quest did not bother to light a lamp, familiar with the space even in the dark. He disrobed, placing the heavy garment over the back of a chair ready for the morning, then washed in cold water left by one of the acolytes. He felt physically weary but mentally alert. He lay down, expecting to lie awake, but instead his eyes closed almost at once as he slipped rapidly and heavily towards sleep, aware at the last of a feeling of excitement.

This was not a normal sleep; there was a different feel to it, one he knew well.

Tonight he would *dream*.

Quest's dreams were no ordinary reveries. He did not wake and remember what he had dreamed, but instead at such times he felt he was both asleep and, at the same time, observing himself at the moment of dreaming, fully aware of what he saw and heard, a ghost-man watching himself.

He wanted to believe his dreams were a form of communion with the gods themselves, but this seemed too arrogant an assumption of the gift he had received in the Barren Lands. Yet it was hard not to believe their origin was at least supernatural, if not divine.

This time, Quest became aware of watching himself emerge from the great house at Wellwater, easily recognised with his instinct as well as his eyes. He was walking fast, agitated, along the path to the pier. It must have been twilight, for the moon was rising, and the watcher could make out the movement of the evening lights far out in the lake, although they seemed muted, mere flickers of their usual brightness.

Kerron stood on the pier, apparently waiting for him as he had seemed to that morning in the real world, a lantern in his hand.

'Should you go?'

Quest the watcher saw Kerron's lips form the words before he heard them – or did he hear them at all? He was never sure. The only thing he knew was that he heard what was said in his dreams.

'I must.' His other self looked angry and distressed, and even Kerron showed signs of disquiet. For once, antagonism was absent from his look and voice, and it came to Quest that his fellow priest was actually feeling sorry for him.

'I hope matters are not as bad as you fear.'

'Thank you.'

No more words were wasted between them, and in his dream time must have passed unheeded, for the next thing Quest saw was again himself, but this time at Arcady, in the company of Ran and Ninian; they were all three in a dark passage on one of the upper floors of the great house. It was a strange feeling, as if he were eavesdropping on himself, and he wondered how he had managed to miss the intervening activity.

'Before you go in, please remember to be careful what you say, and watch your expression.' It was Ninian who spoke; her face was thinner than when he had seen her that morning, and she looked exhausted to the point of despair. Quest's other self experienced no stirring of desire at the sight of her, but only a mounting rage. A feeling of dread crept over the watching Quest, for although in his dreams he could only see and hear, with no use of his other senses, he was suddenly afraid of what they would have told him if this were not a dream.

The great house was eerily silent.

'I warned you this would happen!' He heard rage in his voice. There was hate in the face that glared at Ninian, which gave him pause, for Quest had never hated her, not even when he had learned he was the father of her child, although then he had come closest to it. But that was long in the past.

'Does it matter now?' Ninian's voice sounded bitter. 'Go in, then.'

Quest saw himself brush past without a word and go through the door behind her. Then he was standing in a small room, where the shutters were wide open and a reed fire burned in a narrow hearth. It was quite dark, or else time had moved on further than he realised. No moon- or sunlight entered through the window, but it was possible to make out the bed, and the small figure that lay in it.

'Sarai!' His other self took the few steps to her side, then stopped, checked by the shock of his daughter's appearance.

Even as an observer, Quest felt his stomach contract at the sight of his child, her cheeks sunken, thick hair lank and lifeless against the pillow. He could hear the harsh wheeze of her breathing, but when his own hand touched her he could feel nothing, and was uncertain whether or not to be glad.

'Sarai, you must get better,' he heard himself pleading as he took a seat beside her, his eyes never leaving her face. 'Gods, don't let her die,' came the whisper of his own broken voice, and Quest understood the terrible fear he experienced. 'I gave you my life; in exchange, save her for me.' But there was no response from the still figure, and the other Quest put his head in his hands, and his expression was of one who knew himself abandoned by those he had most trusted.

'What have I done wrong, Father? Why have the gods done this to me?' croaked Sarai; her eyes stared hopelessly up into his. He had no answer for her. The watching Quest felt his throat close in agony.

What sort of gods would do such a thing to a child? And what sort of teaching ensured her first question to him now was what *she* had done to deserve it? The thought jolted him with new terror.

All at once Quest knew he could not bear to watch any longer, that even in a dream this vision of his daughter dying was beyond his capacity to endure.

'Ninian, this is your fault!' he heard his other self say aloud, and wondered if that was at his direction. 'You let Ran bring Maryon to Arcady, and he gave his illness to our child.' He felt in himself a rush of murderous rage towards Ninian as he said all these things, flinging the accusations at her with self-righteous conviction. 'If you'd done as I asked and taken her to my brother, she would have been safe! You should have sent her away.'

He was shaking, feeling his hands curl and harden, fingers stretching out to take their revenge; but before anything else happened, to his astonishment, Quest knew he was awake and no longer dreaming, sitting up in bed and chilled to the bone.

'I must have woken myself,' he whispered, shaken; it had never happened to him before. There had always been an orderly progression from sleep to waking. 'It must have been the shock, seeing Sarai so ill; I never knew how much I loved her.'

As he said it he realised that seeing her so close to death was the reason he felt so cold, and he closed his eyes and thanked the gods with deep gratitude that it had been only a dream, that she was safe. His brow furrowed as he recalled his sensations in the dream, of abandonment and fear and doubt; from where had they come? They were with him still.

'She's alive; she's well,' he whispered aloud to the dark. 'None of this was real.' But as he spoke he knew this was a lesson he could not ignore, and again he gave thanks to the gods for their precious gift, no longer doubting the dream came from them. This was a true warning, and if he did not act on it he was not only a fool, but an ungrateful fool.

As he lay waiting for the first flush of dawn to lighten the sky, he wondered why his dream had shown him Kerron's rare compassion. Could it be that after all Kerron's hard exterior was only a protective shell against fear and loneliness? But as his sympathy for his fellow priest was aroused, so his mind hardened towards Ninian for any chance of hazard to his daughter. She should not be allowed to endanger Sarai.

Slow, self-justified anger began to burn in Quest.

It was a weakness in his nature which had made him vulnerable to Ninian's seduction, which made him vulnerable still through his memories and the existence of their child. Small wonder the gods demanded celibacy from their servants. He would no longer be weak.

Such thoughts continued to occupy Quest's mind for the remainder of the darkness.

Chapter Four

The small skiff was already loaded, Ran holding the oars and Affer, in the stern, the mooring rope, when Ninian came down to see them off.

'Have you enough supplies?' she asked.

'The only thing that worries me is water; if the other lakes and rivers are polluted, we'll have to find spring water, or ration our stocks. That's why most of what we're carrying is liquid.' Ran loosened an oar and indicated the plethora of water-pouches. 'But we should manage.'

'Where will you go first?'

Did Ran hesitate? Ninian was not sure. 'To Weyn overland, I think; it's the closest to us, and furthest from Ismon. Then we climb up to Harfort, and go the long way round.'

'Well, it's your choice,' Ninian said in a neutral voice, certain her cousin had designed a route to allow the maximum number of days' absence from Arcady. 'Are you ready? Then I'll give you a shove to help you on your way.'

It was early morning and still dark. Ninian waited as Ran settled the oars, then waded out thigh-deep into the lake and pushed hard, sending the boat out beyond the shallows. The water was cool so early in the day.

'Thanks.' Ran hefted an oar in salute.

'Take care of yourselves, and come back safely.' Ninian waved back, thinking it a lonely leave-taking for so momentous a mission. For a moment she felt envy, but it was short-lived; a few days away from Avardale was no solution to her own difficulties.

With a last backward glance, she trudged back to the dark shape of the great house, pursued by the sound of lightly splashing oars.

The night air was damp as they pulled away from Arcady. No lights shone that early in the outline of the great house, so it looked uninhabited. Clasping the polished handles of the oars in strong fingers, Ran pulled with slow, steady strokes, taking pride in her strength and precision. Affer sat in the skiff's stern, guiding her with movements of his head if she drifted off course; otherwise, he trailed a hand in the water and was content to be silent.

Sheer Island loomed up on the right, sooner than she expected. Ran directed the boat to the rim which guarded the deepest water to the north. In the dim light, the depths had an oily look, dark and forbidding, seemingly bottomless.

'Please, Ran, let's go on,' Affer whispered. 'Why are we stopping here?'

'There's something I want to do; it won't take a moment.' Shipping her oars, Ran leaned back and reached for something hidden in the folds of an overshirt she had thrown casually over their packs in the bow, then sat up straight again.

'What's that?'

'Just a charm.' Half-ashamed, Ran made a face. 'They say it's lucky to start a journey with a gift to the spirit of the lake.' She held up a figurine made of reeds, then, with a flick of the wrist, threw it out over the deep water. 'It can't do any harm,' she added, as it landed on the surface. Weighted with a heavy stone at the centre, it began to sink at once.

'Quest would say it did.'

'This is Arkata's cliff,' she observed, watching ripples spread out from the centre of the caldera. 'I heard Bellene say she dived from up there, down into the deep water.'

Affer shivered. 'Even you were afraid when you climbed it; I remember you saying so.'

The oily waters of the deeps were suddenly too close for comfort, and Ran knew a flicker of unease; there was something about the unknown depths that was daunting, even to her limited imagination. It was time to move on.

'Remember, our story, if we're asked, is we're delivering medicines to Talfor,' she reminded Affer, naming Avardale's northernmost estate as she took up the oars again. 'But I don't expect anyone will; ask, I mean.'

'It's not the season to travel in trade,' Affer objected. 'People might wonder why we come now.'

'Let them.' Ran was dismissive.

'Look! Look down there.' Affer was not listening but pointing down into the deep water in the shadow of the cliff. 'Can you see the light?'

Ran paused to look where Affer was pointing, intrigued to see, some way below the surface, a slender tail of blue-green light moving down from where her reed-figure offering had sunk. 'What is it?' she asked. 'Can you see?'

Affer swallowed, and in the darkness Ran heard his teeth chattering. 'Perhaps the l-lake has thoughts, too,' he stuttered. 'The Avar Bellene used to tell us about. Perhaps you woke it up just now. Please, Ran, can we go? I don't like it here.'

Suppressing habitual irritation, Ran did as he asked, angling the skiff closer to the Kandrian shore and shallower water. Her annoyance passed quickly; she had, after all, left Arcady for a real journey for the first time in ten years.

The first light of morning came slowly, deep sapphire skies on the eastern horizon promising a fine day to come. At Arcady, Ran would have seen the dawn as herald of yet another day in the prison which was her home, but here, out on the lake, it was a promise, a hope of freedom, and her spirits lifted at the familiar sight of the great house of Kandria. Curls of smoke were already heading up from drying sheds inland, and Ran sighed with pleasure that today, at least, she had no such tedium to contend with. Kandria began work early, earlier than Arcady. Already several men and women were about on the estate, drawing water from the shore. One waved at the passing boat, and Affer waved back, but they were too far out for comfortable speech, and Ran rowed on.

With full dawn, the sun rose in the east in golden splendour; Ran watched its progress in reflection in the lake, blinking at the moment it emerged from its hiding place behind the white peaks of the Toran mountain range, gilding the surface of the water. A pair of fisher-birds, blue plumage bright in the sunlight, swooped near the boat's stern, to emerge with beaks ajar holding small wriggling minnows. Where there had been silence in the darkness, there were now sounds of life, of birdsong, of fish jumping.

'Look by the shore – to your left, Ran. I can see a river-fox,' Affer said excitedly.

Ran saw at once the long brown-furred body and tiny ears. 'Jerom won't be pleased. Look. There're the Kandrian nets. The fox must be after their farm-fish.'

'Should we go in and scare it off?'

Ran considered, for custom dictated co-operation in such matters, but finally shook her head. 'I don't think so, Affer. Jerom would get to hear of it, and he might tell Quest, and we don't want him guessing where we're going. It would only bring trouble for Ninian.'

'Oh.' Affer subsided. He looked less pale this morning, perhaps because he was away from the crowds at Arcady. 'Do you want me to take the oars?'

Ran shook her head. 'Not now.' She felt her body was suffused with rare purposeful energy. 'I'll let you know if I get tired; enjoy the ride. We'll have to use our feet soon enough.'

'All right.' He gave her a shy smile.

In the distance, on the eastern shore, Ran made out the dark shape of the great house at Arbon, north of Kandria, still some distance away. To the west lay Strone, a small estate of only a hundred or so *akhal*, and Malter to the north-west. Talfor, their overt destination, was barely visible at the far end of the lake, where a low mist still clung to the water. Ran calculated that at their present rate of progress they would reach it shortly after noon. It was then that the real adventure would begin.

Ran had no intention of wasting her unexpected freedom in a mere round of the lakes. There was time for a small diversion east, if they walked at a good pace. No one need ever know, and Affer would not mind.

The morning dragged on for Quest. A lingering aftermath from his dream had him listening out every moment for the sound of drums or a bell from Arcady.

By noon his head was dull and heavy, and as he came from the temple after midday service the sight of the lake, glimmering in the pale sunlight, clear and tempting, sent him hurrying back to the great house for fear he should commit an indiscretion.

Impulse sent him to the roof, climbing the five flights of stairs without a pause, holding up the long skirts of his soutane with one hand so he should not trip and fall headlong, as one of the acolytes had done the day before. He met no one, emerging on the paved section at the front of the building only a little breathless.

The flat paved roof was designed with the drainage channels common to *akhal* houses, and divided into two parts, the rear holding water storage tanks, quite empty since there had been no rain for months. They were not important; Wellwater, like the other estates, took its supplies directly from the lake, and in case of real need there was the deep well under the main hall for which the house was named, although it was never used.

The front of the roof where Quest emerged had a high parapet to protect the unwary from a long drop to the ground below. A cool northerly breeze blew against his hot face, clearing his mind as he moved to the edge and stood looking out over the estate, avoiding the glistening water that called to him, tempting him to forget priestly dignity.

To the north, not far from the house but further inland and on higher ground, stood the conical-roofed mews with its dozen or so outside cages. Quest had nothing to do with the message-birds, and knew little about them other than their use. He watched Jordan, the bird-man, leave the building and stand with his head turned north, holding something in his hand which he angled towards the sun. There came two short flashes, then one long one, the sequence repeated twice. Quest could eventually make out the shape of a wide-winged bird in the sky beginning its descent.

Uneasily, Quest found himself wondering what would happen if he went down to the mews and asked for the incoming message to be handed to him instead of to Kerron. Like a whisper of warning, the uncomfortable thought inserted itself that Jordan might not give him the capsule. The birds were under Kerron's command.

And why was that? Because he had acted as Borland's administrative aide ever since his return from the capital, now more master than servant as Borland grew increasingly idle? The function of the Order lay not only in the care of souls but in more prosaic matters of maintaining the rule of law and collecting taxes. The administration of the Wetlands was much less arduous than such a duty in the cities, for the estates maintained their own rule and the *akhal* were peaceful and hard-working in a near-subsistence life, but Kerron had proved himself efficient in running the Wellwater estate and in his wider remit. It was he who preserved communications with the capital, so that physical distance should not separate them from Lord Quorden's instruction and authority.

Why, then, did Quest suddenly doubt his own jurisdiction?

His vision darkened, and he clung to the parapet, unsure why such a doubt should so suddenly assail him. What cause had he to mistrust a fellow priest, one who had never been found negligent in his duty? Quest had always been grateful to be spared the mundane concerns of his Order, free for the higher duties of contemplation, of preaching. Surely the rule of the gods needed both himself and Kerron since it concerned both the bodies and the souls of the faithful?

Kerron was best informed about the political situation in the outside world; there were few traders passing through at present since there was a general prohibition on unnecessary travel, strictly enforced after the Ammon riots; Lord Quorden was determined to restrict the movements of the rebels. Yet later in the year the traders would return, and the lakes would not be so isolated as they now seemed. The Wetlands were self-contained as they were self-sufficient, but a part of the Empire.

Maryon was dead.

Quest had not known there was illness in the north. No one at Wellwater, it seemed, but Kerron had known. Why did that knowledge disturb him . . . ? *Because it made him wonder what else there was that he did not know.*

Quest felt cold. He had believed himself at least an equal partner with his fellow priest in the leadership of the Wetlands; his the spiritual, superior role, Kerron's the practical, the lesser share. His was the public person of the Order among the *akhal*, but was it Kerron who truly controlled Wellwater and its folk?

What if Kerron had lied about the situation in the north?

Quest tried to push the thought aside. It made no sense. Kerron could have no possible motive for lying, but Quest felt his mind whirl, and he hung onto the stone parapet, suddenly groundless. Yesterday, he had been so certain of everything, but today he found himself prey to a rare and irrational uncertainty.

Was it the dream? Was it the fear of losing Sarai, or something else, something he could not remember or did not want to recall? What if he was wrong that the gods had called him to their service? Had he deluded himself?

He was engulfed by a sense of worthlessness, of rare self-dissatisfaction, knowing in that moment that his life was as unimportant as it was without true purpose, that all life was without purpose. What did it matter that he and Ninian had once enjoyed a union in the orange-red dust of the Barren Lands? He was weary of regret, weary of admitting his error, of the physical reminders from his body of his one betrayal. But Sarai had come into being from that union; was she enough to give meaning to his life? Did her existence give value to his own and save him from the terrors of death?

He let his gaze wander further northwards to the long buildings in the distance which housed the guard – some four hundred in total. They were not a particularly active set of soldiers, for the Wetlands were regarded as a way-station whence men were sent on more arduous tours of duty. Who commanded them? It was to Kerron the officers reported, Kerron who allocated the sections of tithe designated for their upkeep. Wellwater, although it might once have been a working *akhal* estate, produced nothing now, except prayers.

Quest's mind played a trick on him, and it came to him, with a cynicism alien to his humour, that it could be said the priests of

Wellwater preyed on the lake people rather than praying for them. It was the physical labour of Arcady and Kandria and Talfor and the rest that sustained the priests and their guard.

'But it is for the benefit of us all, so our prayers will bring the gods to restore the rains and feed the nine peoples of our Empire,' Quest said aloud, as if to remind himself of his purpose.

The swarm of unpleasant thoughts gave him pause, and he wondered if they could be some test of his faith, a temptation to lure him into heresy, perhaps as the dream, too, might have been a test. Were the gods demanding he give up his daughter, jealous of his affection for her? Was that the true meaning of his dream?

All at once, Quest knew what it was that disturbed his peace of mind: not Sarai's illness, but what she had said as she lay dying at Arcady. *What have I done wrong, Father?*

His heart stilled, and Quest did not breathe as he understood what she had said, and why, and his feelings revolted against such a concept of divinity, that preached retribution in place of devotion.

It was only a dream. He forced himself to remember it.

'This is a test of my faith,' he whispered. 'A test. Gods forgive me, for a moment I doubted.'

Slowly, confusion cleared from his mind, leaving him – or so he told himself – as certain as ever of his path and faith, knowing it was the gods who gave meaning to existence. His doubts came from Arcady, from his own fears for his daughter; Arcady was as dangerous to his peace of mind as Ninian was to the peace of his body.

The moment of agony, of doubt, had been only a test, a temptation to show him how empty the world and all existence would appear without faith, how terrible the prospect of dying. The speculations had come from the gods, not from his own soul.

Falling's Pike began as a shallow incline, the river to the west, on his left, but as they continued on and up the path steepened vertiginously. Affer slowed, heaving in long gulps of air.

'Can't we stop, Ran?' he asked between breaths.

'Not yet. This way is completely exposed, and I need to know if it's guarded. We won't be able to see until we reach the ridge.'

'I thought we were going the straight way to Weyn.'

She grinned at her brother. 'Now where did you get that idea?' She was barely breathing hard, her face flushed with the pleasure of exertion. The pack she carried was twice the size of his, and Affer could not stem a prick of resentment that he should struggle so hard to achieve a bare half of what Ran accomplished with so much ease.

In the late afternoon sun the hill they were climbing was all green and gold slopes, themselves perched in apparent precariousness on the steeply rising ridge. The lower wooded sections of the pike were already in shadow, and Affer knew with a tremor of fear that they might still be so perilously placed when the dark came. No one lived on the hills, for there was no source of water and the soil was crumbling and poor. With the wind whistling around his ears, Affer could easily imagine himself surrounded by spirits and serpents: he had never forgotten their encounter with the silver snake on their long-ago pilgrimage.

'Come on. The track broadens out higher up, and I can give you a hand,' Ran called back.

The climb steepened further into a scramble, and Affer was reduced to using his hands to pull himself up the final section, which was discernible as a trail from the fact that the earth had been worn away, leaving only bare and crumbling rock as a path. To his left the land fell away in a terrifying drop, and, when he dared to look down, far, far below, Affer saw the glint of sun on the river as it flowed down the gully joining Weyn to Avardale in the south. The sight made him dizzy, and he swayed forward.

'Don't!' Ran said sharply, pulling him back from the edge. 'You know you don't like heights.'

'Sorry.' For a moment, Affer had thought he was about to fall, and was not quite sure whether to be glad or regret that she had caught him.

Cloud clustered low over the summit, but it was still possible to see ahead. Ran peered down, her eyesight keener than her brother's, but even he could see no guard awaited them. Ran frowned, and he wondered if she was disappointed at finding no challenge to their progress. He sighed.

'We can rest here,' she offered, hearing him.

'I'd rather go further down. The wind's too brisk at this height.'

'We're not going down to Weyn yet; I want to go south and east in the morning.'

His heart sank at the thought of the additional distance; afternoon had stretched into evening, and soon the sun would be going down.

'Where are we going, then?' he asked.

She hesitated. 'I want to see east over the pass,' she said at last. 'In case that green light is still there; that's where Bellene said the old temple of the Plains stood. Do you mind? It won't take more than an extra day or so.'

He sighed, but Ran's desire seemed innocuous. 'No; I don't mind.'

The descent was less sharp than the way up, and although wary of falling, Affer followed Ran with greater ease down the stony path. Below, he had a full view of Lake Weyn, and as it got later he caught his breath in wonder, for the evening reddened as the sun began to sink towards the west, colouring the long oval of the lake and its wooded shores in shades of roseate orange.

The stretch of water was smaller in volume than Avardale, and the glow gave it a warm and inviting appearance, although no evening lights glimmered in its depths. Only Avardale owned that phenomenon.

'Do you think there can be anything wrong down there?' he asked Ran, as he caught up with her.

'It's hard to say from this height. The only way to find out is to go and look after the detour I have in mind. If there's any pollution in Weyn it'll be where the river joins it to Harfort.'

'Those traders, the sandmen who came the day the light shone, mentioned nothing wrong.' It was as if he was trying to persuade himself that their journey was unnecessary, a mere excursion to satisfy Ran's restlessness.

'Remember, we don't want anyone to know we're here.'

Affer shivered. He had tried not to think of what they might find on their travels, concentrating instead on the physical reality of their journey. The reminder of its illicit nature and purpose chilled him.

'Can we make camp here?' he asked, indicating a rare flat space of ground ahead, to the right of the trail. 'It'll be fully dark soon.'

'There's a half-moon.' But Ran made the protest from form, not really intending they should travel through the night. In the twilight she appeared more relaxed than he thought he had ever seen her. Dressed in thin leather jacket and loose trousers dyed pale green and tucked into thick ankle boots, short fair hair blown by the wind, she looked wild and savage, almost elemental. Affer knew a momentary envy, for her thoughts reached out to him and they were exultant: she felt free, capable, afraid of nothing.

Not so himself. As the light waned further, his never restful imagination stirred, creating fears from unexpected sounds and shadows, terrors from the darkness itself.

They made no fire. The hill was dry as tinder, for there had been no rain for months, and Ran said they could eat their food as well cold as hot. The night was cool, not chill, and they were warmly dressed. Affer, who felt the cold, did not complain, but sat cross-legged by his sister as they ate smoked fish and flatbread, and drank Avardale water in the dark. Afterwards, Ran lay down and stretched out on the ground, leaning her head on her pack, looking as comfortable as if she were in her own bed at Arcady. Soon, gentle snores told him she was asleep.

Affer tried to emulate her example, but instead he lay awake half the night, staring up at the stars. Annoin, Arkata's star, glowed brightly, obscuring Omigon, the Dark Star. He felt the ground hard under his spine, and could find no position in which to get comfortable. He was cold, and could not get warm.

He woke, after a short doze, to the dawn, and was grateful for the coming light. It occurred to him that he had more to fear on the journey than any sights he might see. Many days and nights of travelling with Ran, and he might not last long enough to get back to Arcady!

He coughed, amused by his own joke, but decided against waking his sister to share it with her.

'What are you looking at?'

Ninian remained by the north window of the tower, her attention fully caught by the sight of a small boat being rowed to the far side of Sheer Island, carefully avoiding the deep water. She had watched its progress from the landing at Wellwater since the bell sounded from the temple for the evening service, trying to guess where someone might be going at so late an hour. To the island itself? It seemed unlikely. It was too dark and too distant for her to make out who was in the boat, which made slow progress amid the flickering blue-green lights on the lake.

'There's someone out on the water by Sheer Island,' she said, in answer to Bellene's question. 'I was wondering what they were doing there.'

'Crossing to Kandria? Quest?' The old woman's voice was sharp with suspicion.

Ninian shook her head, still watching events on the lake; she had not noticed before how much Bellene seemed to foster the enmity between herself and Quest, as if there was any need for fresh distance between them. 'No, not Quest, because he preaches at evening service; but the boat came from Wellwater. It's already circled Sheer Island twice. That's what's interesting.'

'Circling Sheer Island?' Bellene sounded more alert. 'Odd for one of the priests.'

'That's what I thought, but there's no light on the island, and the boat stays offshore. It just seems to be going round and round.'

'Curious.' Bellene leaned back in her chair, eyeing Ninian's stiff figure at the window. 'Perhaps this has something to do with what I was telling you.'

'About Arcady's guardianship?' But still Ninian did not move away from her place. 'It terrifies me, the idea of guardianship of a lake. Do you really believe the story is true?'

'It's no *story*, as you put it, Ninian; Arkata was a real person, and this is a very real legacy.' Bellene's gaze strayed to the distant cliff on the island, then back to the walls of her tower. 'What was it you said a few days ago – that the lights in the lake were important to the *akhal*? Maybe someone else, someone from Wellwater, also has an interest in the lights.'

'From a boat?' Ninian sounded sceptical.

'If it was a priest who was not *akhal*, for example?'

'Why do you dislike Kerron so much? You were the one who found him, who had him brought up at Arcady. What did he do to make you dislike and distrust him so?'

There was silence as Ninian maintained her vigil. A third time the boat circled the island, then, at last, altered course, heading back to Wellwater. Ninian looked away, at the height of the cliff, then shook her head, thinking over what Bellene had told her, wishing that she could reject her new inheritance.

'You don't care much for Kerron yourself,' Bellene observed.

'No, but only because I don't understand him.'

'I often wonder if I made a very great mistake in bringing the boy up here, at Arcady,' the Steward remarked, looking thoughtful. Age had not dimmed her strength of mind or force of will; it had, perhaps, strengthened both, while at the same time making her unaware that her own manner of thinking might not be universal. 'It might have been better to send him to one of the cities, to his own people. Perhaps he wouldn't have resented us so greatly if I had!'

'He always did. Even when we were children.'

'He was an angry boy,' Bellene said, nodding. 'Angry with the whole world, I think, as much as with us, and that moulded his character. He hated to be less good than anyone at anything; he must always run fastest, learn best, most quickly, win every game. It was hard to *like* him, although he was a clever, strong-willed child, and worked hard.'

'Then why did you keep him here? You could have sent him east to Ammon, or even to Enapolis, once you realised?' Ninian asked, curious. 'It might have been better for him. He was so often lonely.'

Bellene sighed. 'For a good reason, or so I thought: that if I sent him away, once he was old enough to understand, he would believe I rejected him, which would have been true, in a fashion. His pride was always easily offended, and who can blame him, abandoned in such a way as he was.'

'I always thought it strange he came back here, once he was priested. I hoped he'd stay in Enapolis, among his own people, and say good riddance to all of us . . . Except Ran,' Ninian added as an afterthought. 'They were always friends.'

'That he came back is the reason I worry about him,' Bellene agreed. 'I suppose we are insular in our ways here in the Wetlands, preferring our own kind to an outsider, even one brought up among us. Yet I feel Kerron came back for no good reason, that he spies on us for the capital, out of spite or out of envy. He is a powerful man, and could do us great harm.'

'Do you think Affer was right? When he said that there were times when Kerron hated us?'

The old woman nodded thoughtfully. 'I do. And the priests have long arms these days.'

'Quest seems to trust him.' Ninian felt a surge of resentment for the fact. 'Or so he said.'

'I doubt it; not in his heart. But his mind is so taken up with his godliness that he sees little of how others act or feel.' Bellene shot Ninian a sharp, sly look. 'Even his own daughter!'

'He sees what he wants to,' Ninian said bitterly. 'That Sarai loves him is his proof that whatever he wants is right. He doesn't understand how much he hurts her, or me; he just tries to take control of her life as if she were something that belonged to him, and neither she nor I have any say at all.'

'And you, my dear Ninian? Are you so very different?' Bellene's voice was heavy with irony. 'Or would you say *your* concern was just the natural solicitude of a mother?'

Her face flamed. 'Where was Quest when I bore her, when I gave birth to Sarai?' she demanded. 'Where was he when she was growing up? I remember, on our pilgrimage, that after – ' She broke off, remembering her vision of Quest lying naked in the dust, remembering, with unwilling clarity, the sensations he had stirred in her.

'After?' Bellene smiled unpleasantly, fully aware of Ninian's meaning.

'Yes. Then.' She bit her lip. 'He said that perhaps I was a gift of the gods, so he should know what it was he was sacrificing in becoming a priest!'

'Hardly tactful,' Bellene agreed with an amused snort. 'But young men outside Arcady are taught to be self-centred. Or so you must have discovered by now; Quest was not, I think, your only lover?'

'He probably believes Sarai's existence is another gift of the gods to *him*,' Ninian said angrily, ignoring the question. 'As if I had nothing to do with it.'

'He probably does, but at least he cares for her, which is more than some men in his position would do.'

'So?' Ninian was filled with rare anger. She had done her duty and told him about their child, and it was she and Sarai who suffered most as a result, not Quest. 'Am I supposed to be grateful for his generosity?'

The irony was wasted on Bellene, who shook her head. 'You complicated his life, Ninian, or that's how he sees it. You and I may know it was a joint effort which created Sarai, but when Quest came back from Enapolis it was a shock to find himself a father. You did not tell him before he went, and that choice was yours and yours alone. You must admit he did not shirk his duty, that he has acknowledged her as his, and shows his affection for her openly. For a priest, that is no light thing.'

'It might have been easier if he hadn't!'

'For you, perhaps,' Bellene observed acidly.

'And for Sarai.' Ninian flung the words back.

'And leave you with undisputed ownership?' Bellene waited, but Ninian said nothing, so she went on: 'Because we at Arcady trace our lineage through the mother does not mean we ignore paternity, Ninian; only that we prefer the certainty to the possible. Maternal descent is so much more reliable.'

'What are you trying to say?'

'Only that both you and Quest are too busy thinking about your own feelings to consider what is best for your daughter.'

The words were an attack, and for a moment Ninian ceased to breathe, bitterly hurt. She had expected support, not accusation; in the past Bellene had always backed her in her quarrels with Quest. In fact, she generally made them more bitter, for reasons of her own. What was her motive now? A form of vindictiveness, because Arcady must pass in due course to Ninian, and Bellene believed she had already let too much control slip from her fingers? Or was it the simple truth, that she, Ninian, was as guilty of selfishness as Quest?

'I'd not let him send her away from you,' Bellene observed, noting the effect of her words. 'But you should have considered it, as soon as Maryon came here. Don't deny it, Ninian.'

'But Maryon's fever wasn't contagious,' Ninian protested. 'You agreed with me.'

'Perhaps.'

104

And against her will Ninian was struck by the unwelcome awareness that she was by no means guiltless in her motivation, that she had chosen to keep Sarai at Arcady because she believed, with a small part of her mind, that Quest would have won if she sent the girl away. Sarai, she believed in her heart of hearts, was *hers*. She was allowing herself to be tempted by her own wishes against common sense.

Why was there so much conflict between herself and Quest? Did it spring from this cause, that both believed Sarai their own, not herself, not an individual born of them both?

'If I keep her here, Quest will go on fighting me for her,' she said, admitting the truth to herself. 'Bellene, is there any way he could take her away from me?'

There was a long silence, during which Ninian stood absolutely still, afraid to move or breathe. The very fact of the silence gave her the answer, and a wave of cold terror clutched at her heart.

'He is a priest of the Order,' Bellene said at last. 'If he so chooses, he could take Sarai by force on some pretext or other, with the guard at his back. And the priesthood are both executive and legislators in these days, in the Emperor's stead; so much the worse. He could gain custody of her through the law courts, and in any argument between priest and lay, and especially priest and woman, the priest is sure of winning.'

'Then why hasn't he done so already?' Ninian turned away, staring out into the darkness, not wanting to imagine the unimaginable, the bitter ache and misery of loss. 'What's he waiting for?'

'Perhaps for his gods to tell him what to do.'

It was all too likely an explanation. But how, Ninian wondered drearily, how could she counter an influence she did not understand, and against which Quest allowed no argument?

How right she had been all those years ago to struggle against Quest's vocation; his divinities were cold and uncaring, demanding ceaseless sacrifice and submission, with the threat of destruction waiting for those few who dared question their tenets. What did it say about Quest and his fellow priests in the Order that they should devote their lives to deities who seemed so unworthy of worship, so devoid of any capacity for love?

'Quest loves Sarai,' she said, mostly to herself. It was true, and it was also the case that Quest had so far used only threats against her, not following them up with actual force. But for how long? Could Quest distinguish a difference between the will of his gods and his own, if there was, in fact, any disparity between them?

'I hope so.' Bellene struggled to her feet, reaching out with a trembling hand to touch the old hunting horn that hung on the wall; the ring of the Steward of Arcady was loose on her thumb. It was a gesture meant to remind Ninian of her other duty, the secret part of her inheritance. Ninian refused to be manipulated, but the darkness outside mirrored the ache in her heart, and she saw Bellene as an old and bitter woman, who sought to add this, too, and fear for Sarai, to her heir's obligations.

Bellene offered no comfort. She walked unsteadily but unaided to the stairwell and, clinging to the rail, made a slow descent, leaving Ninian alone with her thoughts.

'What should I do?' she asked the empty tower. 'What can I do?'

There was no answer, and Ninian knew that all she could do was her duty, chosen or placed upon her, willing or unwilling; that was what she had been trained to understand.

Whatever came, she must endure.

Kerron rowed back to Wellwater deep in thought. Three times he had circled Sheer Island, and each time caught a glimpse in the distance of lights moving in the deeper waters, but whenever he paused and sought a closer look, they had somehow shifted out of sight and reach. He could not tell how far down their source lay, nor uncover their origins. Among the lakes, Avardale alone enjoyed the nightly phenomenon, but that told him nothing.

He had no capacity for swimming at depth; at lower than ten feet his ears began to ache, and he had no intention of risking his hearing by making any such attempt. This task demanded by the voice was not for his accomplishment; he must have help from *akhal*.

He was curiously relieved at his own inability. While he did not care for any other living creature, he knew himself vulnerable to things of beauty, and the lake lights had always been a delight, compensation for living as an alien among the *akhal*. The lights made the approach of each night something to look forward to, a phenomenon in which he could submerge his affections, certain they would not hurt nor betray him. He did not formulate his feelings in such specific terms, but he knew that was how he felt.

'You must destroy the lights in the lake. If they do not die, then the dark will not come, and your cause will not prosper.'

The voice was disturbing, breaking into more pleasant deliberations; Kerron frowned, annoyed.

'You have no choice in this. Seek out and destroy the source of the lights. Why is it not already done?'

The voice was a bludgeon in his mind, thrusting aside his other thoughts. Kerron wished he could blot out its insistence, or know why it was so concerned with the lights. What was meant by *'the dark will not come'*? He shrugged, mentally and physically, aware his reluctance would be sensed by the other.

'Their beauty is deceit, a disguise for infamy.' The voice seemed to understand his thoughts and doubts better than he did himself. *'You are strong, not to be made weak by bright colours and false imaginings. Where is that strength, if you waste it admiring false images? The lights are unnatural, as are the akhal. You are Thelian; why will you take pleasure in their corruption?'*

Kerron did not even try to formulate a reply, overwhelmed by the certainty in the voice which fought with his own inner confusion. He turned his will to resistance, refusing to allow himself the easy path of submission. Then the odd sense of pressure was gone, and, released, his thoughts were his own again. Kerron shipped his oars and drifted, aware of having come to no more firm decision than to delay compliance with the voice.

He was accustomed to pride himself on his quick decisiveness, but this time he could not agree with the voice. He found himself wondering what could happen if he refused the command? What power did the voice hold over him, after all? It was only a voice.

He did not understand why he resisted, unless it was, as the voice said, that the beauty of the lights had bewitched him. His feelings towards the *akhal* were disdain mingled with indifference; or did he hate them, as the voice seemed to suggest, did he wish them destroyed along with the lights? What would happen if the lights were put out, after all? Why should he care?

The question recurred: what could happen to him if he refused to obey the command of the voice? If he had the strength, and the force of will.

Was he going to refuse?

Chapter Five

1

The descent to the lookout point was very steep. Ran hesitated before starting down as the wind tangled her hair and pushed her away, back from the edge.

The view from the top of the hill was spectacular. North and due east lay mountains, but ahead and below the terrain altered rapidly. To the south-east, Ran could behold the wide immensity of the Plains, the grain fields of the Empire, stretching away to the horizon; they had a dry and parched look, not the waving greenery she had expected. Due south, a series of bleak hills stood between her location and the Barren Lands, and still further off lay the vast desert of the south. She thought she could make out a great golden sea in the distance.

The possibilities open to her took her breath away, and for a moment she felt dizzy. There was so much to see, so many different paths to tread.

'Ran, please come away from the edge.' Affer's voice wavered. 'It makes me sick to watch you.'

'I won't fall.' She peered interestedly over the edge.

It had taken them a second full day and half a morning to reach their present position, the furthest detour she dared make. A sandman from the desert city of Arten had once told her of a place in the hills where the eastern mountains opened up, to reveal a gap through which it was possible to get a sight of one-quarter of the Empire; now she was almost there, Ran believed him.

'We don't have to go down there, do we?' Affer shuffled closer and peered past her with a pale face.

Ran pointed to the shallow flight of stairs cut into the rock. 'There's a perfectly good path. I'm going down.'

Swallowing, Affer looked away from the immensity of the drop back along the way they had come; that path was steep, but not impossible. 'It doesn't look safe,' he said, unable to keep a tremor from his voice.

'You don't have to come.'

At first sight, it looked as if the hill came to an abrupt ending at its highest point, beyond only a vertiginous cliff face where a precipitate descent led to a broad ledge two hundred or so feet down, which bulged out from the rock. The ledge was Ran's ultimate goal, for it was from there the sandman had said it was possible to see the ruins of the old Plains temple. From her present location, a section of distant mountain barred her vision.

'Don't go, Ran. We shouldn't even be here.'

'Stop complaining!' Ran was irritated, not least because it troubled even her nerve to take the first hazardous step along the downward path. It seemed as if she would be walking straight over the edge into thin air. Ran was not afraid of heights, but, omitting the ledge, the drop over which she stood was measured in thousands, not hundreds, of feet. She breathed in a deep lungful of cold air. 'I'm going!'

'No – please, don't go.'

Ran blotted out the protest and took the first step down onto the rocky stairway. For a moment she hung, impossibly, in the air, with no handholds or any other support as she leaned out into space. Then her balance reasserted itself and she took another step down, and another, and after a few more she had the face of the rock at her hand, and the feeling of absolute vulnerability receded.

'Ran, I *can't*,' came Affer's pursuing voice. Ran did not look back, ignoring his gasp of horror. Strength flooded into her legs and arms, and she knew she did not care how her brother felt. Why must she always allow his fears to hold her back? How much had she already given up for his sake? This was her journey, not his; her chance to travel, to explore, to test her limits. Was it wrong to wish she had come alone, that she could leave Affer behind and go on to wherever she chose, that she should resent having to limit herself to his slower pace, to circumscribe her path to allow for his sensibilities? Anger stirred in her.

She did not look down, only ahead; nor did she look back. The steep, open stairway was an obstacle to be overcome. Ran told herself fiercely that she welcomed the cold wind that blew up at her from the east, making her eyes water. The cliff face only seemed sheer, a blank white face of rock; as she got further down Ran found it less alarming, an irregular slope that angled distinctly outwards.

'Ran, come back! I *can't*.' Affer's voice reached her in an anguished whisper.

Strong irritation rose to swamp any gentler feelings. 'No; go back to Avardale if you're frightened,' she called back callously.

'Don't just stand there feeling sorry for yourself!'

'Don't leave me.'

'Do what you like!' Resentment made Ran lose patience with his fears; his imaginary terrors were still fighting to constrict her, where she should be as unconfined as the wind.

She paused to look at her feet, then further, far below, down into the distant valley where the sun shone on a shadowed landscape. Again, dizziness threatened to assail her and quickly she lifted her gaze outwards; the world steadied as the sun got into her eyes.

Ran continued her perilous descent. To counter her momentary weakness she dared herself to loosen her hand from the side of the cliff and trust to the surety of her footing in thin boots ridged at the sole for a better grip on the chalky ground. The stairway did not look as if it was much used; hardly surprising given its vertiginous aspect. Ran was stunned by the expanse of emptiness ahead; one false step would make a long drop and a giddy death. An immense sweep of sky and plain filled her vision, seemingly limitless, and Ran knew a surge of exultant happiness. At Arcady she felt the narrowness of her horizons, but here there seemed no end and no beginning. She forgot about Affer in the joy of the moment. North was a place where the mountain range ended, east there were only cloudless skies and the empty Plains.

'There. That's where I want to go, when this is over,' she confided to the wind. 'And further still, to where the world ends at the start of dawn.' East lay the ocean, some distance beyond the city of Ammon. Ran had always wanted to travel to the sea, unable to imagine a limitless expanse of water. It was said there were seamen and seawomen in the oceans, but for reasons she had never bothered to understand the Order had proscribed them, forbidding contact. She wondered what it must be like to be able to breathe under water, not simply hold her breath for long periods as *akhal* did.

Her nameless yearnings were momentarily appeased by the prospect of such a journey. Ran knew no weariness, no discomfort from two nights spent on hard ground on a cold hillside, momentarily at peace with herself with no desire to rush towards her destination. There was more pleasure in the process of travelling, in the placing of one foot in front of the other, than in the final arrival.

From sounds coming from behind her Ran realised that Affer was trying to follow, but she resisted looking up or back. She had nearly reached the ledge at the base of this section of cliff. To her surprise, the rock wall below was honeycombed with large holes which might even be shallow caves, entrances shrouded by a species of creeping plant.

'Affer,' she called up, half-turning to see how far he had come. 'Come on; it's quite safe down here!' His thin figure was still some way up, leaning against the cliff face, so close he must have been clinging to it with his whole body. She turned back.

Suddenly she was sent flying forwards in the air in a terrifying dive as her right ankle encountered unexpected resistance. There was a moment when she seemed to be borne back, then forwards in reaction, down the last few steps and out onto a ledge covered with tiny shards of rock, where she landed, face down, cracking her jaw and knocking the breath out of her lungs.

For a time Ran lay where she had fallen, trying to get her breath back and not thinking about how very close she had come to going over the edge and down into the yawning emptiness. Her right hand and forearm dangled into space, grazed and sore.

Some time later she found the energy to move. Most of her was sore from the heavy landing, but other than a few abrasions on her face, arms and hands there were no breakages or sprains. The memory of Affer made her struggle up, thinking how frightened he must be. Spitting out blood from a cut on her tongue, Ran rolled over on her right side, then got shakily to her knees.

'Don't move!'

Awareness of just how close she was to the edge of the cliff kept her still.

'You were lucky.' The voice came from close behind, masculine, so low it was almost a croak; it was as if the man was bending over her. 'Turn your face left – slowly, mind!'

Ran obeyed the eccentric command, seeing no harm in it. She turned her head carefully left, wincing at the pain in her jaw.

'That'll do. Just stay like that. And you!' The voice moved away from her, its owner now addressing Affer. 'Take more care how you come down! You'll kill yourself at that pace!'

There was a clatter of footsteps. Ran forgot the order to remain still and twisted in time to see her brother run down the last few stairs in a single spurt, at a pace even she would have described as reckless.

'Ran! Are you all right? Did he hurt you?' Affer asked breathily. He dropped to his knees beside her. 'You're bleeding.'

'Ah – get up, the pair of you!' The deep voice sounded disgusted. 'Come away from the edge. I've water you can use to clean yourself up with.'

With Affer's help, Ran got to her feet, much relieved to discover her legs and ankles were still sound; it was a long way back up the cliff.

'Keep your distance! Don't come too close!'

The person who spoke was very short, perhaps only four feet in height, with arms, head, and legs all in proportion. Red eyes snapped suspiciously in a very white face as they fixed on Ran in some confusion, then, with less doubt, on Affer.

'Who are you?' Affer asked. 'Why did you trip my sister?'

'Sister, is it?' The red eyes surveyed them both, then the head gave a nod of apparent satisfaction. 'You look enough alike,' the stranger admitted grudgingly.

His hair was as white as his face, having a blanched look, making the red eyes all the more startling. His nose and mouth were small, the former flat and pinched, and the hands and feet which emerged from the ends of a spectacularly tattered dark blue garment were stocky and strong. The stranger seemed to be of an indeterminate middle age, but it was hard to tell because his face was very dirty as well as pale.

'Who are you?' Ran asked, realising she had been staring.

'More to the point, who are you?' came the snapped response. 'And what're you doing here?'

'My name is Ran, from Arcady by Lake Avardale, and this is Affer, my brother,' she offered. 'We're travellers.'

'So I guessed!' The small man kept a wary distance, but even so Ran recoiled from the rank odour emanating from his person. 'But what sort of travellers, and why?'

'Are you a mummet?'

The stranger's eyes narrowed as he turned to Affer. 'And what if I am?'

'Then you're a long way from home.' Ran's gaze flicked briefly to the northern mountains, the habitat of the small mountain people. 'I could ask what you're doing here.'

'The same as you. Unless you've not come to take a look at the old ruins? You can see the light, if you've fair eyesight.'

'Can you?' Unthinking, Ran turned north, in the direction of the Plains. 'Oh, Affer! Look!'

The morning air was clear. Ran was able to make out in the distance the markings of buildings and what looked like a broad pathway to the east. There was at least one very long building divided into several sections.

'My eyes aren't so good in the sun,' the stranger muttered. 'But the light's high up on the long building.' And, as he spoke, Ran caught the reflection of the sun on something that glittered green, with a hint of white.

'Is that what we saw a few days ago?' she asked in wonder. 'But it looks so small now. What is it?'

'It must be a lightstone, like the one that used to stand there in the old days; I got here yesterday, and last night the thing shone out bright enough in the dark. Don't ask me how it works.'

'You came all the way from the mountains?' Ran tore her gaze reluctantly away, knowing there was no time to explore further. 'You move quickly.'

'I know the shortest ways.' Suspicion flared in the red eyes. 'What's it to you?'

Ran shrugged. 'Were you trying to kill me?'

Silence fell. Affer turned a startled face to Ran.

'It was a mistake.' Colour came into the mummet's face. 'I thought she was different; but now I can see I was wrong.'

Ran remembered the moment of terror as she fell. 'What do you mean, "different"?'

'I saw your face as you came down the stairs,' the mummet answered, turning to point to a hole in the cliff by the lowermost steps. 'I was in there. You looked wicked, mean. So I tripped you.'

'What do you mean, *see*?' Affer sounded frightened. 'What do you see? How do you see?'

A second silence greeted his query; the mummet stared into Affer's pale face.

'It's like that, is it?' he asked at last. 'Tell me, have you ever been to the dead place?'

'The dead place.' Affer frowned. 'You mean the Barren Lands?'

'It's as good a name as any.' The stranger's eyes narrowed. 'So you have; that explains it; you've an odd look to you.'

'We went there on pilgrimage, Ran and me, ten years ago.'

'I went there, too, in search of the gods, and they gave me a gift. You could call it a curse!' The mummet let out a bitter laugh. 'I read your real thoughts in your face, like a mask of your true self covering your features; not that I need the curse to read you. I'm surprised your sister lets you out at all.'

'I read minds; not all the time, just sometimes.' Affer turned his head away. 'Like you, not the surface, but what's underneath.'

'And you? What did the generous gods give you on your pilgrimage?' the mummet inquired of Ran with a sneer.

She shrugged. 'A general dissatisfaction with life. What's your name?'

He hesitated, then said: 'Storn.'

'Are you a priest?' Ran indicated his outer robe, which did resemble a soutane.

'I was, until I came back from the dead place, a while back.' It was the mummet's turn to look away. 'When I went back to the mountains it wasn't the same; every time I looked at my companions I saw in their faces nothing of any god or good, but only greed and hunger and hate, and I knew there were no gods, and that I could only trust and believe in what I see!'

Affer reached out a hand. 'I'm sorry.'

'Don't be. I can live with it, since I must.' Storn recovered himself, shooting Ran an odd glance. 'I left my people to roam the passages and slopes of the mountains alone, so when I saw the green light I decided to come south and see it for myself. I came around Lake Harfort; they're an odd breed there. Then down the cliffs on the inside, taking the tunnels by the waterfall to Weyn and on to here.'

'Is there sickness around the lake? Or any unusual gathering of weed?' Ran asked, then briefly outlined the reason behind their journey; Storn's travels were no more authorised than their own, and she saw no harm in telling him.

The mummet shook his head. 'Not that I noticed, but you'd best be careful if you mean to go to Weyn, and more if you go on to Harfort. There're guards posted at the eastern end of Weyn, and others at the top of the waterfall.'

'Are you going back?' Ran thought there was a deliberate omission in the mummet's recital, something he was carefully not saying. 'Or are you going on to the Plains?'

The mummet gave Ran a look filled with suspicion. 'None of your business!'

'Are we all so evil?' Affer broke in suddenly. 'Can't you bear to look at any of us?'

'At you I can, little brother!' A smile almost cracked the mummet's dirty face. 'I see nothing bad in you.'

'And Ran?'

The mummet grunted. 'Now? She looks strong and fierce; but at first I saw the darkness in her.'

Remembering the tenor of her thoughts as she descended the cliff, Ran could not deny their ugliness. 'We have to start north again today; we've no more time to waste,' she said quickly. 'Do you want to come with us? We'd be more than grateful if you know a safe way around the lake, and up the tunnels to Harfort, too.'

The sun was high overhead. Storn hesitated, drawing back into himself, retreating to some distant place.

'You'd travel with one who tried to kill you?' he asked eventually.

Ran shrugged. 'You said it was a mistake.'

She turned away and took another look at the ruins of the old Plains temple, glimpsing again a flash of green light. Movement to the south caught her attention, and, with a sigh, Ran turned and watched the bleak landscape where there were several figures moving, tiny, almost invisible figures; Ran counted four. Her heart began to beat faster as she watched, envy growing for their freedom, and she wished with all her heart that she were with them, striding out to distant places, seeing new landscapes and new peoples.

'I wish – ' she began; but Storn interrupted her.

'If you want, I'll come with you.' He held out a very grubby hand to Ran. 'I'll come.'

'Good.' She took his smaller hand in hers; it was warm, even hot. She could smell his unpleasant odour again now he was closer and upwind.

'Good,' echoed Affer, blinking into the sun.

The mummet took back his hand and tucked it inside the wreck of his soutane, and at that moment his eyes were hooded, unreadable. Ran experienced a momentary doubt; what, after all, did they know about him?

She flung off her suspicions, irritated. They had found a guide who knew the hidden ways of the hill tunnels leading from Harfort to Weyn. And she had seen the ruined Plains temple, and the green light. Was it a lightstone? She wished she could have seen it at night.

'I'll go first. Then him, then you.'

Storn did not wait for her concurrence, starting up the cliff face and leaving them to follow.

Ran sighed. 'Go on, Affer,' was all she said.

Affer said nothing. After a while, he set foot on the first step and began the upward trek, following in Storn's footsteps.

It was at twilight, a little before the evening lights were due to begin, that Kerron came out onto the water.

There were the two mixed-race *akhal* from the guard in the boat with him, the best swimmers among the troops stationed at Wellwater. Neither had displayed much curiosity about their task, but seemed grateful for the break in their dull routine.

'Dive as deep as you can, and see what's there – if there's any visible reason for the lights to shine here at night,' Kerron instructed Columb, the younger of the two, who, with his fair hair and the green tint to his skin, might have been full *akhal*, if his unusual height had not hinted otherwise. He was a plain, lethargic young man.

'What am I looking for, Reverence?'

'How should I know? That's what I want you to find out. Go.' Kerron spoke sharply.

'What about me? Do you want me to dive here, too?' The second guard, a red-haired man in his thirties, was more stockily built, green eyes displaying a sly shrewdness. Despite his unlikely appearance, he was a better swimmer than Columb.

'No; I want you further round the island, Elthis, on the other side of the cliff, where it's deeper.'

The man looked up warily. 'I'd rather not, Reverence. It's unlucky to swim in the deeps north of the island.'

'Well, stick to the rim then, for now.' Kerron's nerve was wearing as thin as his enthusiasm for the present venture. 'Just go down as far as you can. There's promotion in it if you find anything.'

Elthis nodded, shooting the priest a calculating look from under pale brows. 'As you wish, Reverence.' He had taken off the leather breastplate and body armour he normally wore and was dressed only in *akhal* leggings and singlet. Without further argument, he climbed over the side of the boat and let himself down into the water. His companion was nowhere to be seen. Kerron shivered empathically, for the water looked cold; he had never really enjoyed swimming.

Darkness was descending at a rapid pace as Elthis swam away at some speed; Kerron could just see his dark head outlined against the water. He wondered how far the man would really go. To the rim of the caldera? He doubted it. *Akhal* were superstitious about the deep water, and even he, brought up among them, was not immune to the suggestions of unseen mythical monsters in its depths: the Avar of old nursery tales, for whom the lake was supposedly named.

'The lights are evil. Watch for them breaking the darkness in the depths of the lake, unknown and unnatural. They must be put out, or the dark will not come.'

Kerron rubbed a hand to his forehead, where tightness at the temples gave a warning of pain to come. He had begun to experience headaches whenever the voice spoke, and he suspected the combination was no coincidence. Ever contrary, the pain strengthened his resistance to their message.

'But why? It makes no sense.' He sat in the boat, oars shipped. The lake was still, barely a ripple disturbing its surface. The looming presence of the cliff reared up ahead, the lake and its surrounding shores cloaked in different degrees of darkness. There was stillness, the brief peace of transition from day to

116

twilight; then the moon rose on Kerron's right, over the top of the cliff which had hidden it from sight, and around the boat the lights began their evening dance.

Kerron peered over the side of the boat, drawn to and frustrated by the movement of the lights as they swept to and fro under his gaze. He reached down a hand in wonder, but the lights were too far down, even if they looked close to the surface.

'I can't find anything, Reverence.'

The hand that grasped the side of the boat made Kerron start, much to his annoyance, before he recognised the fair head of Columb.

'Get in, then. We'll move closer to the far side of the island to collect Elthis,' he said shortly, vexed at being disturbed.

The speed with which Columb slithered into the boat was a reminder of the veneration in which the evening lights were held, and the unspoken prohibition against swimming while they shone. Without a word, Kerron handed over the oars, keeping a lookout as they headed for the rim of the caldera. He found himself continuously drawn back to the movement of the lights, the pain in his temples easing as he allowed himself to experience pleasure in their colours and motion.

'Stop here. We don't want to hit Elthis by accident,' Kerron ordered; his voice carried over the water.

Columb held the boat still, and the two men sat waiting. Lights still flickered below the surface of the water, but further out, near the shores. The waters of the caldera looked forbidding, darker and less inviting than the surrounding shallower waters, as if the shadow of the cliff cast a pall over the depths.

'It's deep, there. And dark.' Columb leaned over the side with a scowl of anxiety.

'Can you see Elthis?'

'No, Reverence.' Columb shook his head. 'Only a sparkle of lights.'

'Close. You are close to the secret, the source. I can sense it is so. Seek in the depths, and you will find that which you must destroy.'

The voice came and was gone in almost the same instant, but even as the sense of it departed there came a sudden splashing in the water.

'What was that? Is it Elthis?' Columb asked. Kerron listened in the stillness, and heard someone gasp for air.

'Elthis?' he called.

There was no reply; instead came ugly gasping breaths and a feeble splashing. Now he could see the man, and Kerron reached down to grasp the swimmer's arm. Cold fingers clutched his own and held. Columb helped to lift his fellow soldier into the boat, which was rocking ominously.

'What happened?'

Elthis tried to raise himself to a sitting position. 'Nothing,' he managed to say between gasps. 'Nothing really, Reverence. I was deep – deeper than I dared go before – and holding my breath well, when suddenly I felt as if my chest was going to burst.' He paused to gulp in more air. 'At the same time, I couldn't tell which way the surface was, which was up.'

'But did you *see* anything?' Frustration added an edge to the priest's voice.

Elthis hesitated. 'I thought I saw something moving, deeper than I could go, but it might have been anything.'

'All right.' Kerron was not sure whether to be angry or relieved that the expedition had accomplished so little. 'Columb, take us back to Wellwater.'

The weather was changing rapidly; suddenly the surface of the lake was no longer still but restless with movement as the wind rose in force. Flecks of spray filled the air, and the boat rocked uncomfortably; Kerron held on to the sides, wiping his face with the sleeve of his robe, surprised by a sudden fancy that the storm was a retaliation for Elthis' incursion into alien territory. Something was aware of his own presence, and its purpose.

Perhaps the voice was right, and the lights were an enemy.

Kerron shivered, not wanting to believe it. He would not believe it. His resolve firmed once more into confused resistance.

'I saw Kerron out on the lake again, with two guards this time,' Sarai commented conversationally as she handed over the jar of dark green liquid her mother had asked for. 'One of them was Columb.'

'That's the second time in two days.' Ninian accepted the glass container. 'Thanks. Columb? That's odd. He's the half-breed from Ismon, isn't he?'

Sarai nodded. 'Can I help?' She danced around the table in an excess of energy. 'Is there anything I can do?'

'Just keep still,' Bellene observed caustically. 'If you bounce about like that you'll jog the table and make your mother spill something precious. These potions are dear to make, in time and effort.'

Sarai subsided, looking resentful as she leaned her elbows on the flat surface and watched Ninian stir a small amount of the green fluid into a bowl containing a second liquid. 'What are you doing?'

'I'm making a fever remedy,' Ninian said, not looking up. As the two liquids combined, small flecks of green were precipitated to the bottom of the bowl – a sign that the proportions were right. The long still-room was lit by a profusion of oil lamps, illuminating shelves of glass jars filled with powders and coloured fluids, all labelled in Ninian's or Bellene's careful script.

'Be careful not to spill. You don't want to get any of that on your shirt, or the table, if you can help it,' Bellene advised from her seat. 'It stains.'

'I know.' Ninian bit her lip and continued mixing with greater care. She was tired and hungry; it was late, nearly supper time, and most at Arcady would have finished their labours for the day. She suppressed the unruly thought that without Bellene's unnecessary assistance she, too, might have finished. 'Sarai, would you fetch me that apron hanging on the back of the door? I should have thought of it before.'

Sarai skipped away, returning with the apron, which she handed to her mother; as she did, by accident one of the ties caught the bowl Ninian was using and it spilled over, spattering its contents across the table and floor, as well as Ninian's white shirt and trousers.

'Blast and botheration!' Ninian jumped back, far too late. She looked down at the spreading green stains with distaste and resignation; it had been tempting fate to work in the still-room dressed in white.

'That was *your* fault, clumsy child!' Bellene snapped angrily at Sarai. 'Whatever possessed you to be so careless?'

'I didn't mean it!' Sarai stood back, hot resentment flaring; Bellene always caught her on the raw. 'It was an accident.'

'I know.'

But Ninian's placatory words were drowned by the Steward. 'You were warned to be still,' she said, voice at razor sharpness. 'Get out of here. You're nothing but a nuisance.'

Ninian turned on her. 'That isn't so.' But the protest came too late. Sarai cast her mother a hurt look, then flung out of the still-room.

'Did you have to speak to her like that?' Ninian asked, trying to keep the anger out of her voice. 'It was an accident, and you know how touchy she is at the moment.'

'She has to learn, just as you did.' Bellene gave a sniff. 'If she's to acquire the skills she needs she must learn to be patient and steady, not rush about like a gad-fly.'

'Maybe so, but she can be told so politely.' But Ninian knew Bellene would not listen. 'She's only nine. She needs her

127

confidence built, not broken, and she was trying to help.'

'A few hard words won't hurt her.'

When she was as old as Bellene, would she, too, be equally impatient, so careless of other people's feelings? Ninian fervently hoped not.

'No girl can be Steward of Arcady who hasn't the skill or patience to brew medicines,' Bellene continued, perhaps realising she had not impressed her heir favourably. 'We've been famous for our potions for centuries; too long to allow a spoilt child to destroy our reputation!'

'You make far too much of a simple mistake.' But Ninian knew there was no point in continuing the argument; Bellene heard only what she wanted to hear. Ninian wiped the table with a clean rag, then prepared to begin the whole laborious mixing process afresh. 'Tell me,' she said after a moment, trying to change the subject. 'Are you worried about Kerron exploring the lights on the lake?'

There was an unexpected pause, an uneasy, heavy silence.

'Yes.'

Ninian's hand paused in its stirring, wooden spoon still. 'Why?'

'You know why!' Bellene gave Ninian a sharp look. 'Kerron must be looking for the source of the lights in the deeps; there's no other explanation. Why should he be doing that, unless he wants to know their secret – our secret?'

Ninian considered. 'Perhaps,' she agreed. 'But surely he won't find anything?'

'There's always a risk.'

'But what could he see?'

Bellene shrugged. 'Who knows? As I told you, as Stewards of Arcady we are guardians of the lake and its lights, which are older even than the Tearstone of the *akhal*. This was the prime legacy of Arkata to her descendants, not Arcady.'

'What do you think was the gift she gave, to become the first guardian?'

'The legend tells that *akhal* and all the other peoples of the Empire were once Thelian, like Kerron,' Bellene began. Ninian nodded, familiar with the tale. 'When our ancestors came here to these lakes, Arkata bargained with the old gods that we should be changed, adapting to our surroundings, so that we should swim better, and hold our breath for long periods, and be in tune with the seasons about the lake, and so we became *akhal*.'

'But nothing about the gift, or the guardian, or the lake itself?'

Bellene frowned. 'I can only recall a saying that the last hope for the *akhal* lies in the depths of Avardale. But that may mean only that we here have the deepest waters of all the lakes, and that Avardale will be the final refuge if drought comes again.'

'The hunting horn you showed me,' Ninian urged. 'The one she was given in exchange for her gift. Do you know from what creature it came?'

'No.' The old woman's voice was dry. 'Nor do I care, but only for its use. I've never heard the call, nor has anyone else since Arkata. Perhaps the summons will never come; we must hope it does not, since it means despair.'

'I hope you don't,' Ninian agreed.

Bellene rose from her chair, a stiff and spiteful figure. 'You, not I; I am too old and frail now for such a duty.'

'I wonder how far Ran and Affer have got.' Ninian thought it a suitable diverson. 'And what they've seen.'

'You are the heir and cannot leave Arcady. Duty binds you, as it has bound me all these years.'

Ninian bent her head over the potion, annoyed with herself for being so transparent. 'I'll finish here, then come on to the hall,' she said shortly. 'It's late. Don't wait for me.'

'I've better things to do than watch you making a hash of that.' Bellene straightened, and Ninian drew in a long, calming breath. 'Very well; I'll see you in the hall.'

The still-room door opened and shut, for a second time with the suspicion of a slam. Ninian kneaded her aching back and wondered where Sarai had gone, and sighed, trying to remember how she herself had been at the same age, how she had felt about her parents. She could recall none of the rage and resentment she sensed in her own daughter, none of the agonising insecurity which welled up and made her blame her mother for every small mishap.

Was it her own fault? Was it the circumstances of her parentage that made Sarai so difficult, so loving one moment, an enemy the next? Most children went through such a stage, but not while they were so young. Surely Sarai knew she was wanted and loved? Ninian had taken care that no other liaison of hers should threaten her daughter; nor, in fact, had she wanted any of her affairs to lengthen into a closer relationship.

Was she afraid to let Sarai go, even as far as Kandria, because she was an only child? That was something Quest did not know, and Ninian had no intention of telling him that the birth had been so hard she could have no other children. At the time it had been a bitter blow, but as Sarai grew it had seemed to matter less, until now. It might have been better if Sarai had sisters and brothers to dilute the attention she received; but there was no purpose in *might*.

The potion was ready. Stirring one last time, Ninian pulled across an empty jar and poured in the contents of the bowl, then inscribed a label, fixing the rough reed paper to the stoppered jar with a sticky substance made from spruce gum.

It was time to find Sarai and try to make amends. Ninian locked the still-room door behind her and set out for the main house, where lights shone out from the open windows of the kitchens, staffed traditionally by the eldest inhabitants of Arcady in monthly rotation. Ninian walked round to the main hall, thinking that for once it would have been a relief to eat alone; but it was not the custom at Arcady, and to order it would only mean another argument with Bellene.

She had forgotten her clothes were stained with splashes of green until she caught sight of a quickly smothered grin on more than one face as she entered the hall. The knowledge made her more cheerful, knowing how her appearance would offend her great-aunt, until she surveyed the assembled inhabitants of Arcady and realised Sarai was nowhere in the room.

'What is it?'

Ninian stared blankly at Bellene, in her usual seat at the top of the high table. 'Sarai's missing.' She looked about the crowded hall, feeling both guilty and angry. 'I knew she was upset.'

Night had fallen on Arcady, and somewhere out in the darkness was Sarai, alone and unhappy. Ninian, though hungry and tired, was aware of an odd sense of urgency to find her daughter, as if she were in danger, although she was a capable girl, and there was little that could hurt her on the estate.

A shiver ran down Ninian's spine. At Arcady there were so many hiding places.

Quest lay prone on the dark marble floor of the temple, facing the twin altars of the gods, oblivious to the passage of time.

He had eaten nothing for two days, and had drunk only a minimal quantity of lake water; now his head felt light, his body finer and less earth-bound. He was aware of the coolness of the stone through his soutane, but remotely; a satisfying numbness was beginning to set in.

The temple was dark, although on each altar a small oil lamp burned, giving out a dim light, enough so that if Quest had wanted to look up he could have made out the stone faces of the gods. His eyes, however, were closed in concentration as he meditated on the true nature of their duality, of smiling Jiva and vengeful Antior, life and death, of men and women.

How was it possible to perceive any extreme of greater value than its opposite, when neither could exist without the other? Mutual dependence argued for equality. As a priest he taught of life after death, a life of eternal service to, and communion with, the gods; yet if that was the ultimate object for his people, then life was of less value than death, since only by suffering death could existence be thus perfected. It was this promise of future being as a reward for faith and obedience which gave meaning to present sacrifice, which surely must mean that life and death were not opposites but the same?

If the gods were all-seeing and all-knowing, was not a believer's intent sufficient to earn reward? Where was the need for an act of sacrifice if the intent were certain?

His thoughts strayed, his mind betraying him, and Quest had a sudden mental image of Ninian and Sarai, as he remembered seeing them on his return from Enapolis. What a shock it had been to learn that Sarai was his own daughter, proof to all of his incontinence. But why did the Order demand chastity of its priests, and why should all priests be male, if men and women were equal in duality? Because the gods were male? But what was *male* and what *female* to the gods? Both were necessary to existence; surely the divinities might have chosen to create one gender alone, to propagate itself as some lake-creatures did, had they so wished. Thus there must be meaning to be found in their choice.

Were priests commanded to celibacy by the gods, or by human agency? The suggestion at the college in the capital had been that physical communication with a woman was in some fashion a contaminant to be avoided. Women were sexual beings as men were not, less than equal, their weakness to bring men low by tempting them with the promise of bright hair and soft skin, lures which must be resisted by any man who wished to give himself to the gods.

But that seemed nonsensical to Quest. If he was tempted by the sight of a woman, how could that be her doing, when the desire arose in his own body? It was hypocrisy to disclaim his own urges by placing them on a woman, a lie the gods would recognise for what it was. Nor were such beliefs common among the *akhal*, who claimed descent from a woman, after all, as Bellene so often reminded him.

He could recall the exquisite sensation of Ninian's skin against his, the firm curves of her flesh as they lay together on hard ground. She had wanted him, but he had been equally as guilty as she, fully as willing, as culpable.

He was paying the price for it now. Never had the sacrifice of his sexual self seemed so heavy, nor so unnecessary. What, after all, was wrong with the physical union of a man and a woman? How else was the existence of *akhal* and the other peoples of the Empire to be continued? Unless the ultimate ambition of his Order was the end of the earthly Empire, the end of his race, and all the other peoples, in order that they might find the greater joys of the next life.

Ninian had chosen to continue her line in the physical world through their daughter, thus giving him, too, a place there. Whether he wanted it or not.

Why was he thinking about Ninian, or about women at all, when it was his intention to give himself fully to the gods, to surrender himself? Or was it a weakness to hope the Lords of Light would think for him, take him over by allowing him to sublimate himself so fully that *Quest* would cease to exist, and be only a part of themselves. Then he would live forever, and he would no longer fear to die the first death.

Why could he not stop thinking?

Quest felt he was going mad. Whenever he tried to sink his will, to submerge his being in prayer, his mind would not let him be but must always question every thought, every action, never at peace. There was no kindness in intelligence, no rest to be found.

He rose to his knees, blinking in the darkness, feeling the air damp in the temple. If he questioned the directives of the Order, if they sometimes seemed less than rational, then the fault lay with the priests, not with the gods, who were without human failings. Errors were human, not divine. The Order existed not only to teach the ways of the gods to men, but also as a political force in forming and ordering society. In that part of its function human mistakes and prejudices could be perpetuated, given divine force in error.

Yet the hierarchy of the world was as the gods dictated. Or was that so? His questioning mind considered his own belief in the structure of the Empire. How could he, or any other priest, know whether or not the word that came down to them was truly the word of the gods? The High Priest was incorruptible *(as he must be, must surely be, to be trusted as the perfect vehicle for communicating divine will to the peoples)*; but, nevertheless, what if he was less than honest, less than impartial, less than a vehicle for the divine word? His mandate would be used to promulgate evil under the guise of divine authority.

The understanding dizzied him.

What if much of what he had been taught was only the

collective opinions and prejudices of mortal men? How could he, a simple priest, uncover which teachings were true and which false? But would the gods allow themselves to be used in such a fashion by mere men?

He had been cold as he lay on the floor, but now Quest was sweating, perspiration dripping down his face and back. He bowed low, agonised at the thoughts going through his mind, horrified at being racked by doubt in such a place.

'Forgive me, forgive me; give me back my faith as pure and full as it was,' he whispered, laying his hot brow on cold stone. But though he waited, he had no sense of the presence of any deity, and at last he gave up and got to his feet, swaying a little, his legs and ankles cramped.

Overhead, the temple bell began to toll, startling him fully awake. Quest looked dazedly about, in no state to attend service. Moving quickly, he quitted the temple by the main door, hoping to meet no one.

The night air was cool, and Quest welcomed the breeze. He felt that even his body was at odds with itself, for he was tired, but at the same time filled with nervous energy. His stomach rumbled, an unwelcome reminder that he was hungry.

'Not for another day!' Quest gritted his teeth; he would allow himself a cup of water, no more. Perhaps he needed to fast longer to free himself from physical temptation. He had not slept for two nights; that was a part of the problem. Tonight, instead of attending service, for once he would allow himself the luxury of sleep. So slight, yet so important a part of existence; food was of less value than sleep.

And before he could arrest the thought, he found himself adding, with desperate passion: 'And please, tonight, no dreams.'

2

It was not a night for sleep . . .

In his cell at Wellwater, Quest was wakeful. Not far away, Kerron, too, lay awake, staring up into the darkness.

He would have slept, if he could, but the voice claimed him, drawing him back to wakefulness from the borders of sleep each time he thought he had won. It had never happened to him before. He had not understood how vulnerable he was to the voice in his mind; without sleep, his own will was dulled, less capable of struggling against the commands of the voice. It no longer seemed to care for voluntary co-operation, instead demanding instant and absolute compliance.

Kerron lay motionless, a natural obduracy struggling against weariness and the endless repetition of the same command. How was it that the voice had ceased to seem a companion, seeking instead to become his master? When had the change occurred? Kerron was aware he had come to dread the voice's advent, shrinking from it, wishing he could shut it out.

He had welcomed it once, long ago, taking it freely into his mind. Why, then, could he not rid himself of it in the same fashion?

With all the force of his will, he fought against being subsumed.

At Arcady, Ninian searched the grounds for Sarai; it had become clear well before midnight that she was no longer anywhere in the great house.

Sarai could be anywhere. The outbuildings, the store-rooms, the infirmary, the still-room and drying sheds, all offered a multiplicity of hiding places, and that was to assume she was still on Arcady's soil. What sort of Steward would she be, Ninian thought, if she could not even keep watch over her own daughter?

She felt a twinge of angry despair. This was not her fault. But it was too simplistic to blame Bellene. After all, why was Sarai so vulnerable that a few harsh words should send her running off? From what cause sprang such misery and uncertainty? Cold fear grew in Ninian, an irrational fear such as might have troubled Affer, that she would never see her child again; but she did not speak the fear aloud, and it was not future truth.

In the darkness, Ninian called her daughter's name, then stood still and listened, hoping against hope to hear Sarai's voice.

No answer came back to her.

Faraway, Affer, too, was afraid.

He lay stiff near Ran's peacefully sleeping figure, trying not to disturb her or Storn, stretched out only a short distance away. He felt ice cold, but that did not stop him sweating as he recalled the previous day's descent down the cliff, where each step had him imagining himself falling, falling out into the waiting void.

He dared not close his eyes. If he did, he only saw again the broad expanse of emptiness. Yet even with his eyes open he still felt the cold stone of the cliff face, the crumbling of the rock as he clung to odd handholds in his terror, as Ran moved further and further away from him, and he knew, in agonised acceptance, that this time she would not come back. This time was different.

126

He glanced at her sleeping form, wondering if she really had rejected him, or if the cold, hard expression Storn had seen had been only one of her fretful moods. Did she even know herself?

Storn could have told him; he saw what Affer only heard in his mind, and, worse for him, saw all the time, unable to shut out vision any more than Affer could shut out thought. Imagining the mummet's plight brought tears of empathy to Affer's eyes, but he blinked them away, despising himself.

He would be stronger. In the morning, in the light of day, he would find the courage to go on, and Ran would not have to be ashamed of him.

In the morning.

Chapter Six

1

A dramatic curtain of white spray, like a fine lace veil, blurred the vista ahead. The trio stood at the mouth of the river where it fed from the north into Lake Weyn, water crashing down from the heights with an almighty roar.

Behind them, the waters of the lake gleamed an impenetrable blue in the early morning light. The colour seemed to Affer subtly different from Avardale, less mysterious, except where the sun lit on queer granite pillars floating on the surface. The islets looked like rafts of rock, spiky and irregular, not true islands but living formations growing from a mineral in the water, their crumbly structures not solid but fragile.

The lake was cool and clear; they had drunk from it earlier, on its southern side, before walking along the western shore to the cliff and the waterfall. Ran had allowed no more than a brief rest since they left the lookout ledge the previous day; Affer looked up at the next obstacle, wondering if he could go on.

'Those are the Apperstan Falls,' Storn said shortly. 'The guards are watching from the top.'

'They could see right down the gorge to here,' Ran agreed.

Storn was in a grumpy mood, snapping and sullen. 'You can't climb up that way; it's steep and unsafe. You'll have to use the tunnels inside the hill.'

'Have to?' Ran lifted a quizzical eyebrow.

'You look like a bad-tempered weasel,' the mummet retorted crossly.

Affer tried to shut his ears to the argument, wishing he could close his mind as easily; whispers of Ran's prickly thoughts broke through to him. She was in one of her more stormy moods; behind her surface thoughts Affer could hear that what she really wanted at that moment was to go on alone and leave both him and Storn behind. The knowledge hurt, as it so often did without her intention. Nor did he want to hear Storn's uneasy anxieties.

He sat tiredly on a flat rock; the empty western shoreline was littered with boulders, in contrast to the east, where tree-lined slopes disguised *akhal* dwellings dug almost invisibly into the hills. There was an empty feeling to the place, but smoke drifted up in the distance, proof of life, and there were a few distant boats moving out on the lake.

Affer quailed before Ran's impatience, almost able to make out in her face the savage creature Storn said he saw; the mummet only scowled. What would he do if Ran left him behind?

The river thundered down with a force like an earthquake through the thousands of feet from the unseen Lake Harfort in swift descent to Lake Weyn. Affer made out a series of staging posts in the falls, deep ledges where the water stilled in its frantic downward progress, only to be urged on by the weight of river descending from behind.

Over centuries the river had forged and widened its own path from the heights, establishing a deep gully down the steep slope to Weyn. Affer thought it might have been climbable if the waters had not been in spring spate, but Storn said his way was easier and safer.

'We should get on.' Ran gave Storn a chill glare. 'By the falls, if I choose.'

'If you want an arrow through your chest!' The mummet glanced down at the water. 'Have you noticed how many water plants there are at this corner of the lake?' he commented more naturally. 'Look at these purple flowers everywhere, all bunching together. I didn't notice them on my way down, and that was only three days ago.'

'I know.' Ran frowned at the sight of a blanket of green weed gathering near the base of the falls. Affer thought he could detect a very faint odour of decay, but said nothing; it was probably only his imagination.

'I'd not drink this water,' Storn observed. 'It's lucky we filled up over the way. This could be poisonous, if what you say about Ismon is true.'

'Dangerous to the lake at any rate; this plant must spread fast, if you didn't see it on your way.' Ran bent down and plucked an errant flower that swirled in the eddies by the base of the falls. 'I wonder if we should try to warn the Weyn folk.'

'They're *your* people, not mine!'

'But none of us has licence to be here.' Ran's thoughts were now calm in Affer's mind, quite different from the other Ran.

'You've changed again,' Storn said, echoing Affer's thoughts. 'The sting's gone, and you look like a cat full of fish!'

Ran shrugged. 'I don't know what you're talking about.' Affer knew she had no understanding of the extent of her mood changes. 'I suppose we'd better not take the risk, not before we know the full story.'

'Good.' Storn pointed up towards the invisible peak of the waterfall. 'And now we negotiate this.'

'How long will it take, the inside way?'

'I came down quick enough, didn't I?' Storn snapped. Affer smelled the acrid odour of his sweat, as if it had been a very long time since the mummet had washed any part of his body. 'This way is a good climb, a day, day-and-a-half.' He blinked in the daylight. 'It'll be a pleasure to get away from this cursed sun.'

'How did you find the way down in the first place?'

Storn did not speak; he stared morosely at Ran, as if she had crossed some unspoken but clear divide between the acceptable and the unacceptable. Her smile faltered, and Affer was glad at that moment that his gift slept. He had read a little of Storn's mind, and it held hidden horrors, buried layers deep. Had he stumbled as he fled the halls and mines of the mountains? Had Storn cursed the gods he once served for their gift? There was a livid scar discernible above his left eye which suggested to Affer he might once have made an attempt to blot out his unwelcome visions in blindness. Who could blame him, either for trying or for failing to destroy that sight which showed him only images of evil? Affer thought he might do the same, if there was any way to destroy thoughts.

'Is it very steep?' Affer asked, trying to delay the evil moment; he had a strong dislike of dark, enclosed places.

'In places.' Storn was watching him, as if he could read the trepidation in his face. 'They're not all dark; you'll see.'

'Then let's get moving.' Ran gestured Storn to lead the way. It was another sharp, clear day, and there was a silence about the lake which might have had something to do with its location, for it was more enclosed than Avardale; it pleased Affer. He had no sense of minds fighting to impinge on his own with their unwanted secret thoughts.

Storn's mind was stormy, his thoughts jumbled, not plain, and Affer was glad, shying away from any contact, for there were mysteries in them he would rather not have made clear.

'The way in's through here, behind this boulder. You two will have to lie down to squeeze through,' Storn remarked, eyeing his much taller companions with an unpleasant expression. 'Don't blame me if you have to bend double much of the way up.'

'Just show us where.' Ran stepped forward; Storn shot her a sly look, then disappeared behind the boulder. Following, Affer saw

130

a narrow gap in the cliff face near the ground, barely as high as his knees and just wide enough to admit the mummet. He swallowed convulsively, trying not to imagine himself trapped in a dark confined space, where he could not see what hid in the darkness.

'I'll go next, Affer, then I'll pull you after me.' Ran was not looking at him, but her bored tone of voice suggested she knew he was in a panic. She crouched down and began to feed herself into the hole feet first, disappearing quickly. Affer caught an errant scornful thought as she waited for him to follow her.

Trying not to think at all, Affer sat down and began to feed his legs through the gap.

Crouching low so as to be hidden by the high reeds that grew on the boundary between Arcady and Wellwater, Sarai shivered.

It was not yet dawn, but there was enough light for her to identify her mother's tall figure as she walked along Arcady's pier; there she stood, obviously counting the boats and rafts to see if one was missing.

'I wouldn't be so stupid,' Sarai whispered fiercely to herself, at that moment hating Ninian with desperate, dark thoughts. Why, she was not sure, except that it was easier to hate her mother than herself.

It was not only that Bellene had spoken to her as if she was a clumsy, stupid brat: that was how she treated all the children at Arcady. It was just that it had come on top of a whole series of incidents, beginning with Maryon's arrival at Arcady, and her mother and father arguing. It frightened her when they argued, making her wonder if it was all her fault. She wished she had never been born.

A solitary tear trickled down her nose, and Sarai sniffed inelegantly. Her insides were stuffed with misery, weighing heavily on her stomach. She had eaten nothing since the noon meal the previous day, but she told herself she was not hungry, although the rumbling in her belly suggested it was a lie.

'No one wants me, no one cares,' she murmured aloud, wallowing in misery. The reed-strewn marshy ground was damp, and her feet were wet and her once clean trousers sodden with muddy water. Sarai bit her lip as Ninian disappeared back towards the great house; she looked angry, her walk stiff, but Sarai did not care. She welcomed the cold and her shivers as proof of Ninian's guilt, of her own very real unhappiness.

She looked at the distant great house at Arcady and hated everyone inside, feeling frustrated rage boil up in her chest. She often felt like that, but she never told anyone; it was better to keep feelings to yourself, for people like Ninian or Bellene always tried to tell you how wrong you were, or that you did not really feel the way you said you did, as if they knew you better than you knew yourself.

She had been a mistake. No one had wanted her. That was why Quest rejected her, even though she knew she looked like him, mostly.

Sometimes, she could believe her father did love her, and at those times she felt grounded, more secure. But there were all the other times, when he was in temple, or in one of his remote moods, a *priestly* mood, that she felt he did not know or like her at all, even though she ached with pride for him, even in his unavailability. Then she shrivelled inside because she knew he found her a nuisance, and did not want to be reminded of her existence. He had never said so in words, but she could sense the feeling clearly enough.

It was at such moments that she blamed Ninian, simply because there was no one else, except herself; and if Quest did not love her, if it was not because of Ninian's shortcomings then it must be her own, which she did not want to be true.

Sarai's lower lip trembled, and she clamped her teeth together. She would not cry. Her father did not like it when she cried.

The skies were lightening perceptibly towards the east, where a band of gold lit the horizon. With a swift look back at Arcady, Sarai got down on her stomach and began to crawl through the weeds to Wellwater. Soon the bell above the temple would toll for the first service of the day, and she wanted to be waiting nearby, for her father usually remained behind to pray after the others had gone. He was a better priest than they were.

Alone, she could talk to him, and he would understand and ask her to come and live with him, and everything would be all right. She suppressed a pang at the disloyalty to her mother, wanting to hurt her. Quest had to want her. He *had* to. She felt on edge with nerves, not wanting to wait, needing to know.

Her courage was ebbing; Sarai began to doubt, after all, that Quest would be pleased to see her. She had thought of running away to Wellwater before, but had never gone further than the boundary; she was forbidden to cross over without permission for the priests did not want uninvited guests.

'But he won't mind me,' she muttered, trying to restore her earlier determination. 'He'll want me.'

If she did not go on she could only return and, a cold place in Sarai's chest told her, she would be in serious trouble if she went home.

The temple bell began to toll, and Sarai eased her head above the rushes, watching priests and acolytes streaming from the house, and, from the north, groups of soldiers marching from their encampment to the temple. They were obliged to attend one service a day, Bellene said, as part of their duties. Her heart beat more rapidly as she saw that her father was one of the hurrying priests. She crouched down, waiting until the doors to the domed building closed, then ran towards it.

There was chanting coming from inside, and the sound made Sarai panic; she looked about for a hiding place, terrified of being sent back to Arcady in disgrace without seeing her father. Soon the day-labourers would be arriving down by the pier, and any one of them might see her.

The best place was the domed roof, which she knew could be reached by an outside stair at the rear; from there she would be able to see who came and went. Shivering, Sarai skipped around the side of the temple and climbed the narrow stairway to the top where she sat down, hidden from the wind and from sight by the parapet. It would not be long before early service was over; it was always short.

Sarai sat and waited, heart thumping, for her moment.

Quest listened as Kerron spoke the familar words of the service, but he did not feel he was really present at all. Another sleepless night had done nothing to appease the restlessness of his mind.

No one noticed his abstraction, although he was guiltily conscious of having gained no benefit from his attendance, and was glad when the brief service came to an end. As was his custom, Quest stayed behind after the others left, resigning himself to another day of mental turmoil, refusing to admit failure.

'Accept my service, Lords,' he said softly as the last priest departed. 'Let me prove worthy.'

The main doors still stood open, but as he moved to the centre of the interior Quest saw no one else inside the temple; he had the wide expanse to himself. A beam of sunlight struck the altar at a point precisely between the two stone representations of the gods, an accident so much in tune with the tenor of his thoughts that Quest smiled as he took his familiar place.

The sense of not being fully present in body stayed with him as he set himself to concentrate once more on the mysteries of the duality. Quest wondered distantly if it could be a sign that he was moving closer to an ideal state of mind as he stood, eyes closed, contemplating the perfection of opposites, trying to submerge his irritatingly assessing mind into an abstraction of accepting thought.

His wits drifted obligingly as, light-headed from fasting, he swayed on his feet. As if at the end of a long tunnel, he thought he could see through the darkness of his mind an image beginning to shape into solid form, and a light that beckoned to him.

'Father?'

It was the touch on the arm that roused him, not the voice. Quest was still for a moment, absorbing the shock before lifting his head and opening his eyes.

'Sarai? What are you doing here?'

He received a second shock from her appearance; she was very untidy, clothes stained and torn, and her face, feet and hands were muddy. 'Is something wrong? Has there been an accident?'

Sarai stepped back, her gaze falling to the marble floor, as if she did not want to look at him. 'There's nothing wrong; I just came.'

'What for?' He did not intend to sound so sharp, but the interruption, just when he believed himself close to acceptance, roughened his tone. He regretted it, and said more gently: 'What have you come for, Sarai?'

Her face was very pale as well as dirty. As he waited for her answer, Quest noticed the grubby footprints her bare feet had made on the floor of the temple.

'What do you want, Sarai?' he asked again, with greater patience. 'Are you in trouble?'

'No!' Sarai's head came up with a jerk, her voice defiant. 'I came to see *you*.'

'Does Ninian know you're here? Sarai,' he went on sternly, 'does anyone know where you are?'

'*You* do!' She looked at him with surprise for his foolishness. 'I've run away from Arcady, Father, and I won't go back.'

At a loss, Quest frowned. 'Is something the matter at home?'

'Yes.' Sarai got the words out in a rush. 'I hate everyone there; I want to come here and live with you.'

'Sarai – ' He was completely taken aback. 'You must know that's not possible.'

'It is, it is!' She stamped her small bare foot defiantly on the floor. 'I know it is. Ninian said you loved the gods more than me, but that isn't true, is it? You only said it because you didn't want to marry her.'

Appalled to have his vocation turned into a means of evading a social responsibility, Quest stiffened. 'Who told you that?'

'No one, but it's true, isn't it?' Sarai looked up at him, desperate for agreement. 'Don't you want me?'

134

The length of the silence that followed her question was his fault; later, he acknowledged it, but at the time he was simply struck dumb by the enormity of the problem. 'Of course,' he said, after much too long a pause; but they were the wrong words, and spoken far too late.

'I hate you!' Sarai's face contorted with the effort not to cry. To Quest's astonishment, his daughter's fists flashed out, clouting him hard in the stomach. They hurt; she was surprisingly strong. He reached down to grasp her hands.

'Sarai, stop this.' She fought him, fury adding to her strength. 'Remember where you are.' Her behaviour shamed him. 'Come outside and we'll talk, but not in here.'

'I don't care!' Despite her best efforts, tears had begun to fall, tracing pale lines down her dirty cheeks. Sarai reached out a slim leg and kicked hard, catching him on the knee, and Quest let out an involuntary gasp of pain.

'Sarai!' He had never seen his daughter in such a mood before, and was shocked she could behave so badly. 'Sarai, don't do that again; it makes me angry.'

'I don't care.' There was a sob in her voice. 'Why should I? When did you ever do anything *I* wanted?'

Movement caught his attention; from the corner of his eye he saw, to his horror, that they were no longer alone. The rear door of the temple was open, and Kerron was standing silently in the shadows beside the altar. Fury rose in Quest, that it had to be Kerron of all people who should witness the embarrassing and deplorable scene.

'Come outside, Sarai,' he said angrily, reaching out to take her arm. 'Now.'

'No!' She pulled back, striking out again, catching him on the forearm. In instant response, Quest's right arm went back, then he brought it forward, smacking Sarai hard across the cheek.

For a moment, neither of them moved, both frozen into immobility by shock. Then Sarai took a slow step back and simply stared at her father. Quest thought he read hatred as well as accusation in the look.

'How dare you? How dare you touch me?' Sarai shouted; then, with a sob, darted past him and out of the open doors. More slowly, Quest followed, but by the time he was outside the building Sarai had already reached the shore and was wading into the water.

He hesitated. Should he call after her? With a sense of scalding shame at her and at his failed fatherhood, Quest could not decide what to do. He swallowed, watching Sarai swim further out into the lake in the direction of Arcady and Ninian.

Quest was torn. He was in no mood to hear Ninian's re-
proaches, however merited. He knew he should not have struck
Sarai; his own lack of self-control was far worse than her
behaviour. She had come to him for help, and he had betrayed
her. He remembered, unwillingly, that Ninian had tried to warn
him that their daughter was troubled by her unusual parentage,
but he had not wanted to hear her, preferring only to see the
adoration in Sarai's face. Her love had been his proof of being in
the right.

With shame, he thought of the leap of smug satisfaction in his
heart when Sarai said she wanted to come and live with him. Did
she really feel so torn between her parents that she felt she must
choose one over the other? He would have liked to blame Ninian
for her daughter's insecurity, but could not deceive himself on
this occasion.

Was this yet another test of his faith, or was such a thought
culpably self-centred? Had the gods sent Sarai to him to test the
strength of his vows? She had said she wanted to live with him,
but that was impossible as long as he remained a priest. He
accepted his duty to the child of his making, but the greater duty
was to his calling, or so he had always believed.

If he had not succumbed to lust in the Barren Lands he would
not now be faced with such a difficulty – but here Quest faltered;
he could not wish Sarai out of existence.

It all went back to that time, to the moment of his temptation,
by Ninian and by his own nature. For his frailty, his child was
suffering.

'Quest?'

Kerron stood behind him, the Thelian's expression impassive,
offering no judgment to Quest's guilty heart.

'What is it?'

'High Priest Borland wishes to speak to you. Now.'

Was there a note of satisfaction in Kerron's voice? Quest
straightened, galled by the knowledge that Kerron should have
witnessed his disgrace. With a curt nod of thanks, he turned and
walked towards the main house.

Kerron shifted so he could observe Quest's retreating back, his
features resolving into an expression of contempt. He could feel
some sympathy for the girl who was Quest's daughter. In her
agony, he had seen a little of his own youthful misery and
desperation, a railing against the cruelty and betrayal of an
unthinking adult world. Sarai had not been abandoned at birth as

136

he had, but nonetheless her position was not an enviable one. To be the child of a priest who had been taught, and who believed, her existence to be a permanent reproach to himself was not a legacy to be desired.

Kerron frowned, surprised at the strength of his empathy for the girl.

'She does not deserve so great a fool as Quest for a father,' he murmured succinctly.

He abandoned the remote figure swimming in the lake. Other concerns pressed around him, none easy of resolution. He found it hard to remember them all, for nothing mattered more than the voice. The problems of the north, of the missing rebel Plainsman, of the possibility of a water-borne plague, none seemed as urgent as the broadening gulf of isolation which separated him from the physical world, leaving him alone with himself, and the other.

'When the lights are put out,' whispered the voice in his mind, *'there will come the darkness, which is power. The lights must die.'*

Abruptly, Kerron moved away from the lake. There was no peace, no true solitude to be found at Wellwater.

Even his thoughts were no longer his own.

Ninian watched at Bellene's bedside, increasingly torn as the old woman's eyes remained stubbornly closed. She wondered if the Steward was doing it deliberately to keep her heir's full attention; she would not have put it past her.

'Why don't you let me keep watch?' asked Aislat sensibly. A distant cousin of both Bellene and Ninian herself, she was a dependable woman in her fifties with a round, capable face and sturdy figure. 'It won't be long before she comes to, and anyone can see you're fretting for Sarai.'

'She's nowhere in the grounds.' Ninian looked distracted, running a hand through her straight hair. 'We've searched everywhere: in all the stores, the ice house, in the drying sheds.'

Aislat sat on a stool on the far side of Bellene's bed. 'Look; there's a little colour in her face at last. It was a nasty tumble.'

'I think she can only have fallen part of the way down the tower stairs, or she'd have done more than break her wrist. At her age, bones are fragile.'

'A pity it's not her tongue that's broken.' Aislat's expression matched her observation. 'Was it that? That sent young Sarai running off, I mean? Was it something she said? It wouldn't be the first time she's been too harsh.'

Ninian sighed. 'I think Sarai's trouble has been coming on for some time. Bellene may have provided the spark, but no more.'

'Well, don't go blaming yourself. You do a fine job here, with both Arcady and Sarai, and don't let anyone tell you otherwise.'

Ninian smiled, surprisingly touched. 'Thank you.'

'Look; she's rousing.' Aislat leaned over Bellene.

Ninian gave a small prayer of thanks. The old woman's fall had knocked her head and broken her left wrist, but as the day wore on into early and then late afternoon, and still Bellene did not stir, Ninian had been increasingly worried.

Bellene's eyes flickered open, and Ninian drew in a deep breath.

'What have you done to me?'

'You fell down the stairs in the tower and hurt yourself; your left wrist's broken, and you bumped your head on the wall.'

'Now will you go?' Aislat interrupted, giving the Steward a sharp look. 'I can manage here.'

'Don't let me keep you from more pressing matters,' Bellene murmured in acid tones.

'Thank you, Aislat, and I'll be back as soon as I can.' Ninian was already retreating before Bellene could change her mind, and she heard a protest even as the door shut behind her. She ran down the stairs, her mind full of anxiety for Sarai.

Where could she be? They knew she had been over to Wellwater in the early morning, but no one had seen her since, and her friends had no idea where she might be hiding. Torn between anger and terror, Ninian tried to think. There was little real harm that could come to Sarai. She was an excellent swimmer and an intelligent child; she had not run off to Kandria, for Jerom and Cassia had not seen her, but there must be other possibilities.

The great house had been searched from top to bottom, as had all the outhouses, including the infirmary: Sarai was not at Arcady. Where, then, could she be?

'Of course!' Why had she not thought of it before? 'The island. Where else would she go?'

Down by the shore, Ninian paused only to discard her sandals and outer clothes before wading out into the lake. There was still some sunlight left as she ducked her head and sank down, immersing herself. Her days were too full to allow her to swim as often as she wished, and she felt a pang of guilt even now at stealing time for her own concerns. But Sarai was worth any quantity of time.

She was not as good a swimmer as Ran, and her arms were beginning to feel weary from the unaccustomed exercise as she neared land. It was a very long time since she had been to the island with Ran and Kerron; perhaps more than a dozen years. The undergrowth was higher and bushier than she remembered, reducing visibility to the minimum.

'Sarai?'

Wind blew from the south, a warm, strong wind which ruffled the undergrowth and disturbed the nesting birds that inhabited the island. Ninian listened, but there was no reply.

'Sarai?'

She struggled through trailing growth inland to the open space where the old temple had stood, stubbing her bare toes on pieces of broken white-veined rock. There was one long fragment which had obviously been part of a hand, two stone fingers still discernible, and another which held a fold that might have been part of the statue's robe.

'Sarai?'

This time, Ninian heard a distinctly human sound above the noise of the wind and the anxious calling of the birds. With a surge of gratitude, as she emerged onto open ground she saw her daughter huddled by the base of the cliff, just past the place where Ran must have found Maryon days before, since the remnants of his fire were still visible.

Unexpectedly, from nowhere the memory of Kerron daring her to climb to the top of the cliff when they were children came back to her. She had refused, ashamed of her fear, but Ran, a year younger, had reached the top. She shook herself; this was not the time for such thoughts.

'Sarai?'

There was an untroubled atmosphere in the clearing, and Ninian thought she could understand what drew Ran to the place so often; but the understanding was forgotten as muffled crying drew her to the base of the cliff, where a small bedraggled figure lay face down in the dust. Ninian's heart gave an uncomfortable leap.

Sarai glanced up, then buried her face again. Her body was shaking, but Ninian realised it was from the aftermath of passion rather than present frenzy, and at last Sarai lifted her head. There were no tears in her eyes, although her face was blotched from crying, and, with shock, Ninian discerned on her left cheek a dark-coloured bruise.

'What's this, Sarai?' she asked softly, lifting her daughter onto her lap and holding her close, as if she was much younger. 'How did this happen?' Her fingers traced the purpling marks along the line of Sarai's jaw.

'*He* did it.' The voice was muffled as Sarai hid her face against Ninian's chest.

'*He?* You mean your father?' Ninian stroked the girl's thin back. 'What happened?'

Sarai hesitated, obviously torn between the need to unburden herself and a desire to try to pretend it had never happened; but her misery was greater than her pride.

'I went to see him, to tell him I wanted to live with him,' she said in a whisper, and it was hard for Ninian to hear what she was saying. 'I was angry with you and Bellene. But he didn't want me, so I hit him.'

'That was foolish, Sarai.' But Ninian spoke gently, trying to soothe the anguish in her daughter's stiff body, understanding the impulse which had sent Sarai to her father. 'Was that why he smacked you?'

'How could he? How *dare* he touch me?' There were renewed tears in her voice, and Sarai's body shook with stormy emotion. 'He never cared about me, never loved me, never wanted me! I hate him.'

'Hush. Hush, Sarai; don't say such things.' Ninian rocked her, trying to find suitable words of comfort. What could she say to ease the pain of rejection? A rush of fury warned her to take care, for she knew, beyond any doubt, that she was glad Sarai understood her father was not the idol she had believed, glad that Quest himself had sent her daughter back to her. Sarai understood at least that her mother loved and wanted her. Yet Ninian was aware that her own feelings were treacherous and potentially damaging; between them, she and Quest should try to salvage what could be saved from his relationship with his child, for Sarai's sake.

'We all make mistakes, Sarai, and do and say things we regret.' Ninian bit back other, bitter words she would have liked to voice. 'This is partly my fault, too.'

'Where were you? Where have you been?' Sarai lifted her ravaged face in a new agony of misery; the depths of her disillusion tore at Ninian's heart, filling her with guilt. 'I wanted you, and you didn't come!'

'Bellene fell down the tower stairs and broke her wrist while we were out looking for you. I had to splint and set the bones, and she was unconscious for a long time; I had to stay with her until she came round.' But as she made the explanation, Ninian was aware of its inadequacy, hearing it as Sarai must, as a further rejection of her own claims to come first with at least one of her parents. 'Please don't think I forgot you, Sarai,' she added, as

140

Sarai's face firmed into bitter rejection. 'I've been desperately worried.'

'I saw you looking for me last night; I was hiding in the reeds, on the border of Wellwater.' Sarai blinked, making the admission with a touch of shame. 'I know you said not to go there, but I wanted – ' Her voice broke.

'I'm sure your father's very sorry, and will say so, if you let him. And he does love you, Sarai, no matter what you think now.'

'I don't want to see him.'

Ninian tightened her arms around the small body, knowing this was not the time to insist, furious with Quest, but at the same time with a touch of sympathy for him, too. Sarai in a passion was not an easy child, and Quest did not know her well enough to read the signs or know how to deal with her.

They were silent, and Sarai began to relax, weariness overcoming the worst of her unhappiness. Ninian allowed her daughter's mood to run its course.

'What do you want to do, Sarai?' she asked eventually, as twilight darkened towards night. 'Are you happy to come back to Arcady with me, or do you want to go and spend some time somewhere else – perhaps with Jerom and Cassia?' It cost her a pang to make the suggestion, and she was rewarded when Sarai uttered an explosive negative.

'*No!* I want to go home with you!' At last Sarai sat up; she was cold and untidy. 'Can we go now? I'm not afraid to swim at night,' she added, as if Ninian had suggested she were.

'I'm ready, if you are.' Ninian stretched cramped arms and legs as she got to her feet. 'I don't know about you, but I missed my midday dinner and I'm hungry!'

Sarai's amber eyes, Quest's eyes, stared broodingly at her. Ninian took her daughter's hand and led her to the clearing.

'Stand on that big stone, and when I bend, climb on my back,' she directed, indicating the rock beside the remains of Maryon's fire. It was too dark now to make out the shape of nose and forehead Ran had mentioned. 'I'll carry you.' Sarai complied, and Ninian let out a gasp as her daughter settled strong arms around her neck. 'Not so tight; you're throttling me!'

Ninian wished Sarai a lighter weight before they stood at the water's edge, and she was glad to put her down.

'Let me get my breath back, then we'll go.'

'There's someone out there, in a boat,' Sarai said softly, pointing towards Wellwater. 'Look.'

The moon had not yet risen, but Ninian knew, with an instinct as sure as if she could see him, that it was Kerron in the boat which was creeping towards the outer edge of the cauldron of deep water. The solitary oarsman seemed to be flinging something into the water, and she wondered what it was.

'What's that person doing, Mother? Was that a weighted line he threw?' Sarai whispered.

'I think you're right. In fact, I'm sure you are,' she murmured. 'I think he must be trying to measure the depth of the deep water.'

Sarai seemed to have forgotten her woes for the moment. 'But it hasn't got a bottom.'

'We should go home.' But Ninian was torn, wanting to stay until Kerron had finished, unwilling to let him know of their watching presence.

'I can see lights shining,' Sarai said softly. 'Look, at the edge of the shallows by the end of the shelf.'

'I never noticed those before; I suppose I've never been here at night.' Ninian stared where Sarai was pointing. 'I wonder what they are.'

'*Oh!*'

Beside her, Sarai stumbled; Ninian reached out an arm to hold her up, but at the same time the earth under her feet seemed to ripple and tremble. The waters of the lake, which had been still, erupted into life and motion, high waves now spreading from deep water to shore.

Ninian, balancing precariously, saw Kerron's boat tossing dangerously. Then the waves seemed to increase in force, stirring the water into a froth of motion, and the boat rose suddenly in the air and turned over, sending the man flying down into the lake.

Ninian held her breath as she waited for Kerron to surface, relieved a short time later to see him come up for air and cling to the upturned boat. The upheavals in the water were already dying away, waves transforming into gentler ripples; the boat was turned right way up again, and a long figure climbed carefully back in.

'What happened, Mother?' Sarai's eyes glowed with intense curiosity.

'Perhaps a small earthquake.' But Ninian hesitated. The part of her which knew and believed Bellene's tales of the lake, of the Avar, whispered that Kerron had disturbed a creature better left in peace. 'Come,' she said abruptly. 'We must get back to Arcady; everyone's worried about you.'

'All right.'

They swam slowly, reaching the edge of the shelf leading to deeper water; instead of going on, Ninian was halted by some flashes of colour below the surface, and she hesitated, treading water.

'Sarai, would you mind waiting a minute? I want to see what those lights are.'

'Quickly?'

'Very.' She drew in a quick breath and ducked down, pursuing the glint of lights deeper than she had expected, perhaps eighty feet. The water was very dark, and she was glad of the guidance of the lights. As she reached the bottom her hands swept the muddy floor, and something hard met her questing fingers; she grasped what felt like a shard of glowing blue-green stone. Putting it inside a pocket, she let her breath go and returned slowly to the surface.

Sarai's strained face met her, and she delayed no further. The lights of Arcady drew them home; Sarai's teeth were chattering from fatigue and cold as they waded ashore at last, and Ninian felt an immense weariness. Sounds of voices spilled from open windows in the hall; they had timed their arrival to coincide with supper.

Ninian put out a hand. 'Come along.' But Sarai stared beyond her, stiffening, and Ninian frowned. 'What is it?'

There was someone else on the shore.

'I've been waiting; they said you'd swum out to the Island.'

Sarai clutched her mother's hand with icy fingers.

'As you see, I found her.'

Quest moved forward; there was distress in his face, not reproach, and it deepened as Sarai shrank back against her mother's body. Ninian's angry thoughts faded.

'I came to say I was sorry, Sarai; very sorry. Will you forgive me?'

The girl said nothing.

'Not here, Quest, not now,' Ninian said, but without anger, understanding as their daughter did not how much the apology had cost him. 'I'm tired, and Sarai's freezing. We can talk in the morning.'

'I had to come and see she was safe.'

'Good night, Quest.' She nodded and drew Sarai on up the strand and into the house. As the door closed behind them, shutting out the draught, Ninian was aware that Quest was still watching them, standing outside on the shingle, facing into the wind. She was surprised into feeling sorry for him. As he stood there, he looked so very much alone.

2

It was dark inside the cave.

They had spent the day in intermittent darkness, for the route along which Storn led them was a mix of caves and tunnels, some open to the skies; it seemed to take forever to travel any distance. Affer was longing for a rest but dared not say so; not after the way Ran had turned on him last time.

'Just up one more passage, then there's a good place to stop for the night,' Storn called down from a narrow opening three feet up from the cave floor. 'In the morning we'll be high enough to see which side of the river mouth the watchers are hiding.'

'Come on, Affer; I'll give you a lift up.' Ran stood below the opening, bent, her hands making a step. Moonlight filtered into the cave through a patchwork of holes, showing him her face, but her voice was almost drowned by the deafening sound of the waterfall beyond the wall of rock, which crashed and thundered in his ears.

Affer obediently lifted his foot onto her waiting hands and felt himself thrust upwards, to be grasped by other waiting hands above, where Storn drew him up once more into the horrors of a dark passage, where his own body briefly blotted out what little light there was. The mummet seemed quite content, but Storn's people lived in tunnels and caves inside the northern mountains; these caves were doubtless more home to him than the open air.

'Can you manage?' Storn called down to Ran, who gave an assent. 'Come along then,' to Affer. 'Best get out of her way.' He began to retreat up the slope, which grew steeper as he moved further away from the entrance. The mummet had his back against one wall, feet on the other, creeping his way up at a slow pace. Affer tried to do the same, but his greater height and length of leg made it difficult and extremely uncomfortable.

It seemed to him eons passed in the darkness. Grunts and noisy gasps from Storn came from one side, Ran's rapid breathing from the other; Affer felt they were crushing him between them.

'Are we nearly there?' he croaked.

'Just now.' There was movement from Storn, followed by a scrabbling sound. then there was the merciful relief of fresh, un-Storn-filled air, and Affer could see again; the tunnel ended at last and there was light ahead. Affer made a final effort up the last section of slope and found himself emerging into another cave, but this time open in one corner of the roof to the sky. He could see the moon shining overhead, and the sound of rushing water was louder than ever.

'Over here.' Storn beckoned, standing by what Affer thought was a wall of pale rock, until he joined the mummet and found that he was looking at a side view of the waterfall itself. Spray spattered him, and Affer smiled, and would have thrust a hand into the current if Ran, coming up behind, had not stopped him.

'Don't touch it. It may be diseased,' she said in his ear. 'There's an odd smell to this place, and we've water enough in our packs.'

'Oh.' He went limp, shamed by his foolishness. 'I thought that was just the cave.' And Storn, he thought privately.

'Don't you want to take a closer look?' Storn said to Ran, ignoring Affer, who stepped back to let his sister by. 'If your eyes are as good as you claim, you may be able to see all the way down to Lake Weyn with the moon on the water.'

She moved closer to the falls, leaning forward with interest. Affer cried out in sudden terror.

'Ran – no! Get back!'

Two small, grubby white hands which had reached out, almost touching her, snaked back, to be hidden in folds of dark material; Storn glared at Affer, his pale face a sickly shade in the moonlight. Ran, unaware of the cause of the dispute, scowled at her brother.

'What's the matter now? I wasn't going to fall.'

'No.' He was sweating, unable to look at her or Storn. 'Please, Ran, move away from the falls. Please.'

His evident terror must have persuaded her, for, with an irritable sigh, she shrugged and came away from the edge. Affer shuddered as he looked at the place, aware how a single push would have sent her out among the crashing water, to tumble down with the river over and over and on to the waiting rocks below, leaving him alone with Storn.

His unwanted talent suddenly woke in him, and in Storn's mind Affer could see a receding image of his sister as the wild, vicious creature Storn perceived her, standing by the edge, and it was as if Affer, too, was able to see that other face imposed on her familiar features. But as Ran's face altered and was her own again, as the mood which had possessed her passed, so Storn's murderous rage dissipated; then it was gone so completely that Affer wondered if he had imagined it, or the fear of something else, some guilty horror hidden more deeply still.

He was sure he had not; it was not the first time he had sensed something dark and unwholesome buried in the recesses of the mummet's mind, knowledge Storn preferred to obscure even from himself.

'This is a good place to stop, Storn. You led us well.' Ran put her pack on the cave floor, rummaging inside for her flask of water.

She found it, unstoppered it and drank. Affer swallowed in sympathy; he, too, was very thirsty.

'Not too much. I know we filled up at Weyn this morning, but who knows where we'll next find drinking water,' Storn advised as Affer drew out his own flask. 'We should ration ourselves.'

'All right.' Affer's thirst was still raging, but he re-stoppered his flask and put it away. He was too tired to care, now the panic was over and Ran was safe, and his mind retreated to more mundane considerations. He ached in every limb, and felt hot and dirty; the prospect of lying full length on the stone floor had a powerful appeal, and he took off his boots and lay back, head resting on his own pack, looking up through the hole in the roof at star-studded skies.

Storn, too, lay down, fortunately some distance away, although Affer could still smell him all too strongly. The mummet's eyes were closed, and Affer picked up no more thoughts, neither from him nor from Ran, who seemed already asleep.

He turned on his side, trying to find a comfortable position, listening to the roar of water from the far end of the cave; and all too soon came an inevitable and increasing pressure on his bladder.

It was almost too much trouble to get up; almost, but, with the noise of the water going on and on, not quite. With a sigh, Affer got to his feet and stumbled to the other end of the cave.

Chapter Seven

1

Kerron, surveying the unusually large congregation at early service, wondered at the cause. He noted the presence of Quest's brother and several other distant relatives from Kandria, but neither Ran nor Ninian; in fact, no one at all from Arcady. Since the temple also served as a meeting place for the exchange of news among the *akhal* such absence was cause for curiosity.

He cast the crystals into the brazier, turning his back, anticipating the moment when the flames would change colour and blaze briefly green, then blue and deep purple as the crystals worked their customary shifts. It was a point in the ritual he enjoyed, and he wondered whose idea the flamboyance had originally been. An *akhal*, surely; a reminder of the lights in the lake.

'You have not fulfilled your duty; the lights still shine nightly and delay the coming of the dark, yet it will come, no matter how the lake defends itself. Beware, priest, if it comes despite your service, instead of with its aid.'

Shock froze Kerron into immobility. The contempt in the voice frightened him, but he would not allow himself to feel his fear as he forced himself to turn and address the congregation.

'And so we make this offering to the Lords of Light, this sacrifice,' he intoned, speaking the familiar words without thought. 'This grain, and this cloth, and this wine, and this gold, which are the means by which we live, that we – '

'There is only a little time remaining for you to accomplish your task.'

The voice thundered in Kerron's mind, drowning out his ability to think; he staggered, reaching out blind hands to the altar to steady himself. He could not remember which part of the ritual they had reached, what he should be doing or saying.

'Let me help you.'

Kerron felt a strong hand under his arm. He blinked, and in an instant of clarity found Quest at his side, guiding him away from the altar.

'We'll go the short way.' Quest led him to the rear of the

temple, to the outside and welcome fresh air. Within the building someone else's voice took up the words of the service.

'You have been commanded, but have thus far failed. There is no forgiveness, no redemption for those who default on their bargain. You will put out the lights in the lake, or pay the price.'

'Price? What price?' Kerron protested, trying to make the voice apprehend his uncertainty and bewilderment, uneasy at the threat. When had instruction become insistence?

'What is it? Are you ill?' Quest's thin face swam in and out of Kerron's vision; for a terrifying moment he wondered if it was *his* voice he heard, but as the pressure seized hold of his mind once more he knew the voice did not belong to Quest.

Nor did this one, which was cold and implacable, no companion or helper but a voice of dominance.

'The darkness is coming, and it abhors the light. The dark comes, and the light will die forever, but first the source of the lights in the lake must be destroyed. That is your task, for which you were chosen.'

'I can't.' Kerron raised a hand in protest, forgetting the futility of the gesture. He swayed on his feet, blinded as well as deaf to externals by the angry, buzzing discourse in his mind.

'Sit down. Here. I'll fetch you some water.' Hands guided him, held him, until he was sitting on the ground; it was soft, slightly damp. Kerron shook his head, trying to regain his self-control.

'This is ridiculous,' he whispered, covering his eyes. There was a cool breeze blowing from the lake, and it revived him, driving some of the mists from his mind.

'Drink this; it may help.'

Quest returned with a pottery beaker. Kerron took it and drank, finding he was thirsty.

'Thank you.' He handed back the cup.

'You look better, or at least less like falling down. Have you been fasting too long?'

Kerron thought the question might more suitably have been addressed to his inquisitor, for Quest's face was the sickly colour that came from abstinence. 'No,' he said slowly. 'I was only dizzy. Perhaps it was the heat of the flames, or the crystals.'

'Perhaps.' Quest was eyeing him closely; Kerron waited until he had finished, his face stiff as he wondered if Quest could possibly know of the existence of the voice. Could he have heard it too?

'I'm well, I assure you,' he said shortly.

'I was worried in case you'd caught the sickness Maryon had.' Quest frowned. 'I suppose there's no more news from Ismon?'

'No.' Dizziness returned, and Kerron put a hand to his

forehead. 'No,' he said more firmly. 'There's been no news; the Plainsman still eludes us.'

'Are you sure you're all right?'

Was the concern genuine? It seemed improbable; Quest had no cause to love him. Suspicion flared in Kerron's dazed mind.

'I need no help.'

Quest shrugged. 'If you say so.'

Kerron knew a violent desire to hide himself, to get away and be completely alone, away from the voice rather than from Quest. Was such a thing possible? He looked at the still waters of the lake, to the high cliff marking Sheer Island and the deep waters beyond, and wondered what had made his boat overturn the previous evening. As he had struggled in the water, a superstitious fear had struck him, and he remembered imagining something else in the water with him, something from Bellene's old tales of the lake. He shivered.

He would have to go out again; the line he had used to try to scale the deeps had not been long enough to measure the drop, even at the edge of the caldera. His eyes closed, and in his mind he seemed to be looking down into the water, fathom upon fathom of depths, conscious of immense weight and mass pressing down on the earth.

What was the *darkness* that hated the light?

Kerron was briefly aware of a flare of loathing within himself and for himself, a feeling so intense it made him clutch his hands to his stomach to ward off the yawning emptiness inside. It passed, and his mind righted itself and he sat back, watching *akhal* file out of temple to the shore and pier, getting into or onto boats or rafts.

Not one craft went close to the deep waters by the island, not even when such a passage would have shortened their journey, as it would for Jerom and the other folk at Kandria. No one ever swam or rowed over the deep water. He felt the prohibition as much as any *akhal*, bred in him by Bellene and the others at Arcady, an inculcated fear which was beyond reason: the deeps were bottomless, would draw down any so foolish as to venture within their bounds.

Kerron's mind shied away from such images. He got stiffly to his feet, turning as he caught sight of the solitary figure by the end of the now otherwise deserted pier. Quest was untying the rope of the boat Kerron had used the night before. Within moments he had launched the craft out from shore, heading east and south, heading for Arcady.

'Perhaps I should send Ninian a storm warning,' Kerron

murmured to himself, remembering the scene he had witnessed between Quest and Sarai in the temple. No doubt Ninian had by now also heard all about it. It was a relief to be able to think about an event in which he was not concerned, and he allowed himself to be amused.

There was certainly going to be a storm at Arcady in the very near future, unless he was a poor prophet and worse judge of character.

Ninian greeted Quest pleasantly when he located her in the tower; he was surprised to find her alone, and said so.

'Bellene fell down these stairs yesterday and broke her wrist, so I'm acting-Steward until I let her get up,' she answered with a smile. 'But I'm not sure how long she'll allow me to enjoy this taste of freedom.'

Quest sat down at the table opposite her. His gaze flitted over the walls, the odd assortment of objects gathered as decoration over the years by the Stewards of Arcady. The hunting horn, one of the least bizarre, caught his eye, the only piece without a layer of dust, which was surprising since it was decades since *akhal* had ceased to hunt, as the rains began to fail and game in the Wetlands became increasingly scarce.

'How is Sarai?' he asked suddenly.

'Tired and sad, but well.'

Rare scarlet flooded his cheeks. 'Did she tell you what happened?'

'She did, but perhaps you'll give me your version?'

He was unsure if she was angry; if she was, she hid it well. 'She came into temple after morning service was over. I was there, meditating; it was a shock when she touched me.' He stared past Ninian out of the window, trying to explain how he had felt. 'She said she wanted to come and live with me. I told her, of course, that it was impossible, and that upset her. I said it badly. She was angry and lashed out with her fists, and she wouldn't stop; I lost my temper.' He fell silent, remembering his anger. 'I smacked her face, and she ran away. I thought she'd come home.'

Ninian looked down at the bare surface of the table; Quest wondered what she was thinking and tried not to feel defensive.

'Do you understand why she was so upset?' Ninian asked eventually.

It was not the question he had expected. 'Why? What do you mean?'

Real annoyance entered Ninian's expression. 'I mean, do you know why your hitting her made her so unhappy? Have you thought about it?'

'I should have thought the fact bad enough,' he said shortly. 'And, of course, she was upset before she found me.'

'Yes.' He had made the statement half in accusation, but she did not respond to the charge. 'Quest, I think you need to understand our daughter rather better. She told me, when I found her on Sheer Island, that the reason she ran away and was so unhappy was because your attitude to her is so changeable. Please.' She held up a hand when he would have spoken. 'Don't interrupt just yet. What I mean is that she feels you've no right to punish her when you don't show her you care in any other way. She's not a baby, and she's quite capable of forgiving you for losing your temper, but she's angry when you aren't consistent.'

'Not this again?' Quest gave a weary sigh. 'I thought we'd said all this, Ninian. My duty to the Order comes first.'

'Then leave Sarai alone.' There was no doubting her anger now. 'If you aren't prepared to try, then stop interfering.'

'And what am I supposed to do?' Quest demanded sarcastically. 'Give up my vows and come to live at Arcady as your companion? Is that what you want? Sarai is still my child, whatever you say.'

'Don't be ridiculous! And she's not *yours*, not in that tone of voice, but *ours*; or herself.'

'You're right.' An appalled sense of his own arrogance rescued him from further foolishness. Quest drew in a long breath, not understanding why he should be doing his best to antagonise Ninian when he had come to Arcady specifically to make peace with her. 'What did you say to Sarai about me?'

'Just that we all make mistakes from time to time, and that I was sure you were sorry.'

He considered, unable to disguise his difficulty in believing her. 'Did you? Weren't you tempted to blame me for everything since the beginning of the world? Didn't you think this an ideal opportunity to persuade Sarai to hate me? Since it would be so much easier for you if she did.'

'Do you want an honest answer? Then yes, I did think of it. Why not? You've made my life difficult with your irrational demands ever since you came back from Enapolis. You come here arguing you want this, you want that, and the gods say you should do this, until I could happily wish never to see you again. But I tried to think how she would feel, not me, and I want her to be happy.'

'How difficult *I've* made your life.' For a second time, Quest flushed. 'Imagine, if you can, Ninian, what is was like for me to come back, to take the place I longed for and devote my life to the gods, only to find you and our daughter here as a constant reminder of my failure to keep my vow of celibacy – one I made myself long before I swore to the priesthood. Do you think it's been easy to forget those sensations we shared, with Sarai in front of me, with you here beside her? Is it so surprising there are times I feel you and she stand between me and my vocation, that the gods themselves despise me for what I did? You sit there, you and Sarai, the living proof, always there – ' He broke off; he had never intended to admit so much.

'Well,' Ninian said at last, perhaps even with relief. 'That explains a lot. What a wonderfully egocentric view of the world you have, Quest. No wonder Sarai feels you resent her at times: you do.'

'No doubt you blame me for that,' he said bitterly. 'As you seem to for everything else. But sometimes, at night, I believe the gods send me dreams; and often they concern you, or her, and I have to stand and watch over Sarai as she dies, or suffers in some way, and I blame myself for her suffering, because that she exists at all is my fault.'

'You have dreams? What sort of dreams?'

A different quality in her voice distracted him from his other concerns. 'Dreams which seem real to me, at the time,' he said, trying to explain the vivid sense of them. 'They've come ever since we went on pilgrimage. Sometimes, I think the gods send them, but at others they seem more a test of my faith.'

She hesitated, then asked: 'Quest, we've never discussed it because you went to Enapolis as soon as we got back, but do you think something happened to us, to all of us, on that pilgrimage? That we were all changed in some way because of it?'

'Perhaps.' His interest sharpened as he understood the question. 'What do you mean, Ninian? Do you, too, have dreams?'

'No; but something happened to me in the Barren Lands, and to Ran and Affer, and probably Kerron, too.' She did not elaborate.

'Aren't you going to tell me?' he asked, after a long silence.

She shook her head. 'No, and it isn't all mine to tell. But I think that the changes that came to us weren't *good* ones. Your dreams sound as if they haunt, not help, you. You don't say what you dream about me, so I won't ask, but it can't be anything to make you feel kindly towards me, or so your attitude suggests. And anything that makes you see harm come to Sarai must surely be evil.'

'Or a warning,' he remarked shortly. 'I dreamed Sarai fell ill, after Maryon came here; that she lay close to death here at Arcady.'

'And you blamed me?' The smile on Ninian's face was not pleasant. 'Perhaps that explains why you're sometimes so antagonistic towards us. Do you really think your dreams come from the gods? Strange gods, Quest. You know what they say: that you bring out of the Barren Lands only what you take there with you. What did we take with us, do you think?'

'Sometimes, I ask myself why the dreams show me such things,' he admitted. It was a relief to say so out loud at last, and he looked across the table at Ninian without antagonism, with no memory of desire. She was familiar, restful even in argument. 'But I should hate to believe it was some flaw in myself that makes me see you or Sarai hurt in any way.'

'You don't look well. Are you starving yourself?'

He was acutely conscious of her scrutiny. 'I fast, yes,' he conceded. 'Otherwise I'm well. It's Kerron who seems ill recently, at least to me; he almost collapsed during service this morning.'

Ninian raised an elegant eyebrow. 'I find it hard to believe his efforts to communicate with the gods would equal yours.'

'I know you never really liked him, Ninian, but I do believe he's in some turmoil. He seems obsessed.' Quest recalled the oddly absent expression on Kerron's face in temple. 'Perhaps he, too, has dreams, and he has no friend to talk to. Perhaps I should ask Ran to speak to him.'

'I've seen Kerron out on the lake, by Sheer Island, more than once recently. In fact, last night he came to the edge of the deep water, and his boat overturned. Sarai and I saw it happen.'

'Really?' Quest was surprised.

'I found this soon after.' Ninian pointed to the table in front of her, where lay a green-blue sliver of shining stone. 'It was at the edge of the shelf south of the island, before it cuts off into deeper water. I suppose it must be a piece from the old Tearstone that was broken up all those years ago.'

'I suppose it must be; perhaps you shouldn't have picked it up.' Quest looked at the fragment, sized about half the length and width of his middle finger; it glowed with an intense, brilliant light. 'I'm surprised it still shines after years in the lake.'

'Bellene says the best lightstones last almost for ever; I asked her this morning when I showed her this. There are probably many more pieces like it in the lake.'

Quest frowned. 'The stone was destroyed at the command of Lord Quorden because it was being used in a malignant design, in a temple dedicated to a false deity.'

'But there's nothing to say the stones themselves were intrinsically evil, only the use made of them.'

'Perhaps not. Do you remember the song you taught me, long ago?' Quest, casting about for past memory, did not observe Ninian's withdrawal. 'I remember now:

'*We brought a stone,*

'*Blue matched with green* –

'I forget the next few lines; something about a serpent goddess.

'*We took the stone*

'*To the high cliff,*

'*To give to the depths.*'

'It doesn't mean anything,' Ninian said, rather breathlessly. 'It's only a song.'

'What happened to your hand?' Her left hand lay flat on the table, and Quest suddenly noticed a large blister on the palm. 'Was that from the stone?'

She nodded. 'Yes; I didn't notice when I first picked it up because my hand was cold and wet, but the stone burns.'

'The Order teaches that the use of these stones in the temples of false deities angered the Lords of Light, and that it was worship of these lights, the Imperial Lights, which drew down on our Empire the failure of the rains and the danger of the second great drought.' Quest frowned. 'Throw it away, Ninian; somewhere it can do no harm.'

'It's only a piece of stone.'

'It was a part of one of the great Imperial lightstones,' Quest said tersely, increasingly concerned. 'There are rumours in the capital that someone is trying to revive the old religion, using such stones to re-light dead temples to restore the old Empire and overthrow the High Priest and our Order. The power of the stones seems linked to the power of the Emperor himself.'

Ninian looked sceptical. 'Do you really believe *akhal* could be involved in such plots? Or that I am, just because of this tiny fragment?'

'Arcady has a name for being different, just as Ismon has a name for disloyalty,' Quest said tightly. 'I'm only telling you what I've heard.'

'While you're here, I meant to ask if you need our share of the spring tithe yet; Kerron said something about a shortage of dried fish at Wellwater.'

Quest shrugged. 'I've no idea. Kerron deals with provisioning.'

'How pleasant to be spared such details,' Ninian said, sounding annoyed. 'I, however, not only have to calculate the tenth we send to support you and your guard, I also have to arrange our tithed labour. I don't know why High Priest Borland doesn't set some of the guard to work the estate, rather than have them idling away at our expense!'

'The guard must always be ready for duty,' Quest said airily.

'If – ' But Ninian thought better about what she meant to say, and broke off. She got abruptly to her feet and wandered over to the windows overlooking the southern part of Arcady.

'Come over here, Quest; you can see Sarai. She's working in the herb gardens this morning, with her friends.'

Quest rose to join her, looking out over the organised chaos which was the inland part of the Arcady estate: the rows of smoking sheds, the distant infirmary, the still-room, the nearby gardens with neat rows of the herbs used in making the medicines which were the pride of Arcady. The familiar smells of smoke rose to the tower, a faintly fishy smell, compounded with an odour of baking bread and a more acrid scent of liquid soap made from a mixture of fish oil and lemon-reed.

Sarai was kneeling in the dirt wearing a ragged pair of trousers and a sleeveless shirt, one of four small figures busy in the gardens. As Quest watched, she wiped her brow with a dusty hand, as if she were hot; it was a bright, sunny day, unseasonably warm. Her companions, two older boys and another girl her own age, were also busy pulling weeds and thinning out the valuable shoots.

Quest frowned. 'She looks tired. Should she be working in this heat?'

'She'll come to no harm, and I always send them off for a swim to cool down when they've finished.' Ninian smiled down at her daughter's narrow back. 'She's a good worker, when she feels like it.'

'I'm pleased.'

'I thought this would be good for her; a back-breaking task to tire her out and make her think less.' Ninian did not look at Quest. 'Go down and talk to her, if you want, but only if you've something sensible to say. Not just that you're sorry, but the reason you were angry with her. Make her understand it wasn't her fault.'

Something, some movement, must have attracted Sarai's attention, for she lifted her head to look up at the tower; Quest brought up a hand to wave, but the head went swiftly down, the figure back at work, digging fiercely.

Her rejection hurt; he had not really believed she would turn away from him. 'Perhaps I should let her alone for now,' Quest said stiffly, wondering if Ninian had told the truth about what she had said to their daughter. 'She still seems upset.'

'It must be hard, to be a father and not a father,' Ninian said, more gently. 'I do try to understand, Quest.'

Her generosity was disconcerting. 'I would have her at Wellwater for a time if it was allowed,' he said, trying to match her. 'But it's impossible. I can only really see her here.'

'A pity she wasn't a boy.'

He was about to voice agreement when he realised she was being sarcastic. As he withdrew his accord, an inner revulsion seized him at his near compliance: there was nothing he wanted to change about his daughter, not her sex nor any part of her. She was herself, no mere extension of himself or Ninian, to be wished this or that at a whim.

'Only for convenience,' he said at last.

Ninian eyed him quizzically. 'Is there anything else, Quest? Because I'm holding an open door later this morning, while Bellene's bedridden.'

He frowned. 'Open door?'

'It's a chance for all our people to come and complain, or ask for a change of task or shift, or help with a problem; I leave the ground floor door to the tower open, and anyone can come up and see me.' She smiled. 'Bellene allowed the custom to lapse in the past year, but I believe it's necessary for all of us to be able to air our grievances, once in a while.'

'Steward indeed.' He remembered his brother Jerom mentioning a similar scheme. 'Children come too?'

'Of course. They live and work here.'

Quest frowned. 'Where's Ran? I wanted to ask her to find time to talk to Kerron, if she would, to see if anything's really wrong with him.'

Ninian smiled. 'How natural you should think of Ran when I mentioned complaints; but you can't see her, because she's not here.'

'*Here*.' His suspicions, for no good reason, were suddenly aroused. 'What do you mean – here at Arcady, or here in the house?'

'Well, neither.'

He waited, but Ninian volunteered no more, and with a sinking heart Quest knew exactly where Ran was. 'She's gone north, hasn't she?'

She hesitated, then nodded.

'So she got her wish, after all.' Quest shut his eyes, wishing he had remained in ignorance. 'They've no licence; if they get picked up, there'll be trouble.'

'She should be back in a few days.' Ninian gave him a look. 'Are you going to tell Kerron?'

'I don't know. Perhaps.'

'I hope you won't.'

She spoke without cajolery, making no appeal to any debt he might owe her. He found he was looking at her simply as a friend, not, for once, as his partner in error. Did she ever recall those eons of time in the dust a decade before, with regret that they could never be again? Had she a lover, or had she enjoyed lovers, over the years since their pilgrimage? There was no reason she should not, although there had been no more children since Sarai. The Stewards of Arcady could marry, if they chose, but most did not, bearing their children alone or with a consort. The customs of Arcady were so long established among the *akhal* that Quest had never thought to question them until he went to Enapolis and saw how very different matters were among the Thelians and other peoples of the Empire.

'If you need help, come to me,' he said, surprising both Ninian and himself. 'If Ran comes to any trouble.' He shrugged. 'Who knows?'

'Thank you.' This time he felt her gratitude was real. 'Let's hope it doesn't come to that, but I'm grateful for the offer. Now, I had better send you away. Would you leave the tower door open as you go?'

He took the dismissal without offence, as he accepted the rapid change of subject. 'I won't see Sarai this time. But give her my love, if you will, and tell her I would have liked to talk to her. I'll come again tomorrow.'

The smile she gave him was warm with approval. 'I'll tell her.'

He reflected that they had never seemed so much in accord concerning their daughter; perhaps after all discussion was more profitable than confrontation.

At the bottom of the stairs he remembered to leave the door open, and as he walked away he saw a woman who had been waiting to go in; Ninian would have a busy morning.

Quest climbed into the boat and undid the mooring rope, but as he pushed off something made him glance back at Arcady. A slight figure stood balanced on one leg at the western side of the house, watching him. Quest smiled with a rush of relieved pleasure, hesitantly lifting a hand in greeting.

There was no response. The small figure stood determinedly still.

Quest sighed, pushing again at the jetty, unable to take his eyes from Sarai. He sat down heavily, then waved again, without much hope.

It was a grudging movement, but one of her hands came up and flapped a feeble response; then, as if she thought he might not have seen, Sarai raised both arms over her head, hands flailing the air. Quest grinned broadly, and thought he heard a distant giggle as she turned and ran off.

He knew himself forgiven, and warmth and gratitude flooded his heart. It was one of the happiest moments of his life.

Ran woke to the grey flush of dawn overhead, opening her eyes to an instant surge of fierce pleasure. The floor of the cave might be hard, the thundering of the waterfall loud and incessant, but every step she took covered new ground. Every sight was new and unfamiliar. At Arcady, nothing was fresh.

The lingering memory of a dream stirred in her, something about the four travellers she had seen from the lookout point. For some reason their images stayed in her mind, as if they and their journey had some greater significance than her own wanderings.

'I'm sure there was a girl with them, younger than me, with dark skin and dark eyes,' she murmured, remembering what she had dreamed. 'There was something about her, light all around her.'

Affer was awake; she saw his eyes open, reflected in them none of her own happiness. Her irritation returned. How could he not find pleasure in their journey, no matter what its purpose? How could he not revel in the physical delight of testing his strength and balance, the extension of his horizons beyond the narrow confines of the home where they had lived too long? He looked, instead, haunted and miserable, and Ran let out a long sigh. He was Affer, and she loved him, and there was no point in complaining about the way he was.

He smiled, and she wondered if he picked up the afterthought. She turned away, uneasy, for she preferred to forget his capacity to see into the recesses of her mind. It surprised her how greatly she resented his unwilling forays into her territory, as if his incursions were voluntary, sly and underhand, as if he spied on her constantly from some hiding place where she could not see him and never knew when he was watching or not.

Storn was still curled up, apparently asleep. Ran did not trust the mummet, but she was not afraid of him. She doubted he had told them the whole truth about himself, not needing Affer's gift to know he was hiding some unpleasant secret, but unless it directly concerned her she did not care what it was.

As if aware of her scrutiny, the mummet stirred, making a great show of waking.

'Are we near the top of the waterfall yet?' Ran asked.

Storn gave her a weary look. 'Not far to go. Stand by the falls and look up, past the overhang, and you can see one of the peaks.'

In daylight, the cave revealed a most peculiar shape, like a crescent moon, the opening through which they had entered half-way up the wall at the centre of the arc. Peering up from beside the falls, Ran made out a steep rock face surmounted by a domed peak, half-shrouded in mist.

'That's called Canton's Fell,' Storn said, coming to join her. 'The other side's known as Ark's Pike. Either would give the guard a clear view over the falls.'

'How do we get up and find out?'

Storn pointed to a narrow opening in the north wall. 'Along that passage, then come out near the top of Canton's Fell, where the rock's not so steep and there's a path of sorts.'

'All right.' Ran moved away as Storn pointedly turned his back; briefly, she envied him the convenience.

'Are we going to eat now, or wait?' Affer was on his feet, stoppering his water flask; Ran frowned.

'I hope you've water left; I don't know where we'll get more.'

'I've plenty.'

'There's smoked fish, if you want, but it'll make you thirsty. If you're hungry, it might be better to eat the hard bread,' Ran suggested. She was aware of only faint hunger pangs in her stomach and decided it was easier not to eat until they reached the top of the waterfall, where she would be in a position to observe the condition of the lake. In addition, there was an odour in the cave which was not entirely pleasant and made her feel slightly sick, although it might only have been Storn.

Their various needs attended to, Storn gathered up his own bundle and led the way out. Ran disliked having to match her longer pace to the mummet's shorter legs, but since she had no idea where they were going she had perforce to follow; Affer coming after, a nervous hand clutching at her tunic.

The passage was dark, although light filtered in at intervals where the rock was cracked. It seemed to Ran that as they made their slow progress up the slope she could see other possible paths leading away into the dimness, and she wondered where they led.

It was impossible to mark the passage of time in the absence of light. Ran found herself unexpectedly disorientated; the tunnel widened and narrowed without warning, so there were times when she could have stretched out her hands and not touched the walls, others when she had to squeeze herself through, scraping against rock. The air was close and damp, unwholesome, as if rarely disturbed, and she found it unsatisfying as she tried to fill her lungs.

Storn stopped abruptly. 'We can rest here a moment; it's warm work in these tunnels.'

The place the mummet had chosen was not ideal; a wide section of tunnel became open space, three passages leading away, all in deep shadow. However, neither Ran nor Affer complained; it was hot, and Ran felt the sweat dripping down her neck and face. Storn moved away, leaning against the wall. Affer was wheezing slightly as he put down his pack, then sat on it.

Feeling restless, Ran decided to explore. She wandered along the passage opposite the one from which they had just emerged, pleased to encounter a light breeze from somewhere overhead.

'Don't go far, Ran,' Affer called nervously.

'I won't.'

She could still hear the waterfall, but the sound was muffled by stone. As she went on, Ran was surprised at how silent the passage had grown. She wandered on, heading idly for a distant shaft of light at the far end of the tunnel. Some trick of the dark must have confused her sense of distance, for although she walked for some time, it seemed a very long way before she came to the source of the light, a place where the passage narrowed sharply, barely wide enough for her to pass.

The light overhead was welcome; Ran gazed up an open shaft that stretched for fifty feet or more overhead, the distance hard to gauge. Blue sky was visible through a circle at the top of the opening. Looking down, Ran took a step back, glad of the light for another reason. Ahead lay a murky darkness, and now Ran could see the gaping void only paces distant, a void which looked as if it led straight into the bowels of the mountain.

'Don't you want to take a closer look?' whispered a voice behind her.

Ran started and tried to turn round, then discovered she could not; the tunnel was too narrow. She fought to retreat further, only to find the press of hard knuckles in the small of her back.

'Who's there?' she asked angrily. 'Is it you, Storn?'

'Perhaps.' But the whisper gave him away, for he was much shorter than Affer, and Ran could not imagine anyone else lurking in the dark passages.

'Stop playing the fool.' She pressed back as she spoke, but again met strong resistance. Ran changed her tactics and tensed, so that she was stuck between the walls of the passage; when the

160

expected shove came, instead of being thrust forwards and down into the dark and uninviting shaft, she was held still. Her breathing quickened as she stared into the gaping hole; not normally imaginative, she could not avoid a shudder of horror at the prospect of plunging down into the dark.

'Do you know how far down it goes?' came Storn's whispering voice.

'How should I?'

There was a movement at her back. She felt and heard motion, then something was flung over her head to fall into the pit of darkness before her; then there was absolute silence as she counted in her head. She had got to sixty before the second sound came, and she swallowed; she was a little afraid of heights, although she never admitted to it.

'Are you frightened? Affer would be, in your place. You don't like it when he's afraid, do you? It makes you angry and your face changes. How do you feel now, little weasel?'

In response, Ran kicked back viciously, and was rewarded by a muffled cry. The mummet's arms were short, and Storn had to be standing close behind her to give force to his shove. She kicked again. There came a muffled curse, and when she kicked a third time her foot met only air; she used the opportunity to step back, away from the void.

The tunnel widened enough for Ran to twist round and face her opponent. She reached quickly down and grasped Storn by the throat with her longer arms and strong fingers.

'You can let go,' he gasped. 'I'll not try again.' Ran released him, but remained on her guard. The mummet put up a hand to rub his throat. In the shaft of daylight his pale, secretive face glared into her own.

'What game are you playing?' she demanded, moving along the tunnel, pushing him in front of her. 'Why?'

'Ran?'

Affer's frightened voice came from down the passage. 'Here,' she called back. 'We're coming.'

'Where were you? What happened? What was Storn trying to do? I heard something in his mind.'

'I think our guide was trying to persuade me to take a long trip down into the mountain.' Ran gave the mummet a push that sent him staggering, to land in a crouch in front of Affer.

'I was only trying to frighten you,' Storn said sullenly, but Ran saw real malice in his expression. 'I wouldn't have hurt you.'

'That's a lie!' Affer shouted the denial. 'You tried to hurt Ran, as you wanted to last night, when you tried to push her down the falls.' Storn shot him a sly glance. Affer went on breathlessly: 'You've killed before, haven't you? That was why you came south, not because you wanted to see the green light, but because you're a murderer.'

Storn reached up a dirty hand which was almost a claw, aimed at Affer's face, then thought better of it and sank down again. 'And what if I have?' he asked with a snarl. 'I can see into the heart of any man and know him by his face; or woman, too, just as you can know their minds, little brother. Are you telling me your sister's so perfect she's never had an evil thought? Have you never seen her face when she's angry with you, and would desert you in the nearest wilderness for half a copper coin?'

'I make her angry,' Affer whispered. 'I hold her back and always have, but she's never deserted me. So what if she's thought of it from time to time? It's the deed, not the thought, that matters.'

'Is that so? Storn took a step nearer Affer. 'But the thought comes first, doesn't it? She may not have acted on it yet, but you know she will. Don't you? *Don't you?*' He laughed, throwing back his head. 'I've seen it in her face; the hunger grows.'

Ran was silent at first, angrier at the truth in Storn's words than at his attempt to kill her, but the same rage compelled her into speech.

'Why shouldn't I be free, after so many years of servitude, no matter that they were service to my brother, whom I love?' she spat out. 'Am I never to be free just because he imagines such terrors that even the prospect of a swim in our lake frightens him? Is his life of so much greater value than mine that I must subjugate mine to his? I never wanted a man, or a child, or any other tie of the flesh, but only to be free.'

'Listen to her mind, not just her words,' Storn said softly. 'As I look into her face and see her for the savage she truly is. You know what I say is true, Affer.'

'*No.*' But he was shaken; Ran knew that despite his denial Affer was aware Storn spoke the truth, and it was too late to call back the words she had spoken.

'What does it matter?' she asked wearily. 'I'm here, and it wasn't I who tried to murder my companion.'

'No?' The malevolence left his face, and Storn looked blank, quite ordinary again. 'Shall we go on?'

'Ran!' Affer was still in shock. 'We can't trust him.'

'If he's in front we can.' But Ran softened her voice, seeing her brother's state. 'Don't be frightened.'

Affer paused, then picked up his pack and balanced it on his shoulders. It was a display of courage of a kind Ran knew she would never understand. She shot Storn a quizzical look.

'After you?'

The mummet shrugged. 'Please yourself.'

He shouldered his own burden and led the way up the widest of the tunnels. In total darkness for the first hundred paces, it then curved and opened up and out, where sunlight fought a way in through gaps in wall and ceiling, picking out motes of dust that floated in the fresher air.

'We climb through that long vent there.' Storn pointed to a gap in the wall about the height of his chest. 'It comes out on the side of the mountain. There's a sort of path, mostly hidden from view by rock and an overhang; from there we can climb to the top and have a look-see down the falls without the guards look-seeing us.'

'Is this the only way?' Storn nodded. Ran approached the gap warily, the mummet close behind; a flicker of a smile on his pale face challenged her, but she ignored him.

One glance at the path outside confirmed the truth of Storn's statement. There was what amounted to a sheltered passage, a narrow path between falling water and the cliff face. Ran poked her head out briefly and looked up, and saw that part of his account, too, was accurate: the top of the cliff overhung the path at an acute angle before curving round the side of the peak. From there, presumably, it was possible to clamber up and on to the top.

'You first.' She stood back. 'Just in case.'

'Up to you!' Storn made a mocking bow. He strode past her and climbed out of the gap, with some awkwardness because he was so short; he had to jump to gain leverage before disappearing through the hole.

'I'll go next.' Affer slung his pack through the vent; Ran wondered if he was simply afraid of being left alone in the tunnels. Affer spat on his hands, levered himself up, then turned sideways and slipped outside.

Following his example, Ran took off her pack and passed it through the hole; Affer's hands came up to take it from her. She breathed in damp air, relishing the prospect of full sunlight, listening to the sound of the falls as she jumped up, balanced, then let herself down on the far side.

There came a loud whistling noise. As her feet touched the ground, Ran saw Storn, standing a little way up the slope, give a small cry. She ducked instinctively, pulling Affer down as the mummet fell backwards, landing hard. Above the sound of the waterfall there was nothing, and when she glanced round there was no one else in sight; but, as Ran watched, a dark stain began to spread from Storn's arm.

Near the mummet's elbow, a thick wooden bolt from a crossbow stuck out among the flesh, tendon and bone of his left arm.

2

There were never many cases to hear before the court, and that morning there were only a handful, most disputes concerning boundaries or quotas exceeded. Jerom was there, unusually without his wife for they normally travelled as a pair, but there was no one from Arcady, so Kerron realised his quarrel must lie with a northern neighbour. Quest greeted his brother with a curt nod.

The main hall at Wellwater was long and dark; the narrow windows that faced east and north let in surprisingly little sunlight. Dark wood panelled walls and floor, except at the centre where a large square slab of stone covered the opening to the deep well which had originally given the estate its name. It was not used now; there was no need since water was drawn from the lake. The part played by the well in the deaths of the *akhal* inhabitants of Wellwater in the early days of the Order remained theoretically a mystery, but Kerron's cynical soul thought poison the most likely cause.

For once, High Priest Borland was officiating, having decided on a whim not to delegate the rather dull task as was his wont. The *akhal* priest sat on the old, broad chair used in the past by the Steward, almost a throne, his pale face tinged with green, his acolyte standing shyly behind him. The boy was young and slight and pretty, with a narrow face and limpid grey eyes fixed on his master. Kerron caught Quest glance with disgust at Borland and the boy.

'I wish to complain that Jerom of Kandria allows lake-foxes to spawn on his land. I've lost half my breeding stock, thanks to his negligence!' A tall but corpulent *akhal* whose name Kerron had forgotten, spoke angrily, giving Jerom a haughty stare. 'I've asked him more than once to scour his shores for lairs, but he claims there are none, that he's too good a Steward.'

'Well?' Borland gave Quest's brother an indolent nod. 'What do you say, Jerom?'

Jerom, looking more than ever an older and more stolid version of his brother, swept thick fair hair out of his eyes with an irritable gesture. 'What I said to Caddir there is there're no lake-foxes on my land,' he said impatiently. 'They have their homes in the marshy section on his own estate; I've seen them. Caddir's just too idle to set his own people to work.'

Kerron tuned out the voice, the subject not holding his attention. *Akhal* were rarely active in serious infringements of the law, and lesser violations, such as petty theft, were usually dealt with privately by the Stewards of the estates. The courts of law through which the Order enhanced its authority in the Empire were of little use for such a purpose in the Wetlands.

Quest looked ill; Kerron could see his fellow priest was still fasting, a nonsense he himself despised. Then Quest's face seemed suddenly to blur, to grow out of focus and become less than real; Kerron felt dizziness sweep through him as his surroundings dimmed into insubstantiality. He wondered, distantly, if he was going mad.

Of late, he seemed to be losing control over his thought processes and his other faculties, so that when the voice spoke in his mind he was not always certain whether the thought came really from the voice, or from some deep, unregarded section of his own consciousness. Yet, conversely, the voice seemed more real to him, much of the time, than his fellow priests. In the past, the voice had come to him only intermittently; now, it was always present, a pressure against his mind which nothing could relieve except compliance with its commands.

Other things about himself were changing, too. His eyes troubled him constantly, feeling sore, as if he spent too much time staring into the sun, and his head ached, the pain oddly distant. Kerron clutched at the arms of his chair, the familiar smooth sense of wood beneath his fingers an assurance he was real, was still in the hall at Wellwater.

The voice repeated incessantly that the darkness was coming, but at times Kerron felt it had already arrived, and he was living inside it. Which was real: Wellwater and Quest and everything else, or the gradual diminution of his self-command? He thought feverishly that the voice in his mind knew the answer, but did not speak.

Light would penetrate the darkness.

He thought about that. Was that what the voice feared, that the lights in the lake had the power to hold back the coming dark? Perhaps, if he put them out, then the voice would go away and leave him alone. He wished there was someone he could talk to about the voice, but he was isolated in the solitude of his own making. There was only Ran; he thought he might talk to her;

perhaps he could. The idea was soothing. She had been with him on the pilgrimage; she might understand.

Was this dark in his mind a warning, a means to force him to the will of the voice? Kerron put a hand to his forehead, wondering if the skin could really be stretched as tight as it felt from inside his head. Was he ill? He sighed, forgetting where he was, wishing the answer could be so simple.

'Did you have an opinion, Kerron?'

Through the fog in his mind Kerron recognised Borland's lazy voice.

'No, nothing, Reverence,' he said, in a voice barely above a whisper.

'Kerron? Are you ill?'

There was some sort of commotion to his right, beyond Borland, but although his eyes were open Kerron could not see in the darkness of the hall, blinded by the pain and pressure in his head. A cool hand touched his hot face, and there came a low exclamation.

'I'm not ill,' he said hoarsely.

'You must destroy the lights to prepare for the coming of the dark. There is little time left to you, unless you fulfil this duty. I cannot protect you if you continue to refuse it.'

For a moment, Kerron thought the voice was Quest speaking; many times he had tried to put face and figure to the voice, and failed. But when his mind was clear, he knew Quest's was not the image he sought.

Then mind and vision cleared and he blinked, staring about the hall, suddenly aware of being the focus of much interested attention.

'My apologies, Reverence,' he said smoothly, turning to the High Priest. 'I felt faint.'

Quest made as if to speak, then checked himself; Borland merely nodded, not sufficiently interested in any but his own affairs to make further inquiries. 'Then shall we move on?' he asked, a little testily, as he surveyed the two remaining petitioners. He put a hand on his stomach, and Kerron, observing the bulge disfiguring the line of the soutane, realised his superior was thinking only of his next meal and of the inconvenience of the court, and wondered how Borland had ever risen to his present status. Had he ever been an ambitious and hungry man, or had his appointment come about because along the way he had made no one hate him?

Kerron sat up, noting obliquely that Quest still watched him, and that Jerom, too, was staring at him with a puzzled expression, the two brothers in accord for once. He stiffened, wary. No one else had ever heard the voice. No one else knew about the voice. Kerron knew the secret would remain his alone, as if to share his knowledge would be to lose it.

Did he want to lose it?

Stubbornly, Kerron set his mind on the case to which Borland was listening with such a lack of enthusiasm.

He would not be forced to another's will, even to the will of the voice. The choice, when it came and he made it, would be his; no one else's but his.

Chapter Eight

1

Affer barely had time to blink before he was lying face down beside the rocks bordering the path overlooking the waterfall.

'We should be safe here,' Ran said, above the rush of water. 'Storn, how badly are you hurt?'

'It's my arm.' The mummet pressed a hand to the bolt protruding from the fleshy part of his arm above the left elbow; his face was paler than ever, sweat beading his forehead. 'I just didn't see them.'

Their present position was relatively secure. A natural wall of uneven rocks hid them from the sight of the opposite peak, as the overhang protected them from above. However, they were safe only as long as they remained crouched by the rocks; the moment they set foot beyond cover and onto the path they presented easy targets for archers on the far side of the falls.

'I'll bind your arm to stop you losing any more blood.' Ran edged forward on her stomach, then, with less caution, knelt beside Storn. With quick efficiency, she made a tourniquet about the mummet's upper arm with strips torn from the spare shirt in her pack, then set about cutting out the protruding section of arrow.

'I can't pull it out. The end's probably barbed, and would only do more damage.' She made a rough sling and bound the arm close to Storn's chest; he grunted.

'I'd as soon leave it.'

'There are two men up there,' Affer commented. 'I feel them.'

'Pity you didn't before!' Storn grumbled.

'It's no one's fault but our own; we were careless.' Ran looked calm, quite in control of the situation. 'If you can move, Storn, we can't stay here. This place is a potential trap, and we have to get out as soon as possible.'

'They'll be watching for us,' Affer objected. 'If we move, they'll shoot.'

'We may be able to move away without being seen. The rocks

give good cover.'

'But what happens at the end of the path when we have to stand to get round and up onto the peak?' Storn objected. 'They'll be able to pick us off one by one.'

'I'll go first.' Ran shrugged, challenging him to find a better solution. 'Well? Would you rather stay here?'

Storn's gaze went to his injured arm. 'I'd as soon not have its fellow in me.'

Ran lifted her head, revelling in the excitement of the risk she was about to take; she felt charged with energy. 'Given the size of you, that guard must be a good shot. Come when I call.'

Further downhil the path disappeared off the side of the cliff at a dizzying angle. If she slipped, there would be no second chance. Ran moved up the slope with a slithering grace, indifferent to the risk, pulling the pack behind her, still invisible behind the wall of rock.

The ground was covered with pebbles and rough grass. Affer clung to it with stiff fingers as he advanced up the slope in Ran's wake, ahead of Storn, who had turned on his back and was pushing himself up with his feet, uttering occasional grunts of pain.

'Can you tell if the guards know we've moved, Affer?' Ran hissed down.

'No.' Affer shook his head, looking frightened.

'Oh, never mind!' Ran tried not to sound impatient. 'Look; this is the difficult part. We leave the shelter of the wall for open ground for about a dozen paces, to the point where the path curves around the peak. It's uphill, and steep, which means the archer or archers will have a clear view.'

They had left the waterfall below, and were now perched above it. A narrow crack between the rocks gave Ran a view of rushing water pounding on rock.

'Storn?' she asked, looking past Affer. 'Can you manage this?'

'I must.' Blood already stained the sling she had fashioned for him; the mummet lay on his side, looking exhausted.

'Should we wait?' Affer asked anxiously.

'Probably not.' Ran frowned at Storn, 'What do you think?'

He tried to shrug, then winced. 'We'd better try.'

Ran was struck by something unpleasantly furtive in his expression and wondered what he was not saying. She sensed an immense anger emanating from him, at herself, at the world. 'Why did you come with us?' she asked suddenly. 'You could have let us come here alone.'

'Why not?' The rage was in his voice. 'There's nothing left

for me now.'

Affer blanched, as if the thought behind the words had entered his mind. Ran frowned, then said: 'What have you done?'

Storn looked away. 'You guessed I'd killed a man.'

'I don't want to know,' Affer said in an agonised whisper. 'I don't want to hear you.'

'I'm not ashamed of what I did.' Storn glanced at Ran. 'Perhaps you're still fool enough to believe in goodness, but there's none in the hearts of men and women. I know. I know what I saw in the faces of my people, with this precious sight the gods, or whatever they are, gave me. Not kindness, nor gentleness, but greed and envy and misery.'

'I wonder what you would see if you could see yourself?'

Ran's interjection brought the tirade to an abrupt end. 'I don't look,' Storn said softly. 'Never.'

'Who did you kill?'

'One was a man who stole from our grain supplies at night; we were all hungry, but he cared only for himself.' There was no awareness of guilt in Storn's expression. 'I saw his true face and knew who the thief was; the next night he went prowling, I rid us of him.'

'Were there others?' Affer looked sick, but Ran felt untouched by Storn's madness; she was almost ashamed to be so indifferent to his evil.

'Nosy, aren't you?' But Storn did not object to the question. 'One was a priest, like me, but a spy, always sending to the Order in Enapolis, informing on who spoke for the Emperor.' The mummet spat. 'He rose in rank with each betrayal, but what good did it do him? I strangled him in the dark ways, past the dead mineworkings.'

'I can see it, Ran,' Affer breathed; his face was a mask of horror. 'I see the memories in Storn's mind, a narrow passage where dim light shines from a cracked amber lightstone, the light blurred by the figure of a man, a priest, taller than Storn.' But it was evidently not this vision alone which frightened Affer. 'But his face – he's not a man. His eyes are black, staring out from a face so white it seems to have no colour. He has long teeth, like a snake's fangs, and a long tongue slithers in and out. He looks hungry, hateful, but I see a second face, like Storn's, overlaying the other, but it's only a mask – ' He broke off, trembling, and in pity Ran looked away.

'Is that all?' she asked.

'There was a woman; she was no better,' Storn said abruptly, and it was evident he thought he had said enough. Ran saw in her

170

brother's horrified face that he was still in intimate contact with the mummet, hating what he learned.

'What else, Storn? Even without my brother's talents I can tell you're hiding something.'

'No!' Storn was genuinely agitated; his good hand chopped the air for emphasis. 'No.'

'I don't believe you.'

Storn gave her a shifty look, but said nothing.

'Affer?'

Affer glanced at Ran, then swallowed. She had never seen him so pale, as if he were deathly unwell. He shook his head, unable to speak.

'Leave him be!' Storn looked as if he would like to kill her, too. 'It was meant for them, not for you,' he snapped at Affer.

'What was?' Ran felt suddenly cold, as if she was balanced on the brink of a chasm.

'Never you mind.' The mummet was watching Affer, seeming to dare him to contradict. 'Well?'

Affer opened his mouth, but nothing came out; he shut it again and shook his head hopelessly. Apparently satisfied, Storn turned back to Ran.

'We must move.' Ran knew there was no point in questioning Affer when he was in such a state, but she felt an ominous curiosity about whatever it was he had learned from Storn's mind. 'Get ready.' She hefted the pack onto her shoulders for protection. 'I'll call when I think it's clear.'

'Ran – ' There was a note of panic in her brother's voice.

'Don't, Affer!'

Suddenly, she was angry with him. 'Not now.' He subsided, and she moved away.

At the end of the rock wall, Ran stooped, then stood up straight and dashed across the open section to where the path curved around the hill. The noise of the falls obliterated the sounds of her footfalls on the dusty earth.

She felt exhilarated, and, momentarily, content.

'She's safe,' Affer whispered, hardly daring to believe it.

Storn gave a dismissive snort. 'Her sort always is!'

'She's brave.'

'Brave? No imagination!' The mummet grinned. Affer thought it seemed impossible he could smile, when he bore so awesome a responsibility on his soul. 'You imagine the worst all the time, don't you? You've the real courage.'

'Me?' Affer wished he could die; had died before he had seen inside Storn's mind.

'Will you tell her?'

'Tell her what?' But Affer knew he was prevaricating.

'That it was my doing.' Storn stared at him with a mesmeric expression. 'You saw, didn't you?'

'Not saw; heard.' Affer gulped painfully. 'That you meant to kill your people.'

'They deserved it,' Storn said, but in a flash of appalled understanding Affer knew that it had been only an impulse, now long regretted. 'I couldn't bear to look at them, you see; not with what I saw. You can understand that, can't you? You most of all.'

Was he asking for sympathy? Affer turned away. 'How?' he asked tonelessly.

Storn shrugged. 'I got the idea from a healer; he showed me how he made a culture with moss to make theriac, which is good against poisons. Soon after I found a colony of diseased rats, and wondered what would happen if I tried to do the same with their blood; I got something that spread like wildfire.'

'And you put it in your water supply?'

Storn hesitated. 'Not at once; it was after I killed the woman the idea came to me. I gathered all the moss I'd used and threw it in, and the bodies of the rats; in my home in the mountains we take most of our water from the source of the river that feeds your lakes. I was just curious to know if it would have any effect.'

'When did you do it?'

Storn considered. 'A month or so back, before the spring surge. I noticed at the time there was a bit of weed on the surface.'

'What happened then?'

'I don't know. They found the woman's body, and I came away south.'

'So your people may be dead?'

Again, Storn made the mistake of trying to shrug. 'It's possible.'

For the moment Affer could think of nothing to say, frozen by the possibility that Storn could have poisoned his people and the *akhal* on an impulse. 'Why?' he said at last.

'Where's your sister got to?' Storn was staring up at the overhang. 'I don't want to stay here forever. Why? Because at the moment I did it I thought people didn't deserve to live.'

'And now?'

'Now?' Storn puffed out his cheeks. 'I don't know. Every time I look at someone I think I was right, when I see their true face. I wondered, since, if that was why whatever it is in the Barren Lands, as you call them, gave me this gift.'

'And to hear your thoughts, was that why they gave me my

172

gift?' Affer asked, in agonised tones. 'To bear this knowledge? I can't.'

'That's your sister now. You go; I'll follow.' Affer hesitated. 'Go on!'

Affer was almost unafraid as he crept to the edge of the line of rocks, then prepared himself to risk the open path beyond. He felt numb, as if he had received too many shocks to be able to fully experience any more. Nothing seemed quite real, least of all Storn's confession.

'Go. Now!' Storn's whisper urged.

It surprised him that he should obey; Affer stumbled on. It was only, as Ran had said, a dozen paces to the point where the path curved. He reached it, and saw he was not yet safe; another similar stretch lay between the start of the curve and the top of the hill, and the overhang offered no protection from his present angle. He paused, then began to run, just as something struck the ground in front of him, pitching dust up into his eyes.

'Come on; now.' It was Ran's voice; he went on. 'You can stop now.'

Affer stopped at once, still feeling dazed, to discover he had reached the overhang and was safely behind it.

'The bolt missed you; the archer couldn't allow for your stopping like that.' Ran spoke tersely. 'You did well, Affer.'

He blinked. 'Someone shot at me?' That did not seem real either.

'What's the matter?' Her tone sharpened, and Affer realised Ran thought it was the shock of nearly being killed that was making him behave so oddly.

'Nothing.' He shook himself. 'Why are they shooting at us?'

'How should I know?' She shrugged. 'Perhaps Kerron ordered Harfort to be isolated as well as Ismon.'

'There's a funny smell here; have you noticed?' Affer lifted his head and sniffed.

'Not now, Affer.'

She often said that to him, but for once he was profoundly grateful for the dismissal. Inside he shuddered, wondering what would happen when he saw Storn again. Affer listened, waiting for Ran's call.

'Now,' she said, under her breath. Then, '*Now!*'

The sound of Storn's boots on the path came quickly. Then another sound, a sort of whistling cry, and a groan. Finally, ragged steps came on again, and Affer saw Storn appearing round the bend, hunched low and moving fast. Then the mummet pitched forwards, sprawling flat on his face.

'Storn!' Ran was on her feet at once; Affer followed, swallowing bile. A second bolt protruded from the mummet, this time between the shoulder blades.

'He's alive.' Ran knelt and put a hand to Storn's neck. 'There's a pulse.'

Affer felt sick. 'Will he be all right?'

Ran shook her head. 'I don't see why he's alive at all.'

'Can he hear us?'

It was a shock when Storn's head suddenly moved; then a tremor ran through him, and he grew quite still. Ran felt again for a pulse. 'He's dead.'

'What shall we do now?' Affer asked in a trembling voice.

'Do?' She sounded angry. 'Carry on.'

Affer opened his mouth to explain that he had meant what were they going to do with the knowledge that the pollution of Lake Ismon had been Storn's doing, then realised that Ran still did not know. He alone knew, now Storn was dead. Guilty gratitude surged through him that the knowledge need not be shared; after all, what good would it serve? There was nothing either Ran or he could do; it was far too late to change what had happened, and the man who bore the responsibility for the pollution was dead.

Affer must still have been in a state of shock, for his reasoning felt perfectly sound. It came to him that perhaps the strange conversation he had had with Storn had been only in his mind, that he had imagined the whole. That, too, was consoling.

'It never happened,' he whispered, as Ran stood, stony-faced, looking out to Lake Harfort. 'None of it. I dreamed it all.'

Affer walked away from Storn's body without a backward glance. Ran frowned, as if something in Affer's behaviour puzzled her, but she made no comment.

'Are you ready, Affer?' she asked eventually.

He shook himself, but the numb feeling was still there. 'I'm coming,' he said.

Quest knelt on the marble floor of the temple and tried to meditate on divinity, but his mind was weary of the effort and would not rid itself of more mundane concerns.

He sat back on his heels, too accustomed to the pose to find it uncomfortable, and his head drooped. Quest's eyes closed as his arms sank limply to his sides and his mind filled with the peaceful emptiness he recognised dimly as the prelude to sleep. After yet another wakeful and unsettled night he thought he would welcome the catharsis of repose, which might, in this place, be gods-given.

'Let me sleep, then,' he murmured, allowing his thoughts to drift away. 'If that is your will.'

It was with no sense of pleasure he became aware of the first symptoms of dreaming, yet he had no power to halt the process. One part of him, that part he thought of as his true self, separated in spirit and sentience from the dreaming Quest to observe the inferior remnant left behind. From a distance, immeasurable in space or time, he watched.

The other Quest rose to its feet and quitted the temple.

Although it had been late morning in the real world, in the land of his dream the day was edging towards twilight. Quest watched his own tall figure walk down to the pier and step into a waiting boat.

Distant figures of other *akhal* busied themselves about the shores of the lake as the small craft swept smoothly on; Lake Avardale was still and peaceful. Quest looked down into the face of the Quest in the boat, a face he could never really think of as his, for all its familiarity; it seemed to belong to a stranger who was not *Quest* at all. There was something watchful and wary about the intent expression he did not like.

Time passed, unnoticed. The other Quest landed the boat on Sheer Island, pulling it up as if he feared to lose it to an imaginary tide. It was a long time since the watching Quest had visited the island, perhaps more than a dozen years. Once he accepted the call to priesthood he had never thought to go there, site of the forbidden gods of the past. Yet the watching Quest found he remembered the island well; the landmarks were unchanged, the high cliff, the open area where the temple had once stood.

It was growing dark by the time the watching Quest distinguished the sleek head surging smoothly through the water to the south. His other self stopped pacing and stood waiting by the shore. The swimming figure reached the shallows and stood up, but Quest had already recognised Ninian; it was as if some part of him knew her as well as he knew himself, this the only woman with whom he had ever been intimate. The shape of her body had changed over the years, softening in outline, but only a little. In his present guise, the watching Quest could look on her without desire, but never without interest.

'You're late.'

Ninian had been smiling, but at the other Quest's tone she frowned. 'Am I? I had a great many other things to do.'

Her companion looked impatiently up at the sky, where the sun hovered above the western horizon. 'Perhaps it doesn't matter,' he said shortly. 'How is Sarai?'

'Well, no thanks to you.' Ninian's face took on a familiar expression. 'I asked you to leave her be, Quest, unless you were prepared to make a real effort with her. You hurt her with all your changes of mood.'

'With you to poison her mind against me, that hardly surprises me.'

There was something singular about the other Quest, something in face or manner that struck the watcher unpleasantly.

'I shall take her from you. It's what you deserve.'

Ninian frowned. 'What is this nonsense? I thought we'd agreed – '

'You thought you'd deceived me,' the other Quest broke in angrily, spitting out the words. 'All that talk about *her* welfare, and how you cared only for that. Did you think I believed you? I know you better than that, Ninian.'

She stepped ashore, and her feet left damp footprints on the dry earth; the light was going as dusk drew on. 'Why are you saying this?' she asked, sounding perturbed. 'When you chose to become a priest, you left behind any rights you had to Sarai, other than to her affections, which are hers to bestow, or not, as she chooses.'

Stop, thought the watching Quest, suddenly afraid. *Run, run away –*

Ninian's voice died as the other Quest's hands reached out and took her throat in fingers which were strong and bony. Her mouth opened as she struggled to draw in breath, but the other Quest pressed tighter still as she began to choke, scrabbling at his hands with her short nails.

Stop! This isn't real!

The watching Quest struggled to gain control of this other self, and, when that failed, to place his insubstantiality between Ninian and her attacker. Panic drove him, but as in any dream he had no power to influence events, and with terrifying speed it was already too late, and he could only watch Ninian's limp figure collapsing to the ground, held between that other Quest's angry, grasping hands.

He let her go, then bent to pick up her body, placing it in the boat; then he climbed in. He rowed south, then west and north, headed for the rim of the deep water on the cliff side of the island. Quest watched his dream self reach the edge and ship his oars, letting the boat drift over the deeps to a point somewhere directly below the centre of the cliff.

More time passed, unnoticed by the watching Quest; he was

176

shocked and stunned by what he had seen, by the violence he perceived within himself. He knew cold terror at witnessing so sudden a death, so instant a cessation of being. Ninian had had no time to prepare herself, no time to know anything but fear as she died. He himself might preach of the rewards awaiting the faithful in their next lives, but in that moment he knew that he dreaded the prospect of dying, that nothing he preached touched the depth of his horror of dissolution.

The spectacle of the evening lights began, and Quest's heart lifted at the display, as though their colour had the power to soothe tumultuous spirits. It soon became plain the lights meant something also to the other Quest, who sat up and, in what seemed no time at all, lifted Ninian's body and put her over the side of the boat.

Worse followed . . .

The water in the caldera began to bubble, and boil; the evening lights, usually spread out over the entire surface of the lake, seemed all at once to shrink, to retreat towards the centre of the deep water, there to be confined within its limits. Individual tendrils of greenish-blue light snaked out here and there towards the edges of the caldera, only to fade and wink out.

Soon, there were no lights left in the water at all.

The other Quest waited until the lake was completely dark, then calmly dipped his oars and began to row away, undisturbed by the bubbling turmoil, which had begun to die down.

'It isn't possible!' The watching Quest struggled to tear himself from this horror of a dream, to wake and obliterate what he had seen. 'This didn't happen,' he whispered. Surely there was no part of him that hated Ninian so? Why had her death put out the lights in the lake? He did not understand why he was being shown this vision, unless he was being tempted, tested; unless it was a warning to him not to use the authority of his office to enforce his will when dealing with Ninian, or his daughter? What would he gain through Ninian's death? Sarai? He thought about those hands, those fingers, their strength, and he shuddered in revulsion, knowing himself afraid.

Quest woke, drenched in sweat, cramped and kneeling in temple before the altar.

It was a struggle to get to his feet. Dizzy and weak, he managed shaky strides to take him outside to fresher air. Quest looked up at the sky, then down at his hands, trying to comprehend the events he had dreamed, which, surely, had not taken place?

'It was so real,' he whispered.

He did not hate Ninian. He could be angry with her, but he had never hated her. There were times he felt a conviction that Sarai should be brought up according to his own dictates, but common sense as often brought him up sharply and told him the only rights he possessed were those Ninian and Sarai chose to grant him. His vows to the priesthood obviated the physical fact of paternity, and by his own choice. Ninian had been generous, on the whole, in sharing their child, although at times she must resent his presence and demands, and the loss of a portion of their daughter's love, if love could be so measured.

Why had he dreamed of killing her, and in doing so extinguishing the lights in the lake? What had one to do with the other? Or was the dream merely a product of his lengthy fast and shortage of sleep?

The peaceful waters of Avardale gleamed a dark, clear blue. Quest drew a deep breath into his lungs. He had prayed the gods would speak to him, but nothing spoke, except in his dreams, and to those false lures he would not listen.

'Are they products of my own mind?' he asked in sudden terror. 'Could a part of me be so lost to common sense, and justice, and fairness, as to believe that only what I want is right, or true?'

A dizzying perspective came to his mind, a vision of a world where all his certainties were turned upside down, where he could take nothing for granted, not even his vocation nor the gods themselves; the vista shook him, so that he called aloud, '*No!*' He could not, dared not doubt, or nothing would remain but the certainty of death.

That fear restored him.

Quest's rapid breathing slowed, and he felt calmer. He had only one true choice, which was to trust in the Lords of Light; if he did not, then there was only chaos and the void of terror and uncertainty he had glimpsed.

With steadier steps, he returned to the temple, and knelt once more in his place before the altar.

Bellene looked a great deal stronger, Ninian decided, with a mingling of regret and satisfaction. The old woman was sitting up in bed, a small handbell at her side, of which she made constant use with an imperious disregard for those she summoned.

'And where are you going?' she asked Ninian haughtily; the bandaged wrist lay lightly on the covers of the bed, a mute reproach.

'Out onto the lake. Sarai will stay with you, and run any errands you have, since you say you're so much better.'

A sharp look rewarded such slyness. 'If you can be sure she

won't run off and leave me!'

'She won't.' Ninian exchanged a smile with her daughter; Sarai was still subdued, but the closeness they had found on the Island had not yet faded.

'If she does, she'll be spinning flax for a month,' Bellene warned. Sarai, who loathed spinning, made a face.

'Well, go off and enjoy yourself. I'm not yet so old I can't deal with any problems that arise without *you*!'

'Thank you.' Ninian managed to extricate herself with a further smile; Sarai followed her from the room.

'Where are you going?' she asked anxiously. 'Will you be long?'

Ninian touched a hand to her daughter's head. 'Not long.'

'I'll stay here.' It was a promise.

'You're a good, kind girl, and don't let anyone tell you otherwise.' Ninian gave a rueful smile. 'Bellene only says nasty things to make herself feel better.'

'I know.' There was no answering smile in Sarai's face. 'Be careful.'

'I will.'

It was a warm afternoon and Ninian was pleased at the prospect of a swim as she walked down to the shore. Behind her, the house and its environs were a hive of activity, but she felt no guilt at absenting herself: she worked as hard as the others, harder since she was always available to the people of Arcady at any time of day or night. That was the first duty Bellene had taught her, and perhaps the hardest to learn, that her own concerns should be placed lowest on the scale: only over Sarai had Ninian rebelled. Bellene had never had a child, a misfortune rather than by intent, although she had treated Ran and Affer's mother as her own daughter, with a jealous affection which resented her children's calls on her.

Ninian waded straight out into deeper water. There were a few boats far out, well past the Island, as she filled her lungs and dived down below the surface. Schools of tiny pink fish darted away as she swam lazily through the water.

When she reached the edge of the sloping shelf south of Sheer Island, Ninian trod water, considering her next move.

'I wonder,' she said aloud. 'Will I see anything?'

She would swim to the edge of deep water west of the Island, where she had seen Kerron's boat on more than one occasion. The prospect was not inviting, for she felt about the deeps the same way she felt about high places, a sort of dizzy giddiness that made her disorientated and sick; it was an annoying weakness she tried to ignore, believing it shameful. But despite the inducement she offered herself, Ninian could not help retreating from the edge of the caldera when she reached it; it was so very dark, so easy to imagine herself floating over a bottomless void. It took all her courage to force herself to dive below the surface.

The pressure intensified as she went deeper; an uncomfortable but not yet painful sensation in her ears and against her skull. Ninian could not see the bottom, although she had swum down a long way. Ahead, terrifying in its impenetrable dark, lay the caldera. Although she had no real need of air, Ninian nevertheless felt a tightness in her chest.

Far below, deeper than she had imagined possible, Ninian thought she saw something move: something that glittered before its brightness was once more obscured. She summoned her courage to carry on, but as she tried to swim towards the lights panic seized her, and she had the sudden conviction she was no longer alone. The water that slid over and round her body became alive, as if cold fingers reached out to caress her skin with icy detachment; in revulsion, Ninian let out her breath in a single, frantic protest.

Pressure pushed her up to the surface, just as she feared she could no longer tell which direction was which. She reached the warmer water, then at last the surface, where she floated, drawing in desperate gulps of air. Ninian shook the excess water from her head and knew a passionate longing to get out of the water and on to dry land.

She struck out for Sheer Island, her fear of the water irrational but intense; unwanted imagination had long trailing weeds, or worse, something alive, slithering along her sides as she swam. When she reached the Island she pulled herself out of the water with frantic speed, shaking with disgust.

Looking back at the water, she wondered if she had the courage to get back in for her return to Arcady.

'I don't know,' she muttered, despising her cowardice and indecision. 'Perhaps Bellene shouldn't have chosen me. What use is an *akhal* who fears the water?'

She found herself envying Ran, who was afraid of nothing, who had no responsibilities except Affer; who hoarded her talents for herself, was not forced to spread herself thinly for the benefit of all the souls at Arcady. Ran, who had the prospect of freedom ahead if she had the patience to wait.

Rebellion surged in Ninian against the burden she carried which could never be put down, against the duty of the Steward who was also guardian of Avardale, and the terrifying nature of that guardianship. She glanced back at the tall cliff with resentment.

'I never asked for this, for any of this,' she said fiercely. 'Why *me*?' Suddenly she was angry; no one had ever asked her what she wanted. The pleasure of self-righteous anger swept through her, a heady feeling. Why should she not abandon the duties imposed upon her and leave them all behind, leave the Wetlands, too, and Quest, and everyone who thought they had a claim on her? Why should she not have a taste of liberty, of self-indulgence?

She could not.

Her rage died as suddenly as it had arisen, startling her into conjecture as to its source. She remembered Quest as she had seen him the previous day, the agony in his face as he admitted his failure. He might be often at fault, not through malice but a genuine conviction that he was and had the right; he, too, loved Sarai, and had never, despite his threats, really tried to take her away from Arcady and her mother.

She felt a powerful temptation to blame him for all the ills in her life, but to do so would be both dishonest and foolish. Emotion drained away as she accepted her responsibilities once more, without resentment.

She looked down at the lake, her fears dispelled with her anger. There might be some creature lurking in its depths, but it had no reason to harm her. If it existed, it, too, was a part of the circle of life and death, no more nor less important to the continuance of the world than she was.

Bellene's teaching decreed that everything that lived possessed an equal value. Men and women of the *akhal* were buried in bare earth when they died, their deaths enriching other lives. Such a creed appealed to Ninian far more strongly than Quest's preachings of eternal servitude to the gods, because it gave meaning to her existence; by the single accident of being born she shared in life's purpose.

The lakes were mother and father to the *akhal*. Ninian thought she could argue with Quest that they were god to them also, if to be god was to own the power of life and death and to give meaning to life. The creed of the Order was dedicated to hierarchy and subservience.

'How can Quest not understand?' she asked aloud. 'How can he be a priest in a religion of jealousy and anger, believing in vengeful gods no better than ordinary men and women? Or is it only that he doesn't want to understand, because to do so would diminish his image of himself?'

She was no longer afraid as she walked into the shallow waters, and dived down to begin the long swim back to the southern shore, to Arcady.

2

They kept to the high ground, concealed from sight below by dense evergreens covering the slopes. North, they caught frequent scenes of jagged snow-capped mountains in the distance; at such times, Ran stopped by any gap in the trees and stood, yearning.

All her life she had wanted this. Affer would have had no need to read her mind to know the sight of the mountains acted as a powerful lure, drawing her to abandon her duty, to him, to Ninian, to Bellene.

'Let's go down to the lake here. There's no sickness flag flying in that village, if that's what it is.' She pointed to a cluster of small, neglected-looking stone houses on flat ground bordering Lake Harfort. 'Perhaps they can tell us how far the pollution has spread.'

They had avoided all contact with *akhal* around the lake thus far. After leaving the peak, and Storn's body, it had early become evident it was not only green weed which infected Harfort and its people; the yellow-green disease flags which were a warning of contagious illness flew from several points around the lake. The powerful odour of decay, stronger as they travelled further west, warned them that the lake itself, as well as its people, was diseased, not just weed-clogged.

They descended the slope with care, keeping a line of trees between themselves and the tiny village; Ran was wary of their welcome. The rank smell intensified as they drew closer to the lake, and Affer covered his nose with his sleeve.

There were only a dozen houses in all, with two, presumably communal, smoking sheds, all built from the same slabs of slate that littered the shore. They were basic-looking dwellings, with only one or two windows apiece and a single door, all huddled so close together that from a distance they looked almost like one single great house.

'I can't see a flag,' Affer whispered to Ran.

'No.' She frowned, for the sun was in her eyes as she peered at the village. From the sound of their raised voices, three men and two women standing in a group by the smoking sheds seemed to be engaged in a vigorous argument. Ran was not afraid, but there was a mean look to the place, to its inhabitants, which was disturbing. 'Let's go, then.'

Affer followed, as ever. Ran walked down through the trees, making enough noise to give warning of their approach to the strange *akhal*, in appearance much like any of their people, except these were broader built and fairer skinned. All five stopped speaking and stared as they drew nearer, leaving the safety of the trees to emerge onto open ground. The lake beyond the village was green, with a sprinkling of purple and white, and stank.

'Who are you? I don't recognise you.'

It was the shortest of the men who asked the question; he looked a little like Bellene in his overt belligerence.

'We've come from the south, from Avardale,' Ran replied composedly. 'We heard about the pollution of the lakes, and the sickness that goes with it, and came to see for ourselves what could be done.'

'Sickness? What sickness?' The man's eyes were sly, those of his companions downcast. Ran observed that they were all poorly dressed, their clothes little better than rags; the material was torn and stained and worn. One of the men and the younger of the two women, both of whom must have been close to her own age, cast hungry looks at her pack; their broad faces were thin and pinched, and there were cracks in the skin around the woman's mouth.

'Ran, I think they're thirsty,' Affer said carefully in her ear, sounding frightened. She nodded, annoyed at the interruption.

'The lake sickness,' she said loudly. 'I can see from here that there's weed covering your water.'

'That?' The man, who seemed spokesman for the villagers, cast an unconvincing look of puzzlement at the lake. 'It's only a flowering plant, not a weed. There's no sickness here.'

'We've seen warning flags out at other villages,' Affer put in.

'What've we to do with them?' the man snapped. 'Strangers, they are, and fools, too. We keep ourselves to ourselves here in Stark.'

It occurred to Ran that he meant exactly what he said; on closer inspection, there was a similarity of feature about all five men and women too great for coincidence. They were, presumably, all close blood-kindred. With only a dozen houses, and presumably only three or four dozen *akhal* inhabitants, they must be close kin indeed; if none of the people bred out, it was no wonder they were all so alike. The thought was oddly repellent, against all Avardale custom, which dictated a breeding pool of no fewer than a hundred.

'Is there something the matter with *akhal* in other villages?' Ran asked, curious as to the cause of such hostility. 'Are you enemies, or have you some quarrel with them?'

'Enemies? Only when they over-fish our waters, or try to take what's ours,' the man answered coldly. 'But we've no truck with them. They're no kin of ours.'

'No doubt you know your own business,' Ran remarked, but, recognising the man's antagonism, changed the subject. 'Do you have well water in your village? Or do you take your supplies from the lake?'

'What's it to you?' The man took a step forward, menacing for the first time.

'Because the sickness we were warned of spreads through water.' Ran held her place. 'If you've a well, and you don't take food or water from the lake, that would explain why you're free of it.'

'And you've come to tell us this? All the way from Avardale?' The man exchanged a look with his companions, who moved closer, until they all stood together. Such proximity exaggerated the likeness between them, and Ran had a sudden and deeply unwelcome conviction that their minds were as closely linked as their bodies.

'No!' At her side, Affer took a step back; Ran guessed he was alarmed by the villagers' evident suspicion and distrust.

'Stay still,' she said sharply, putting a hand on his shoulder, annoyed at his public show of weakness; but she, too, sensed the others' innate dislike of strangers, of anyone who was not of the same blood kin as themselves. To them, she and Affer were the enemy, simply because they were unknown. These were *akhal* unlike any she had ever met, so obviously inbred there could be no taboo on breeding between generations of the same immediate family.

'How did you come here?' The spokesman sounded fretful. 'We've few visitors in these parts.'

'I'm not surprised, given the warmth of your welcome.' Ran pulled herself up, remembering why she had come. 'We came through the tunnels to give you warning.'

'To us?' There was disbelief in the man's tone. He spat, but it was an effort, his mouth obviously dry. His companions followed the flight of his spittle with hungry eyes. 'We want no help, not from any outsiders. If the drought is coming, as the priests say it will, then we're better off alone here, where we drink the water from our own lake and fish our own fish. We want no strangers here to steal what's ours, to drink our water.'

'We live or die together, we *akhal*, or so I was taught,' Ran observed. 'But perhaps manners are different in Avardale.'

'Perhaps they are.' It was the younger woman who spoke, from her place at the spokesman's left shoulder. Her voice was very like his, the same defiant tone; they might have been brother and sister. 'I heard it said the people of Arten city in the southern desert will break from the Empire, conserving themselves and their water from outsiders, when the great drought comes. Why should we not do the same?'

'A whole city is not the same as your village. How many of you live here? Two dozen? Three? And how many such villages are there around Harfort, each set apart by pride and ignorance?' Ran felt no kinship with the quintet, more alien in mind to her than any travelling trader from outside the Wetlands. 'If the drought comes, then it's hardly likely to spare only you, as you seem to think, and leave the rest of us to die.'

'How did you get here?' Suspicion in the spokesman's voice warned that the question was not as straightforward as it appeared.

'As I said, up from Weyn, through the tunnels,' Ran answered shortly.

'And you had no difficulty on your way?'

'No.' She looked him in the eye as she lied. 'Should we?'

The flare of anger told her what she needed to know; the archers who had lain in wait for them were not priests' men but *akhal* like these, who would kill to keep out anyone who did not belong to Harfort. Isolation had produced a sickness in them quite as fatal to outsiders as Maryon's fever.

'We should move on before dark.' Ran sensed the villagers were quite willing to attack, only her blind confidence deterring them. The knowledge exhilarated her, the sense of pitting herself against the world, until she remembered she was not alone. Affer was there. Resentment rose, but the habit of protection was strong. She gestured him back to the tree-line.

'Careful,' she cautioned under her breath. 'Don't walk so fast. They haven't made up their minds yet.' She rested her fingers on the handle of the dagger at her belt as she followed her brother in retreat.

'Ran, are they following?'

'I'd heard Harfort *akhal* were different, but not how different! I could have sworn those five were all brothers and sisters, if one of the women hadn't been pregnant.'

'Was she?' Affer had reached the trees and his pace slowed; Ran risked a backward look, but the five villagers still stood by the smoking shed, heads close together. Evidently they had decided on discretion since their visitors had shown themselves willing to leave. She glanced ahead.

'Affer, look!'

He peered past her up the slope. 'What is it?' Then saw, and gagged.

A body, not *akhal*, clad in a dark soutane of plain blue lay on the open hillside, partially covered by pine needles. It was in an early state of decay, which meant little in the warmth of spring; the priest might have been dead only a few days.

'But the villagers must know he's here,' Affer whispered.

'Probably because they killed him in the first place.' Ran shrugged, not really surprised. 'They said they didn't like outsiders.'

'What shall we do?'

Ran turned on him, suddenly angry. 'Do? We do nothing but carry on to Ismon. Unless you want to go back?'

She wanted him to go back, to Avardale, and go alone, and made it plain; any protest Affer might have made was silenced. Ran experienced a new, deeper resentment than any before that her brother should continue to act as a brake, as a conscience, a constraint. Without him, she would be tempted to forget her mission and go where whim should take her, never returning to Arcady and Avardale.

Freedom. Never to know where the next day would find her. No one to remind her of duty, or to force on her the tedium of regularity, no one to tell her what she should be doing, or where she should be.

'Ran?'

She turned on him, words of dismissal on her lips. 'What is it?'

'Ran – ' he began again, eyes pleading with her. 'Please, don't go on without me.'

She hardened herself, counting each glimpse of the mountains a strike against him, and would not listen. 'Why shouldn't I?'

'It wasn't my fault,' he whispered. She softened, not understanding him but knowing that whatever the error it would never occur to him to blame for it anyone but himself, binding the guilt to him. Yet even with that understanding, she wished she could go on alone.

'Come, if you're coming.' Ran tore her gaze from the sight of the northern mountains, resisting their allure with immense difficulty. She felt bitter, against herself for failing to seize her one chance to be free, and against the awareness of responsibi-

186

lity which would not let her take it. Perhaps, all those years ago, Kerron had been right when he accused her of self-deception.

After a little time, Affer followed.

They travelled on through the belt of trees, away from the villagers and the body of the dead priest. As they walked, Affer had the strange understanding that there was less of him now than there had been at the start of their journey, that he was in some way diminished. He did not know precisely why, unless it was a new flaw in himself, perhaps contagion from unwanted contact with Storn. He had lost the stronger part of himself, leaving only his imagination and terrors to go on to Lake Ismon. And whatever they would find there.

'Gone? But where has she gone?' Kerron demanded. 'I gave her no leave.'

'To Ismon, or so Ninian let me understand.' Quest shrugged. 'I suppose we should have expected it.'

'*You should have known there would be no help for you from her,*' whispered a voice in Kerron's mind, one he could have sworn was his own. '*Ran is no kin of yours, no true friend to stand by you; remember that day in the Barren Lands, remember what she said to you then. You cannot trust her; you can trust no one. There is no one to help you. You were alone then, and you must stand alone now.*'

With an effort, he hid his despair from Quest, covering his feelings with a mask of cold anger.

'She should not have gone,' he said crisply. 'Arcady will pay for this. They had no leave, and they knew the area in the north to be sealed off. If Ran comes back, I shall see that she and Bellene understand they cannot choose to flout the authority of our Order.'

'As you say.' Quest seemed indifferent, as if his mind was otherwise occupied. Kerron let him go, back into the temple, and stared blindly north, to the far end of the lake and beyond, where the river fed from Ismon.

'*She has betrayed you,*' whispered the voice. '*She chose to go against your ruling, to desert you in your time of need. She does not trust you or like you; she once told you Bellene should have left you in the lake to drown, not brought you as a cuckoo to Arcady –*'

'Be quiet!' Kerron put his hands to his ears, struggling to silence the voice of poison in his mind, which would not allow him even hope. But what it said to him was true, for Ran was gone, and there was no one else to whom he would speak, no one else he would ever ask for help. Pride and his deliberate self-isolation bound him in silence; except that there was now rarely silence in his mind, only the constant urgings of the voice.

Chapter Nine

1

Quest could sense the presence of the press of people behind him as he opened his arms wide to the altar, lifting his gaze to meet the smiling stone face of Jiva, the furious scowl of Antior. This was no special ritual, only the usual morning service, but an air of disquiet seemed to be spreading about Avardale, with the result that many *akhal* had come to Wellwater in search of reassurance.

'Speak through me,' he murmured. 'Let me speak your will to my people.'

His mind was clear, with a sharp edge of detachment that came from another night spent without sleep. Although aware of the *akhal* in the temple, Quest felt himself to exist in a state remote from them, at peace for once as he reached out in body and in spirit to the graven images of the Lords of Light. Their outlines seemed to him to deepen, as if they might at any moment pull free from their confining stone, made flesh in response to his offering of absolute submission, so that they might come to him, and in that instant he would become one with them and know all they required from him. There would be no more fear, no more uncertainty.

Quest shut his eyes, offering himself with a blind fervour and humility born of acceptance of his weaknesses. He knew himself human and imperfect, he acknowledged it yet strove for improvement, hope and belief in the ultimate generosity of the Lords of Light conquering despair.

He felt empty, a willing receptacle. Physical and mental fatigue were restful, stilling the incessant questioning of his nature.

'Fill me. Let me speak your words,' he said, so softly no one could have heard him. The moment was close when he must turn and face the people and preach to them, Borland once again having delegated his duty. Ordinarily, Quest would have considered his subject matter deeply before the time of the ritual, but this time he was offering himself in pure faith; only a vehicle, if the gods would accept and make use of him.

A gong sounded. Quest shuddered and turned to face the waiting *akhal*, not seeing the rows of faces lifted towards him, some anxious, others afraid, all expectant. There was nothing in his mind, no message. For a moment his legs felt as if they would no longer support him, and he was afraid of falling; there was a blackness in his head that swirled invitingly, a roaring in his ears so loud it astonished him no one else seemed to hear it.

'Help me,' he prayed silently. 'Help me.'

He was answered.

Quest closed his eyes and entered his dream state; there was the familiar objectifying of himself, the separation of his body into two distinct selves. He was able to look down on his second self, the tall, thin figure in the dark soutane that swayed as it stood before the altar and began to speak.

'Brothers and sisters in the Light.'

The watching Quest was surprised at the power of the voice which was his and not his; it had a hushed, magnetic quality.

'You are fearful, as we must all be, of incurring the anger of the Lords of Light, and of the coming of the second great drought and with it our deaths, our dry deaths, which we born *akhal* must always fear above all else. You dread these things as you must, for all that lives fears to die, clutching and clinging as we do to the slightest thread that binds our spirits to our physical bodies, until that thread at last snaps and we are sent out free, to be with our Lords in faithful servitude for all eternity.

'You fear these matters, yet for all that you do not fear enough.'

There was a sudden change in the tone of the voice, a deliberate verbal slap. The watching Quest saw a passionate intensity enter the face of his preaching self, a defiance and fanaticism as he surveyed the congregation he intended to rebuke.

'Lord Quorden, whose very name declaims him guardian of all the peoples of the Empire, taught us that submission and sacrifice are required of us, that we should listen and obey in accordance with the hierarchy laid down by the Lords of Light through the medium of their servants. Yet do the *akhal* listen, do they conform to this hierarchy, rendering their duty to those who stand above them?' The preaching Quest paused, as if waiting for an answer; none was forthcoming. Continuing his tirade, he raised his voice:

'Not one of you knows your duty. Not one of you truly serves the gods. These trifles you bring in sacrifice, these fish, these weeds and herbs and spices, these are as nothing to the gods, if you do not submit yourselves. Why, then, should our Lords withhold their anger from us, when you offer them nothing but trash?'

190

The watching Quest saw shock on the faces of the other priests at the altar, only Kerron's expression absent, as if he heard nothing out of the way. He himself was shocked. The *akhal* were good and generous supporters of the Order and its priesthood, never stinting in sacrifice or day labour. True, they did not attend services with the assiduity of the population in Enapolis, but their working day was long. His people were devout and law-abiding, undeserving of rebuke.

A chill ran down his spine. Were these the words of the gods? He was both ashamed and uncomfortable. He had not envisaged that the gods would make use of him while maintaining his awareness, speaking words through him while he must observe, with no sensation of communion with them.

'Where is that willing duty which alone protects us from the drought that may yet come, unless the gods in their generosity withhold their righteous wrath? Where is that order which they command, when even among ourselves we see children rebuke their parents, wives their husbands, where our Lords have commanded that there should be respect and compliance?'

The watching Quest looked into the faces of the congregation, hitherto overlooked, aghast to discover who was present to hear this ungenerous sermon. Not only were his brother and sister there, but also Sarai and Ninian, as well as others from Arcady. He saw anger begin to build up in Ninian's eyes, and those of others of her kindred, at what must seem to them a deliberate insult aimed at the heir to Arcady. Nor did the other *akhal* seem any better pleased with the sermon. They looked less fearful than affronted: this was not the way they expected to be treated.

'The gods demand you should atone for your shortcomings; for they, in their generosity, are willing to forgo their vengeance on those who break faith with them, asking only that you should from now on give them all, not a mere semblance, of their due. We should not struggle against the gratitude and duty we owe, but give what we have willingly, and with our whole hearts.

'Lastly, you should look among yourselves and seek out those at fault, and name them straightly and without false honour, for they are an offence to the gods, and must be brought to reason and rightness. For no man has a higher duty than to bring his wife or sons or daughters to full obedience to the gods; and if he fails in this, then the larger failing is his, for he stands to them as the gods to himself, he the guardian, they his charge.'

Sarai bent a tight face to Ninian and whispered a question. Ninian shook her head and placed a restraining hand on her arm. Quest struggled, deeply shamed, against the invisible bonds which kept him from his own body and forced him to observe this parody of himself mouth teachings which sounded at best foolish, divisive; doctrines which made no sense, and made the gods appear mindless, vengeful and greedy, no more than selfish men intent on their own pride.

Had he ever said or believed such things of his free will? Did he usually sound so pompous and tendentious?

'For the manner of a woman is not that of a man; she is more bound by nature than he, more enslaved to her womanhood. She is temptress, too, in her weakness, made to lure a man from his bounden obedience by means of her round softness and the frailty of her will. Through her, his purity may be defiled, for he, as he stands closer in image to the gods, may offer them more perfect service. Yet she, too, may give herself to them, in her willingness and her obedience, in bearing her husband's children and in serving his will. The Lords of Light hold her spirit equal to his in her duty.'

The watching Quest was aware of a stirring in the congregation, his attention drawn unwillingly away from an appalled observation of his other self's misogyny.

Ninian had stood up and reached down for Sarai; the girl looked puzzled and hurt. Ninian, with lips compressed into a very thin line, stepped out of her place and into the centre aisle, where there was space to walk, turning her back on altar and preacher.

'Where do you go, woman?' the listening Quest heard himself ask, in loud tones of exaggerated self-importance.

There was a pause; Ninian checked. Even the set of her shoulders was furious, the hand that held Sarai's curled tightly around her daughter's fingers. She was not a woman to ignore a challenge; Ninian turned back to face the preaching Quest.

'I have heard enough.' Her voice, too, was loud enough to fill the temple. 'We came here to listen to the words of the gods. Instead, we are harangued with nothing more than the bias of a man whose conscience chooses to blame others for his own mistakes, who cares more to invent excuses for himself, and to create gods in his own image, than for the people he claims to serve.' The listening Quest had never heard so much anger and bitterness in her voice.

'That you find what I say unpalatable does not make it untrue,' the preaching Quest said sternly, his features composed into a mask of arrogance. 'You have defied the gods, not once but a thousand times. You forced a man of vowed celibacy to break his promise, yet deny him those rights in his child which are by nature his. You stand as heir to Arcady, an estate that in its lineage goes against the common practice of our land and the dictates of the gods. Your defiance is an offence, and the Lords of Light will strike you down unless you surrender to their will.'

There was contempt in her voice. 'To you?'

'No.'

Sarai pulled her hand away from her mother and stepped back. She glanced up at the man she called her father with a look so agonised the watching Quest felt a stab of pain that she should have been subjected to so shameful an episode. He fought to gain control of his body, to repossess physical mastery so he could at least ensure he said no more, but there was a barrier between him and his corporeal self that he could not cross.

The watching Quest was never sure who made the first move; it might even have been his own brother. Whoever it was, one by one the men and women and children of the *akhal* rose to their feet to follow Ninian, for she was well liked and her position as heir to Arcady gave her status among them. There was no question as to the meaning of their actions. The preaching Quest watched silently, without dismay or apology.

'I want to go home.' Sarai's painful whisper could be heard by everyone. With a final contemptuous backward look, Ninian gathered her daughter close and led her out of the temple. More than half the congregation, including Jerom and his wife, went with her. The watching Quest was unsure how he felt. Half of him was proud of his people, that they should not allow this false self to rant against a woman and child who did not merit such abuse; but the other half was ashamed, of them or of himself, wanting Ninian to share in his defilement and degradation. To add to his self-disgust, as she walked away, in his mind's eye he saw again her naked form, pale flesh powdered with orange-red dust, lying in the abandonment of desire on the ground in the Barren Lands. With even deeper loathing he looked at his other self, sensing that Quest, too, knew a stirring of desire; he wondered how much himself this twin really was.

Was it the gods who had spoken through his other self? Quest was a prey to doubt. It shook him to think that the thoughts expressed by his preaching self might be his own, suppressed but nonetheless owning their origins to himself. Had he, in his heart, ever blamed Ninian and Sarai for his own difficulties in maintaining the required celibacy? Yes, he had, to his shame; he knew it was true. And did he, in his heart, believe women and children were the possessions of men, subordinate and somehow less by reason of their difference? Honesty required him to respond that he did not, but that he might wish it were so.

The Order taught that the gods had ordained a hierarchy, the rightness of which could not be questioned; yet in the Wetlands this hierarchy meant little, for women and men and children worked together to maintain themselves and their kin, all a part of the same circle of subsistence. While he believed in the opposing qualities of woman and man, Quest had not, or at least not consciously, believed one of greater value than the other, both necessary for completion of the circle. In the cities, he was aware that values were different, but for the *akhal* life had not changed in centuries until the coming of the Order.

He had, somehow, managed to uphold some of the teachings of his Order while ignoring those with which he did not agree. Was this his punishment for such selectivity, to be forced to preach to his own people and despised by them for speaking the truth? But what was the truth? What he saw, what he had known all his life, or what the gods taught: or Lord Quorden taught? How could he know which was which? Once more, all the questions he had relegated to the back of his mind rushed to the forefront of his thoughts. He was only a man. The gods had called him, and he had done his utmost to answer their summoning, opening his heart and mind to their will. Yet after ten years he was still unsure of their resolve, unable to distinguish between the will of man and god.

'Help me,' he whispered.

There were still a few *akhal* and guards left in temple, but no one he knew well. In visible reproof, no one from Kandria or Arcady remained. His preaching self stood silently aloof, apparently ignorant of, or indifferent to, the offence he had caused.

In that moment of comprehension Quest hated himself for the injury to his daughter, wounded a second time by his incapacity to accept responsibility for his own actions. It made no sense that his vocation, even if it was real, should be imperilled by the engendering of a child. In a rare moment of rebellion, he thought he could understand what Ninian meant when she argued that human and divine love had the same origins. Why should his love for Sarai detract in any way from that other love, when it possessed the same quality, the same necessity to put self aside?

'Help me,' he whispered again, as the temple and its interior began to swim in a dizzying blur. 'Ninian,' he said, half a plea. 'Help me.'

As the darkness closed in on his mind, Quest wondered fleetingly that he should dare call on her, when this other self had so openly denied her and their child. Hopelessness suffused his thoughts as he sank into the depths of mindlessness, which was more welcome than conscious reflection.

His mind blurred and the barrier between himself and his body fell away, and they were one again. He staggered, as if he had fallen into himself. Quest saw, in one pellucid moment, that he must make a choice and cease the endless prevaricating which ate into his spirit, so that he never knew from one instant to the next what, or who, he should be.

He was a priest, and he was a father. They were the same man, but each separate in existence. He must find the means to join his own duality in one man, or tear priest, or father, from his heart.

Sarai was not crying, but her face held a bewildered look, as if she was trying to make out why her father should speak against her.

'Is it true?' she asked eventually, once they were down by Wellwater's pier.

'Is what true?' Ninian fought to conquer her own rage and hurt, for Sarai's sake.

'That I was born because you tempted Father, not because he loved you, or wanted me?'

Well, Ninian thought bitterly, given the sermon Quest had preached, the question was a fair one. 'No, of course it isn't true,' she made herself say calmly. 'Your father and I came together because we wanted one another, and thought we loved one another, and you were born because of that love. He didn't know about you until you were two years old because he was away in Enapolis, but that doesn't mean . . . '

'What?'

But Ninian could not bring herself to continue, too filled with a sense of deep injustice to attempt to be fair to Quest. Angry words hovered on her lips, the truth for Sarai, which was that although Quest did love her, at the same time he seemed to wish she had never been born. It would, at that moment, be very easy to make Sarai hate her father for the rest of his life, and the temptation was strong.

'I'm sorry, Ninian. I apologise on my brother's behalf, since he seems incapable of common courtesy.'

She turned, flushed, to find Jerom addressing her, his expression filled with an appalled anger. He looked very like Quest, and, unexpectedly, like Sarai; Ninian breathed in deeply and remembered she had no quarrel with him.

'Thank you; it's good of you to say so.'

'How could he?' Jerom was outraged. Cassia, with a glance of compassion for Sarai, came forward and laid her hand on his arm; Ninian was surprised at the look they exchanged, one so filled with mutual understanding and affection that she was consumed with momentary envy.

'Ninian, he must be ill, or he wouldn't speak so.' Cassia's voice was low and pleasant, evidently sincere. Ninian, who had always thought both Jerom and his wife detested her, found herself unwillingly grateful for their support.

'Thank you.' She laid her hands on Sarai's rigid shoulders.

'He'll regret this, and say so.' Jerom's expression was coldly angry. 'And in public, too, or I'll not call him my brother.'

Ninian wanted to say it did not matter, because she would never go to Wellwater again, or receive Quest at Arcady; but, with Sarai listening, she held her tongue. 'Thank you,' she said again, forcing a smile; she gave Sarai a gentle push along the pier to their waiting boat. Silence marked their departure. Tingling with furious embarrassment, Ninian nonetheless understood the intended compliment. She took the oars while Sarai cast off, giving the pier post a violent shove.

'Look how many flowers there are on the water,' Ninian remarked after a moment. 'I don't think I've ever seen so many.' The area of lake north of Wellwater was dotted with floating green plants, each with a single purple and white flower. 'Do you remember the old saying, *green weed, great need*'?

'What does it mean?'

'Oh, I think it's just a general warning not to allow plants to silt up the waterways; you know rivers, and even whole lakes, can be clogged by some kinds of weed.' She made a mental note to order them to be gathered away, and if there were any plants near Arcady waters. Sarai, however, was not so easily distracted.

'Why did he say it, if it wasn't true?' she asked, a betraying wobble in her voice. 'I don't understand. You can't both be telling the truth!'

Rage returned, but also reason. 'In the cities, customs differ from ours,' Ninian began, hoping Sarai was old enough to understand. 'And it was in the great city of Enapolis that your father was taught by the Order. Some of the other peoples of the Empire believe that if a man looks at a woman and is physically aroused by the sight of her, even a lock of her hair, then it's her doing, even if it's unintentional; that's why they make their women wear concealing garments, or stay in their houses, so no one can see them.'

Sarai scowled. 'That's silly.'

'It is, isn't it? But people often believe what they want to, not what's true.'

'Why do they want to believe it?'

Ninian sighed. 'That's a good question, Sarai. I can't tell you the answer, unless it comes about because such people project their own weaknesses onto those they then blame for being weak.' Sarai looked puzzled. 'It's surprising how many foolish things people can believe, and if they do so for long enough it gets called tradition, or custom. Once that's the case, it doesn't matter whether belief is rational or not, since almost anything can be justified by *custom.*'

'Like women ruling at Arcady?'

Ninian laughed. 'Like that, yes. If you find you need to decide whether a custom or tradition is sensible or not, try to think whether it would still be sensible if you changed *man* to *woman*, or *akhal* to *Thelian*, for example. Imagine if your father had preached that men, not women, were tempters, out to seduce women from their duty by showing off their ankles, or their hair. Doesn't it sound ridiculous? Always try to think of the meaning behind the words, don't just accept the familiarity of the saying.'

'Oh.' Sarai bent over the side and trailed a hand in the water.

Other boats were following in their wake; the remainder of the Arcady contingent was also returning home.

'But does Father believe that, then?' Sarai asked, not looking up. 'Is he silly?'

Ninian sighed. 'At times, yes, Sarai; as we all are.'

'Was he angry with us today? Why?'

'Why?' Ninian repeated. 'I don't know; he didn't look well. You'll have to ask him, Sarai, not me.'

'I hate him.' But the words lacked conviction. Ninian saw that it lay in her power to make them reality, but again, when the angry, vengeful words came to her tongue, she could not speak them.

Not in anger, she thought. If she was going to poison Sarai's mind against her father, it must be done coldly, with deliberate intent, in full awareness of what she was doing and why. Yet the temptation was strong. Ninian wondered if she were ever to be allowed the loosening of her own anger, or whether she must keep it inside herself forever for fear of hurting those she loved or were in her care. Was that a part of the duty of a Steward of Arcady?

Words were nothing in themselves; it was action which gave proof of real intent, and she would not act in any way which would sink herself, in her own esteem, to Quest's level.

'Try not to hate him, Sarai,' she said gently. 'I don't.'

The child looked at her, and as she did Ninian became aware of a real alteration in her daughter, as if she had never before thought of her mother as a person with feelings of her own. It was evidently a revelation to her, one not entirely welcome.

'I'm sorry.' Sarai blinked, then sniffed. 'I didn't mean it.'

A rush of love warmed Ninian's chilled heart, and she smiled. 'I know.' For once, she felt she had received a reward fully worthy of her sacrifice.

'You're going too far out; we'll be over the deep water if you keep on this pattern.'

The change to the prosaic almost made Ninian laugh, but she saw Sarai was right. They were almost at the rim of the caldera, and she set to correcting their course.

'Whatever happens, and no matter what anyone says, re-member you were wanted,' she said, reverting to their earlier discussion. 'I knew the moment of your conception, and it was then that I knew I would call you Sarai.'

The child looked startled, for she had never been told the full story. 'How did you know?' she asked. 'That it would be me?'

'It was the first time I ever spoke a future truth, although I didn't understand then what it was. It was a surprise to me.' She smiled, remembering the shock and pleasure of the revelation.

Sarai relaxed. 'Why didn't Father know too?'

'Do you know something?' Not for the first time, Ninian was surprised by her daughter's acuity. 'I wonder that myself.' What was it Quest had said? That he had dreams which sometimes came true. Why had his dreams never told him about Sarai? The thought lodged in her mind.

They progressed in peaceful silence, soothed by the regular slap of the oars. The sun was high, for it was close to noon, and the day was very warm. As they passed the island, Ninian noticed a few of the floating plants beginning to gather in the shallow waters; there had been some over the deeps, too.

The light was very bright, and the sun on the water dazzled her as small ripples moved to a regular rhythm in the wake of their boat. Ninian blinked, feeling suddenly sleepy and in no hurry to return to Arcady, where there would be questions and anger and decisions to make. She looked at Sarai, and was about to say something of the sort, when the world went suddenly dark and colourless, as if a hand had grasped the sun and blotted out the light. Frightened, Ninian loosened her grip on the oars and cried out.

'I'm here. What's the matter?' There was a reassuring touch of wet fingers on her ankle, but Ninian could see nothing at all.

'I don't know. It's so dark.'

'No, it's not.' The small fingers clutched her leg. 'It's a bright day, Mother. What's wrong?'

'It's the darkness. The dark is coming to Avardale,' Ninian whispered. 'I can see it.' She could feel it, too, a cold darkness that gathered her up and hid her in its depths, blinding her. She was speaking a future truth, and this time it terrified her.

'What can you see?'

The boat rocked; Ninian felt Sarai's narrow body move alongside her own. Small hands took her arm and shook her.

'Nothing,' she whispered. 'I can see nothing. Just the dark.'

Ninian shut her eyes, so that at least the darkness was her own. She tried to concentrate on feeling the warmth of the sun on her arms and her face, relieved to find she still could. She raised her head, lifting blind eyes to the sun, when suddenly brightness dazzled her. Ninian took the frightened Sarai into her arms and hugged her.

'Don't be afraid, Sarai; I couldn't see for a moment, but it's all right now.' Sarai's expression was filled with doubt; but Ninian went on: 'It must have been a part of the truth I spoke, about the coming of the dark. I've never seen the future before, just said what would come to be.'

'I want to go home.' Sarai pulled away.

As she took up the oars, it struck Ninian that while she was still very angry with Quest, the worst of her fury had abated. What he had said in temple seemed now far less important than it had before she had been granted her vision of darkness.

Quest might be a priest, but he was only a man, whereas who knew from where this dark vision had come? Perhaps from his gods, perhaps some other source. It mattered more that it was true, or would become true, than who or what had sent it. And, if darkness came to Avardale, whatever that portended, was it for that purpose that the Stewards of Arcady were guardians to the lake? Would it mean the fulfilment of that other duty beholden on Arkata's heir?

She would not think of it; there was no purpose served in anticipating fear. That was Affer's trick, and it led to inaction and terror at every unexpected sound and shadow.

The bow of the boat grated on the pebbled shore. Sarai scrambled out and ran into the house, leaving Ninian to order two men to pull the craft up on the shore before following, at a more sedate pace. The next part of her day's trials was about to begin. Ninian braced herself, knowing others who had attended service at Wellwater would already have spread the news.

She waited for the first, inevitable question.

Kerron took the message capsules from the birdman but did not open them. Jordan noticed he only glanced at them before putting them in the pocket of his robe as he strode off up the hill, away from the mews.

The wind blew from the north, bringing with it a hint of something not entirely wholesome. Kerron breathed in, his heart labouring, feeling only half alive, perhaps even less than half. The greater part of him had been, was being, consumed by the power of the voice. He, as Kerron, existed, in a world alone with the voice, more isolated than he had ever been by his own design.

There had been some fuss in temple during the morning service. He had noticed Ninian get up in the middle of Quest's sermonising, looking drawn and angry, taking Sarai with her; but he could not remember why she was angry, and it did not seem important.

He climbed to a high point on the hill north and west of the great house, with an excellent view over the lake, the source of all his present troubles. Avardale glimmered, boats and rafts bobbing over its surface, all much as usual. Kerron blinked, sight blurring, until all the shapes and colours wavered and grew indistinct, unreal and distant. He was so very tired.

The message capsules in his pocket were cold and heavy. Reminded of their existence, he drew them out, without much interest. There was a small knife in the same pocket, one he used to pry the halves of the capsules apart; he took that out, too.

The seals on the capsules told him their origin. Without surprise, Kerron noted there was still no news from the north, neither from Ismon nor Harfort.

'*And will be none; you know there will be none,*' whispered the voice in his mind. '*You knew from the beginning it would be so: out of sight is out of thought. It was already too late when you made your choice and did nothing.*'

'But I thought it was only a spring-fever and would pass.' Kerron's protest was feverish. 'And I had my orders to seal off the lake.'

The voice was silent, but even its absence had a fretful, spiteful quality; its silence condemned him. Kerron swallowed and took up a capsule, using the point of the knife to break it open.

It came from Ammon. He decoded the message mentally, registering it as merely a repeat of an earlier request to keep watch for strangers. He shrugged; if any rebels escaped to the Wetlands he would find them. Strangers could not be hidden long among the *akhal*, especially not Plainsmen, nor the dark-skinned woman the message described.

There were always stories about rebels; it was another of the

Order's tricks to effect conformity, to invent imaginary charges of an ambiguous nature against anyone who questioned authority. No doubt true rebels did exist, but not in the Wetlands, backwaters of the Empire.

He opened the second capsule; the seal gave its origin as Lake Weyn. He decoded it with a certain wariness, but it was only a reply to his query regarding the outbreak of disease. It reported a few cases of fever and mentioned polluted water and a build-up of green weed.

The third and last message was from Enapolis, the capital, from a priest named Accufer, a Thelian of similar temperament to his own; they had become acquainted during Kerron's two years in the city, both recruited for political service within the Order. The message read:

'Greetings, brother in the Light.
In my last communication, I told you of our Lord Quorden's disagreements with the Emperor; they have reached such a pitch that now Lord Quorden believes the rebels intend to strike hard and soon, perhaps south, in the desert city of Arten, or else further west, even in your Wetlands. There is some plot afoot to make it seem the old religion has been revived, the temples brought back to life. The green light seen on the Plains has started up the ancient stories that the Imperial Lights will bring back the rains. Since you are not so far distant from the site of the Plains temple, I send you this advisement: you will gain favour with Lord Quorden if you dispatch any known dissidents to Ammon or Enapolis for questioning.

There is further trouble here. The Seafolk, the forbidden people, disrupt all trade by sea around the coasts. As you may imagine, this has caused great consternation as well as loss of income to our Order, and it has been agreed that all trade in grain must be by land until the problem is solved.

There is an uneasy mood here, at the court and in the temple complex. I sense that both the Emperor and Lord Quorden are only paused in their conflict, biding their time until a new weapon comes to the hand of one or the other. There is some scheme I have heard, involving discredit to the heir, Lord Hilarion himself, but it may come to nothing.

These are difficult days. I urge you to protect your position, if you can; no one's head is safe, unless it is on the right side to be counted.
Farewell.
Accufer, Priest.'

Kerron folded the paper and replaced it in his pocket, frowning over the contents. It did not seem so very important, yet for

Accufer to have written suggested it would be wise to follow his suggestion. Surely there were *akhal* who sided with the Emperor, discontents like Maryon, who could be sent for questioning and give proof of his own zealous allegiance to the Order? Around Avardale, Arcady had always been the prime source for such dissidents; its very structure was anathema to the Order's teaching, and its unconventionality made it and its inhabitants vulnerable, no matter how much Bellene might prattle about Imperial Charters.

But none of it seemed urgent. The only part of the message that really interested him was mention of the Imperial Lights. Bellene had told them all the stories of the distant past, a time when the skies of the Empire were filled with rainbow colours, lightstone calling to lightstone from the old temples, their own Tearstone a part of the whole.

'Fool! You have looked, but you have not seen.'

'What?' Startled, Kerron asked the question aloud.

'Look below. The darkness is coming, and may not be halted nor stayed. The lights in the lake must die. Fool! See what is being done, under your very eyes!'

Kerron had small will left to disobey the vicious scourge of the voice. He glanced up to the guard compound; the long stone buildings and open yards showed him only scenes of everyday activity, men engaged in drills and mock combat.

'No, not there! Look away, to the east!'

The impatience held an undertone of contempt; Kerron half-turned and looked out on the lake, where several men had taken their boats along the shore; between them, on a line, they seemed to be holding long, fine-mesh fishing nets.

'There; it is there!'

It was a moment before Kerron realised what the men were doing, which was gathering up the mass of floating plants which had converged near the shore over the past two days.

'Stop them gathering the weed? But why?' he asked, puzzled.

'Can you not see and understand? Have we made, then, so poor a choice of servant? The darkness is coming, and this is a part of it all!'

Comprehension came at last; Kerron stared at the clumps of weed. 'You mean I should let the weed cover the lake?' he said in a dazed voice. 'But the men are gathering it up.'

'Then go down, fool, and stop them. Make any excuse, but stop them!'

Kerron hesitated; he did not want to obey the command, if only to prove to himself that he could resist the compulsion. He stayed where he was, on the hill, looking down at the boats and the nets, beginning to sweat as pressure built up inside his skull.

'You will do as you are bidden. Go, or learn the true cost of your foolishness.'

Still Kerron did not move, trying to believe he was invulnerable, if he chose dissent. The voice was only a voice.

'Numbskull! It was better you should comply of your own volition, but if you will not, so be it.'

Kerron felt his first jab of real doubt; the voice sounded so very certain.

His right hand lay curled inside the pocket of his soutane. Kerron's fingers straightened and felt about, searching for the handle of his little knife. It was very sharp at the point, quite blunt along the sides. The right hand drew it out holding the handle in a tight fist, point down.

Kerron's left hand and arm stirred into motion, without his will. The arm bent at the elbow, extending the forearm, palm uppermost, at the level of Kerron's waist.

'What's happening?' Kerron whispered, terrified; he tried to move his left arm, but it would not obey him. He tried to loosen the fingers of his right hand, but they would not let go of the knife. He strained his will until his head ached, but his body was no longer his to command.

'I'll go,' he whispered. 'All right. You've won. I'll go.'

'Not until this lesson is complete.'

The hand with the knife came slowly up to shoulder height, then began to slope down across his chest, drawn to the bare flesh of Kerron's exposed left wrist.

'No! You can't; you're only a voice.'

The sharp point of the knife touched the skin of Kerron's left wrist, digging in with a brief stabbing movement. A small speck of blood appeared.

'No,' Kerron cried out. 'It isn't possible!'

'Learn from this, that there is no difference between my will and yours, for what was yours is now mine. Then obey.'

Kerron's whole body shook as he fought to regain his freedom, but power over his hands was, as the voice had said, no longer his.

The right hand raised the knife, then brought it down in a sharp and angry slash along the inner wrist. The cut was carefully drawn, deep enough that blood began to drip down the wrist and fingers in a steady flow.

'Now go; and remember this lesson, for our bargain, once made, and willingly made by you, is not to be broken. Go, and do as you are bidden.'

His sense of restraint, of being bound and manipulated by invisible strings, was suddenly lifted. Kerron let the knife fall from lax fingers as blood continued to flow down his arm and hand. He stood, dizzy, not wanting to consider what had happened. Then he began to walk downhill to the shore.

There was a frozen part of his mind which would not allow him to forget, or thrust fear aside. It jeered at him that he had thought himself favoured, special, believed himself the master of the voice. And now? Now he could no longer trust even his own body, which made him servant or slave, not master. Kerron's pride burned in him. How could he fight something he could neither feel nor see, but which was able to use his own hands against himself?

He stood on the shore and called to the men: 'Hi, you! Stop what you're doing. Who gave you orders to gather these plants, instead of your usual work?'

'Priest Manfred,' called back the man nearest to shore, a day-labourer from Arcady. 'It's what we usually do with weed.'

'Well, let those nets go. There're not enough plants to worry about, and there's far more urgent work ashore.' Kerron racked his brains for some suitable task.

The labourers, most from Kandria and Arcady, paused, but did not drop their nets. It was obvious to Kerron the *akhal* did not intend to comply with his order without protest. The men furthest from shore were muttering to one another, and one made a gesture with his fingers to his head. Kerron felt a surge of anger at the insult.

'Come,' he called loudly. 'High Priest Borland has ordered the temple dome be scoured and repainted, and at once.'

It was a foolish and unnecessary task, but it was the best he could invent; his other choice was to enforce his order with threat of the guard, but that would look strange for so minor a confrontation.

There was a moment when he thought the men would continue to defy him, but, slowly and unwillingly, they finally loosened their nets and the captured plants floated gently away from the shore.

'*You were barely in time. There must be no repetition of this; the weed must come to Wellwater, to all the estates, until it covers the waters of the lake. Then the darkness will come.*'

The voice knew, as did Kerron, that the balance of power between them had shifted permanently, unless, he thought, it was only now that he understood where the true mastery lay. He had thought the voice an ally, a gift that marked him out from all other men and confirmed he was special, of greater worth, but he no longer believed it.

'Ran?' he said, speaking her name softly. 'What would you say to this? What would you do, if you were me?' But thoughts of what Ran might do in his place could not help him; she was gone, unavailable to him when he needed her. His thoughts hardened.

'What will happen when the darkness comes?' he demanded of the voice. 'When even the lake is dark? What happens then?'

Silence was his reply. The voice did not speak in his mind.

There was coldness in the silence, freezing out the warmth of the sun.

2

The river which flowed eastward from Ismon to Harfort coursed sluggishly, its surface covered with a mass of greenery which did not conceal the fetid odour of the water. Ran and Affer were thirsty, but neither considered drinking from such a source.

It was a long day's walk from Hartfort to Ismon, along a track which inclined steadily to the south of the river. Ran had never travelled the way before and enjoyed the unfamiliar scenery, most of all the comparative closeness of the mountains to the north.

'I imagined it,' she heard Affer muttering to himself. 'I didn't hear it.' He looked as if each upward step were a struggle, a sense of guilt bearing down on him. She wished he would be quiet, weary of his ceaseless uncertainty.

She called a halt and Affer collapsed on the ground, breathing heavily. Ran was not tired; she found activity stimulating, and only the boredom of everyday life at Arcady in the pursuit of subsistence wearied her spirit. She walked to the river bank, ignoring the smell, and stared at the distant mountains, their peaks and upper slopes clouded in snow and mist, and felt a yearning deep in the pit of her stomach. Affer once said the evening lights at Avardale called to him, and these mountains called to her, in their beauty and their silence and their solitude.

She had never been so strongly tempted. Ran glanced back at Affer, but he was slumped in his own thoughts, apparently indifferent to hers, and she turned back to the vision of her dreams.

Why should she not cross over the river and go to the mountains, leaving her brother and Arcady and Bellene behind? Did she care if she never saw any of them again? At that moment the answer was no. Duty was not enough to bind her. Affer could fulfil their mission, and it might be good for him to be forced to go on alone and cope for himself. The sloping ground where she stood was no place to dally, the dun-coloured rock friable. The wind whistled down from the north in icy, frost-laden gusts, so that the trail was warm enough in sunlight but in the shade it was cool, almost cold.

Ran felt intensely strong; her hair was stiff with dust, her nose burned by the sun, but she had never felt so vital, so much that her feet positively itched with desire to follow her inclination. Practical considerations, such as supplies of food and water, she refused to consider, certain she could find both in the north. She took a step to the river bank, ready to wade through the weed-strewn waters to the far side, reckless with the knowledge that this was a chance which might never come again.

'Ran, how is the Steward of Arcady also a Guardian?'

She froze in mid-step, foot balanced over the water. 'What?'

'It's something I heard in Bellene's mind, once.' Reluctantly, Ran drew back from the river and turned round, but, despite her suspicions, Affer was not looking at her but at the ground; he had not been reading her thoughts.

'In what context?'

'It was when we were in hall once, with Quest, and I caught just the tail end of her thoughts: *"perhaps in Ninian's lifetime there will be a need for the Steward of Arcady to fulfil her duty as Guardian"*, and I wondered what Bellene meant.'

Guardian? Ran felt an odd excitement, a curiosity, at the word. A guardian was a keeper, a protector; in what capacity was the Steward of Arcady also a protector, and of whom, or what? Of Arcady, or something more? Memory stirred, and Ran thought she could remember hearing her mother speaking the word in the days when she, not Ninian, had been heir to Arcady. There was some secret, something not known to other people, in that duty; a secret now presumably shared by Ninian, not herself. A rare moment of jealousy shook her composure.

'I don't know what she meant,' Ran said slowly. 'Why do you ask?'

Affer shrugged his narrow shoulders, and she understood what he would not say, that he was thinking once more of his own inability to follow his conscience; but this time, instead of impatience, she was filled with pity for him, and affection, knowing that even in this trial he never once blamed her, but only himself.

'Look – a snake.' Affer suddenly pointed down the slope, where a narrow black string was wriggling along the way they had come. Affer was terribly pale, and Ran remembered he had been terrified of snakes ever since their pilgrimage, when Kerron had disturbed the silver serpent.

'It won't hurt you, Affer,' she said. 'You know those aren't poisonous. It's probably more frightened of you than you are of it.'

'I doubt it.' He shivered. 'Sorry.'

She could not desert him. As he sat on the ground, Ran could not avoid seeing the fear in his eyes, the fragility of his physique, his terror that she would abandon him, and she could not do it, no matter that to resist the lure of the mountains was a physical agony.

'Are you rested? Then let's get on,' she said finally, reaching down a hand to help him up. Affer was worryingly lightweight.

'Thanks.'

It was odd, to her, that he seemed to have no knowledge of how much difference his casual intervention had meant to her. His ability to read thoughts might have been absent, yet instinct must have taken its place, to speak to her at precisely the moment of her decision.

With an aching heart, Ran led the way up the slope.

The scene before them was hideous.

Lake Ismon lay in an oval depression ringed by hills to the south and mountains to the north. Ran stood at the top of the slope and looked down, covering her nose and mouth with her sleeve. Affer joined her.

'Oh.'

Far to the west, beyond its centre, the lake glowed, reflecting the fading sun, but the rest of its waters were almost entirely covered by green weed. The north and east were most heavily clogged, with scarcely a gap, as Ran should have expected since that was where the lake fed in spring from its mountain river source.

'I suppose the houses must have been built before the rains failed,' Ran commented, breathing through her mouth. 'You can see where the water level used to be, but it's retreated and left them stranded.'

'There're no boats out on the lake.' Affer's voice sounded thin.

Ran realised he was right at the same moment she noticed yellow-green flags flying from masts on the roofs of all the houses at the eastern end of the lake, their colour bright against the dull slate.

Nothing moved, except for hordes of tiny insects which buzzed around her face and eyes, so that the air seemed full of their fat, bloated bodies. They were the only creatures subsisting around and off the lake that did move. The rest had died wherever their bodies failed them. The grassy slopes down to the lake were littered with decaying corpses of birds and rodents and even another black snake, curled in a rigid circle.

'Everything is dead,' Affer breathed.

'No. Look down there, to your left; there's someone moving by the pier of that long house, and you can see smoke rising from another, further north. In fact, I think that's Carne, Maryon's home.' Ran felt her heart lurch as she surveyed these scant evidences of continued life, because for a moment she had been afraid Affer was right, and everything was indeed dead.

'What should we do?'

Ran looked into her brother's blank face and had no answer; nothing had prepared her for this. She had been thinking of the journey as a pleasure designed for her gratification, not as it really was, a desperate mission.

'I don't know,' she said at last. 'We should go down and see if we can help.'

'I wish Ninian was here.'

With a new humility, Ran thought that she echoed Affer's wish.

Carne was a charnel house, for all the smoke Ran had spied. As she and Affer moved from room to room they found no one living. Many of the *akhal* who lived on the estate must have died in close proximity in time, for although a few bodies lay untended, most must have made up the massive funeral pyre, the remains of which they came upon in the grounds.

'Will they all be like this?' Affer whispered painfully. 'What if there's no one left, Ran?'

She did not answer but climbed the stairs to the roof of the dead house, eager to escape from its confines and its contents. Maryon must have left before this worst of all disasters, the end of his kin and clan.

A cool wind blew away the worst of the smells, but it was not the wind that startled her as she stepped onto the flat surface, but the figure that lay by the message bell.

'Affer, come up here!' she called down, hurrying across the roof. The reclining figure was long, big for an *akhal*, and Ran was not really surprised to discover the man was an outsider, a Plainsman from his appearance, for he was built to a large scale and had the fair skin and blond hair of his people.

'Is this the rebel Kerron spoke about?' Affer asked, eyes wide open with surprise.

'I think it must be. He's still breathing, Affer.'

'What should we do with him?'

Ran put a hand on the man's forehead; it was very hot, and his breathing was loud and heavy, but he seemed strong and might survive. She wished again, more fervently, that Ninian were with them, for she would know what to do, but they had come with only a small supply of the more common medicines, none of which seemed in any way adequate for this.

'We'll take him away from here, at any rate. Ring the bell, Affer, and see if anyone answers.'

Affer pulled at the rope and sound boomed out, very loud so close at hand, two long and two short tolls for a question requiring a response. They waited.

'What if no one answers,' Affer whispered. 'What if there's no one to answer.'

'Shut up!' She rounded on him, suddenly furious. 'Don't make this worse!'

A bell tolled from the south, then another from the west; then another, also from the far side of the lake. They waited, but in total only five of the twenty houses around the lake responded. The implications of such a failure were so monstrous that Ran would not allow herself to consider them as she and Affer lifted the unconscious Plainsman and carried him down through the house and out to the pier, where they laid him in the bottom of one of the longboats.

'What are we going to do now?' Affer asked uncertainly.

'Find out how many people are left here, then decide.' Ran thought she was beyond feeling, seemingly incapable of taking in the loss of so many of her own people. She felt numb, if she felt anything at all.

'Then what?'

She wondered why Affer was asking so many questions, then realised it was because he, too, was unable to cope with the immensity of the disaster. She held the boat for him to climb in, then sat down herself, taking up the oars; it would be hard work rowing through the heavy weed, but it would be quicker than walking carrying the weight of the Plainsman.

'You can see what Maryon said was true,' she commented. 'The weed came from the north; that's why it's so thick up here, but it's spread west, too. And south.'

'To Avardale,' Affer agreed softly.

Ran made out the shape of two figures standing waving at the end of the pier of a house further down the eastern shore. That made three survivors thus far. Those numbers seemed more real than any count of the ones who had not survived.

What would have happened if she had followed her inclination and left Affer to come on alone to discover all this desolation? What would he have done without her? For a moment Ran's imagination was almost as vivid as her brother's in the terrible vision displayed to her. Gratitude that she had not abandoned him mingled with guilt that the choice had been so nearly made, commingled with a rising sense of anger.

'Kerron lied,' she said in a hard voice. 'He's little better than a murderer. If we hadn't come here, despite him, we'd have no warning of the extent of this plague, if that's what it is. And even warned we don't know how to deal with it.'

'He can't have known.' The shadows on Affer's face were dark, his eyes filled with agony. 'I never read this in his mind.'

'He lied to us; he must have known.' Ran made no effort to contain her growing rage and revulsion. 'Look at all this, Affer; he must have known.'

A deep sense of betrayal tore at her; Kerron should have told her. They had been as close friends as either of them could or would allow, but this, this omission, was as evil as anything she could imagine. So many *akhal* had died, and for what? Because of one rebel Plainsman, who could hardly represent any substantial threat to either Kerron or his Order.

'Please, don't,' Affer whispered. 'Please, Ran; I can hear you, and it hurts.'

She could feel no sympathy for her brother, her earlier pity for him obliterated by the confusion in her own mind. 'Look down there; I can see some cats. We'll take them with us too; I'd not leave anything here to die.'

'What do you mean?'

Ran gestured with her head to the mouth of the River Thun which coursed south to Avardale, taking· the weed-infested, polluted waters of Ismon to their home.

'Whatever, whoever we find alive, we'll take with us and go south; we don't have to worry about taking the sickness with us, Affer. By the time we reach Arcady it will have travelled there ahead of us.'

This, then, was the end of her dreams. Even she could not choose her own freedom over the disaster which awaited them. She counted back, and discovered that only something like a dozen days had passed since the appearance of the green light from the Plains, since she had discovered Maryon on Sheer Island. So much death had come about in an impossibly short space of time. Time. How much time was there left for Avardale?

The question was almost as disturbing as the desolation around them.

Chapter Ten

1

Affer watched Ran counting heads and allocationg places, marvelling at her capacity to withstand the enormous pressures within herself, all the boiling anger and resentment which spilled over to him, but was nonetheless more welcome than the thoughts of the other *akhal*. Open and defenceless, he stood and let their agony fill his mind.

'I'm sorry, but if you stay here you will die,' Ran was saying to the Plainsman, who had recovered consciousness and was lying on the pier of the big house beside the mouth of the river which was to take them south, with the current. 'The choice is yours, of course, but we can't stay here just for you, and although you're welcome to any medicines we have, you're not strong enough to fend for yourself.'

'Then I suspect I shall die in any case, once the priests get hold of me.' The big man's voice was stronger than he looked. 'I was in the riot in Ammon, you see.'

'What happened?'

He shrugged. 'One of my friends organised a raid, during one of the periodic grain distributions to the poor; we stole a cartload from under the nose of the priests and their men. They don't forgive that in a hurry, being made to look such fools.'

'Is that all? Is that the only reason they've been looking for you, and why they sealed off this part of the Wetlands?' Ran sounded disbelieving.

'Do you think they care for your people more than for preserving their own power? If you do, you know little about life outside these lakes.'

'Well, that's true enough,' Ran admitted grudgingly. 'So you are a rebel, after all.'

'Rebel? Only in their eyes; I should call myself an Emperor's man,' the Plainsman retorted. 'All we want is the restoration of Imperial authority, and for the Order to meddle only in matters of religion; let them answer to their gods, but leave us to rule our own lives. You can't imagine how many in Ammon and other cities go hungry while the priests hoard their grain jealously, begrudging every mouthful, as if they'd grown it themselves.'

'But what did you hope to achieve?' Affer heard the impatience behind the question. 'And how?'

'Do you think I'd tell you?' The Plainsman's thoughts were weary and confused as he struggled to concentrate. 'Doesn't what you've seen here convince you that anything we can do is worth it, any injury we can inflict on these priests?'

Ran was silent, and she was not alone in the involuntary glance she gave the deserted shores of the lake. The thirty-odd men and women gathered on the pier were all that remained of a once-thriving population. The lake itself was dying, its people and other dependents with it.

'But it makes no sense,' she said at last, her thoughts as bleak as her voice. 'What could possibly be worth all this death, all this desolation?'

'Fear.' The Plainsman leaned on an elbow, his face flushed. 'Fear of losing control of the Empire, fear of the unknown, fear of the light that came from the Plains, and what it may mean. The priests rule by force and fear, by engendering division, where the Empire was founded on unity. They treat us like cattle and pretend it is the will of their gods, threatening us with extermination in a second drought if we dare to challenge them. But I believe a god must be more than man, not less. Whatever it was that spoke to the first Lord Quorden, I am sure it was no god.'

'But there is something there, in the Barren Lands,' Ran said, and Affer could hear her confusion. 'We went there once, my brother and I.'

'But did you hear the voice of a god?'

'I felt something.' Ran glanced at Affer. 'But no, I never thought that, although whatever it was that inhabits that empty place is as vengeful as those we hear about in temple.'

'They say you take your own fate with you if you visit the Barren Lands; it makes you wonder what dreams the first Lord Quorden took with him, when he visited that place.'

Dreams, Affer thought, looking at the emptiness round the lake, altering the scene in his imagination to a land as dry as dust, with a wide red sun beating down on him. What had been his dreams that day long in the past? He had been afraid, and had not wanted to be alone. Was his gift the result of that fear, ensuring he could never be wholly alone?

What had Kerron wanted, and Quest? He did not know, and had never asked; nor, as far as he knew, had Ninian. Each experience was so personal it had been hard enough to tell Ran what had happened to him. Was it his own doing, his own fault, that he endured such tormenting weakness?

Dawn had come to Ismon, but brought with it no hope. Mists hung over the weed-infested lake, from which rose the by now familiar stench of decay, not, Affer decided, from the weed, but from some underlying cause. Ismon breathed out death.

Ran and two of the stronger *akhal* were organising the boats, helping people to sit or lie as they must. From his sister, Affer received almost overwhelming impressions of self-hatred, and did not understand their cause until another thought reached him, a wish for Ninian's presence and calm competence, and a hitherto undreamed-of humility and self-contempt so strong the feelings frightened him.

'We should reach Arcady by nightfall,' Ran said, helping the Plainsman onto the raft she intended to command. But the prospect brought Affer no pleasure as he took his own place in one of the boats, surrounded by memories of death and despair.

'Do you know, Affer, how long it has taken for Ismon to come to this?' Ran's voice, low and angry, came to him from his left. 'Fewer than twenty days since the weed first appeared, they say; that's all.'

He made no reply. What was there to say? A dull hopelessness settled over him as he picked up the oars, as if there was no point in caring what would happen in the future, that there might well be no future for the *akhal*, that the Westlands were coming to an end. The aching desolation in his heart might have been his own, or had its source in any one of the survivors of Ismon who lined the boats, eyes closed and stony-faced, refusing to take a last look at their erstwhile home. What was there to see, after all?

The stench of death travelled with them, south along the River Thun and out into Avardale.

'This negligence from Wellwater is a disgrace,' Bellene pronounced, standing on the Arcady shore beside the lake. She sniffed in disgust, looking down her nose. 'What are you doing about it?' A pause. 'Well, Ninian?'

Sarai and several of her friends were busy gathering up any floating weed that reached Arcady's waters. Ninian watched them until she was satisfied they were doing the job properly.

'I'm sorry, Bellene; what did you say?'

The old woman turned snappish eyes on her. 'I asked you what you were doing about this green mess!'

The bulk of Sheer Island's cliff hid from view the distant shapes

214

of the boats making up the flotilla, but Ninian had seen them from Bellene's tower when the warning bells had sounded from northern Talfor: Ran and Affer were coming home, it seemed, and not alone.

'I've withheld our day-labourers from Wellwater since yesterday in protest; I imagine the boat soon to land at our pier is Kerron coming across now to ask why,' Ninian answered absent-mindedly. 'Sarai and her friends are doing fine work keeping our own waters clear.'

'That may be so.' Bellene subjected her young relative to close scrutiny. 'And is that the only quarrel we have with Wellwater?'

'The only one that need concern you.' Ninian kept her gaze on her daughter's fair head; she was swimming some way out. 'Are you sure you're well enough to be up, Bellene? That was a nasty crack on the head.'

'But not an excuse for you to keep me in my bed forever, no matter how much you might prefer it!' Weakness seemed to make the old woman testier than ever. She shifted her wrist uneasily in its sling, as if it ached; there was a bruise on her cheek, another legacy of her accident.

The bruise on Sarai's face had nearly faded now. Ninian wrenched her thoughts away from that episode.

'I thought we were discussing Wellwater,' she observed.

Bellene's voice was querulous. 'We were.'

'Look. That is Kerron coming here.' She pointed to the boat approaching the pier. 'He seems to have brought help with him.' She made out several members of the guard in the boat with him, and frowned. 'Do you want to deal with this, Bellene, or shall I?'

'Which of us do you think he likes least?'

Ninian considered, unable to resist. 'You, probably.'

'Always truthful, aren't you?' It was not a compliment. 'All right. Leave him to me.'

'No wonder he brought his own army.'

'Oho!' A gleam appeared in Bellene's eye. 'Not so gentle after all, my young heir; that observation was worthy of Ran.'

Ninian sighed audibly. 'It was only a joke.'

'Stop taking yourself so seriously! You do your duty well enough; why shouldn't you rise to the bait occasionally!'

Ninian was so taken aback she bit her tongue, making her eyes water. Bellene gave a malicious laugh.

'That surprised you, didn't it? You thought I didn't know how tiresome I can be. Well, I do, and why shouldn't I be? If I can't say whatever I want at my age, when can I? I've served Arcady for fifty years, putting the estate and my kin first; now it's my turn, and I mean to enjoy it!'

Ninian smiled in genuine amusement. 'And I thought you were trying to set us a good example with the sweetness of your nature,' she said pleasantly. Bellene let out a cackle of delighted laughter.

'Your point, I think! Ah, I see Kerron approaching. How rude shall I be to him, do you think?'

'Be careful, Bellene.' Ninian was suddenly uneasy. 'Remember what he is now. And he looks ill.'

'What's that to me?' Bellene asked callously. 'If he doesn't do his work properly, he should be told, priest or not; the customs of the *akhal* are a great deal older than the Order.'

'Hush.'

Kerron was approaching. To Ninian's relief, he had left his guards on the jetty and come on alone. She watched his approach, disturbed by a visible alteration in his appearance. Like Quest, he was certainly thinner, but the change was more than merely physical; his expression was haunted, the green eyes darker and duller. His arms were crossed at the wrist, hands hidden inside the sleeves of his soutane, and Ninian was certain, without knowing how or why, that it was because he was afraid his hands might shake that he held them so.

'I see all Arcady has stopped work to witness the return of your absentees.' Kerron held his head high, the wind clearing his face of the dark hair, emphasising the high cheekbones.

'Rather more than that, I think,' Ninian said quickly, then realised her mistake as Kerron stiffened.

'Arcady has failed in its duty.' It was not clear if he was addressing her or Bellene; both received a glare of chill disapproval. 'For two days you have not sent your quota of day labour. As Administrator of Wellwater, I call on you to make good this omission; I shall require twice the usual number of men for ten days in reparation, and a cord of reed-logs.'

'Will you, indeed!' Bellene drew herself up to her full height, not so far from his. 'And I should like an explanation, Kerron, of the reason why you feel entitled to claim reparation for our absences when you so signally fail to fulfil your own responsibilities.'

'What are you talking about?' He sounded irritated, but Ninian thought his attention was only superficially engaged.

'Have you observed what our young people are doing?' Bellene swept a majestic arm at the lake. Piles of weed already littered the shore, waiting to be dried, then burned. 'We at Aracady know our duty to keep our waters clear, where you so patently do not. We even sent messages through our men to request your compliance at Wellwater, but received no reply.' The old woman paused, but Kerron was silent. 'I am told there is a heavy concentration gathering in the area of deep water; it must be dealt with, Kerron, before the build-up endangers the purity of the lake.'

Kerron did not seem to see her; it was almost as if he was listening to quite another voice. 'We are not your servants, old woman,' he said coldly. 'Deal with your own problems, and don't come whining to me. Leave it all. What does it matter?'

Shock momentarily silenced Bellene, but against her better judgment Ninian was seized with sudden compassion for the man who had been the companion of her childhood. It was as if she could sense in him a loneliness she herself had never had to endure, and she understood that even within the ranks of the Order he had found no real fellowship.

'Are you ill, Kerron?' she asked. 'Is there something I can do to help you?'

'You?' He recoiled, and the look he bestowed on her was without gratitude. 'What are you talking about? I need nothing.'

Ninian put a hand lightly on Kerron's covered left wrist; he flinched, the reflex jerking the sleeve of his soutane, displaying a bloodied bandage. Kerron recovered it at once.

'I came for the labour owed to Wellwater,' he said shortly. 'Nothing else. I have brought the means to enforce your duty, if you try to refuse.'

'Did you never listen to me, Kerron? Were you deaf while you were growing up here at Arcady?' Bellene shook her head in despair. '"Green weed, great need" we were brought up to believe. Look at your own shores – they're covered with greenery. Do you want the lake to silt up, the fish to die?'

He ignored Bellene's interruption. 'Two days ago, you walked out of the temple in anger, Ninian, before a host of witnesses. I myself have heard you speak against the Order and its teachings.'

'What are you saying?'

He favoured her with a frosty smile 'I have orders from Enapolis to keep watch for evidence of rebel activity in the Wetlands. You should be careful, Ninian. If I must search out enemies of my Order here at Avardale, I shall look for them first at Arcady.'

She almost laughed. 'On what grounds, Kerron? You know, and who better, that we have always been loyal to the Emperor and paid our dues to the Order. We tithe our tenth and send you our men, even though it means your acolytes and guard spend idle days doing nothing but contemplating their calling. What cause could you possibly find to accuse us of treachery?'

'Do I need a cause?' A smile played about his lips, but Ninian had the curious conviction that he was not serious in what he was saying; it was almost as if he was playing a game with her. 'When the Lord Hilarion, the Imperial Heir, visited the Wetlands last year, you or Bellene saw him in private; you must have done, or you'd not have been able to persuade him to endorse Arcady's charter. How can I tell what else you may have discussed with him? Even the Emperor himself is not secure from the power of our Order, and certainly not his heir, if they could be proven to be plotting treason against the gods, and Lord Quorden, who is their spokesman in this world.'

'Treason? The Emperor and his heir?' Bellene snorted with disgust. 'What nonsense you prate, Kerron. Without the Emperor there is no Empire. How is it possible for him, or the Lord Hilarion, to be accused of treachery against himself?'

'You are an ignorant old woman who knows nothing of the power of the Order in the capital.' Kerron spoke without rancour, but that did not reduce the level of offence. 'Lord Quorden rules the Council, not Emperor Amestatis. To speak against the Emperor may be treason of a kind, but to speak out against the Order is a more dangerous form of sedition, for you offend the gods themselves.'

'I have said nothing which could be construed as treason,' Ninian said calmly. 'Nor has anyone here at Arcady.'

Kerron nodded absently. 'Perhaps not.'

'There's another boat from Wellwater.'

The warning came from an open window at the front of the great house, from which a young woman leaned at a precarious angle. Ninian felt her heart skip a beat.

'Why should he come?' Kerron frowned, turning to observe the incoming vessel before returning to Ninian, eyes alive with suspicion. 'Why is he coming? Did you send for him?'

It was growing perceptibly darker as afternoon lengthened into night, and the sun began to sink behind the Wellwater estate, burnished orange lighting up the dome of the temple. There was something infinitely final about the scene.

Further movement caught Ninian's eye. 'Look, Kerron.' She pointed to the lake, where the flotilla was now visible as it passed to the left of Sheer Island. 'They're coming.'

A watching stillness settled over the mass of people on and about Arcady's shore. Kerron stood as if apart, a tall, brooding figure engrossed in his thoughts, his expression so tormented

Ninian gave silent thanks she did not possess Affer's capacity for reading thoughts.

Sarai came out of the water, deposited her bundle of weed, then crossed to her mother. Her friends followed suit, leaving behind a shoreline free of weed.

'Thank you all,' Ninian said warmly. 'You've done well.'

'But we'll have to do it all again tomorrow,' one boy objected, face angrily mutinous. 'Unless – '

'Be silent!' Ninian glanced warily at Kerron. 'Go inside, Shan.'

The boy, who was only ten years old, hesitated, but went as he was bidden; it was not the custom at Arcady to question the rule of the Steward, or the Steward's heir.

There were heads in every window at the front of the great house; it seemed all of Arcady's people were waiting to welcome Ran and Affer home.

'I can see her, on the raft,' Sarai whispered excitedly, reaching for her mother's hand, but Ninian had noticed the second boat from Wellwater tie up at Arcady's pier, and her attention strayed.

There was an uneasy tension as the boats and rafts of the flotilla made their slow approach to Arcady, a prolonged hush, as Avardale held its collective breath, as if everyone and everything that lived about or in the lake was aware of the imminence of a moment from which the course of their existences would never be the same again. Tiny waves broke against the shore; the sound of Quest's firm steps on the pebbles was unnaturally loud.

The eight boats and three rafts were spread out along a line, Ran's craft marginally in front. The light about the lake changed, growing dimmer, now only a pale luminosity; the flotilla was no longer visible as a collection of craft but had become all one single shadowy outline of irregular shapes and angles which seemed to be drawing shadows to it, as if the return of the travellers heralded the coming dark. Ninian, recalling the nightmare of her vision, caught her breath. Sarai grasped her mother's hand more tightly as Quest neared. His advance halted, and he, too, stood staring out at the lake.

Kerron had not moved; even Bellene was silenced. Ninian could feel the racing of Sarai's heart, and her own. The sun disappeared fully behind the western horizon, and darkness began to settle and fall.

The evening lights began to sparkle deep in the waters of the lake.

When the warning bells first sounded, Quest was lying, feverish, unable to sleep; nor did he want to, for fear of what dreams might come. He wished with all his heart the incident in the temple had been only a dream, that he had not shamed himself; being humiliated was no lesson in humility, but only in self-recrimination.

His mind was set on his own ties among *akhal*, his bonds to the Wetlands: his brother and his and Cassia's family; his own daughter, and the woman he had once loved. If being forced to alienate them forever was the punishment sent him by jealous gods, then they knew his weaknesses better than he knew them himself; until that day, he had not believed himself so earth-bound.

Ws it really the total rejection of all human ties of blood and affection which alone would satisfy the gods he served?

The bells broke his train of anguished thought, and he got up from the bed and went outside. Ran and Affer were coming home.

'What is Ran bringing down on us?' Quest asked aloud, and knew a sudden fear for Sarai, and for himself.

Down by Wellwater's shore floated a heavy mass of green weed; there was more, too, out towards the centre of the lake, and in the caldera of deep water north of Sheer Island.

'Kerron should have set the men to clearing it,' Quest murmured, frowning. *Green weed, great need.* That was the *akhal* saying. For a moment, Quest considered finding the other man and insisting action be taken to clear the waters, then saw he was too late as a longboat was launched from Wellwater's pier. He recognised Kerron in the bow at once, and wondered why he felt the need for half a dozen guards at his back when he was heading only for Arcady.

Quest drew back. Would they receive him at Arcady, if he went across, if only for his priesthood, which had once been the most vital part of him? After all he had done, he knew he did not deserve to be received as a man.

'But I am *akhal*,' he whispered passionately. 'Not a god, but only a servant of the gods, and I am not removed from feeling. How can it be right for me to want my own child to reject me? If I cannot inspire love in her, then how can I hope even for acceptance by the gods, who are so much more than human?' And, for the first time, it came to him that he did not understand the nature of divine love, that he had been thinking of it as exclusive, not inclusive, jealous in place of universal.

Was that failure a flaw in his own nature, or the teachings of the Order he had not the capacity to comprehend?

'I will go to Arcady,' he breathed, making the words a promise.

'I would rather know my fate there than imagine it. I would rather atone than expect forgiveness because I believe it to be my *right*.' He slammed his fists down on the stone parapet, feeling the pain as his narrow bones bruised on the hard surface.

Kerron was standing beside the shore, near Bellene, with Ninian and Sarai, when Quest finally reached Arcady, but no one seemed to be aware of his own arrival, or else they deliberately ignored him. The flotilla was coming on, drawing the dark behind it.

The waters of Arcady were clear of weed; Quest noticed the difference at once, even the air felt fresher. He hesitated to cross the shore to join Ninian; he did not think he could endure a public rejection, if that was to be his lot, and there were a great many people about.

Yet he had spoken worse against her, and in temple. Bracing himself, Quest squared his shoulders and headed down to the shore, the loose pebbles scrunching beneath his sandalled feet.

Out under the lake, the evening lights began to glow.

Ran was used to the pain of the blisters on her hands as she pulled and pushed the heavy paddle. Her four passengers, three *akhal* women and the Plainsman, lay motionless, asleep or unconscious, but they were close to Arcady now. Her eyes, red-rimmed and tight, stared at the shore ahead, registering the whole of Arcady, even Avardale it seemed, waiting to see them back home.

She glanced aside to see how Affer was faring with the oars of the boat immediately to her left; he was lucky enough to have a man able to spell him from time to time, but in the fading light she thought his hollow face looked worse than those of their passengers. Something in Affer had broken, even before they reached Ismon. Ran could not find it in herself to be impatient or angry with him. A pair of swimming cats crouched low near Affer's feet, thin and wary, but at least alive.

They were nearly home.

Light had passed from the sky and the land, but Ran realised, with weary pleasure, that in the lake the lights were just beginning, and she stopped paddling to observe the spectacle. Green-blue sparks darted everywhere, and Ran was shaken at how relieved she was to find them still alive, as if in her heart she had believed Avardale would be as dead as Ismon.

Figures were wading into the water to pull her own and the other crafts the last distance to shore. The lights of Arcady were not yet lit, and she was too tired to recognise or identify who came to help.

'Ran?'

Quest gave her his hand, and she stepped from the raft to shore. She nodded at him, wondering what he was doing at Arcady, but fatigue blurred her thoughts.

'Are all these people ill?'

Ran blinked; Quest's face had been replaced by Ninian's. 'Yes. The same sickness Maryon had.'

'Should we isolate them?'

The question seemed irrelevant; Ran stared blindly at her cousin.

'What's the matter with you?' Ninian was insisting. 'I must know if they're infectious.'

'Does it matter?' Ran rounded on her, suddenly angry. 'These are all there are, Ninian. All the *akhal* left from Ismon. Isn't that more important?'

She saw the shock register; Ninian paled. 'All?'

'These are all Affer and I found alive. We searched the lake, all the houses. We rang the bells. There's no one else left – *nothing* else.'

'This man is no *akhal*,' Bellene observed; two men were lifting up one of the passengers from Ran's raft. 'Who is he?'

'I don't know his name; a Plainsman. We found him at Carne, the only thing alive we did find there.'

'Kerron's rebel, I suppose. Well, no matter.' Bellene's face was stony. 'He is welcome here.'

Someone pulled up Affer's boat and helped him out. He stood swaying on the shore, a haunted, fragile figure; when someone would have taken his arm, he shied away.

'Is Affer ill?' Ninian asked, turning back from giving orders for the bestowal of the sick. 'Ran, he looks dreadful.'

'You know him, Ninian. Imagine, if you can, how he must feel, travelling with these people and their thoughts of all they suffered.' She did not say that there was more to it than that, because she did not understand what had happened to Affer, but was afraid it was her fault.'

'Would he be better in the infirmary with the others? But no.' Ninian shook her head at her own stupidity. 'Of course not. We'll put him somewhere well away from the rest.' But Affer was not to be persuaded away from the shore, where he stood, staring at Ran with watchful eyes, until she wanted to scream and ask him what he wanted from her.

Time passed in odd segments, as if there were moments when she slept. Ran opened her eyes to awareness that all the Ismon *akhal* had been taken away.

222

'I asked if you knew anything about the progress of the disease,' Ninian said patiently, and Ran guessed she was repeating an earlier question.

'There seems no sense about those who survive and those who don't, except that all the children of Ismon are dead.' Ran's voice cracked as she succeeded at last in shocking herself.

'Of the survivors you brought with you, two must be well over sixty,' Ninian remarked, with a composure that jarred Ran's uneven temper. 'The other, the Plainsman, is as ill as the rest, so obviously it isn't only *akhal* who are affected by this plague.'

Ran listened, cosseting her rage. People came and went along the shore, intent on various errands. Night had fallen, and the stars were out. She thought the time had come, and walked towards Kerron, who stood apart.

'Did you know, Kerron?'

The priest stirred. He had remained utterly remote during the landing and unloading of the *akhal*, cloaked by darkness and his soutane, a silent observer.

'Know what?' he asked distantly.

'That there was plague at Ismon, and death, too, and at Harfort; that half Ismon and the rivers are covered by green weed?' Her voice sharpened. 'It's coming here, to Avardale, Kerron. This plague creeps along the rivers and infects the lakes, with the stench of decay. Will you lie, Kerron? Will you lie, even now, when everyone can hear you and know you lie?'

A chill crept into his eyes; lights spilling out from the hall showed Ran his face, drawn and pale, as pale as Affer's.

'You may not say such things,' he said softly. 'We make allowance for your natural grief, but you must not.'

'There were many of your own people, priests, among the dead. You locked them up with the rest, with the plague. The people at Harfort believe the end of the world has come.'

'You will not accuse me.' Kerron's head shot up. 'You may not. I did not know the extent of this disease, and you may not say otherwise.'

'I do accuse you.' Ran spat the charge out. 'I asked you, before Maryon died, what was the true situation in the north, and you lied then as you lie now.'

'Enough. Be silent!'

Ran hesitated, struck by something unexpected, his tone making the words a plea rather than a command. She frowned, puzzled, as her eyes met his, and it was as if he was begging her to hold back, and for her benefit, not his.

Affer gave a convulsive shudder. 'Ran – ' he whispered.

'Well, Kerron?' she said, more naturally. 'Will you help us? We'll need grain and other supplies from you, if we're to turn Arcady into an infirmary.'

He gave her a stiff nod, yielding unwillingly. 'Very well.'

'And what else?' The grudging nature of his response re-lit barely banked fires, and her voice rose. 'What else, Kerron, what else can you offer the people of Ismon, who have lost everything, their homes, their kin, even their means of living, thanks to your negligence? Ismon is dead and foul.'

'Be silent.' Kerron's expression changed again, the plea becoming a command. Quite a different person now looked at her out of the green eyes, dark and fathomless. 'I am not your friend here, but a priest of the Order, and it is the Order you accuse when you arraign me. Perhaps Ninian never told you I came here in search of rebels, but it seems to me I could prove you, at least, guilty of treason. You have travelled beyond our bounds without licence.'

'Me?'

'Ran,' Kerron interposed softly, a note of urgency in his voice. 'Say no more. If you are silent, I will forget what you have said, but there must be no more.'

'Me?'

He flung up a violent hand. 'There has been enough.'

'How dare you?' Ran blazed, a new fury driving out fatigue. 'What have I done or said that you dare accuse me of betrayal, when you betrayed all the *akhal*? Why? Because of some deep-hidden sense of personal injury? After all, what did we ever do for you, except give you a home when you had none?'

'I hear you attempting to stir up rebellion against a priest of the Order; you make accusations against those set in authority over you, not only by decree of the Emperor but by the gods themselves.' But for all the threat Kerron was still speaking to her as an equal, and he sounded hurt rather than angry. 'What is that if not the basest treason and betrayal of your people, when in defying the gods you seek to bring down divine wrath upon us?'

'*Don't! Don't, Ran,*' Affer cried out, burying his face in his hands.

What had he read in Kerron's mind? Ran heard him, but she refused to be bound, neither by her brother's fears nor by the tyranny she heard Kerron attempting to exert.

'Hypocrite. Liar, too. Is that what it means to be a priest, to use empty rhetoric as if it were the only truth, when you understand no difference between truth and falsehood, except convenience? To think I believed we were friends.' Ran could not contain her bitterness and rage. 'I call you murderer, Kerron. I wish you'd drowned before Bellene found you and brought you here to Arcady.'

Sarai, suddenly afraid, ran from Bellene to her father; Quest opened his arms to her. Silence enveloped the shore.

'Do you, Ran?' Kerron spoke intimately, pleading with her for something more than forgiveness; perhaps acceptance. In another mood, Ran would have taken back her sharp words, but she answered him without giving herself time to think.

'I wish you had never been born.'

Kerron made an odd gesture, crossing his hands at the wrists; Ran had a glimpse of the left, bound and stained with blood. The intensity of his regard made her heart miss a beat, and she was almost frightened.

'There was a time before when you made me angry; but I forgave you. You called me a hypocrite once before; but I forgave you. So I give you this one last chance.' Kerron made the appeal to her alone, speaking as if they were lovers. 'Remember, Ran; remember that other time, so many years ago, and take back what you have said. Don't do this.'

It sounded to her more like a threat than any offer of absolution. Ran saw again in her mind's eye the carnage at Ismon; bile rose in her throat.

'Not this time.' She drew back her hand and slapped Kerron's face, deliberately reminding him of that other quarrel.

He did not recoil, but the expression in his eyes was ghastly in the pallor of his face, a sick terror that surfaced for only an instant. A random flash of lightning lit up the night, giving Ran in its trail clear pictures of her brother, mouth agape: of Quest and Sarai, close together: of Bellene, a thin hand held up in protest: of Ninian, face shadowed by anxiety. All the images seemed frozen in a brightness which faded almost at once, leaving Ran almost blind.

'Calloran of Arcady, I arrest you, in the name of the Order of Light, for high treason against the Empire and the rule of the gods.'

Ran felt Kerron's cold, strong fingers reach out to take her arm; she saw nothing, still dazzled by the lightning.

'You will be taken to Wellwater, and from there to the prisons of the Order in the eastern city of Ammon, for questioning.'

There was a pause; Ran blinked, unwilling to believe what she heard.

'You know this is nonsense.' Ran recognised Quest's voice, sounding incredulous. 'Let her be, Kerron.'

'This is not your concern. Your care is for souls, mine for the flesh.'

Ran rubbed her eyes, and vision returned slowly; she could see Affer on his knees on the shore, head bent.

'Well, Ninian?' It was a challenge born of old dislike. 'Will you fight to keep your kin, or let her go without argument?'

'Let her alone, Kerron.' Ninian's voice was ragged. 'Why don't you accuse Affer, too, and everyone else at Arcady, if you're going to let a few angry words turn you into a vindictive fool.'

'Ninian, he means it.' Bellene had noticed Kerron's gesture to the guard on the pier.

Ran held her head high, too proud to ask for her freedom. 'Let him take me then, and make his accusations; he is more guilty than I.'

'A woman, and *akhal* at that, to challenge a Thelian priest in the courts of the Order, in a city of the Plains?' Kerron sounded almost amused. 'Oh no, Ran; I think not.'

There was movement round the shore. Shadowy figures drew in from several directions, from the pier, from the house, from near the entrance to the tower.

'Tell them to keep back, Ninian.' Kerron had seen them too. 'You have a choice: you let me take Calloran in peace, or your *akhal*, with no weapons, must face my fully armed guard. Not only will your people lose, but you will lose Arcady; I will have you arrested as an accomplice. Is that your choice?'

Bellene did not allow Ninian time to respond. 'Take her, then, priest,' she said scornfully. 'For now. But we will have her back, unharmed, or your head will pay for it.'

Kerron ignored her. 'Well, Ninian?'

Ninian nodded, gesturing her supporters away; Ran wished she could think of something to say, understanding at last that she was leaving her cousin with a weighty burden, and had added to it.

'Look after Affer.' Ran bent to her kneeling brother and touched his shoulder; he did not look up. She could feel the tremors coursing through his thin body, but could not help him. Ran was beginning to understand his fear.

They were going to take her to Wellwater, and lock her in a small cell, with four walls closed around her. Kerron was well aware of what he was doing to her. It suited his concept of revenge to treat her in this way, as if she was really a traitor, fully aware of her horror of confinement. She had thought Arcady a prison.

Lights now shone all about the lake, from Wellwater, from Arcady, from Kandria. In her last moments of freedom, Ran looked up into cloudless skies where Omigon shone most brightly; only over Sheer Island was there absolute night. Ran stooped to scoop up a handful of water from the lake, then spat it out, not liking the taste.

'Come, Calloran.'

'It won't be for long,' Ninian said quickly, as the guard moved forward. I promise, Ran.'

'I know.'

Quest, Sarai beside him, watched her pass in silence. Bellene glowered, daring her to complain. Affer clung to the strand, hiding his face. Ran knew she was leaving him to cope with his nightmares alone, and guilt stabbed at her.

How could she endure, closed in a dark cell with the door barred against her? Ran thought she was well paid for her selfishness.

Lights shone from Wellwater, casting long gilded trails on the surface of the lake, like coloured streamers glowing in the wind, but for all that the night was dark.

Ran walked to the waiting boat without protest. She was so tired that nothing seemed real, not least this unimaginable conclusion to her journey.

'Was that all?' she asked bitterly, addressing any power beyond humanity, perhaps the spirit of the lake. 'No journey to mountains for me, no sea, but only this ending in a dark cell?'

There was no answer. If any deity inhabited the waters of Avardale, it slumbered on, indifferent. Ran sat down in the stern of the longboat opposite Kerron's seat with a raw sense of betrayal.

She allowed herself to consider only the breeze on her skin, the air she breathed and the sky overhead.

A word, taken or given, could have saved her from this fate; but she had not uttered it.

A word unspoken could have saved her from this fate; but she had spoken it.

In her own nature lay her fate, as she had learned in the Barren Lands, as they had all learned, a decade before.

She was the mistress of her fate; it was a bitter knowledge.

2

Kerron's mind was surprisingly cool and clear, as if the tangled strands of his thoughts which had troubled him had somehow become woven together in one smooth single strain, all the divergent parts of himself joined into a coherent whole.

Kerron dismissed Affer from his thoughts, and had no effort to spare for Bellene, who was old, and would soon die. It was only Ninian, and Ran herself, who gave him a moment's perturbation, and now, with Ran effectively caged, even that anxiety was much reduced.

She had been the only *akhal* who mattered to him; perhaps the only person for whom he had ever felt more than a fleeting mercenary or political affection. Even after the pilgrimage, when they had both said things not to be forgiven, he had been able to forget and forgive precisely because they were both equally guilty, neither able to claim a moral superiority. If both were guilty, both were also equally innocent.

He dismissed the memory. That was no longer so; Ran had betrayed him. She had returned from a prohibited journey in order to do so, to accuse him of murder. No matter that it was the plague, not he, who had killed her people. She had tried him and found him guilty and returned to pass sentence.

Except that he was judge in the Wetlands, not she. And without the leavening of his protection, she was vulnerable, for he was a priest of the Order and she nothing, not even heir prospective to Arcady.

Kerron wanted to laugh aloud. What price that heirship now, when Avardale itself would die? If the lake died, so would its people, along with every other form of life. What value had the *akhal* that they should go on living when their land, their lake, was dead?

'Their existence is only a drain on the resources which remain in the Wetlands. Why should people live when their habitat dies? Why is there unease in your thoughts? The Empire holds too many peoples, too many people, and you are Thelian, not one of them.'

Kerron let the words of the voice seep into his mind. Were the thoughts his, these dark, hating thoughts which seemed to live in the secret recesses of his mind? Safe –

Safe? But from what?

'Forget the akhal. *Think only about the lights. Now the dark is coming, and only the lights in the lake stand between the dark and its convergence.'*

His thoughts, or his voice, or that other voice, went on and on, repeating the same commands. Kerron wondered again if he was going mad; or whether it was only now that he was becoming sane.

Affer heard Kerron's thoughts flowing in an unstoppable flood into his own head, a dam burst crushing his poor mind under their weight.

He had had no such doubts.

He was quite certain he, or Kerron, was going mad.

Quest knew, the moment Sarai pulled away, eyes accusing, that she had expected him to rescue Ran, and only now realised he had failed her yet again.

He let her go, saddened; she was right. His new self-knowledge would not allow him to deny that he had permitted a great wrong to be enacted at Arcady. Ran was innocent of all offence but insensibility.

No dreams had shown him dead *akhal* at Lake Ismon. He was deeply shaken.

Again, he pondered the question: if his dreams were not sent by the gods, then from whom or whence did they originate?

Or if the gods had sent them, were they the divinities to whom he wished to dedicate his life and service?

Ninian watched the boat disappear into the night.

Sarai came and tucked a small hand in her mother's elbow, warm and firm. Ninian was glad and touched that she should care; she had rarely felt so alone.

'Quest?' she asked.

'I'll find a way to get her out,' he said at last. 'I swear it, Ninian.'

'I know.' Ninian looked down at Sarai trying to pretend she had not heard, unable to hide the faint flush of hope that her father was not, after all, quite without honour. 'I need her, Quest.'

'I know. I'm sorry.'

Ninian gestured Sarai to where Affer knelt; the girl let go her mother's arm and reached down to pull him up.

'Come in with us, Affer,' she said, in a surprisingly gentle voice. 'We'll take care of you, until Ran comes home.'

Blindly, mutely, Affer allowed himself to be raised; he looked little older than Sarai, and less substantial. He gazed at Ninian blankly. His trust, which Ran had bequeathed to her, suddenly terrified Ninian, reminding her of her other legacy.

'I can't do it,' she said under her breath. 'When the time comes, I shan't have the courage.'

Had she said *when*? Ninian shivered. She should have said *if*.

Chapter Eleven

Dark Fall – Day Two

1

Low mist clung to the waters of the lake, solid and opaque. Ninian had hoped it might lift by midday, but instead it seemed to have expanded, so that the sun overhead was visible only in outline amid thick grey cloud. Ninian shivered, for the fog was damp as well as cool.

'Keep the water coming,' she ordered. A dozen men and women stood in a line from lake to shore, filling wooden buckets from the lake and passing them along. 'We must boil every drop, not just for drinking and cooking, but for everything, in case this plague is spread by water pollution.'

'I don't know how long our fuel supplies'll last at this rate,' grumbled the young man at the lake end of the chain.

'I know. The children are all twisting reed-logs, but of course those give out far less heat than wood or burnstone. But we daren't take risks, Haym.'

'The water certainly smells bad enough!' Haym sniffed noisily. 'And look at all these weeds. We only cleared our section yesterday, and already there're clusters of the things; they seem to breed overnight.'

Ninian strove for patience. 'First things first; we need water, and we've thirty more people to cater for now. Once that's done, we can think about clearing the lake again.'

'You'd not think things could get so bad in just two days.' It was one of the women who spoke, rubbing an aching shoulder.

'Is it really only that?' Ninian had hardly slept since Ran's return with the Ismonites, all her energies occupied with the newcomers and the necessity to protect Arcady from suffering the same fate.

'Where are the labourers I requested?'

Ninian started back as Kerron's tall figure seemed to materialise from the air as he emerged from the fog, his dark soutane a darker shadow in the mist.

'Kerron! You gave me a fright – I didn't hear you.'

'The fog muffles sound. I see you are well occupied; an excellent idea, and one we shall adopt at Wellwater.'

'Aren't you here to bring me the supplies you promised? If you recall, Kerron, you said we should have grain to help feed our visitors.'

'Ah yes, those visitors.' A small cloud of mist floated past, obscuring Kerron's face. 'I came to ask after the Plainsman; is he well enough to question?'

Ninian shook her head. 'He's not conscious.'

'Will he live?'

'How do I know?' Ninian said wearily. 'He's no better and no worse than many of the others. Did you bring our supplies, Kerron?'

'I am no acolyte to be sent out on errands; when I give the order, your supplies will be dispatched. I came to exact the labourers you have yet again failed to provide.'

Ninian looked at him blankly. 'But I need them here, Kerron; as you see. I need every hand at the moment, with so many ill, and so much extra food and drink and fuel to find.'

Frowning, Kerron gestured to the line of men and women. 'Surely the children could do this? Send me the men I require, and we shall forget the omission.'

'But you have nearly four hundred men of the guard standing idle.' Ninian found it hard to take the demand seriously. 'Can't they boil their own water? Or are they so helpless even that has to be done for them!'

Kerron's expression grew absent, as if he had withdrawn all attention from her, and Ninian fell silent, watching and waiting. She had a sudden sense that the man she knew had undergone an alteration, so that what had been familiar was now entirely strange, a change that made her most uneasy.

'You will send me the men, and I will send back your supplies,' the priest said at last. 'And if the Plainsman recovers, send me word at once.'

'Kerron?'

He had turned to go, already half submerged into the mist. 'What is it?'

'Will you let Ran go?'

He stood quite still as waves of mist eddied round him, giving his presence an unreal quality, as if he existed as no more than a ghostly shadow of himself.

'Let Ran go?' he echoed. 'Oh no, Ninian; I don't think so. No, I don't think it would be safe.'

Before she could make any protest he had turned back and was gone, surrounding himself with fog, an obscure shape receding in the distance.

'It'll be too dark to see anything soon,' Haym grumbled. 'How did he get here?'

'I don't know.' Ninian stared after the retreating shadow. 'All right, since we've no choice, you men gather up another half a dozen and head for Wellwater. We need those supplies badly. I'm sorry, but there's no alternative. Kessa, can you find more women to help here?'

The woman nodded and put down her bucket; Haym, with an exaggerated sigh, did the same. Ninian allowed herself the luxury of a pause before continuing with the next most pressing task.

It was not the inconvenience of Kerron's demands, nor all the other difficulties she faced, not even the loss of labour and sheer volume of work to be accomplished, which disturbed Ninian most; it was Kerron himself. The cuckoo of Arcady had changed, revealing himself in a new guise as not only predatory and parasitical, but also capable of poisonous malignancy.

'The woman is more than she seems,' intoned the voice. *'There is that in her which could prove a danger to the coming of the dark.'*

'But what?' Kerron asked, weary of flat statements without further explanation. 'What do you mean?'

'She is more.'

'Well, Ninian has enough to keep her occupied at Arcady, with no time to interfere beyond her borders,' Kerron said shortly.

'You must hope it will be so. You have received warning.'

The mists crowded in, so Kerron could hardly see his hands. He felt more isolated than ever, but the fog was curiously restful, producing a solitude which was more substantial than any company. Except that he was not alone, for there was always the voice, and that did not, would not, leave him.

The fog had found its way into the temple, seeping in through cracks in the double doors and any other opening wide enough to allow it entry. The heavy mists swam in the air, hovering above the marble floor, dispersing into vaporous wraiths that crept towards the walls before expiring, leaving behind an odoriferous reminder of their presence.

Quest stood before the altar, the congregation comprising his fellow priests and acolytes and a few of the guard; the weather militated against other attendance at afternoon service. High Priest Borland was officiating for once, by his own choice, perhaps feeling at such a time of crisis that he should perform his duty; he looked dreadful, both fat and unhealthy, pallid face glowing with sweat above the gold neck of his robe.

'For as much as the gods spoke to the first Lord Quorden, revealing to him the means to preserve our people against the coming of the second drought and our own dry deaths, so they speak again, this time to us all, in the form of this plague which has descended upon us. In anger at our faithlessness and disobedience, Antior directs at us that vengeance which fair Jiva sees as just and allows to fall, sent by the Lords of Light in due retribution.'

Borland's voice suddenly faltered and he swayed, face sweating more heavily than ever. The High Priest bent and lifted a hand, as if to ward off sudden pain, then relaxed, straightening, as the spasm passed.

'This evil is sent to us in warning, that we must more strictly observe our promise if the gods are to find us worthy of salvation. For – '

Again, Borland faltered. He reached out a hand on the stone altar for support, knocking over an oil lamp. Shass, the *akhal* acolyte who was the High Priest's favourite, let out a cry as the High Priest's corpulent figure slowly toppled, collapsing onto the altar and spilling burning lamp oil on the stone floor.

'You there – put that out!' Kerron directed the nearest acolyte, who used his robe to smother the flames.

Quest took a step forward, only to find his path blocked by Shass. The white-robed acolyte was staring at his fallen master, his own face as pale and as sickly; as Quest tried to move him aside, the youth began to retch.

'What's the matter with him? Can't he control his stomach?' Kerron asked irritably.

'It's more than that – ' Quest began as the youth gave a final, violent heave, then collapsed in his turn. Quest knelt to feel for a pulse in his neck, but there was none.

'Borland, too,' Kerron observed calmly, standing back with a look of disgust. 'What is it? The fever?'

'I shouldn't think so; it's far too sudden.' Quest frowned. 'It looks more like poison.'

'Reverence?' It was another of the acolytes, a young *akhal* named Cater, who spoke, a plain, sullen-looking boy, with spots on his chin and discontented eyes.

'Yes?' Kerron snapped. Cater swallowed.

'Reverence, I think it may have been the water.'

'What water? What are you talking about?'

A sly expression came over the acolyte's face. 'It was this morning, Reverence. The High Priest said he did not like the boiled lake water, so he ordered Shass to draw some clean from the old well in the great hall. He did, and they both drank from the same pitcher. The High Priest said the level of water in the well was low, and there would not be enough for all of us, so Shass was to close it up again, but to draw enough for their needs.'

'Well water.' Quest looked at the contorted dead face of the High Priest. 'Then perhaps the old story is true.'

Kerron gave a cold smile. 'It's the only solution that makes sense.'

'But to kill them all – ' Quest could not bring himself to continue, shaken to learn his Order had gained Wellwater through such a trick, no matter how far distant in time the event.

'What should we do, Reverences?' Finn, the next ranking member of the priesthood, looked doubtful. 'Who is to take the High Priest's place? Who is to command the Wetlands?' An *akhal* of over fifty, he was a worrier, lines of perpetual anxiety crossing his face. His bloodless voice sank to a whisper. 'Is this a visitation from the gods?'

'I think not; rather a visitation from the past,' Kerron observed dryly. Finn frowned, not understanding the allusion. 'And as to your question, neither Priest Quest nor myself decides the succession: that is for Lord Quorden. He will, of course, be informed.'

'But I thought – ' Finn turned towards Quest, groping for a more specific response.

'The matter will be decided in Enapolis. Have these bodies taken to the High Priest's rooms. They might as well be laid out together.' Quest ignored Kerron's amusement at the unfortunate turn of phrase.

'Uncharitable,' Kerron observed quietly, as the others hurried to carry out the orders.

'So, the well was poisoned.'

'Did you ever doubt it?' Kerron gave a shake of his head. 'How else did you think Wellwater came to our Order?'

'Through the gods, perhaps,' Quest said, with a sigh. 'But I see it was foolish of me to believe it.' He thought of Ival and Isma, the last *akhal* holders of the estate, resisting the priests until their drinking water was poisoned and they died, with all their people. It was a shameful knowledge he would rather have been spared.

'So, the well offers us no safe alternative to the lake,' Kerron observed. 'Ninian orders all Arcady's supplies to be boiled before use.'

Quest looked at Kerron's thin face, wishing he understood him. 'How shall we proceed until word comes from Enapolis?'

'Continue as we are.' Kerron shrugged. 'You have jurisdiction here in the temple, but the administration of the Wetlands and the estate remain in my control.'

'Very well.'

Something dark flickered in Kerron's eyes. 'This changes nothing.'

'We need help as much as a new appointment.'

'Do you think so?' Kerron sounded distant. 'But no one will come here now, not with the plague raging at Harfort, and Weyn, too, and here soon, no doubt. You heard what Borland said: it is a punishment on the *akhal*, sent by the gods.'

'Do you believe that?'

The two men stared hard at one another; Kerron smiled.

'You should tour the lake, Quest, to let our people know the reason for this sickness, since the fog prevents their attendance here. They will need such knowledge and consolation from their most beloved priest.'

As Quest hesitated, into the silence came muffled sounds of a series of regularly phrased drumbeats.

'Trouble at Arcady,' Kerron remarked. 'Probably one of the Ismonites has died.'

Quest frowned, his thoughts instantly of Sarai. 'I should go across.'

'I think not. It would not look well for you to show a preference for Arcady, not at this time.'

'Very well.' Quest's tone was bloodless, understanding the choice presented to him, yet again to be either father or priest.

'Your duty is to the whole of our people,' Kerron went on smoothly. 'Do as I suggest and tour the lake; I will send others to Weyn and Harfort, but this charge is yours.'

'Are you so sure of the outcome?' Quest shook his head. 'What if Lord Quorden should prefer me to you?'

'With your child and her mother so obviously still your concern? You know how strong a count against you that must be to our master. He has no sympathy for such weaknesses.'

Defeated, unable to deny it, Quest sighed, feeling deep resentment at his situation. 'Very well.'

Kerron made a mocking salute. 'May the gods be with you on your journey.'

Quest wondered, as he left the temple, how he could have lost so much without even a struggle. Had he come to a turning point in his life, where a final choice was to be forced from him?

It had been dark in the temple, but it was darker still outside in the fog.

He could not believe his people deserved to die, no matter what Borland had preached; his opinion of the late High Priest had sunk to a nadir as he listened to that pronouncement. The *akhal* were neither faithless nor evil, less devout than those in the cities, perhaps, but their lives were hard, barely above subsistence. Sweat gathered uncomfortably on his forehead and at the top of his spine as he struggled to understand what was happening to him and around him, ever since Ran had returned from Ismon two days before. Quest swallowed against his suddenly dry throat.

'Show me what I should do. Gods, tell me what I should think, think my thoughts for me,' he whispered. 'I am afraid of my thoughts, afraid of what may come of them. Help me; help all of us.'

In performing his duty to his people, in consenting to the task Kerron had given him, was he betraying Sarai and his promise to her, and Ninian, that he would help Ran? Where was his duty first of all? He was a priest, sworn to the service of the Order.

The understanding reassured but did not comfort him as, with great reluctance, he went to gather his belongings for the journey ahead.

Ran could see out through gaps in the square of bars high on the door of her prison, wide enough for her fingers to grasp. She beat against the heavy wood with all her strength, but the door scarcely shook, and all she achieved was to bloody her knuckles.

The surge of rage passed; Ran slumped against the door, closing her eyes in despair.

In the two days that had passed since her incarceration, mist had descended on the lake; light at first, a soft cloud on the surface of the water, as time passed it had settled and grown denser. It was now a solid fog, clinging to land and water alike, and by early afernoon of the second day it obscured all but the outlines of the long huts to her left which housed the guard. Every other part of the camp was a blur of thicker or thinner patches of fog.

There had been mists at Ismon, and the same sickly, sweetish smell in the air. How could it have come so far so soon? Surely it should have taken more than two days for the pollution to set in?

The two half-*akhal* among the guard, Columb and Elthis, came and brought her food and water. Ran ignored them, unable to eat the salty dried fish and the stale bread. The smell from the fog destroyed her appetite as surely as the cage of her prison broke down her spirit.

The agony of confinement closed in on her. There was a pallet, even blankets for her comfort, a large covered pail for other physical needs, but even with bars in the door letting in the air Ran felt she could not breathe. The locked door and solid walls between her and the world outside choked her, and she gasped for air with real panic, as if she were drowning.

The fog-ridden air was clammy and cool. Ran pulled herself together and ran a hand through her hair, which was thick with dust. Her clothes were dirty and torn, and she felt empty with loneliness and despair.

Somewhere in the fog, the temple bell began to toll.

'Were things really so bad in the north?' inquired a low voice beyond the door.

Ran looked up, startled, as the cell darkened and a face appeared behind the bars.

'Who are you?'

'Elthis.' The man stood back so she could see him more clearly; his red hair identified him. 'I wanted to know if matters were as bad as they're saying. Were they really all dead?'

Ran swallowed. 'Except those we brought back with us, yes.'

'Get away from there.'

The half-*akhal* stepped back from the door at the command. Ran did not see who had spoken.

'Who told you to come here?' came the angry voice.

'No one.' Elthis sounded sullen. 'I was passing, and I thought I heard the woman call out.'

There was the sound of a blow; Ran peered through the bars to see Elthis sprawled on the ground, a hand to his nose. Standing over him was a well-built Plainsman, blond and powerful, who wore the badge of a captain of the guard.

'Keep away from this one. She's for the priests in Ammon, not for you!'

'I was sent by Priest Kerron himself to watch over her,' Elthis gasped.

'Then keep your distance!' The captain gave the smaller man a final kick, then turned away, leaving him groaning. After a time, Elthis got to his feet and staggered off, leaving Ran alone.

The fog deadened sound and obscured sight. The tolling of the temple bell at regular intervals reminded her of the slow passage of time. The day endured, the afternoon far beyond its usual length as the mist gave little indication of the coming of night.

Drums spoke in the stillness; drums from Arcady. Ran ached, wanting to know what was happening as the sound swelled in volume.

Sickness at Arcady.

Ran listened, but there was no answer from Wellwater. The bell above the temple tolled again, but it was not the time for service, and Ran wondered why, but there was no one to ask.

The afternoon darkened further; the fog shaded from grey-white to grey proper, dense and chill, damp and unlovely. Ran hated it, feeling it close in on her, and panic surged up again. She fought it down, making herself hum lines from an old *akhal* song Bellene had taught them all as children.

> '*On a stormy night*
> *When the wind was high*
> *When the lightning flashed*
> *And the lake was wild,*
> *Arkata awoke*
> *From her sun-filled dreams,*
> *Aroused by the sound*
> *Of the Avar's cry – '*

Ran's voice faltered. It was an old story from Arcady, a piece of lore designed to teach the legend of the first *akhal*. How did the other verses go? It was so long since she had heard or sung it, she had forgotten most of the words.

> '*For she was afraid*
> *Of the howling storm*
> *And the dark and the deep – '*

Ran shook her head; the next part told of Arkata's sacrifice, then of the old goddess of the island temple, and the bargain made between them. Arkata had asked that her people be given strong lungs and cool blood, to be made a full part of life around the lakes as they became *akhal*.

'Ran?'

It was so dark in the cell that the appearance of a second visitor did no more than obscure the gloom.

'Quest?' Ran came to the door. 'What is it? Is something wrong?'

He shook his head, then, perhaps realising she could barely see him, said: 'No, or not as far as I know. I came to tell you I'm going away for a few days; Borland is dead, and I am being sent around

238

the lake to spread word of the cause of this plague.'

She clasped the bars. 'How did Borland die?'

Quest did not reply.

'Was it the sickness?'

'Not that, thank the gods.' The swift answer puzzled her. 'Ran, you should be safe until I get back; Kerron has much on his mind at present, and sending you to Ammon is a low priority. Elthis and Columb will make sure no harm comes to you.'

'Why are you going away? Surely, if Borland is dead – '

'I've no choice!' He sounded bitter. 'Don't ask questions, Ran; I'm sorry, very sorry you should be here. This is nonsense.'

'Why – ' she began, but too late; Quest had retreated into the mist. Ran frowned, wondering what was happening at Wellwater, and why Quest had not been more specific. Wisps of fog seeped through the bars into her prison; it was cold, and Ran shivered.

'Let me get out,' she breathed. 'I can't stand being shut in.' She closed her eyes and tried to picture the mountains, imagining herself climbing their icy slopes. She was not afraid to risk her life for the adventures her soul craved; the gamble, the challenge, they were what called to her. But her mind stayed stubbornly in the cell.

Ran berated herself that even in prison she was selfish, not thinking of Ninian and the problems she must be facing with the plague, with so many extra people to care for, and there was Affer, abandoned.

She would not believe her confinement would last for long; that way was despair. She would think of the future and her freedom, and what she would do with it, and hope would expand her horizons beyond the prison bars.

Sound brought her back to the present.

Drums spoke again, once more from Arcady.

'Do you think anyone will come?'

'Of course they'll come,' Ninian said, with some impatience. Aislat was one of her most capable helpers, although the older woman's pessimism was wearing. 'But it may take some time for anyone to respond to our summons. The fog's so dense it's hard to see anything at all on the lake.'

'It's all of a piece; the weed's getting so thick you can hardly move. I went down to the pier this morning and there was hardly a clear stretch of water anywhere.'

Ninian breathed in deeply. 'The weed is the least of our problems just now, Aislat.'

Unexpectedly, the door to the infirmary slammed open, to admit Affer, out of breath. 'Ninian, can you come at once?'

She braced herself for more bad news. 'What is it?

'Bellene.' Affer's pale face was taut with strain; Ninian remembered Ran had left him to her care, and experienced a pang of guilt.

'Has she had an accident, or is she ill?'

'I don't know.' Affer looked ghastly, the pupils of his eyes enormous. 'She collapsed in the hall, and I was sent to find you.'

'All right; I'll come.' Ninian turned to Aislat. 'Can you manage here, if I send you another helper?'

The older woman counted on her fingers. 'Fifteen, sixteen – yes, I can cope; I've young Kerr, and Shura, so one more should be enough.' She sighed. 'There's little we can do for the Ismon folk as it is.'

'I know. Thank you, Aislat.' Ninian turned to Affer and pushed him gently towards the door. It was dark inside the building, and not much better outside. The mist had settled in dense patches all round Arcady, depressing and damp.

'I hate this fog,' Affer volunteered in a small voice. 'I wonder how Ran is.'

'I don't know.' Ninian had hoped Quest would come across with news, but she had heard the temple bell tolling for Borland, and guessed he had no time to spare. She wondered how Borland had died, and hoped it was not from the plague; but the onset of the disease was rapid, if erratic, or so she had learned from the Ismon survivors.

She went directly to the hall, where she found several children gathered closely around Bellene. One of the boys had made a pillow for her head from some rushes, and put a covering over her thin figure. When Ninian knelt and felt her brow, it was obvious Bellene had caught the sickness; she was burning hot, her skin taking on a greenish tinge.

'We need to take her to her room. You, Affer, and you.' She pointed to the biggest of the boys. 'Carry her carefully, and I'll be up in a moment. Make sure the windows of her room are closed; she needs to be kept warm.'

Glancing around the hall, Ninian noticed someone had had the sense to close the shutters against the fog. By the hearth, the children had gathered an immense pile of rushes, and two girls had already recommenced their plaiting. A second, smaller pile of the reed logs lay on the floor.

'Good girls, Carla and Sass,' Ninian said, forcing a smile. The children of Arcady had always shared the work of the estate, now more than ever as they fought for their very survival. What weapons would they find in a battle against an unseen enemy that struck at will, attacking the strongest as well as the weak? Bellene was not the first casualty of the day; already three others had been taken ill, two men and a woman Ninian's own age.

'Is there anything else we can do?' Carla looked up earnestly, an intelligent girl of ten.

'Just carry on here; we need fuel as much as food.'

Ninian left them to their work and went to the small store room in the passage in the hall where the common supply of medicines was kept. She frowned at the meagre supplies, the prospect of one more task suddenly impossible. Ninian knew a moment of despair, wishing Ran were at Arcady, for despite her wanderlust her cousin was capable in still-room and sick-room.

As she climbed to Bellene's room, Ninian felt the weight of weariness of two hundred *akhal* at Arcady, with now thirty more from Ismon, all to be fed, watered, nursed; the fields and gardens to be maintained, the house provided with a minimum of cleanliness. Herbs must be gathered, the breeding fish cherished, stores regulated, fish smoked, and now all their water must be boiled and more medicines distilled. The full extent of her responsibilities threatened to overwhelm her.

'Ninian?' The voice was hesitant.

'Sarai? What are you doing here?'

'I – I don't feel well.'

'Come here.' Fear clutched at Ninian's heart; she put a hand to her daughter's forehead, but it was cool. 'Do you hurt anywhere?'

'I ache.' It was almost a whine; Sarai's eyes were filled with unshed tears. 'All over.'

'Oh, Sarai!' Ninian bent to hug her, not knowing what was true.

'I'm tired.' Sarai pulled away.

'Can you put yourself to bed? I'll be along to see you as soon as I've taken a look at Bellene; she's caught the fever.'

'Can't you come with *me*?' Amber eyes, so like Quest's, demanded her primary allegiance.

'Ninian, can you come?' Affer's head appeared in the dorway of Bellene's room.

Ninian glanced uncertainly at Sarai. 'Sarai – '

'I'll go by myself!' The girl hunched her shoulders in angry rejection. '*She* always comes first!'

'That's not true.'

Ninian knew her duty was to Bellene. 'All right; I'm here,' she said wearily, wishing Affer were not so helpless in the sick-room. 'Affer, I need someone to help Aislat in the infirmary,' she said, remembering her promise. 'Can you find out who's free? I'll need someone here, too.'

'Who?' Affer asked helplessly.

Her patience snapped. 'Just find out who's not too busy at the moment!' Seeing his face, she regretted her harshness. 'Please, Affer,' she said, more gently. 'It would be a great help.'

'I'll try.'

'Then come back, as soon as you can.'

He nodded and disappeared.

'Oh, Bellene, I wish you had chosen someone else to carry this burden,' Ninian said to the recumbent steward. Bellene lay under a thin covering, turning and twisting her head uneasily; she looked etiolated and parched, cheeks sunken. Like a child, she had so little flesh and energy to spare that the plague was instant in effect.

'Take this; it may help.'

With a practised hand, Ninian administered the syrup she had brought, a concoction of wellbane and wine.

'I found Hal. He said he'd help Aislat,' Affer announced with pride, peering round the door. Ninian tried not to sigh, for Hal had to be given any order at least six times for the meaning to sink in, and even then the outcome was doubtful. Aislat would hardly be grateful.

'Stay with Bellene, while I see Sarai,' she remarked.

'All right.'

'I won't be long.'

'Wait.' Affer grasped her sleeve. 'Please, have you any news of Ran?'

'No, Affer,' she said gently, pausing. 'I'm sorry.'

'She will come back?'

'I think so.' Even to Affer she would not make assurances which might prove false. 'I'll send to Quest tomorrow and ask after her.'

'Would you?' He seemed to relax. 'Thank you.'

'Ninian, the Plainsman from Ismon's been talking, and I think you should hear what he's saying.'

Trapped against Bellene's door, Ninian felt momentarily as tormented as Affer. 'Yes, Amori? Can't it wait?'

The younger woman frowned; at eighteen, she was a capable person with a clear gaze and calm bearing. 'I think you should, Ninian. He keeps saying something about grain, and arms, and the Emperor.'

242

'Wonderful!' Ninian cast up her eyes. 'All right, Amori, I'll come.' She had a desperate sense of failing in her duty, putting no one first, but only dealing with each disaster as it struck. She thought of Sarai, of Bellene and her legacy, of Ran.

'He's along here. If you remember, we decided to keep him away from the others,' Amori remarked. 'Kerron said he wanted to question the man.'

'I'm coming.'

'Ninian?'

Feet clattered on the lower stairs. Ninian stiffened, wondering what new catastrophe awaited. A tall, formidable figure advanced towards her, others following.

'Cassia?' she said incredulously. 'Is there something wrong?'

'No more than we can cope with; we've a trio taken the fever so far, but bearing up. We heard your call for help and, being nearest, I thought I should come and offer our aid. Tell me, what can we do first?' A cool eye surveyed her. 'You've more than your own share of troubles just now. I've brought half a dozen women, so just tell us where we can be most useful.'

Ninian could hardly believe her good fortune; relief at such capable assistance swept over her. She thought of Aislat and the infirmary, then found herself saying:

'Cassia, could you go and see Sarai? She wasn't well, but I don't think it's the fever. Otherwise we need help in the still-room, and infirmary; we've four taken ill today, and I expect there'll be more to come.'

The older woman gave her a look. 'Are you sure, Ninian?' She was not talking about the fever.

'Quite sure.'

The two women's eyes met in mutual respect. Cassia nodded.

'I see you have your hands full. Go on with what you were doing, Ninian, and we'll talk when you've time.'

Cassia swept her women before her; dazed, Ninian shook her head, feeling herself relieved of an immense weight. Cassia was more than capable; she was effective. Quest had not come himself, but his brother's wife was almost more welcome in their present predicament.

Ninian wondered why Quest did not come.

Affer heard the bells boom over the temple at Wellwater. Sickness rose in his throat as he listened to their message of death, even though it was for Borland.

'Ran, I wish you were here,' he whispered. Did Ninian know he could see into her thoughts, that he read his worthlessness in her mind? He wondered what she would say if he told her about Storn and the origins of the plague, but knew he could not. Since he alone knew the cause, he felt the guilt, too, was his; it was illogical, but it seemed true.

He felt lonely. He climbed the stairs to the small room Sarai occupied. She, too, was unhappy. He felt he could keep her company, doing that much, at least, for Ninian, but outside her door he stopped. He gave a tentative knock.

'Sarai? I came to see how you were.'

She was not alone. Cassia from Kandria sat at her bedside; there was an air of intimacy about the pair that seemed to exclude him.

'Come in, Affer,' Cassia invited with a smile. 'How kind of you to come.' *What is he doing here? Has he nothing better to do, with Arcady in this turmoil?* Her unspoken thoughts reached him all too plainly.

'I'm sorry,' he stammered. 'I'll leave you and go.' Unable to think of an alternative, he bolted.

Poor Ninian. With men like Affer, no wonder she has to call for outside help. This time the thought was more acerbic, and Affer flinched.

No one cares, no one wants me; I wish I were dead! Sarai's thoughts, coming on top of the others, felt leaden, heavy and oppressive, as if she dragged them with her through every day of her life.

'But it's not true,' Affer whispered to himself, unable to escape the solid pulse of her misery. 'I swear to you, Sarai, it isn't true. They both love you.' But he could not help; he was an afterthought to everyone but Ran, and she was not there.

Since he had talked to Storn, the burden of other people's thoughts and feelings had increased, rarely leaving him in peace. Distance alone served to free him, but he felt terrible guilt at absenting himself with so much to be done. Ninian needed every spare hand; even his. Affer shuddered, desperate for respite from the tumult of voices.

In the hall, laid for the evening meal, children were still busy making reed logs; Affer passed them and went out by the side door, to be instantly swallowed up by the fog outside. It was not yet night, and the darkness held a different quality of obscurity, the air dense and heavy. It was possible to hide in shadows, to imagine an absolute solitude.

Affer walked aimlessly, terribly alone. He put his hands over his ears, retreating into the emptiness of the fog, a cold sweat breaking out over his body.

'No, please,' he moaned. 'Leave me alone. Please, go away!'

He was close to the infirmary. Thoughts and sensations pursued him relentlessly, battering against his mind, overwhelming any resistance. There was the agony of a woman who tried to breathe air into tortured lungs, remembering all her children were dead. Affer shared tormented thoughts of a man whose head was bursting with unbearable pain, along with other feelings, of loss, of pain, of desolation; from nowhere came any thought of hope. He was spared nothing.

'*No, please; this isn't my doing. I didn't mean this to happen,*' he cried, clutching at his ears, his imagination added to other despairing voices, to Storn's voice.

'Affer?'

He did not know who called to him; Affer turned and fled through the fog, running blindly until he tripped and fell on a patch of uneven ground. He did not know where he was, and did not care. He could smell the fog, and the odour of decay blowing from the lake.

The fog surrounded him with silence, its clammy tendrils creeping over his face and hands and bare forearms, and he shuddered, barely sane enough to comprehend the mist was not sentient, but only air and moisture.

'Ran, come back,' he begged, as the fog ate his words. 'Come back.'

His words evaporated in the grey stillness. Affer breathed in deeply, wishing he could catch the sickness from the damp air, to leave the choice to deity or fate whether he should live or die.

'Let Ran come back. Let her be free,' he begged; he wept, without shame.

No one answered, or gave him comfort, and, bitterly, Affer knew no one would ever come. He was of use to no one, not even himself. He was alone, but never alone, helpless in the face of a possession he did not want, so great a curse that death held a greater allure than to live with the torment of knowledge.

'Ran?' he called. 'Ran? Help me. Why was I born, if it was only to this?'

The fog swallowed his words and let him alone, kneeling on bare earth in the mists of despair, in much the same posture he had adopted in a very different place, ten long years before.

2

The service was over.

Kerron watched, wondering what thoughts were going through the minds of his fellow priests. What did they believe about the plague, about this sudden violent alteration in their lives? Did they blame him, as Ran had done, for the deaths of the Ismonites, or were they, like Borland, willing to credit their gods with the deed? Did they feel they would be spared by reason of their calling, or were they afraid? He thought that in one or two faces he could certainly discern fear.

He left the temple to climb onto the roof, standing by the parapet. The lake was obscured by fog, but it seemed to be lifting as night fell. Kerron made out the pattern of stars in the north, tracing the constellations of Columb and Sythera; Omigon, the dark star, was clear, too. There was a black patch of sky over Sheer Island, without any light.

The Wetlands had been imprisoned all day by fog. It was, Kerron was sure, the first physical manifestation of the darkness which was coming to the *akhal* and to Avardale.

'The weed covers much of the lake,' the voice said. 'When there is darkness on the lake, it will be dark in the lake, and the secret will not matter.'

'The secret. What is this secret?' Kerron asked impatiently. His gaze swept east, and for an instant the mists lifted. Sparkles which must be the evening lights flickered under the surface of the lake, dimmer, obscured by the green blanket of weed.

'The lights are dying as the darkness comes. The weed will succeed where you failed, and bring back dark to the lake. The water will die as the lights die; the dark will come and the secret of Avardale will be destroyed.'

Kerron experienced renewed irritation at the refusal to answer his question. What was the secret? What could represent a danger to the power of the dark? The lights?

'It is not for you, not for you to choose,' hissed the voice in his mind. 'It is not for you to know, or choose to know.'

Kerron shook his head wearily. Sometimes it seemed to him there were two people living in his mind, or perhaps two constituents of the same person. He wondered if the one he thought of as *Kerron* really existed, or had he become only the personification of, or for, the voice? Were his thoughts ever his own?

The *akhal* of Avardale were succumbing to the plague with terrifying speed. Even Kerron was startled by the rapidity of the change, in only two days, as if Ran had drawn the weed and decay and plague after her with her flotilla. Borland was dead, killed by drinking water all the stories should have warned him was poisoned. Kerron had sent to inform Lord Quorden of the plague and the death of the High Priest, but he did not think any external help would be forthcoming.

246

Did becoming High Priest matter now? Did he still care? Something in Kerron no longer believed it did, or that he did.

Several members of the guard had already fallen ill, but Kerron felt extraordinarily hearty. The illness might rage in the temple, among the guard, on every estate around the lake, but he was sure it would never touch him and his charmed existence. The disease would pass him by.

The evening lights had finished, and fog descended once more. In the darkness, the waters of Avardale were being covered by the clogging weed which poured down the river from Ismon in a relentless tide. Kerron felt a momentary chill as he thought of what had happened at Ismon. So many had died.

His thoughts returned to the mysterious secret the voice told him had something to do with Arcady, with the Steward, and the old days.

How had the song gone, the lay of the *akhal*?

> *'When first we came*
> *These lands were dry,*
> *Though there was water still*
> *In the deepest places*
> *So black a blue*
> *We could not see,*
> *Not in the depths*
> *Where the shadows lay,*
> *As we looked down*
> *From the high cliff,*
> *Afraid of the dark.'*

Bellene had taught them that song, with other legends of the old times, of Arkata and Columb and Sythera. She had taught him and Ninian and Ran and Affer, all the children of Arcady. What had the high cliff to do with it, and the deeps? He could not recall the other verses of the song, the words lost to memory.

There was ice in the pit of Kerron's stomach, something about the idea of *lost*. He wondered how Ran was in her prison, bound by stone walls and barred door. Was she afraid?

The prospect of her being hurt, being given pain by some stranger priest in Ammon, gave him no satisfaction. Kerron shied away from such a vision. There was something in Ran which was linked to a part of himself, and he was reluctant to let it, or her, go.

'Perhaps she knows Arcady's secret,' suggested the voice in a sly aside. *'She is close to the Steward's heir, daughter to the heir previous. Ask her the secret.'*

Not for the first time, Kerron found it impossible to distinguish between his own private thoughts, and the voice. So often, now, the two were too deeply intertwined to be differentiated.

Chapter 12

Dark Fall – Day Six

1

Ninian pushed open the shutters, letting mist and damp evening air into the room, which was stuffy and smelled of sweat and burning tallow. The man on the bed struggled to sit up.

'It's dark; is it night already?'

'Not yet; this is the fog I told you about. It came down the morning after you arrived from Ismon and has never completely lifted since.' Ninian stared at the mass of grey cloud, feeling dispirited. 'It seems to loosen its grip as night comes, at twilight, then sets in again.'

'How long has it been?'

'Six days.' Ninian sighed. It was close to sunset, and in the west there was a leavening of the mists, but she knew it would not last. It was as if the fog which covered Avardale possessed an existence entirely its own, that it had chosen to descend on the *akhal* to isolate them inside the Wetlands with the plague and the weed covering the lakes.

Was it the darkness she had foreseen, that day on the lake? Something in her mind told her it was not, that such dark had been absolute, not this mere shadowing.

'What are you looking at?'

Ninian turned back to the man on the bed. He was, or had been before the fever struck him down, of sturdy build, young, with flaxen hair, fair skin and the bright blue eyes which marked him as an outsider, a Plainsman. 'Nothing; the fog hides everything.'

'It smells nearly as bad as it did at Ismon.' The Plainsman wrinkled his nose. His cheeks were flushed, but Ninian judged the colour arose from exertion, not a recurrence of fever. She did not understand why he survived when others as strong, and as young, had died. There had been more than a dozen deaths at Arcady over the past four days, Ismonites and one of her own

249

people, and many more now lay ill with the plague. The rate of mortality was so high that Ninian allowed herself to wonder, in her worst moments, whether any of them would survive.

'It isn't only the fog; it's something in the water, and the weed on the lake,' she said in explanation. 'It covers most of the surface; I never knew anything spread so fast.'

'Faster than at Ismon.'

'What were you doing there?'

'Hiding.' He managed a grin, which made him look much younger, perhaps only twenty.

'From the priests?'

He gave her a wary look, then shrugged. 'As you say.'

'You know they want to question you? So far I've said you're too ill, but I don't know for how much longer it will keep them away.'

'I reckon I can trust you; after all, you took me in and saved my life.' He hesitated. 'I was involved in a demonstration in the city of Ammon, against the Order; we stole barrels of grain from them on a fair day, to give a proper distribution to those who needed it.' His face grew more flushed. 'You can't imagine it, not here, but there are so many in the cities who go hungry. But the guard came looking for us; someone must have betrayed us, because they knew our names.'

'I see.' Ninian regretted what she was about to say. 'You know I can't hide you forever; I can't risk the lives of our people for one man.'

'They tell me one of your kindred was taken up by the priests.'

Ninian nodded. 'Ran, my cousin; she and her brother were the ones who brought you from Ismon.'

'And that was her offence?'

'That, and a little more.' She could see in his face that the Plainsman had a very real fear of capture. 'What would they do to you, Carrol, if they caught you?' she asked. 'Was the theft so serious a crime?'

'They'd hand me over to the inquisitor for questioning. They've no love for rebels in Ammon just now; it was another reason I ran off.' The flushed face grew pale, and Carrol's voice wavered. 'I daren't be caught, not with what I know. We were only waiting for the sign – '

He broke off. 'What sign?' Ninian asked, seeing he was silent.

'For word to seize the city.' Carrol bit his lower lip. 'Perhaps I shouldn't tell you, but it might make you see how important it is that I stay out of the clutches of the priests. We were waiting for the sign to rise, and not only those of us in Ammon; those in

Femillur to the south, too, will revolt with us against the Order.'

She was astonished. 'And what then?'

'Do you follow the Emperor here?' Carrol asked, in a low voice.

'We are *akhal*,' Ninian said simply. 'We are loyal to the Empire and the Emperor, but those are very distant concepts to us most of the time; especially now, when the outside world seems to care as little for us as we for them.'

'We fight for the restoration of Emperor Amestatis to his rule, and for the cities to return control to the old lay Administrators. We want the law to reflect the needs of the peoples and not the whims of whoever claims to hear the voices of invisible and unaccountable gods.' He spoke quickly and with passion. 'It seems to me – to us – that the rule of the priests has as its end the destruction of the peoples of the Empire, not their good, and that only the Emperor can save us. The light on the Plains was the first signal; another will follow. I believe that the old Imperial lights will shine once more across our skies, and the rains will come again.'

'Imperial lights? We had one here in the old days, the Tearstone; it stood on the island in the middle of our lake.'

'It will be restored and will shine out, light calling to the other lights throughout the Empire, as the old temples are brought back to life.'

'The priests claimed the light on the Plains was a portent of good harvests to come,' Ninian said slowly, wondering what Quest would have said if he were present; but he had not come since the guard had taken Ran away, and had sent no word. 'A sign of favour.'

'Nonsense.' Carrol dismissed the suggestion with a wave of his hand. 'The harvest will be the same as it has been for the past few years – poor, but not so poor as they make out. No, the priests have some scheme of their own in mind; this light surprised them as much as everyone else. There's something else at work to counter their evil, something beyond their control.'

A flicker of hope stirred in Ninian as he spoke, perhaps because he seemed so very certain of his cause. For a moment she was tempted to confide in him in her turn, to speak of her own fear and sense of being burdened by a duty beyond her courage, but realised she could not; the responsibility must remain hers alone.

'Then I shall have to try to keep you safe,' she said practically. 'Thank you for telling me.'

'Are matters here as bad as at Ismon?' The Plainsman seemed eager to change the subject.

'Not yet. The drums and bells speak of sickness on all the

estates, and the fish in the lake are dying, but we've brought our own breeding stock ashore to the tanks. For the most part, we're managing to exist on our stores, for at least the sickness came in the middle of the summer and not winter's end, when we should have been hard pressed.' Ninian shrugged. 'You survived, and you were as ill as any who came from Ismon. That's cause for hope.'

'What's that?' Carrol sat bolt upright, peering out into the fog.

Night had fallen. As Ninian turned to look out of the window she saw the mists had lifted somewhat, and it was possible to see the flicker of blue-green lights out on the lake.

'Our lake lights,' she said. 'They appear each evening after sunset, although the weed seems to be affecting even them; they used to be much brighter. And now,' she went on as she closed the shutters, 'I must go. I'll send someone with some supper for you, if you feel you can eat.' He nodded. 'And I'll send warning if the priests come, so you can put on you're dying.'

'You have my thanks,' Carrol said with a sigh as he lay back, looking weary. Ninian shut the door quietly as she left, sure he would sleep.

Affer jumped up from a crouch by the door, startling her considerably.

'Ninian?'

'Why didn't you come in and fetch me, if you wanted me?' she asked, irritated. 'Have you been waiting long?'

'His face creased. 'I – his thoughts hurt, Ninian.'

She sighed. 'Never mind. What is it?'

'Cassia and Sarai are with Bellene; Cassia thinks you should come.'

The summons was not unexpected, but nonetheless apprehension stirred.

'I'll come.'

The rush lights along the passage flickered, casting strange shadows across Affer's face; Ninian could not tell if he looked worse than when she'd last seen him. 'Please, Ninian, may I go out?'

'If you must. Affer – ' She put out a hand to stay his flight. 'Is there something wrong? You look terribly unhappy.'

'*I can't!*' His voice shook.

'Can I help?'

But Affer turned away and ran down the passage; Ninian hesitated, unsure whether his need was greater than Sarai's or Bellene's.

'I wish there were three of me,' she said under her breath. 'And even those wouldn't be enough.' The onus of Arcady had never before felt so burdensome. Ninian caught herself wondering what benefits ensued from her efforts, what greater good, when all she seemed to achieve was to watch her people sicken. The great house felt empty and dark and cold, transformed in so short a space of time from home to a vast infirmary, isolated by surrounding mists and filled with fetid air.

Sarai sat beside Bellene's bed, her eyes unusually dark and frightened. Cassia was with her. As her mother came in, Ninian read relief in her expression.

'I tried to give her water, as you said, but she won't take it.'

'I'm sorry.' New guilt stabbed at Ninian. Should Sarai who was ill herself be sitting with a dying woman? Yet how could her daughter grow into a woman to be proud of if she did not understand the reality of death?

'Will she die?'

Ninian looked down at the still figure of Bellene; the only sign of life came from the faint wheeze of her breathing, the slow but steady rise and fall of her chest. The old woman looked peaceful; when Ninian felt her hand, it was cool, not hot.

'I think so,' she answered steadily. Bellene's tired old body was no longer warring with the sickness; it was hard to believe so cantankerous a woman could give up a fight.

'Does she mind?'

'I doubt it. Can you imagine her lying there so peacefully if she did?'

A small hand slipped inside her own. 'You won't leave me alone with her?'

'Do you want to stay?' Ninian surveyed Sarai's face; she had a frail appearance, black shadows outlining her eyes. 'You may find it very upsetting, Sarai.'

'If you're here, I want to be with you.'

'Thank you,' she said, meaning it, and nodding gratefully to Cassia that she could leave now.

Sarai lifted her head. 'This will be her last night, won't it?' she asked in a whisper. 'Then you'll be Steward of Arcady.'

Ninian pulled up a chair beside Sarai's stool. On a low table by the bed a rare oil lamp flickered in the darkness, more efficient than the tallow candles allowed to others. The flame lit the heavy thumb ring placed beside it, too large now for Bellene's gaunt hand, inset with green carnelian carved in the shape of a fish, but with wings rather than fins. Arkata's ring; her only other tangible legacy. Ninian looked at it, the insignia of the Stewards of Arcady. It was a heavy piece, probably uncomfortable and inconvenient.

What if the call came tonight? Ninian, looking at the still figure, knew it would be for her, not for Bellene. The old woman had no strength left.

'Ninian?'

She looked into the frightened eyes of her daughter. 'I'm sorry; I was thinking. What is it?'

'I was thinking, too, about dying,' Sarai whispered; her small body gave a shudder. 'About what it was like. Are you sure Bellene isn't afraid?'

Ninian hesitated, a chill of doubt giving her pause. What did she know, after all? One moment to be a person with thoughts and hopes and desires, the next to be nothing but a shell, food for the creatures of the earth, was a prospect so briefly terrifying that her mind went blank. Surely the promise of the priests was better, the hope of an eternity of willing service to the gods, for it contained the assurance of continued conscious existence. But Ninian knew Bellene had long ago rejected such spurious comfort, preferring the prospect of glorious adventure or nothingness to what she termed perpetual slavery.

'I hope not,' she found herself replying. 'Sarai, I can't give you a promise she's not afraid; to travel into the unknown is frightening. But if we see it as an adventure, then perhaps it becomes something we need not dread.'

Sarai nodded, her thick crown of hair bobbing low over her forehead. Silence fell between them, and they sat and watched Bellene's breathing, each engrossed in private thoughts as they waited for the final change.

They had been sitting so for some time when Affer came in to join them, slipping in without a word, his face set and determined.

Quest strained his eyes into the darkness, peering at the shoreline and beyond.

'Don't bother to make the pier. Just get me close enough to shore and I'll jump out,' he said to the guards who rowed the long-boat. 'Then you can go on to Wellwater.'

'It's after midnight,' muttered one man, sounding less than pleased.

It was heavy work forcing the boat through the covering of weed. In the four days since he began his circuit of the lake, Quest thought the drums had rolled and bells tolled ceaselessly with their melancholy messages of death and disease. Jerom had wanted him to spend the night at Kandria, but Quest would not stay, consumed by a desire to go on to Arcady.

254

'Are you sure you want to get out here, Reverence?' one of the men asked, as the bottom of the boat scraped against the shallows.

'We're close enough in,' Quest answered shortly. 'Just hold the boat steady.' He clambered to the bow, balancing a moment before making his leap. Fasting had reduced his substance, and he felt as light as air as he launched himself up and out, landing with a stumble on the pebbled shore.'

'You don't want us to wait? Then we'll be getting along while we can still see, Reverence.' Quest waved an impatient hand, and heard the splash of oars.

Why had he come?

He was too exhausted to think clearly; he felt almost as if he were in one of his dreams. Perhaps that was the answer; the moment was very like a dream. He did not wish to remember the suffering he had seen on his travels, nor his inability to console or assist the sufferers. There was no consolation and no assistance to give in the face of death. He was a priest, and yet he feared the ultimate dissolution more greatly than any he had striven to comfort, for all he was in good health.

Why had he been so insistent on coming to Arcady? To seek solace from Ninian?

A bell tolled out from across the water, from the north: another death. The Steward of Arbon; he had been very ill when Quest saw him, taking the plague with terrifying swiftness. Quest lowered his head a moment for respect, for the man had been a good and resolute Steward.

Before he died, Borland had preached that the sickness was sent by the gods in retribution for sins of omission by the *akhal*. Could he have been right, that foolish, selfish man? But the *akhal* were neither evil nor corrupt, wicked nor vicious. If he was right, what did that signify about the nature of divinity?

Quest strode towards the great house, trying to blot out his thoughts. The darkness reminded him of his dream of coming to Arcady on just such a night, to find his daughter dying. He hurried on, afraid the dream might now become reality and entered the main hall, which was not quite deserted.

'Where will I find Ninian?' he asked a young man lying beside the hearth, half-asleep.

'In the Steward's room.' The man blinked and sat up, sleep fleeing. The hall was dark, only embers of the fire and two rush lights brightening the shadows. 'Keeping watch.'

His words brought Quest up sharply. 'Is Bellene dying, then?'

'So they say.' The young man swallowed. 'Shall I go and tell her you're here, Reverence?'

Quest shook his head. 'No, I'll find my own way.'

'As you wish, Reverence.'

His eyes were accustomed to the dark, and Quest had no difficulty in finding his way. Three watchers waited in the passage outside the door of Bellene's room; he recognised Aislat, one of the older women, and Amori, a slender girl who reminded him a little of Ninian.

'Have you come as a witness, Reverence?' Aislat demanded in a low voice, looking surprised. 'Ninian is with our Steward now; she still lives.'

'I will go in and see her.'

'Very well.' Aislat moved politely aside, but her expression was unfriendly, as if he intruded.

Ninian turned as he opened the door, and he thought she looked weary, Sarai apprehensive.

'What are you doing here?' The angles of Ninian's face were prominent in the lamp light, and she sounded almost hostile.

'I've just come from Kandria.'

He thought she relaxed a little. 'Cassia has been more help than I can say.'

'They've been luckier than most so far,' Quest agreed. 'I've been round the lake since we last met, and the plague is everywhere.'

'I heard the drums from Arbon.'

Silence fell again. Sarai gave her father a quick glance from under her lashes; Quest was appalled at her frail appearance.

'Can I speak to you alone?' he asked Ninian abruptly.

He thought he heard a sigh escape her, but at last she nodded.

'If we walk a little way along the passage we won't disturb anyone. Affer,' she added, 'come and fetch me if there's any change. Stay with Sarai. We shan't be long.'

Quest followed her from the room and out of hearing of the watchers at Bellene's door. It was dark further down the passage, making it easier to speak without reserve.

'What's the matter with Sarai?' he demanded. 'Why are you making her sit at this deathbed with you? Can't you see how tired and frightened she is?'

'Sarai,' Ninian responded coolly, 'is with me because she wants to be. At present she doesn't like to be alone, and even you have to agree I must stay with Bellene tonight.'

'Has Sarai the plague?'

'Obviously not. Or do you imagine I would force a seriously sick child to watch a death just for my own amusement?'

The memory of his dream, of sitting by his dying daughter, came vividly into Quest's mind, and without further thought he reached out and caught Ninian in an angry clasp.

'Are you sure? Can you swear it?' Panic rose in him. He remembered how vivid the dream had seemed, how sure he had been that it was a warning. 'Why does she look so ill? The gods are punishing me for her, revenging themselves because I broke my vow.'

'Be quiet, let me go . . . ' Ninian stepped back. 'And keep your voice down.'

'Ninian?' Quest blinked, and his surroundings firmed into greater reality.

'What's the matter?' But she did not sound as if she cared what troubled him. 'Was there something you wanted to tell me?'

'I'm sorry: I didn't mean to hurt you, but I had a dream once, a dreadful dream in which I saw Sarai dying, here at Arcady.' His throat closed against the memory of anguish. 'Ninian,' he whispered, 'was the dream a warning from the gods? Or did I imagine it all?'

She frowned. 'How can I know?'

'Do you believe this plague is the vengeance of the gods on the *akhal*?' Suddenly, he needed her answer. 'Why else should all this have happened, Ninian? Why are they killing us?'

'You want *me* to tell *you*? Oh no, Quest; that's your province, or so you've always said.'

'But what if it's true?' he persisted. Somehow, he thought, if she would tell him it was true, then he would know, and there would be no more doubt. 'What if this is the vengeance of the Lords of Light for failing in our duty, so that we have no more right to live? Could it be true?'

'Why ask me?' Ninian answered, sounding very angry. 'You were the one who knew everything. If you stand between us and the gods, they can hardly speak to us, only to you. Answer your own question.'

'But what if the gods are not merciful, or not as we understand it? What if they are not even *good*, as we mean the word?' Quest asked, his voice trembling. 'What if I have wasted my whole life in worship of beings whose nature I cannot hope to understand? What if they care nothing for us, for any of us? Then I have sacrificed my life in praise of creatures who would kill my own child without a thought, my people on a whim.'

Ninian stared at him in blank astonishment. 'What do you want me to say?'

'How can I preach, now Borland is dead, that each and every

one of the *akhal* is important to the Lords of Light, if the gods make it plain they care nothing for our suffering? Help me, Ninian; help me, or I think I shall go mad.'

'Help you?' she asked incredulously. The chill in her voice brought him back to the present. 'You ask me to tell you what you should believe, when Bellene is dying, when I spend all my days and nights caring for the sick, and you want me to help you worry about the state of your soul? How dare you, Quest? How dare you come here and place this burden on me? What do I care for your doubts, for the waste of your life? If this is what you came for, go away, and stop wasting my time.'

Rage began to simmer in the pit of his stomach. Quest heard her out, each word freezing his hope into despair. He had come to her for solace, but she cared nothing for his torment.

'Are you too stupid to understand what I'm saying?' he demanded. 'If we fail to comprehend the true nature of the gods, we may risk all our lives. If this plague is the result of their anger, it's destroying us. Is that too difficult a concept for you to take in?'

'Oh no, Quest, I think I understand better than you,' Ninian snapped back. 'You think that if you can persuade yourself this sickness is sent by the Lords of Light, and if you can understand why they sent it, then you can plead with them for forgiveness of whatever sin you imagine the *akhal* to be guilty, thereby saving us all. That's what you want to believe.'

'You're wrong.'

She swept aside his angry protest. 'I have to deal with the here and now, Quest. All of us are struggling to save what we can from this disaster, and we've no time for the luxury of asking what we may or may not have done to bring it down on ourselves.'

Her scorn struck him to the quick; he would not agree with her unwelcome understanding of his deeper motives. 'What is life, if there is no more to hope for than this bare existence?'

'Haven't your dreams told you?'

'No.' He was suddenly so angry he could barely speak. His thoughts blurred together, making it hard to formulate ideas with any clarity.

'Your dreams were only ever what you wanted them to be,' Ninian went on with chill brutality. 'You always had a talent for self-deception.'

'You were never a true believer,' Quest managed to say. Rage pulsed in his mind, blinding him; his hands curved and stiffened. 'Small wonder Arcady and Sarai are cursed.'

She frowned. 'Cursed? Only by you, I think.'

'How dare you? She may be dying.'

He did not think. In an instant his hands were around Ninian's neck, just as they had been in his dream of the island, squeezing, cutting off air and voice. His vision clouded; he went on squeezing his hands together, ignoring attempts to push him away. The sensation of power over her was sexual in force, his hands on the softness of her throat as potent as their union had once been, in the Barren Lands, where his flesh had conquered hers and been conquered in turn, and sudden desire raged through him, struggling for release –

'Ninian!'

Affer's anxious summons broke into consciousness through a haze of physical excitement that was both overwhelming and deeply shaming. Uncertain, Quest released his grip on Ninian's throat, then felt his hands torn away by hard fingers with sharp nails. Shaken, he took a step back, dizzy and lost.

'Get away from me!'

He shook his head mindlessly. Ninian's face came into focus; she was breathing in quick, painful gasps.

'You tried to kill me.'

'No.' But Quest could not go on, unsure if his denial were true. He looked down at his hands in bewilderment, feeling as if he were only now really waking from his dream.

'Ninian – come; come and look!'

She looked uncertainly from him to the distant Affer. Quest shook his head.

The door to Bellene's room stood open, and inside the watchers had gathered around the window, where the shutters were open, facing south over the herb gardens and the infirmary.

'What is it?' someone gasped.

Filling the frame, Quest saw not the blackness of night but a column of pure red light, deep and rich and brilliant.

'A light – an Imperial Light!' The voice was Bellene's, weak but sure. 'From the desert.'

Quest needed only one glimpse, one moment of ultimate revelation. He never knew what it was about the light that dissolved the self-imposed barrier by which he hid from himself all his doubts and fears, his refusal to accept that he was only a man, and must die. He only understood that his eyes were opened to that truth at last, and he sank to his knees, his gaze never leaving the column of light.

'Forgive me,' he whispered. 'Forgive me.'

He knew now he had tried to kill Ninian as he had seen himself destroy her in his dream, an evil dream sent by an evil temptation. It was his own doubt, his own fear he had really wanted to kill, but he had personified them in her.

'I wanted to believe I was chosen by the gods,' he said, bemused and dazzled. 'I made myself believe it.'

His dreams were no messages from the Lords of Light but temptations, not prophecies but admissions of his own secret desires. His dreams told him Ninian was his enemy, that she was evil and must be destroyed; that his hardships stemmed from her existence, and if she were gone they, too, would disappear.

'I believed a lie; all my life, I chose, wilfully, to believe a lie . . . ' In a moment of perfect understanding all Quest's old faith, his credence in his gods shrivelled and died, leaving him alone and empty and afraid.

A great wind blew up from the south, bringing cleansing breaths of dust-scented air into Bellene's chamber.

Quest knew an agony of self-reproach. What sort of deities had he and his fellow priests created, in whose image, that they should envisage them as jealous and vengeful, as unyielding as the priests themselves? Or had they not created them at all, but accepted instead demons or other evil beings, and set them up as gods simply because he and his fellows preferred to worship power, not goodness, nor any other concept worthy of adulation? Because they were so afraid of death, of ceasing to exist, that the prospect of perpetual servitude was preferable to such a fate? Could his whole Order exist only as a denial of the reality of death?

'I wanted to believe; I wanted to believe I lived for a reason, that I was someone separate, important.'

Was it possible that he and his people, all the peoples of the Empire, were not as consequential as they conceived themselves? Was it possible they existed as no more than tools in the mind of some greater force, to be used or put aside or destroyed at a whim, like a grass plucked from the bank to make a pipe? Or was even that assigning them too great a purpose? Did human capacity for thought mean nothing?

Quest kept his gaze on the column of light, but his eyes were wet with the threat of tears. He felt emptied of everything, of all sensation and emotion other than bitterness; most of all of any sense of self-worth.

'I am nothing,' he breathed.

Never had Quest been so humbled. Never had he so questioned his own worth, preferring to allow his spurious gods to endow him with value as their servant.

But there were no gods. This light, this Imperial Light, was somehow more real than any god, possessing the power to clear his mind of self-delusion. Quest thought he could understand why his Order had so feared the old temples, the old lightstones and their force, their focus. Even if he had not been able to see it now, he thought he would have been able to sense the presence of the light, as if it were more than it appeared, more solid and impenetrable.

His past claims to authority, to the reflection of divine superiority in every sphere, shamed him so greatly he wished he could die when he remembered them.

Affer gave a strangled cry. He stared down at Quest with an agonised expression, as if he did not want to see what he was seeing, to hear what he was hearing. It was as if the younger man could somehow reach into his mind and read his bitter, self-destructive thoughts.

A new and utterly terrifying humility kept Quest kneeling rigidly on the floor as Affer fled and the door to the room slammed, the south wind blew against the shutters.

Bellene stirred, then opened her eyes.

'Then it is true,' the old woman breathed. 'It's all true. A light, an Imperial Light from the desert. The lights have come back.'

Ninian had somehow forgotten Quest, sunk to his knees, no longer posing any sort of threat. She glanced at him, and had the sense that the man who had tried to strangle her was not the Quest who knelt in Bellene's room. That was the false, this the true man.

There was a change in the quality of the light; no, it was that other lights had joined the scarlet column, a green-white brilliance from the east, and from further off a chain of deep blue, all three colours merging and joining in one vast triangle of light.

'The Imperial Lights,' Bellene whispered again. 'Is this the beginning of the second end of the world?'

'The wind's getting up,' Aislat observed.

At first there was only a light breeze, warm and refreshing, which rose rapidly to howling, and the shutters of Bellene's room rattled frantically against their bolts. It cooled suddenly as gusts of dusty air filled the room in a brief visitation, then died away, and the lights faded, and there was nothing more to be seen in the outside world but the night sky.

'Look. I can see the stars again,' Sarai cried out. 'The mist's gone.'

Ninian leaned out of the window. The air was warm, as it should have been in mid-summer, and both Annoin and Pharus shone brightly amid clear skies; the remnants of the moon's quarter gleamed over the herb gardens and the infirmary.

'It's all gone,' she said, marvelling. 'The wind blew away the fog.' Then more words came from her, in a different voice. *The wind rose with the light, and sent back the dark.'*

Her words hung in the air, a truth unacknowledged.

'Ninian. Come here.'

Bellene's voice was very weak; Ninian, after one quick look at her, obeyed, kneeling at the bedside. The old woman lay flat, no colour in her face at all, but she managed to find the strength to lift her right hand and place it on Ninian's head.

'You, all of you, Aislat and Amori and Farse and Sarai, all bear witness, and you, too, Priest Quest.'

'No,' Quest said softly. 'No more a priest.'

Bellene ignored the response.

'You all bear witness to my naming of Ninian, my heir, as next Steward of Arcady; to her care I bequeath it all, house and hall, lands and lake, she to be their guardian.' She lifted her hand from Ninian's hair and fumbled on the table at her side for the thumb ring. 'Put this on,' she commanded. 'Take it, and with it the duty of Arcady.'

'I will do what I must,' Ninian said softly, and felt the ring's weight on her hand.

'Restore the lights to Avardale.' Bellene's voice sank so only Ninian heard her.

Aislat shook her head, and Bellene's chest rose in one last massive heave, followed by a long silence.

'Is she dead?' Sarai asked, her teeth chattering.

'Yes.' Ninian held out her arms and Sarai came and buried her face in her mother's shoulder.

'I'll stay and watch the rest of the night,' Aislat said softly. 'You take Sarai. Farse can go and ring the bell.'

'You see? She knew, and she wasn't afraid,' Ninian whispered into Sarai's ear. 'There's no need to be frightened of death.' But Sarai did not speak, clinging more tightly still.

'Let me help you,' Quest offered, sounding as if he did not hope for, or expect, a positive response. He had the air of someone awaiting a dismissal, anticipating it, knowing it was what he deserved. Ninian's brief doubt died.

'Thank you.' She struggled to her feet, loosening the thin arms that encircled her sore throat. 'Will you carry her?'

'Will she let me?' A small spark of anguished hope leaped into Quest's eyes.

Ninian nodded. 'She's tired; it's been a long night.'

Quest bent to Sarai and picked her up. She did not resist, but lay passively in his grasp, head lolling loosely against his chest. Ninian drew in a sharp breath, oddly jolted by the sight of father and daughter together, wondering if she had just lost something infinitely dear; then knew it for a selfish thought and strove to banish it. If Sarai loved her father, it did not diminish her feelings for her mother.

'Are you coming?'

'Of course.' Ninian put out a hand to Sarai's cheek.

'I won't touch you, Ninian. You don't need to be frightened of me.' Quest's expression bespoke his sincerity. 'I never would have hurt you, not in my right mind.'

'Let's imagine it was a dream and never happened. I believe that.'

Sarai turned startled eyes to her mother, and a very little colour crept into Quest's white face.

'Is there anything I can do, for you or for Arcady?' he asked unsteadily. 'Tell me.'

'Bring Ran back to Arcady.'

'I can't promise; she's in Kerron's charge, not mine; but I'll do what I can.' A darker flush covered his cheeks. 'If I can.'

His new humility made her gentle: 'That's all any of us can promise.'

'And light to banish the dark.'

She nodded, wondering how much he knew or understood. 'Perhaps.'

On her right thumb, Ninian felt the heavy weight of the ring of the Stewards of Arcady, reminding her of the full burden of duty it demanded. That knowledge was something she shared with no one, now Bellene was dead.

She was now Steward of Arcady, and Guardian to Arcady's secret, and she was afraid.

Ran was not asleep when the light appeared. The sounds of drums and bells were a constant disturbance, and lacking exercise she was restless.

She paced the short distance from door to rear wall, unable to settle. After six days of imprisonment her moods swung wildly from listlessness to rage and futile fits of energy for which she had no outlet.

Her uselessness to Ninian and everyone else at a time of crisis was another source of anger. The drums told her the situation around Avardale grew daily worse, even the numbers of the guard in the camp diminishing as they, too, succumbed. It was as if the passage of time had accelerated since her return from

Ismon, so that each day was several.

She saw no one apart from her guards and sometimes Kerron. Ran stared hungrily at the lake, where the mists had settled down again with the coming of night; it was dark, starless, confining.

Ran had always believed Bellene held her prisoner, but now she knew the reality of confinement of mind and body. She could have freed herself from Arcady, if she had been willing to pay the price, but from this prison there was no release.

As she stared out through the bars, lonely and desolate, she fought a rising understanding of her own worth, and it did not comfort her. She, who had always been strong, who had dreamed of flight and travel and freedom, had been nothing more than selfish, as Kerron had once said to her. She had been proud of her self-assumed superiority, but if she were to die now, what would she leave behind? No tales, no deeds, but only the memory of a woman who had accomplished none of her visions, whose life had given her only the illusion of difference. The admission was a painful one.

Ran could not have said at what point the change came, when a small amount of light came to counter the gloom and the dark. It began as a gleam from the south, burgeoning to become a pillar of red light, a dense column rising up to join the earth to the sky, dispersing the mists and the dark.

'But how beautiful,' Ran whispered.

A deep blue glow rose from the eastern horizon, drawing with it from somewhere nearer a green-white brightness; both in turn joined to the red column in the south. Between them they formed a triangle of light, each shade distinct, yet at the same time merging in a harmony of colour.

A sharp wind suddenly gusted from the south, blowing dust into Ran's face, and she blinked, unable to see. By the time she could open her eyes again the triangle of lights had gone, but so too had the mist.

'What does all this mean?'

Elthis, the red-haired half-*akhal* guard on night duty, started at the sound of her voice, and drew near the door of her cell.

'What did you say?'

'Where did the light come from?' Ran asked, glad of company. 'What was it?'

Elthis gave a furtive look to left, then right. 'They say someone is lighting the old temples,' he said, speaking low. 'That it's a sign for the Emperor, not the priests. That light must have come from the southern desert. Did you see? It looked like a chain that linked the earth to the stars – ' He broke off, but Ran nodded.

264

'I thought so, too.'

'It was a fine sight.'

Ran realised she was feeling quite different now; the wind had blown away her depression as the light had restored her some optimism.

Had Affer, too, seen the light? Her conscience smote her again, knowing he must be very unhappy and lonely, much of his sadness of her making.

She was shocked when the drums began to roll at Arcady, telling her Bellene, Steward of Arcady, was dead. Ninian must now stand in her place, facing alone all the duties and responsibilities of an estate at its lowest ebb.

The sense of peace Ran had experienced evaporated as she reproached herself for being absent at a time she should have been at Arcady to offer her strength and support to her cousin. But what use was strength without something more, be it generosity, or wisdom, or even simple kindness?

She had no tears for Bellene; it was not in her nature to submit to a display of feeling she accounted in herself a weakness, something to struggle against rather than a catharsis. But if she could have done, she would have shed tears for herself as she stared in despair through the bars of her prison for the long hours of the night.

In the first flush of dawn the mists drew in once more, light fading to dark. Grey fog rolled in to swallow the whole.

'This is a hesitation, not a defeat.' The voice was menacing in tone. *'This light will be broken again as it was before, where the dark may not. The war has only begun again.'*

'What do you mean – what war?' Kerron stood facing south on the roof of the temple, eyes watering, unable to endure the spectacle of red brightness which dispersed the concealing, protective grey mists around him.

'The war which is being fought in the Empire on many battle-grounds.'

'But what is it?' he asked, shutting his eyes. The red pillar of light suddenly hurt his eyes, which had grown more sensitive of late. Kerron shaded his face. There was a power source behind the light that he could sense even if he did not see it, and at the thought a powerful wind blew up, plastering his soutane against his body. It was warm, dust-scented.

'All war concerns power.'

'But who is fighting whom? My Order against the Emperor?' Kerron queried, startled. 'I don't understand.'

'The minds of men and women are as fitting sites for combat as this land, this lake, no more and no less. There is only one struggle, one war.'

'For what?' His heart was beating quickly, and he felt himself, for once, close to a real understanding of everything that had happened lately. 'What do you want from me in all this?'

'Arcady's Steward holds a secret, a weapon to be used against us, a promise made to the akhal in the old days after the first drought in exchange for a gift. You are the power here in the Wetlands; it is for you to see it cannot be used.'

Kerron listened, not surprised to learn that Bellene had kept a secret from him, the *cuckoo in Arcady's nest*. Yet the appellation no longer stung; the past seemed to mean little to him now.

He recalled a snatch of song as he considered the question of a secret.

> The empty night
> Filled up with colour,
> Imperial Lights.

Imperial Lights. That must be what he had seen so briefly, some of the lights which were said once to have filled the Empire's skies in the long-distant past; but they had gone out long before the coming of the Order. He wondered why they had existed, if they really had, and why the voice seemed to fear them.

'But how can they come back?' Kerron protested. 'If they were real at all.' But he had a sudden conviction that they had been real, just as he knew the voice was real, perhaps both representing the duality preached by the Order. The Lords of Light who fought against another sort of light? But, he caught himself thinking, what is *light* about the gods of the Order? Their titles were mere words, a jest, perhaps, made by the masters of the coming dark. Or, if not masters, representatives.

'Ask the woman Ran for the secret of Arcady; she may be used as a shield against it.'

'Ran?'

The lights and the wind were gone, taking with them the heavy mists. Kerron could see the stars and the outline of the great house at Arcady, feeling himself oddly exposed without the fog to cover him.

'Ran?' he asked again, feeling an instinctive resistance in his heart to any plan to harm her. In his mind he could see her face when she had landed at Arcady, with the Ismonites, and in his heart – if not his mind – knew that even then she would have liked to believe him guiltless of the countless deaths.

266

The drums began, sounding from the east.

Bellene was dead. Ninian was now Steward of Arcady.

'She will tell you the secret,' whispered the voice. *'She has a daughter.'*

Kerron felt again the struggle in his own mind, knowing that the voice was right, yet despising himself for his willingness to use Sarai against her mother. He had no feeling for children, other than perhaps mild dislike, but instinct revolted against such an action. His own parents had abandoned him, but Ninian kept Sarai close, seemed to love her.

'Which makes her weak.'

'Yes,' Kerron breathed. 'That is so.'

'Human frailties are not for those who would hold power. Love is weakness, friendship a chain to bind. Only the dark is free and strong.'

It was true, and that knowledge tugged at his mind, willing him to agreement. He, who had always stood aside from his companions, knowing himself different, was free and strong; that was who and what he was. To dissent was to destroy everything he had built, the very foundations of himself.

With the coming of day, Kerron knew he would go to Arcady.

2

Affer had no thought for where he was going in his headlong flight. He was suffocating, crowded round in body and mind by fear, by misery, by desperate hope and anguished humility.

'Ran,' he moaned to himself, 'Ran, I wish you were here.'

He fled down to the hall and outside, heading to the shore at a run. After so many days of fog, it was a surprise to be able to see the stars and moon in the night sky. Sheer Island reared up in the distance. Affer found it easier to breathe now, as if the clearer air were somehow lighter in his lungs.

In the past, distance had effectively shut out such thoughts, a solitary form of relief from despair, but this time it was different. These feelings would never leave him; nothing could protect him from them.

'Why?' he shouted despairingly at the sky. 'Why did you do this to me? What did you want?'

His gaze slid west to Wellwater and Ran, but even she could not have answered his anguished question. Perhaps there was no answer. What function had his life served, after all? He had been of no use or value to anyone. No wonder Ran had wanted to leave him; he had continuously hung on her heels and kept her back, limiting her to his own slow pace, more snail than fish. Even the horrifying ability to hear others' thoughts had not been any use; he had run from it as he ran from everything, too afraid even to tell his sister what he had learned from Storn. Whatever good it might have done was nullified by his panic.

The appearance of the light from the south had not given him strength. Affer thought of Quest, changed from priest to mere man, alone and unsure. Quest feared death, but from somewhere he had found the strength to confront his dread, and in that opposition could learn to live. The light had changed Quest, perhaps healed him, but he himself had seen beauty, and found only despair.

Affer was so sick in heart there could be no consolation.

Somewhere not very far away, he felt Bellene slipping away into the peace of death. For a moment, envy seized him, a deep envy so acute it shook him. Bellene had gone and left him behind, bound to the thoughts of all the other souls at Arcady.

He knew Sarai's flare of panic; felt, with Quest, the emptiness in his perception of himself. He sensed Ninian's trepidation as she put on the ring of the Stewards of Arcady, the deeper terror he would not hear, but could not refuse to feel.

There were no gods . . .

Quest had found it out, and now Affer knew it too; there was no one to call on, no one to beg help from in extremity. Affer felt he should have understood it the first time he found he could hear thoughts in the Barren Lands. They had been born of his terror of being alone, of the knowledge of his own weakness and worthlessness which he had taken there with him. Perhaps it was a fitting punishment. He had no value; he had been born for nothing.

Something, some entity in the Barren Lands, had seen him and found out his weakest places, and cruelly given him his curse. Was that something not a god? Could a god be malign?

'You're killing me,' he whispered in agony. 'Since then I've been dying; every day I feel less and less of a person. Everyone is more real than I am; everyone matters more than I do, because I don't really exist. Because of you, whatever you are, I never learned how to know my own feelings and thoughts.' He bent double against a blow which might as well have been physical. 'Oh, Ran, why aren't you here?'

Affer tried to calm himself, breathing deeply. Pain could not last for ever; even agony must ebb.

The thoughts of others returned in force, beating at his mind.

In the house someone was afraid, very afraid. Ninian . . . it was height that terrified her, the idea of falling. Her fear was infectious, and Affer shivered.

Other thoughts rushed into his mind, other terrors, of age and death and the inevitability of the circle. There were many people at Arcady with the plague, all sentient, all forcing him to share their suffering. One man was afraid of pain, of torture; he foresaw it, anticipated it.

'Shut up. Please, shut up and go away,' Affer moaned, clutching at his ears, but the clamour in his mind went on and on.

'I want to be left alone; alone,' he whispered.

But Ran? What about her?

'You'll forgive me, won't you?' he asked the air and the night. 'You'll understand?'

There was no more time. He was in danger of allowing the voices to overwhelm him; Affer knew he was too weak to carry more burdens than his own, and Storn's secret was too heavy to bear, too heavy to share. Awareness crystallised into determination. There was no moment of decision, for his mind had been made up long ago; it was only that the time for action presented itself, and he recognised it for what it was.

He bent to scour the shore for the largest stones; it did not take long. He put each heavy stone in any pocket large enough to hold them. Their combined weight was greater than he expected, and he was pleased. He stumbled down to the water line.

Weed had invaded Arcady's shore, but Affer thought that if he waded out he would find clearer water. He slipped off his sandals and stepped into the water, trying not to slip on slimy leaves. The noxious smell from the lake no longer disturbed him, for he had been breathing it for days, and he experienced only a mild distaste as he trod on the purple flowers.

Further out, he saw flashes of blue and green light, bright sparks. He had always believed the lights held a message for him, if he could only read and understand them, as if they offered something. Now, Affer was quite sure they were summoning him, inviting him to join them as they sparkled about the lake.

'I'm coming,' he called softly.

The further from shore, the less forceful was the press of voices in his mind. A sense of peace began to spread through Affer, releasing him from the fetters which bound him to Arcady and its people.

After a time, Affer swam, struggling to stay afloat because of the weight of the stones, his arms and legs pleasurably weak and sluggish. From land came a sudden roll of drums, high up; Arcady was sending out word of Bellene's death.

He could hardly stay above the surface for the weight of the stones. Affer had a sense of deeper water beneath him, but he could not be very far from shore, and it did not seem right or fair. Then it came to him that he did not care, that it made no difference how far he had come, for he had no more strength. It was almost too much effort even to draw in breath. He felt warm and safe, cocooned by the familiar waters of the lake.

'I'm coming,' he said fuzzily, thinking he spied a spark of light down below. His body felt heavy as he slipped under the surface, forgetting to breathe. Habit brought him up again, but only briefly. He managed a ragged swallow of air, then sank down again.

The weight of the stones carried him further down into the lake, where the water was colder. He was almost happy. Affer sensed that although he had left the mass of jangling voices behind on the surface, he was not really alone. Some other creature shared the water with him, something which did not disturb his new-found peace, nor share its thoughts with him, but a friendly presence which accepted his lax body as rightly belonging in the lake.

One of Arkata's children . . .

The thought was restful, and the absence of sound and sensation stilled his blood. Dreaming now, Affer let go his fear, welcoming a very different silence from his experience in the Barren Lands. He had failed to live, failed in everything that mattered, but the guardian of the lake had left him this choice, to become a part of it and thus make good all his omissions.

He breathed in water, and there was pain, but it did not last, and soon he was no longer aware of sensation. Affer felt nothing at all. There were no voices, no feelings, no fear, no pain, no confusion. Only the peace of oblivion.

His body drifted gently amid the waters of the lake.

Chapter Thirteen

Dark Fall – Day Seven

'It's getting lighter.' Quest peered through a chink in the shutters of Sarai's room, which faced north. 'But the mist's back.'

Ninian frowned. 'Thick?'

'Not yet.'

Sarai lay deeply asleep, curled on her side with a thumb close to her mouth. Quest looked at her and sighed.

'I should go back to Wellwater.'

'Are you in a hurry, or have you time to talk?'

'Of course.' He did not seem eager to go.

'Come outside; I don't want to wake Sarai.'

He shrugged. 'As you like.'

In the hall, two young men lay asleep by the hearth, and Ninian hesitated. 'Shall we walk in the grounds?'

Quest nodded. 'It would be quieter.'

Arcady was beginning to stir. Work would soon begin on the morning meal and the day-labourers would be getting ready to go to Wellwater. A pile of wooden barrels lay in readiness by the side entrance to the hall.

'Where do you want to go?'

Ninian was looking east, only half listening. 'You know, I'd almost forgotten what a sunrise looked like.'

The air around the lake was very still; dawn had not yet come, but already the skies were lightening with the promise of day.

'The mist's beginning to settle again,' Quest observed. 'We might as well enjoy this while we can.'

'It's not coincidence, is it? That this fog should have come at the same time as everything else.'

Quest shrugged. 'I sometimes think this must be the beginning of the end of the world.'

'That's hard to believe this morning.' Ninian drew in a deep breath. 'The air smells cleaner.'

'What do you think really happened last night?'

'They say that in the old days lights shone over the Empire's

271

skies, protecting us.' It was not really an answer, but Quest nodded. 'Like a rainbow, after a storm,' she continued, not quite sure what she was trying to say. 'The Tearstone too, from here, as a part of it all. I wonder what it was like.'

Quest looked across to Sheer Island; fog clung to it in dense clumps. 'Do you believe it was true?'

'Can you hear anything?'

Quest listened. 'Only birdsong.'

'I've not heard that for days.' Ninian stiffened, then relaxed; for an instant she had felt someone was listening. 'Was what true?'

'About Arkata, your ancestor. The one for whom Arcady was named.'

Ninian turned away, twisting the ring new to her right hand. 'What about her?'

'You remember; there was something Bellene once said, about a gift, and a promise. She was supposed to have built the temple on Sheer Island and set the Tearstone in place.'

'I wonder how she knew; about the Tearstone, and what to do with it.'

Quest seemed not to notice her evasion. 'I felt the power last night, Ninian; if I believe in anything, I believe in that. The Imperial Lights mean something.'

Ninian fell silent for a time, then said: 'I felt it, too.'

'It drove away the fog in my mind as well as the mists out here.' Quest shook his head with self-contempt. 'How could I have been such a fool?'

'It makes me wonder if we have all been fools, the Emperor with the rest of us.'

'What do you mean?'

Ninian rounded on him. 'Doesn't it occur to you to wonder about the purpose of your Order? If your gods don't exist, or not in the way you used to believe, what are their intentions? Why does the Order have such authority through the Empire?'

'Because – ' But the words died on his lips. 'I don't know.'

'The first Lord Quorden visited the Barren Lands, and it was there his gods spoke to him. I won't and can't deny that there is something there,' Ninian said slowly, 'because it affected all five of us who've been there. I've thought since that it was as if we were all being tested, but for what I don't know.'

'I felt that, too.' Quest was thoughtful. 'What you're saying is that the Order may be based on a false premise, so that while it claims to speak for the gods who will save us from the present drought, it cannot do so.'

'More than that. Think of the light last night, and how we all reacted to it. What if the old ways were right, and the Order stands in direct contradiction to them.'

'Then its intent would be to destroy us, not to save us.'

She nodded. 'It may sound silly, but it makes an odd kind of sense to me. It makes me begin to question all the accepted truths and go back to the tales Bellene used to teach when we were small. What if all the myths were true, and the Order is wrong? What if Arkata did meet the goddess on the island and speak to her, and the temple and the Tearstone did serve a real purpose? And the Order had the old temples and lightstones destroyed precisely because they were powerful and a threat to them?'

'The lights could be nothing more than luminous stones, a natural phenomenon, and the goddess Kerait and her temples no more real than the Lords of Light.' He glanced at Ninian, but she did not look annoyed.

'Perhaps, but think back to the stories of the first drought.' She smiled. 'The silver serpent appeared to the men and women gathered round the last spring and offered them a bargain, that in return for their worship she would bring back the rains, and the lightstones which lit the old temples were a part of it all. If that was true, then the stones must have played a part in the fulfilment of that bargain.'

'How?'

'Perhaps the stones are the medium through which power passes, a sort of intermediary.'

Quest was interested. 'What sort of power?'

'What if the stones were specifically chosen for geographic location by colour? The Tearstone was blue-green, like the lakes. The desert stones were red, I think, the light we saw last night. What if they have something to do with the elements?'

'You mean some unknown creature or deity uses the stones to control the air, or the water, or the earth? But why, and how?'

'I don't know. Yet it might explain why the Imperial Lights were so important in the past.'

'But how did they fail? How have we survived so long since?' Quest objected, forcing down the part of him that would like to accept what Ninian was saying, not least because to do so would give him back a sense of meaning. 'Because they did, and long before the Order was formed.'

'Because the peoples forgot their bargain, believing it was only a story,' Ninian said instantly. 'And so they stopped going to the temples, as they had promised, and the rains began to fail. Not, as the priests claim, because we had been wrong all the time to worship the old gods, but because we didn't.'

'How does that make the old any better than the new?' Quest sounded and felt distinctly sceptical. 'They sound very little different.'

'Nonsense. In the old days there were no priests, no hierarchy and no set of divine rules demanding endless sacrifice and ritual,' Ninian argued. 'There were only the temples and the stones, and they were tied in somehow with the Emperor. Perhaps one thing you preached was true, that prayer is powerful. Perhaps it's important.'

'Do you remember the serpent on the hillside, on our pilgrimage?' Quest asked suddenly.

'How could I forget?'

'Someone, I think it was Ran, said then that perhaps it was trying to stop us going on, to the Barren Lands.' But the idea seemed too improbable, and Quest frowned. 'I'm not sure what I mean.'

'It was a silver serpent.' Ninian looked startled. 'Quest, that would mean that whatever we found there, or anyone else who went there, would have to be evil, wouldn't it? Or dangerous.'

'What did it do to Kerron?' The question shook him as he asked it, reminding him of other, earlier doubts. 'Ninian, what do you think it did to him?'

The mists were beginning to close in again as the sun rose, the fog struggling to shut out the light.

'Quest,' Ninian interrupted suddenly. 'Look at the lake.'

Visibility had deteriorated, softening the outline of the cliff as dense grey-white fog gathered at the centre of the lake and began to spread out over Avardale. Quest gazed out.

'What's happening?'

Ninian swallowed. 'I'm not sure.'

The lake had been still, but now, from somewhere in its depths, large air bubbles began to erupt on the surface; strong waves formed and made for the shore. There was no wind, no visible reason for the disturbance, but a sense of violence pervaded the scene.

'It's like an explosion under water,' Quest murmured. 'As if the lake was trying to rid itself of something.'

The turbulence was already dying down as the fog continued its steady advance. The waves calmed as they were subsumed by grey cloud, and the day darkened.

'I can see something solid floating out there.' Ninian's voice was not quite steady. 'I think it's a body.'

'Where?' Quest strained his eyes.

'Over there.' Ninian pointed. 'I want to go and see what it is.'

Quest followed her down the strand to the shore; the object of her interest bobbed up and down in rough water only a little way out.

'What is it?'

'I don't know.' Ninian slipped off her sandals and waded out.

'Don't go in – ' But Quest's protest died on his lips.

'Affer. . .'

Quest waded out to join her, careless of his heavy robe. 'How?'

The body lolled loosely in the water, drifting closer with every wave, as if the lake was returning him to his home. There was no expression on the white, drowned face, relaxed in death as it had so rarely been in life.

'Affer,' Ninian said again, in a whisper. 'Ran gave him into my care, and see how well I looked after him.'

Quest stooped to lift Affer's narrow body in his arms, the sodden weight unexpectedly heavy. A stone dropped from one of the pockets of the white tunic. 'He did this deliberately,' he said, in grim tones.

'How can I tell Ran?' Ninian looked stricken. 'How can I possibly tell her?'

'This isn't your fault.'

'Isn't it?' she asked shakily. 'How can you know that?'

Quest laid the limp body on the shore, remembering how Affer had seemed to be reading his mind as he knelt in Bellene's room. 'Perhaps Bellene's death was the reason.'

'He was very unhappy; I knew it.' Ninian's voice was unsteady. 'But there was always something else to do, someone who needed me more than he did.'

'Don't blame yourself, Ninian; that's the worst sort of arrogance.' Quest spoke gently. 'You must allow Affer control over his own life.'

'But how can I tell Ran?' she asked again.

'I will, when I return to Wellwater.' He had no more liking for the mission than she had, but he owed her that much at least.

'I – thank you.' Gratitude surged into her face. 'You don't know what it's like to have you offer to help.'

The stark admission surprised Quest. 'I was so busy worrying about the state of my soul, I forgot there were other problems to be dealt with,' he admitted, feeling guilty. 'You said that to me once, and it was true.'

'There've been times when you made me very angry.' She spoke in a low voice, and there were tears in her eyes.

'And I never said I was sorry for all the grief I caused you.' It appalled him that he had forgotten the disgraceful episode in the temple, until then. 'Especially my sermon. I don't know why I said what I did, but at least you can take comfort in that I'll never preach again.'

'But what will you do?' Ninian looked at him. 'You won't tell them at Wellwater how you feel? You know how dangerous it would be?'

'Do you really think me such a fool?' Quest was saddened by her lack of trust, but could not blame her. 'I can act the priest while I must.'

'For Kerron, at least.'

Their eyes met. Quest said abruptly, 'For Sarai, rather. I'll find a way out.'

'It may not matter.'

The grim reminder brought him back to full attention.' We will survive this, Ninian; I feel sure of it.'

'There's a boat drawing in, from Wellwater.'

Quest straightened. 'It might as well be now.'

'It's Kerron; he must have come for the Plainsman. He sends daily to see how the man is.' Ninian looked down at Affer. 'Quest, I can't let him take Carrol.'

'Is that his name? Why not?'

'He's a rebel; he told me some of their plans.' She did not elaborate, and he did not ask. 'We can't let Kerron take him,' she reiterated.

'How will you stop him?'

'Say he's still in a high fever. Back me?'

Quest hesitated, then nodded, making himself trust her judgment. 'As you like.'

Ninian sighed. 'Perhaps I'm wrong, and he's come to offer his respects to Bellene.'

'I don't believe it; Kerron detested her.'

There was the ghost of a smile in her eyes. 'True. I'm glad you're here, Quest.'

He was warmed by the admission, and by the new friendliness with which she turned to him; it appalled him that he should have found it so hard over the past ten years to think of her as the old Ninian. Looking at her, he found no hint of desire in himself, as if the absence of the prohibition which had vanished with his faith had lifted yet another layer of falsehood from his mind. He wanted only to help her, as a friend should.

They stood side by side, keeping watch over Affer's body as they waited for Kerron's approach.

'Is this an official visit?' Kerron remarked dryly, looking from Quest to Ninian. 'Or a family reunion?'

There was something different about him; Quest realised belatedly it was Kerron's soutane, which now had gold at the neck as well as the hem and cuffs. Once, he would have been desolate at being overlooked; now, it meant nothing to him. He felt nothing.

'My congratulations.'

Kerron bowed. 'Word of my appointment came soon after you left Wellwater.' His gaze went to Ninian. 'And mine to the new Steward.' He looked down at the strand, at Affer's sodden figure, brows tightening into a frown. 'What happened?'

Quest thought there was a hint of something that was almost regret in Kerron's posture.

'He drowned himself, after Bellene died.'

'I find it hard to believe him overwhelmed by sorrow at *her* passing. The old woman always despised him!'

'Did she?' Ninian asked flatly.

'You know how very hard he took everything,' Quest observed, thinking how cold an epitaph Kerron's words framed. 'He felt too much.'

'Poor Affer.' The new High Priest's expression was oddly bitter. 'It gives me pain to find him like this. When so many are dying of the plague, it seems unnecessary to lose another to despair.'

'Let me tell Ran.'

The moment he spoke, Quest became aware that he had made a mistake. Kerron's green eyes clouded over, growing dark and impenetrable.

'Your concern is touching.'

'Why are you here, Kerron?' Ninian interrupted.

'For the rebel Plainsman you're sheltering, to take him back to Wellwater.' His expression sharpened. 'You've put me off long enough.'

'He's in a high fever, and in no state for visitors.'

'Oh?' Kerron lifted elegant eyebrows. 'But I think I will see him, all the same.'

'Is this how you perceive your duty, to force your way into a house of mourning and bully the sick?' Ninian's voice expressed outrage. 'You were born and bred here, Kerron; have you no respect?'

'*Respect?*' His green eyes glittered. 'What is Arcady or Bellene to me? I grew up here grudgingly. Bellene called me an unwelcome cuckoo that she dared not, or could not, throw from the nest.'

'Do you think she was gentler with the rest of us?'

'Do I?' Kerron seemed to consider. 'Perhaps not. At what hour did the old woman die?'

'Just after the red light faded,' Ninian said, then bit her lip. Kerron's eyes narrowed in suspicion.

'What did you make of it?'

'Nothing,' she said quickly. 'We were told to expect another portent. Perhaps it brings hope in all our troubles.'

'No doubt you will tell us its meaning in due course,' Quest added smoothly.

'Perhaps.' Kerron eyed him. 'You seem different.'

'In what way?'

'Less naïve, perhaps.' The acuteness of the observation made Quest instantly uneasy. Kerron frowned. 'Why are you here, Quest?'

'I came to Arcady, as to all the estates, to offer what comfort I could, as you requested. This was my last visit.'

'True; I had forgotten.'

Kerron looked drawn, tense and uneasy; given he had now achieved the position he had sought for so long, Quest wondered what really motivated him. Insecurity? Ambition? But surely not belief; never that.

'Is there any news from outside, Kerron?' he asked.

'Ah, perhaps I should have told you first.' Kerron veiled his eyes. 'I'm afraid there will be no help for us; the rebels have rioted in the city of Ammon, and in Femillur too, and there is a fear that disorder will spread to other Imperial cities. I await commands for the guard; they say a contingent will be sent east. Our own difficulties must wait on the greater good.'

'Greater good?' Ninian sounded disbelieving. 'Kerron, unless we have help we may all die. This sickness has no cure, or none that I can find.'

'Perhaps you should try harder.'

Quest put a hand on Ninian's arm. 'That was not a just remark, Kerron,' he said quietly.

Kerron inclined his head to the shadowy outline of the pier. 'There's a boat waiting, and an escort. We need you at our services, Quest; your absence has been our loss.'

Quest bit back a refusal, wondering briefly what would happen if he declared his change of heart. But Kerron would not perceive it as a bar to priesthood, and it would only provide him with another weapon. Quest thought he had lied to himself for a dozen years or more; what difference did it make if he must act a part for a time?

'Are you coming with me?' he asked in neutral tones.

'I wish to speak to Ninian, in private,' Kerron added. 'Go on ahead.'

'Then again, I tender you my respects, Steward.' Quest bowed to Ninian. 'May Arcady prosper under your guidance.' There was nothing he could do to help her except to hold his tongue.

The full extent of his powerlessness swept over him as he made his way to the pier. All the authority he had believed himself to possess had come from the gods and his priesthood within the Order; without it, he was nothing, less than Kerron, who was now his superior with full control of life and death in the Westlands.

If he was not a priest, what was he?

'Just myself,' he said under his breath.

He looked back to where Ninian and Kerron stood in close conversation. It seemed to him that the mists had grown peculiarly dense about the shores of Arcady, enshrouding both figures in a grey world of their own. He would speak to Ran, immediately he arrived at Wellwater.

'Kerron – '

'I have a question for you; a bargain I want to make with you.'

Wary, Ninian waited for him to go on; the mists muted the sound of their voices.

'What is it you want?' she asked, as he did not continue.

'I want your secret.' Kerron turned to her and folded his arms inside the long sleeves of his robe. 'The secret of Arcady, that you and Bellene hid from me.'

'I don't understand.'

'I want the secret of Arcady. In return, you may have Ran, even the Plainsman, if you want him; I don't care what happens to either of them.' Kerron lowered his voice. 'But if you refuse me, I will send Ran east, to Ammon, to be questioned by the Inquisitors. I will take your daughter away from you and give her to Quest, even to the Order.'

'But there is no secret, or if there is, I don't know it!' Ninian bit back with panic and weariness. 'Perhaps Bellene knew something I don't, but, if so, she died without passing that knowledge on to me.'

'Do you really think me foolish enough to believe you?' There was no doubt in Kerron's cold voice. 'I give you this choice, Ninian; tell me the secret, or you will lose your child. I am not Quest, to be deterred by mere words; I am High Priest of the Wetlands, and the rule here is mine.'

'Why are you doing this?' There was a look to him she did not understand. 'Ran once saved your life, on pilgrimage. Don't you feel you owe her better than this? Don't let your pride stand in the way of what you ought to do.'

'I told you; I want your secret.' But she had hit a nerve; he looked away. 'I must have it.'

He was very pale. Ninian watched, unexpectedly sorry for him; for once he seemed vulnerable, easy to wound. 'Are you ill?'

'Ill?' he repeated blankly. 'Not in that sense, no. But I think I may be dying – '

At first, Ninian thought he broke off because he regretted what he was saying, but soon realised he was in real distress and struggling to hide it.

'Kerron? What is it?' She was increasingly alarmed. The muscles of his throat were working hard, but he was gasping, as if he found it hard to breathe. 'Kerron?' She put a hand on his bare arm, where the sleeve of his soutane had caught and folded back.

An intense and powerful shock spread all the way from her hand, up her arm and to her shoulder. Ninian tried to pull away, but for a moment she and Kerron seemed fused together, one flesh. The pain startled her; Kerron, too, recoiled.

A moment of empathy flared between them. Ninian tore her hand away, appalled at the rolling confusion she sensed in the priest's mind, at the forces of rage and resistance which struggled for control. Ninian thought if this was what Affer had heard all the time, she understood his desire for peace in death.

'Kerron,' she said softly. 'Let me help you.'

'You? What can you do?' But the words were bitter, not contemptuous. 'You're too late, Ninian. Give me what I ask for; give me the secret.'

'There is no secret.' Pity filled her. 'Believe me, Kerron, I would help you, if I could.'

'Perhaps you would.' He was breathing normally again, his cheeks flushed pale pink. 'If I thought – '

'What happened to you?'

He was a stranger again; her pity died.

'Do as I ask, Ninian. Think of Sarai, and tell me what I want to know.'

There was no longer any temptation, no moment of being torn between inclination and duty. She sensed that to give way would be the very worst betrayal of all, that if she did she would lose more than her daughter. 'There's no secret,' she repeated dully.

'Very well.'

He seemed to be considering his next course of action. Ninian waited, wondering what new trouble he saw fit to fling at her.

'I will give you time to bury your predecessor, and this one.' Kerron gestured to the shingle and Affer's cold, still body. 'Then I will come back, and I will ask you again.'

His forbearance was as surprising as it was welcome. Ninian

said nothing, wondering why he held his hand.

'It will make no difference, in the end. The dark is so close, it is almost here,' he whispered suddenly, and for an instant he was another man again. 'I can see it.'

A cold wind sprang up from the north, blowing gusts of thick fog to Arcady. A terrible and terrifying silence surrounded her, as if the whole world were gone and she was left alone in the mists with only Kerron for company, a Kerron who was not a man, neither Thelian nor *akhal*, but a thief, a stealer of souls.

'Kerron – ' She put out a hand, forgetting what had happened between them.

He stepped back. 'No! No, Ninian.'

He seemed to disappear into the mist, becoming one with the fog. There was no sunlight, only grey. She had not noticed quite how dark it had grown.

'I will come back, to hear your secret,' she heard him call as his shadow receded further and further away, adding to the illusion of insubstantiality.

She looked out at the lake to where Sheer Island should be, but it was invisible. She was surrounded by an uncanny silence; it was as if Avardale slept. Ninian felt utterly alone, weighed down by the responsibility Bellene had bequeathed her, by fear for Sarai, for Ran, and for Quest, too.

'The summons hasn't come,' she said aloud. 'Not yet. Give me courage, Arkata. Give me your courage, when the moment comes.'

She inhaled deep breaths of damp, noisome air.

Ran did not look up as Kerron entered her cell. Thanks to Quest she was at least prepared for what would come.

'I've news for you.' Kerron was watching her with an intensity which made her skin prickle.

'Have you?' Her voice was dead, flat.

'From Arcady.'

She sat on the pallet, the only seat available, eyes downcast. She did not think she could bear to look up. 'Have you?' she asked tonelessly.

'Are you ill, Ran?'

She had not expected the tone of concern and looked up to meet Kerron's gaze, surprising an unlikely compassion in his green eyes.

'Not ill, no, but very weary of these walls,' she said at last.

'Your face is dirty.'

She shrugged. 'Does it matter?'

'Perhaps.' He moved closer. He looked gaunt, almost as haunted as Affer.

'Tell me, if you would go free, Ran, what do you know of the secret of Arcady?'

She evinced puzzlement. 'Secret? What secret?'

'If I knew, would I ask you?' Some of his habitual acerbity returned to Kerron's voice. 'Something Bellene knew, and now Ninian knows. I hoped you did, too.'

She shook her head: 'Is that why you came to see me?'

'No.'

She sensed uncertainty in him, as if he hesitated in the task of informing her of her brother's death, and wondered why. There had been so many; what was one more?

'Ran – ' He broke off, then went on, 'Ran, Affer is dead. I saw his body myself this morning at Arcady. He drowned, and it seems it was by his own wish.' He paused. 'I didn't think it was easy for an *akhal* to drown.'

She was silent for a time, and he waited for her to speak. She thought he did regret the news he bore, but for her sake, not because Affer was dead.

'Anything is possible if you want it enough,' she said eventually. 'Poor Affer. He suffered so many torments.'

'You don't seem surprised.'

'Don't I?' Again, she blessed Ninian and Quest, who had allowed her to endure the first sharp agony of loss in privacy, without Kerron's observant eye upon her. Now, she tried not to believe it was true; it was the only way she could sustain the knowledge that Affer had left her. 'How would you know how I feel, Kerron? And why should you care?'

It was his turn to shrug. 'Perhaps for the sake of the past.'

'Is that why you came to tell me yourself?'

'I came because I grew up with Affer, and you, and Ninian, and I thought it right.'

'Then I thank you.' Ran fell silent once more.

'Do you blame me? After all, I had you brought here, leaving him behind.'

'Why did you put me in here?' Angry resentment flared at his question, for she did blame him. 'Why, Kerron? You know I'm no spy.'

'You betrayed me; you called me a liar. You said you wished I had never been born. What else could I do?'

'Are you saying I was wrong?' She could not keep the bitterness from her voice.

'It was all because of you, you know.' He spoke in conversational tones. 'All this. It came about because of you, because of what you said to me once.'

'What . . .?'

'Don't you remember, Ran? In the Barren Lands, when you slapped my face, and said Bellene should have left me on the lake.'

She could not bear to let him go on. 'I remember.'

'It was after that; after we separated. Nothing has ever been the same since.'

She frowned, not understanding him. 'It was just a quarrel,' she said impatiently.

He smiled, as he used to in the old days. 'You don't change, do you, except to be more yourself? Perhaps after all you're stronger than I am.'

'Oh, I changed, Kerron.' She did not want to recall the past, nor consider the present. 'What do you want?'

Kerron stiffened and stared down his nose at her, a trick which always annoyed her. 'I want you to make Ninian tell me Arcady's secret.'

'Why do you dislike her so much?'

'She reminded me that I owe you my life.' For a moment he softened, but the expression passed. 'I have a proposition for you.'

Wary, Ran looked away. 'What?'

'You want to be free. If you give me your word to do as I ask, I will let you go.'

'My word to do what?'

'To give me the secret of Arcady.' She said nothing. He went on, speaking with rare passion: 'You never lied to me. If you asked her, Ninian would tell you. Swear to let me know this secret, and you may go free.'

It seemed to Ran there was desperation hiding behind his eyes, as if he was pleading with her. His thin face was taut with strain, and there were dark smudges of sleeplessness round his eyes. Remembered friendship stirred.

'Why do you want to know this secret, if it exists?' she asked, forgetting for a moment that this was not the old Kerron. 'You seem worried. What's the matter?'

'Worried?' There was sweat on his brow, though the day was cool. 'I must know this secret or have no peace. Do you know what it's like to be torn in two every moment? To have even your own thoughts turned against you?'

'You're ill, Kerron.' His body was trembling.

'Ill? I'm not ill, not unless you believe illness is someone else living in your skin, controlling your body and your mind.' But he was speaking feverishly, to himself rather than to her. *'My right hand doesn't know what it does, nor the left –'* he whispered, the fingers of his right hand moving to touch what Ran saw was a scar on his left wrist. *'The secret will bring silence.'*

'Silence?' Ran echoed, and it came to her suddenly that he was suffering from some trial he had brought with him from the Barren Lands, that he, like the rest of them, had not emerged from the place unscathed.

'Affer suffered, after we came home,' she said obliquely, but she saw he understood her. 'He could hear other people's thoughts, and it was driving him mad.'

'Did he?'

Ran thought she could detect in the slyness of his expression a similar desperation lurking behind Kerron's eyes. 'He heard things he didn't want to know about other people, all the angry thoughts, the dislike, the daily annoyances,' she went on. 'He couldn't shut it off, or them out. You know what he was like, how much it would hurt him.'

'Then he's lucky, isn't he? He's dead!' Bitterness engulfed Kerron's features. 'No one can make any more demands on him.'

'You're stronger than he was, Kerron; can't you fight back where Affer failed?' Ran could almost feel his despair; but he did not reply to her question, instead abruptly recovering his earlier composure.

'Well? What have you to say to my proposition?'

'But I don't know if there is a secret, and if there is, it belongs to Arcady,' Ran said wearily. 'Not to you. What good can it do you?'

'Yes or no?'

Ran sighed, remembering, with a tightness in her throat, what Affer had asked her before they reached Lake Ismon, about the Guardian of Avardale. That was the knowledge Kerron sought; she was certain of it. The walls of her prison closed around her. 'Then it must be no.'

Kerron nodded, as if he had expected her refusal. Again, she was struck by the torment in his expression. 'I'll ask again,' he muttered. 'If Ninian won't tell me, I'll ask again. I told her I'd take Sarai –'

He could not threaten Affer. Affer was dead. Ran gasped, 'No!' as the pain of her loss struck home. 'Let me go, Kerron,' she asked in despair. 'Let me go, leave us alone.'

'I can't.'

She thought at first she had misheard him. Ran stared, uncertain.

'Can't?' she repeated.

Suddenly, his face was the colour of the fog outside, a dark and sickly grey. 'Agree, and you will be free. Refuse, and you die a prisoner.'

When she did not respond, Kerron turned and knocked on the cell door; it was opened for him, then slammed to. Ran caught a glimpse of Elthis' red hair through the bars.

She slumped back on the pallet, weary and confused. She could not mourn her brother. He had gone to meet his death with open arms of welcome, and she was not surprised; his life had been a misery since the gift first came upon him. Now he was at peace, and she would try to be glad for his sake, not selfishly unhappy for her own. His death was no one's fault, not even her own; she had an inner conviction that Affer's life had been measured in mere moments from the time he had set foot in the Barren Lands.

'And Kerron's too, perhaps,' she said aloud.

What was Arcady's secret, the *Guardian*? Ran frowned, for a moment angry at her exclusion from whatever knowledge Bellene had passed on to Ninian, but the impulse faded.

'Poor Ninian,' she murmured. 'I wish I could help you.'

She wanted to shout a protest at the futility of it all. What did ambition matter, what was the purpose of vengeance, or hatred, or even love? The plague from Ismon, the miasma which filled the air and the waters of the lake with disease and decay, had brought death. Now the reality was only the fog, darkness and death, and no Lords of Light, nor any other divinity, to save them. Nothing could save them.

Memory stirred again.

Arcady had a secret.

Ran looked up at the bars of her cell, thinking about Ninian, and about Arcady, and the old legends of the *akhal*.

Something about *Arkata's legacy*. She had heard those words spoken once, in connection with a light, and the island, and a bargain.

'Don't let me die here,' she said aloud. It was not an appeal so much as a desire for justice, for a reason for living. 'I would do anything, anything, if it will make amends.' She was not sure why she felt the need to atone, or for what, save being herself. '*I will be free!*'

She cried out in passion, half-shouting, then buried her face in her hands. Her skin was hot, her eyes dry. She was consumed by a sudden terror of abandonment and an agony of loss, unfamiliar fears she did not understand.

Affer had loved her. He had loved her, worthy or unworthy, kind or cruel, thoughtful or thoughtless. No one else would ever feel the same way, no one else could ever feel the same way about her.

Ran wrapped her arms around her body, forcing her misery back and down, refusing it release.

Chapter Fourteen

Dark Fall – Day Fourteen

1

'We had our orders at first light, if you can call it that. We move out for Ammon tonight, when the fog lifts, all those who can be spared; say half a company.'

'Are you supposed to be taking me with you?'

Elthis shook his head at Ran, red hair bright. 'No; there's been trouble in the city. They say rebels have seized most of the levels, keeping the priests and guard prisoner on the uppermost; but they've the granary there, and water, and can hold out. We're the relief.'

Quest frowned. 'What do the rebels hope to achieve?'

'We heard they made demands to Lord Quorden himself, wanting the old Administrators back to run the cities in place of priests; and they want the Emperor to take back his rule. Someone told me Amestatis himself is rumoured to be behind these moves.' The guard brought himself up. 'But I'll not leave you here to rot,' he added to Ran. 'Even if the Reverence here hadn't asked for my help.'

The fog had settled in once more, and the day was dark. The air around and in Ran's prison cell felt heavy; Quest wondered if he was only imagining that he found it harder to breathe. He picked up a piece of bread from the tray of food Elthis had brought for Ran's supper and crumbled it between his fingers.

'Are you sure it's safe to talk here?' he asked, keeping his voice low.

Elthis paused, then said bluntly: 'As safe as anywhere tonight.'

'How and when are you going to let me go?' Ran asked. Quest thought he had never seen her so dispirited. Her hair and face were dirty, her clothes torn and dusty, and there was a weariness in her expression which spoke of despair.

Elthis scowled, thinking. 'If we leave the key in the lock,

Reverence, will you turn it? Then I'll not be breaking faith with the guard; it could just be carelessness.'

'If that's the way you want it.' Quest was satisfied. 'Soon, I think. Before your company moves out.'

A nod. 'But you'd better not be caught. The new High Priest's not a forgiving man.'

Quest was suddenly curious for a view less personal than his own. 'What do you think of him?'

'As an administrator, he's fair; a bit heavy-handed, but knows what he's doing. Supplies are always plentiful. But lately?' Elthis shrugged. 'Ever since the weed appeared I've thought he was going mad; he'd not let us clear it away, you know. And once he took me and Columb out to the island and made us swim down to see if we could find the source of the evening lights.'

'What did you find?'

Elthis shivered. 'Nothing. I'd not go down there again, Reverence. Never. There's something down there that didn't like me paying it a visit. He wasn't a good enough swimmer himself; "*half a fish*" they call us here in the barracks, me and Columb.'

'You'd better go. Even in this fog it's foolish to take more risks than we must. My thanks.'

Elthis managed a smile; his thought processes were not precisely rapid, but straightforward good nature shone out from eyes as blue as Affer's had been.

'Take care, Reverence, and you, mistress. Get out as soon as you can, and hide yourself in this fog. It shouldn't be hard to get past the compound gate; there's only one man on duty, and he's paying precious little heed tonight, with us getting ready to leave.'

Ran pushed a hand through her tangled hair. 'I'll never forget this.'

'They can't send you to the Inquisitors in Ammon, not now, at any rate; but there're other cities, and they're not all up in arms.' Elthis gave the closed door a nervous glance. 'I'll be off now; I've to pack up. Good luck to you.'

'There's the bell for the ritual. It must be close to twilight.' Quest frowned. 'I should be there; Kerron notices these things.'

'But you can't!' Ran pulled at his sleeve in panic. 'Not before you let me out.'

He gave her a wry smile. 'I've no objections to missing a service; I'll stay.' In the eight days since his return to Wellwater Quest had struggled to disguise his new-found loathing for the rituals which had once been his reason for existing. He had even, at Kerron's request, preached on three occasions, despising himself for the hypocrisy. 'I shall have to go to late

288

service tonight; Kerron's officiating.'

'How does he seem to you?'

'It's hard to say. Why?' He looked questioningly at Ran. 'He's been to see you, hasn't he? He comes most days?'

She nodded. 'I don't understand him any more.'

'I'm going.' Elthis sounded anxious as he pushed cautiously at the door of the cell. Moving quickly, he stepped outside into the fog and disappeared almost at once. How the men were to march to Ammon in such conditions Quest could not imagine.

'There are drums again,' Ran observed.

Quest had learned of his sister's death, along with countless other losses around the lake, by the same means. They both listened, dreading what might come. Among the guard, too, the rate of attrition had been high, and two acolytes and Priest Manfred had also died.

'It's Arcady, Quest,' Ran said softly. 'Listen.' She put a hand to her mouth. 'Children – '

'Not Sarai!' Quest closed his eyes, taking in a deep breath. 'Not Sarai,' he repeated.

They waited in silence. Drums ceased, and there came the moment of stillness that heralded the coming of dusk, although there was no noticeable change in the quality of the light.

'It's always dark now,' Ran said, with a catch in her voice. 'Quest, is it time yet?'

He moved across to the door. 'Elthis left the key, as he said he would. All right; it might as well be now. Where will you go?'

'Arcady first, to Ninian. After that?' She shrugged. 'It depends what she wants.'

Surprised, Quest realised that Ran seemed to share some of his own new humility, a characteristic he had never thought to find in her. His sympathy increased. 'Kerron will send men after you.'

'I'll not be found.' The old certainty came back to her voice. 'Don't worry; I won't add to Ninian's difficulties.'

'Wait here, then.'

He stepped outside, for a moment disorientated by the fog. There came sounds of distant commotion from the barracks, loud voices and shouts. Overhead, Quest could make out the darker shape of the sun as, heavy and leaden, it fell rather than sank to the horizon. The lake lay directly ahead, beyond the guard post; he could smell it, a rank, powerful aroma.

'Head for the lake, then along the shore; otherwise you might lose your way,' he called back softly into the cell.

He hesitated, wondering if he should go with her. Uncertainty assaulted him. What of Sarai? Nothing in his nature prepared him for subterfuge, the need for skulking in the dark.

Ran made the decision for him. Slipping out of the cell, she stood beside him for a moment, breathing deeply. She looked instantly more relaxed, and he realised just how hard confinement had weighed on her.

'I'm going now, Quest.'

She bent low and glided away into the fog, moving swiftly and silently, like any wild creature, and Quest thought that at least he had accomplished one small thing. It was not a great deal, but better than almost anything else in his life thus far.

'Good fortune go with you, Ran,' he said under his breath as he shut the cell door; he left the key so it would appear, as Elthis wanted, a simple oversight. Moving away, he turned back, thinking he still saw Ran's tall figure in the distance.

A solid shape cannoned into him, knocking him flat on his back. He lay on the ground, winded, unsure what had happened.

'Who're you?'

Quest looked up, dizzy and confused. A guardsman stood over him, large and heavy, with a captain's colours on his sleeve.

'I said, who're you, and what are you doing here? This is the woman's cell.'

Quest was about to reply when a foot landed on his stomach. He gasped.

His aggressor's voice came again, hard and suspicious. 'Stay there!'

'If you look carefully, you'll see I am a priest.' He might, after all, be supposed to possess some authority. 'I came to visit the prisoner.'

'Get up. Show me your face.'

A hand came down and grasped the thick stuff of the soutane, lifting him forcibly to his feet. A dark, heavy Thelian face came down to his, and he smelled ale-laden breath.

'I know you.' The hand that held his robe tightened, but the voice grew faintly more respectful. 'Why's the door open?'

Quest realised he had not shut the cell door properly; unlocked, it had a tendency to drift outwards. He did not know what to say. A boneless lethargy seized him, disappointment threatening to crush him.

'Where's the woman?'

'I don't know.' He could only hope Ran still had a chance to get away. 'I found the door like this.'

'Did you, indeed?' The huge guard shook him, lifting Quest off his feet. It was evident he had no respect for the soutane, and enough intelligence to recognise a lie when he heard it. 'I think

I'll just put you in this hole, little mouse. The High Priest shall hear of this; they say he's an interest in the prisoner.'

Before he could protest, Quest found himself propelled unceremoniously into the cell; the door slammed shut.

'Well, well; the key's in the lock. Someone's been very careless!'

Quest heard the key turn, and moved to bang on the door. 'This is an outrage – ' he began; but the guard had already gone. He stood back, stunned. It had all happened so quickly.

'Let it not be for nothing,' he said aloud. 'Let Ran get away.'

The guard had not respected his priesthood, but why should he? He, Quest, had used the Order's ugly concept of divinity to promote his own authority, and for what? As compensation for inadequacy? Fear of dying and of being nothing at all?

Quest stood by the door, grasping the bars with long, cold fingers, seeing the flaws in his own nature with icy and unforgiving clarity. He recalled the things he had said and done to his child, to Ninian, and the recollections threatened to overwhelm him.

But that was to betray them once more. The only possible reparation lay in action, not in guilt; but shut in a prison cell he could not act.

The fog seemed to close in on him. Across the lake another drum began to sound, this time from Kandria, and Quest closed his ears to more news of death, sick at heart. There seemed so little time left for his people, yet disaster had come about in a matter of mere days. How long was it? He thought back, and found it was only fourteen days since Ran and Affer had come down from Ismon with the flotilla, eight since he had knelt in Bellene's room and lost his faith.

The darkness of the fog had entered the souls of the *akhal*. It extinguished all light, blotting out all hope.

Were the plague, the weed, the fog mere accidents of nature? Quest wanted to believe they were, that there was no designing hand involved in this genocide. Nor could he find any reason for the murder of his people. The *akhal* kept to themselves, troubling no one. Who or what could consider their extinction preferable to their continued existence, feeding on their deaths?

He shook his head wearily, wondering if Ran had managed to get out of the compound. Quest clung to the bars, listening for sounds to warn him that she had failed in her attempted flight; but no raised voices reached him, no outcry. He waited, and after a long time there was still nothing. Yet he stayed by the bars, looking out, watching and waiting, not knowing for what it was he waited and watched.

At last, far out on the lake, his attention was caught by a gleam of light, shining out through the clouds of grey fog. It was a bluish-green light, beautiful and sharp, strangely cheering.

When night fell with its blanket of dark, he could still see the light. It glowed, a pin-point of bright colour in the middle of obscurity.

Ran crept close to the ground as she made for the lake, sure of the way even if she could not see it. She was close to the guard post at the compound gate; once past, she would feel truly free.

She stayed low. Her heart hammered as she moved cautiously forwards, aware of the dangers as well as the benefits of the fog. She might not be easily visible, but nor were any potential captors. And she had to hurry; when it grew dark, ironically, she would be more easily seen, for the mist lifted at night.

She could make out a pair of leather-encased legs coming towards her. Ran froze in a crouch, hardly daring to breathe as the legs stopped, mere paces distant.

'Are you heading out tonight, then?' came a deep voice to her left. Ran started; she had not known there was anyone else near.

'Thank the gods, yes. You?' The lighter tones belonged to the legs.

'No.' The deep voice was suffused with gloom. 'I've to stay.'

'Rather you than me. This is a gods-forsaken, disease-ridden swamp.'

'Tell me about it!'

Ran held her breath, realising she must be nearer the guard post than she had thought. The fog was thicker than ever; she breathed in through her mouth, wanting to cough.

'If I never see this place again, it'll be too soon.' Legs again. Ran wondered if he was planted there for the duration, but his last sally had apparently exhausted the conversational possibilities between the pair. The legs moved away to her right, barely missing her. Ran got to her knees and began to crawl forward.

She did not feel safe until she reached the lake, after a long and agonisingly slow creep down the hill and over shingle. At one point, drums blotted out all other sounds, the announcement of deaths from Kandria adding to the urgency of her escape.

By the shore, the water was weed-clogged and smelled foul. Ran hesitated. It made sense to walk around the lake, hidden by fog, until she reached either the boats of Wellwater or carried on to Arcady. It would take longer to walk, but it should be safe,

292

unless she was unlucky, safer in any case than trying to take a boat. The fog was so dense she would need the lake as her guide; by the time night fell, which would be soon, she should be beyond the house at Wellwater, free.

Yet Ran hesitated.

Far out in the mists a light caught her attention. In the midst of darkness it was unexpected, a beacon drawing her gaze.

Common sense told her to be cautious, to take the way along the shore to Arcady. She was wasting time.

But still she hesitated.

Out on the lake, there was a light where no light should be; a blue-green light, probably on Sheer Island. It pierced the fog, lifting her spirits after days of darkness. There was something else, too, a pulse that beat in her mind.

Ran glanced down at the weed-clogged water; the rank smell was more concentrated at the lake's edge. A shiver ran through her. This was no water for swimming, this filthy, despoiled lake, which was no longer Avardale.

Ran hesitated.

Affer had swum in it; he had chosen to drown himself in the lake. He would not have been afraid at the end, she thought. For once he had led where so often – in fact, all his life – he had followed. Was she a greater coward than he? Could she not, just this once, dare to follow where Affer led?

Ran closed her eyes and shook off her sandals, then stepped into the water. It felt disgusting, slimy and unclean. She gave a shudder of revulsion, hesitating once more, then took a step forward, then another, and another, until she was up to her knees in weed and water.

Far out she still saw the light.

The water was cold after days of darkness. Ran went further in, making herself think of Kerron, and his fury when he discovered her gone. She tried to think about other things and kept her gaze on the light in the distance. It seemed very far away.

She might have been the only living thing in or about the lake. She was surrounded by fog, dense grey mist clinging to the water's surface; it revolted her. She looked at the light. It still shone, drawing her on, as the pulse in her mind beat a steady rhythm.

A strand of weed caught and clung to her legs; briefly, Ran imagined it to be a tendril of some mythical creature, struggling to pull her down, to drown her as Affer had drowned in some form of nightmarish retribution. But she had not come to the lake to drown; she had come because of the light.

She pulled free, and the terror passed.

Ran swam on.

The day had rushed towards its end at dizzying speed, as if time itself could not endure longer.

'Sarai, please drink this.' Ninian put the cup to her daughter's mouth. 'Come along now.'

'Let me alone.'

Sarai's lips remained firmly closed, her expression stubborn. Her cheeks were flushed and Ninian tried again, fighting her dread, keeping her fear from her face.

'Just one mouthful. It'll help you sleep better, and you'll wake up feeling well again.'

The amber eyes that met her own were hard with disbelief. Sarai dared her to make the promise, knowing it false. 'It tastes revolting, and it doesn't do any good.'

'Sometimes it does.' Ninian's throat closed, knowing Sarai was right. There was no effective remedy for the fever. Some lived and some died, their fates dealt by an entirely arbitrary hand.

'Did you make Jan and Bissa drink some?' Sarai named her friends fretfully; only the previous day she had helped to nurse them.

'Of course.' The enormity of the lie brought a stab of pain; Ninian thought of the two small bodies which now lay stiff and still. Her fear doubled, trebled, at the sight of her own daughter, ill with the same fever.

Sarai swallowed the dose, accepting the lie for truth. Ninian wondered if she would ever be forgiven for the deception, then realised she did not care, if only Sarai would survive to be angry.

'I can't breathe.' Sarai turned restlessly on her pillow.

'I've left the brazier steaming, and Amori's going to stay with you until I can come back.' Ninian watched, seeing her daughter's eyes slowly cloud over as the sleeping draught took effect. She bent and kissed the hot face, aware, with a sudden stab of agony, that she might quite easily never speak to Sarai again.

'Do what you have to, Ninian,' Amori said softly as she took her place. She had aged a dozen years in appearance since the night Bellene died; her eyes were battle-weary, but she was strong. Ninian thought she could not have managed at all without Amori. 'You did the right thing just now.'

'Did I?' Ninian shivered.

'What is it? Don't you feel well?'

'Just tiredness.' Another lie. Ninian knew she had a touch of the plague herself, but it might as well be fear of what lay ahead that made her feel so cold. She, who had taken life so directly, was now afraid of many things; she had learned that there were boundless degrees of fear. 'Thank you for staying, Amori. I'll be back as soon as I can.'

'Have a rest. Gods know you need it.'

Ninian hesitated, wishing to share her burden, to tell Amori where she was going and why; but what was the use? If she failed, it would no longer matter.

The call was there, in her mind, in her ears, but no one else could hear it. It was a summons for the Steward of Arcady, for the Guardian of the lake alone.

'Thank you,' she said. With a last look at Sarai, she left the room.

As she climbed the stairs to Bellene's tower, now hers, the call seemed louder, a shout rather than a cry.

'A voice that she alone could hear,
That summoned her –'

Arkata's legacy, carried with her ring, with her blood. Ninian shivered again, feeling the fever burn in her head.

Her lamp held some of the last of their precious stores of fish oil. It appalled her how rapidly their carefully hoarded supplies had been exhausted, and she thought bitter thoughts about Kerron and Wellwater, of the existence of four hundred guardsmen, who must be fed and watered and warmed with Arcady's stores.

The only thing Kerron had not taken from her was the secret, the secret of Arcady. It puzzled her that he had accepted so long a delay, but tomorrow he had told her he would take it, or Sarai; now, the threat was irrelevant.

The summons was loud in her ears.

She put the lamp down on the table. Night had fallen, and an easterly breeze had blown the mists out of the tower room. The eccentric collection of decorations on the walls flickered in the lamplight as the flame blew about in the wind. Ninian moved across to the northern window and looked out.

There was a light out on the lake.

'Blue-green,' she said in a whisper. 'As the Tearstone must have been.'

There was an unusual quality to the light, which grew brighter as she watched, gaining in size and intensity.

'We brought a stone,
Blue matched with green
A star in the dark,
As had long been foretold
By the serpent god –'

She spoke the words of the song aloud, the old song of the *akhal*, a link between herself and her forebears, between herself and Arkata, her ancestress. It was true; it must all be true, not legend.

> *'Below the cliff,*
> *On the island,*
> *We set up her temple.*
> *A lady's form, her hand*
> *Holds a stone of light,*
> *A second stone,*
> *Blue and green, shining*
> *Witness to our people.*
> *The empty night,*
> *Filled up with colour,*
> *Imperial Lights.'*

'A second stone,' Ninian repeated. 'I wonder?'

The call came again, a cry of loneliness and sorrow. It filled her skull and her mind with its pain.

The wind freshened abruptly, and the lamp flame blazed, lighting up the fish skull, the coloured barb, the bone hunting horn on the walls. Ninian reached out a hand to the horn, then drew back.

It was very ordinary to look at, a yellowed, stubby horn the length of her hand, with a thick piece of leather, surprisingly long, attached to a hole at the narrow end. Arkata's horn. Whatever creature of the lake had once owned it was long dead. Ninian took the horn from its hook.

A powerful gust of wind filled the room, rushing through the windows and extinguishing the lamp, leaving her in the dark. Ninian clutched the horn in her hands, cold against her skin, feeling as if the wind was urging her into motion. It seemed there was going to be a storm, a rare occurrence.

'On a summer's night, when the wind was high,
And the lake was wild and the storm full force –'

'No; oh no,' she whispered, putting a hand to her mouth. On such a night had Arkata heard and answered the first call. Where had she found the courage? Ninian stood in the tower, clutching the horn, trying to force herself to move.

A roll of thunder broke her trance; the noise, so unfamiliar and so close overhead, made her jump.

The wind gusted more strongly still as she left the tower for the pier. Ninian put her head down and pushed against the force of the gale, right hand clutching the horn. Waves had broken out on the lake, stirring the dead waters into uneasy, angry motion.

Far out across the water, the light still shone.

'Reverence, most of the troops have gone; I've no one left to send in search of the woman. The rest of my men are sick.' The captain, a large, solid Thelian with a broad, ugly face and an anxious expression, frowned. 'And there's a storm coming up.'

'You should have found her long before the troops left for Ammon,' Kerron said coldly. He sat in state in the Great Hall of Wellwater, his tall, high-backed chair centred at the long table, but he was alone, except for the captain. 'Did you question the priest? He must know when she escaped, and where she was heading. Find some men and take them to Arcady. She must have gone there.'

'I'll try, Reverence.'

'You will not *try*! You will find her.' Kerron's tongue lashed the older man. The captain bowed as he retreated.

'Yes, Reverence.'

He was alone again.

A candle in a wooden holder stood to either side of his place; oil lamps glowed along the back wall. Kerron sat stiffly upright, arms resting lightly along the wooden arms of the chair as he listened to the wind rising outside, battering against the shutters.

He thought about Ran, out in the storm, unsure of his feelings. Was he glad she had broken free? It seemed more fitting than keeping her in a cage for his own pride. But that it should be Quest who had helped her –

'*But she refused to discover the secret for you,*' the voice whispered insistently. '*She deserved her fate. She betrayed you.*'

'But she saved my life once,' Kerron murmured, trying to fight back, but feeling appallingly weary. 'She was the only person who would have risked herself for me, and without a second thought.'

'*She was without fear; she would have done the same for anyone, not only you,*' sneered his opponent. In his rational moments, that was how Kerron now thought of the voice. '*Why should you think she cared for you? Are you not content with solitude?*'

'Because she did. Because she wouldn't have been so angry if she hadn't thought better of me, hoped for better things.'

The voice was briefly silenced.

If she had fled for safety to Arcady, then she had played into his hands; he could use her to obtain the secret from Ninian. It would be his in the morning.

'Fool! You are too late for that! Look outside. Look and see. The time has come.'

Kerron did not resist the pressure to rise from his seat, to walk across the deserted hall to the shutters which opened out onto the lake. He undid them, letting them swing back, crashing against him with spiteful violence, until he managed to fasten them.

He looked out.

There was a light shining out on the lake. The mists were lifting, and he could see across quite clearly to the shape of the cliff on Sheer Island, close to where the light shone with a curious, not quite real glow.

A second roll of thunder crashed down on him, and the wind tore at his robes; the light did not move. The elements had no effect on it. A small, hidden part of Kerron warmed to the light.

'The woman has gone to the island with the secret. You are too late, too late.'

The menace in the mental tone was chill; Kerron could not suppress a convulsive shudder. His chest was tight, as if he had forgotten to breathe, and he had the sense of something building out in the night, some force which would rise and crush him.

'Why did you delay?'

'Delay?' As he repeated the word, Kerron glanced again at the light out on the lake, then regretted it as his throat tightened, involuntarily, as if squeezed by a powerful hand. 'Did I?' he forced out. 'But Ninian would say nothing, and Ran refused to help me!'

'Such stupidity. Were you not taught that anyone can be forced, if the right weapon is found? You have acted as a sentimental weakling, as if the lives of these akhal *had a value, when it is their destruction and the coming of the dark which are the only matters which should concern you.'*

'The lake is dead, and its people dying. Isn't that enough for you?' The hand at his throat had temporarily relaxed its grip; Kerron realised, with horror, that it was his own. 'Why are you so concerned with death?'

'Death is life to the dark. Why should the akhal *live if their lakes are dead? What value have they in themselves? They claim to be a part of the cycle around the lake; let them be. Let them die as the waters are dying, and bring life to the dark.'*

Kerron had once imagined only such a disaster would satisfy his undirected need for vengeance, but the wind seemed to clear his head. He could not remember exactly why he should hate the *akhal*. The thought brought with it a sensation of extraordinary peace, as if for the first time in his life Kerron believed he could let

298

matters pursue their course without him either resenting them or trying to change them.

'No,' he said softly, his words blown away by the wind. 'No. A whole race to die because of me? Because I resent what I was born, and how, because I fear loneliness?' The idea was ludicrous, as if he had used a boulder to swat a fly. He seemed to be waking from a long sleep, his mind stretching beyond the narrow bounds within which he had chained it. 'You wanted me to destroy the lights because you said they were evil, but they are beautiful; and in the dark there is nothing to see.' His voice was incredulous. 'What are you, voice? My evil demon?'

'Perhaps. But you give yourself too much credit. Do you truly believe the death of the akhal *is your doing? You were only a means, not a cause, a willing weapon to our use.'*

The response was so unexpected that Kerron thought to look about, as if he might discover a physical form to which the voice was attached. He felt a separation inside himself, a tearing, as his mind struggled to divorce itself from the mind of the voice. The pain was acute, and Kerron gasped.

'You cannot be rid of me; I am more a part of you than you of me,' spoke the voice, vicious and hateful. *'Anger formed me; hate nourished me; darkness feeds me. You feed me.'*

'No.' But Kerron already sensed what would be the ending of what he had begun.

'Go on. Tear this weakness from within yourself and discard it, leaving behind only what is strong and certain. The sickness that takes the akhal *has passed you by,'* hissed the voice. *'The lights have gone out, and the shadows lengthen. Let in the dark!'*

'But you said it was too late, that Arcady's secret –'

'It may yet be defeated. The light is dying, it flickers and weakens.'

'You said it had gone out,' Kerron managed to say.

'You know nothing! There is more than one light in this Empire, more conflicts than one. Or did you think your petty soul the only battleground?'

Kerron gasped at a stab of pain in his head.

'What is happening?' he asked breathlessly. 'What goes on in the lake, and what goes on inside me, my mind, my body?'

'They are no longer yours to control!' Triumph rang in his mind. *'Begone! You have no more place here, for you are mine. Go, out into the darkness where you belong, and be dispersed in it. Go!'*

With a cry, Kerron fell to his knees. Agony tore at him. He felt as if he was being broken into tiny fragments of himself, that each bone and sinew was being torn apart; but they did not want to be sundered, and they dragged against the strain. He screamed, but the sound was lost in the wind.

Then the wind, too, rushed into his mind, and his existence was sent whirling into a pool of darkness from which no spark of light emerged, where he could not see and could not feel, and could only hear the shriek of victory which rang inside him, and he thought he would hear it for ever as he spun round and round in the emptiness of the pool.

'*You are cast out, out into the dark!*'

Yet even as the scream rang on, he saw a gleam of light in the far distance. He possessed no body, no physical self, yet Kerron began to try to swim towards the brightness, yearning towards it as if it alone could save him from an eternity of night.

It was not yet too late.

Ran pulled Ninian's canoe up the shingle.

There was very little mist on the island, an oasis of clarity in the night. Overhead, three stars burned brightly; Annoin, Arkata's Star; Pharus, the Imperial Star; and Omigon, the Dark Star.

The green-blue light shone inland and to the west, more like the memory of brightness than an ordinary light, the image printed on the eye after the lid comes down.

'I've been waiting. I thought you'd come.'

The wind was less strong on the island, the tall cliff serving as a break. A crash of thunder came from somewhere not far off, but no rain fell.

'How did you get here?' Ninian asked.

'I swam. Quest and one of the guards at Wellwater let me go; I saw the light, so I came.'

'Why here, and not Arcady?' Ran looked dreadful, soaked through, with her hair a matted mess. 'Ran, you shouldn't have swum in the water.'

'It doesn't matter.' Ran turned away wearily. 'I came because of the light, because I felt drawn to it.'

Ninian swayed, dizzily. 'There's so little time left, Ran; we're all dying at Arcady.'

Ran took one of Ninian's hands; her own were cool, but Ninian's burned. 'You're ill,' she said sharply.

'Not so ill that I can't do what I must.' Ninian turned her face to the high cliff inland, and her free hand fell to the horn tied with the leather strips round her waist. 'Make Arkata's dive.'

'Dive? What dive? Is this Arcady's secret?'

'How did you hear of it?'

'Kerron. He asked me if I knew anything about it, and I remembered something my mother once said.'

Ninian started as a flash of lightning lit the darkness. 'Bellene told me, not long ago, while you were travelling with Affer, that Arcady had a secret,' she said, glad Ran was there to tell. 'She said that the Steward of Arcady was also Steward to the true Guardian to Avardale, because we were the first colonists of the Wetlands, and because of Arkata's dive. She dived from the high cliff, here.' She pointed inland. 'This horn the Avar gave her in thanks for her gift,' and she touched it again, 'is our secret. In time of need, when the Avar calls the Steward of Arcady must answer. She must climb to the high place and dive into the depths, as Arkata did, and blow the horn.'

'Dive? From there?' Ran gave her an incredulous look. 'But Ninian, you're terrified of heights.'

'I don't have a choice, Ran. The lakes are polluted beyond life, and we are all dying. Tonight, I heard the Avar's call, and saw the light, and knew this was the last chance. Tomorrow Kerron said he would come, and I must tell him Arcady's secret or he would take Sarai away.'

'What if it's only a tale?' Ran demanded. 'Are you willing to kill yourself for nothing?'

'Not for nothing. And if it's true, then Arkata survived. Why shouldn't I?' Ninian shivered, unwilling to admit how the prospect of the dive terrified her. 'I have to do it.'

'This is a strange night.'

The wind, which had whipped the surface of the lake and the weed into urgent action, suddenly died away. Ninian became aware that the quality of the air had changed, leaving it warm and light.

'The mists have gone,' she said quietly. 'Look. Everything's so clear.'

'There are boats coming from Wellwater.'

West, as Ninian looked, she made out the shapes of three longboats heading for the island, dark and indistinct. Without the wind, she heard the sound of their oars as they dipped in and out of the water.

'They're coming fast,' she said, striving to sound calm. 'I had better begin my climb.' She managed a laugh. 'They're quite an incentive.'

'I'm coming with you.'

Ninian did not argue.

Moonlight lit their path. They walked rapidly over the brushy terrain to the flat space by the base of the cliff. Ninian was infinitely relieved not to be alone, the plain fact of Ran's presence enough to reduce the level of her fear. They walked to the site of the old temple, drawn by and to the light.

'What is it?' Ninian breathed. 'Is it real?'

'I don't know.' Ran moved closer, lifting a hand to try to touch the source of the light, but her fingers met only empty air. The light was intangible; it hung in the air above her head, a luminous half-globe of green-blue stone, not a true lightstone but only the memory of one.

'The story said Arkata gave the Guardian of the lake the other half of this stone,' Ninian said softly. '*"A second stone"*; that's what this was, the Tearstone.'

'But what is it we see?' Ran said, awestruck. 'And how can we see it, when I couldn't touch it?'

'I don't know, except that on such a night as this anything could happen. Isn't it glorious, Ran?' The warm glow calmed Ninian's fraught nerves. She thought she could see the wavy outline of the figure of a woman, hand outstretched to hold the light. 'Can you imagine what it must have been like in the old days, when the Tearstone was here, shining out over the lake?'

'One of the old Imperial Lights,' Ran said unexpectedly. 'I remember Bellene talking about them. And then it wouldn't have been dark.'

'We can't stay here.' Yet Ninian thought she would have liked to stay, looking at the light. 'Ran, where's the best place to climb the cliff? You know, because you did once, didn't you?'

'When Kerron dared me, yes.' For a moment, Ran was still, her face sad; then she shook herself. 'I'll lead. Will you be able to follow, watching where I put my hands and feet? It's not an easy climb.'

Her mouth was suddenly dry; Ninian nodded. 'If you don't go too fast.'

'You'll manage.' But Ran had no fear of heights, and could not understand those who had.

'Now, quickly,' Ninian managed to say, her words instantly drowned by an immense crash of thunder directly overhead. The green-blue light wavered and faded, but just as Ninian thought it would die, it recovered, although glowing with less than its earlier force, and she was afraid.

'Before the light goes out,' she heard Ran mutter.

'I think this is our last and only chance,' Ninian said aloud, and knew it for a statement of truth. 'Or the light will go out forever.'

The climb was a nightmare, and without Ran Ninian would never have made it. Her eyes and hands and fingers were far less adept than her cousin's at discovering necessary holds, and several times Ran had to lean down and pull her bodily up when she could not find the way.

'The boats are halfway to the island,' Ran called down, but Ninian, clinging desperately to the rock face, did not dare look out or down, giddy with fright and fear of falling.

'How much further?' she shouted.

'About a third more. You're doing well; don't worry,' Ran called back. She moved easily, apparently enjoying herself; Ninian could not help envying her physical confidence.

As she climbed higher, the wind blew up again, from the south this time, plastering her to the rock. No plants grew in the crevices, no signs of life except for the occasional empty bird's nest, or rock slimed by droppings. Moonlight came from her left, lighting her way.

'It's all right; you've made it.' Ran reached down and pulled her up the final length. 'Well done.'

'Thanks.' Ninian was winded and aching in every limb.

'The boats haven't reached the island yet,' Ran remarked, holding the rock with one careless hand and swinging out over the drop to see better. 'We've made good time.'

Another roll of thunder sounded, followed by a rare flash of lightning that temporarily blinded Ninian. She swayed, losing her footing, then felt her right wrist being seized and let herself go, trusting Ran. When she could see again she was half kneeling on a flat space some four paces wide, overlooking a vertiginous drop. Ran stood at the far edge, hands on hips, looking down as the wind pressed at her back.

'Ran –' Ninian protested, her heart leaping.

'I can see a light in the depths,' Ran called back. 'Look down there.'

'I'm sorry, I can't.' She could not move, paralysed by the fear that if she did she would instantly fall, down into the deeps. She found the degree of fear was worse than her imaginings. In the past, her experience suggested that action was far less frightening than the prospect of action, but it was no longer true.

'Ran!' she called desperately.

'What is it?' Ran moved away from the edge of the cliff to where Ninian knelt. Her expression was exultant, eyes glowing. 'Isn't it wonderful up here?'

'No.' Ninian could hardly get the word out.

'There isn't much time.' Ran looked out and past her, down the cliff face they had climbed. 'The light below is growing weaker.'

'And if it goes out, I shall be too late.' Silenced by her own future truth, Ninian felt deathly sick. Even with her eyes shut she could feel herself falling, falling from a great height, the world lurching around her.

An extraordinary weakness overcame her, and she put a hand to her head, then felt her pulse; it was racing from either fear or fever.

'Let me help you stand up; it's not as bad as you think.' Ran's strong hands came down to take her wrists. 'Truly, Ninian. Look out instead of down, and you won't mind the height.'

It was the hardest, most terrifying feat Ninian had ever accomplished. Her skin was clammy with sweat as she allowed Ran to pull her to her feet. She swayed, clutching desperately at her cousin for support.

'Gods, you're hot.' Ran frowned, but did not make the obvious comment. 'See, there's lots of room up here.'

Her voice failed to convince; Ninian knew they perceived their positions from perspectives so far apart they would never meet. She managed to open her eyes, but instead of staring ahead, her gaze fell instantly down, drawn to the giddy drop to the deep water, where she had a momentary glimpse of a flash of light.

'I don't know if I can,' she whispered. 'Not even for this.'

Ran turned her face away. 'It took more courage from you to climb up here than I ever possessed. Do you think I don't know that?'

'Give me a moment, and I'll manage.' Ninian swayed again, suddenly sure it was the fever and not her fear alone which weakened her resolve. 'I'm sorry; I feel so odd.'

'I heard the call, too; or felt it.' Ran stared out at the lake.

'If I fail, we all die.' Her legs would no longer hold her up, and she sank to her knees again. 'Just a moment.'

'Ninian, there's no more time. The light below is flickering. If we wait any longer it'll go out.' Ran paused. 'You said if it went out it would never be lit again. Let me go in your place, now. Your life is worth a hundred of mine.'

'You should have been Steward,' Ninian said feverishly, willing herself to feel stronger. 'Bellene chose your mother first, before me.'

'You know me better than that, and so did Bellene.' Ran shook her head. 'I'm not generous enough to be Steward; I would always put myself first. But this, this is something I can do, something for you and Affer and Arcady, something to make it all worthwhile. It would be the ultimate test, don't you see?'

Ninian looked into Ran's face, certain she was not speaking the whole truth.

'You're wrong about yourself, Ran,' she managed to say. 'Help me up.'

Ran gave her a crooked smile. 'You can't stand, so you think you might as well fall?' She reached down to Ninian's waist and untied the leather cord that held the horn. 'Don't fight me in this, Ninian,' she said, as Ninian struggled with her. 'Affer's dead, and no one else really needs me. Don't argue, but let me go; because there's no more time. The light is nearly out now.'

'Ran – ' Ninian spoke the name as a plea as Ran knotted the leather around her own waist, shrugging off her outer clothes and pulling her vest down to cover the horn for protection as she dived. She had her back to Ninian as she steadied herself, as confident as if she stood on solid ground and not on a narrow ledge several hundred feet up, where the wind threatened to blow her off at any moment.

'Ran – ' Ninian called again, despairingly. She could not move, her legs simply wouldn't support her.

Her cousin turned back to her, at the same time taking a step towards the far edge overlooking the deep water. 'Don't worry about me, Ninian. This is the only thing I can do to help you, so let me do it.' There was absolute determination on her face. 'Don't call me back. There's no more time.'

'*Ran!*' Ninian shouted. A new crack of thunder drowned her cry. In that instant, Ran turned to face the deeps, took a short run, then launched herself up and out, reaching back her head and stretching out her arms like wings as she began her plunge to the deeps and the light that flickered fathoms below.

A flash of lightning lit the sky. Ninian lay close enough to the edge to be able to look down at Ran's plummeting figure. A great ache grew in her chest, a pain greater than any she had ever known, and she would have liked to howl out her grief and despair to the wind and the thunder, at the wildness of the night and the dying of the light.

Down below, on the island, the bluish-green light flickered, but continued to burn.

2

Ran had never dived so far.

There was time to be aware of the force of the wind as she dived, to make the automatic corrections of her body so that she would enter the water straight, arms over her head.

For a very brief instant it felt like flight, and Ran thought it glorious. Beneath her, all was dark except for the reflection of the moon and the glimmer of lights far below the surface of the lake.

She kept her arms stiff and straight over her head, and hit the water in a perfect angle, going on and down. The water stung on entry and the pressure and rapidity of the first part of her descent forced air from her lungs. Ran could see nothing; it was too dark as her body sped downwards.

Pressure gathered as her speed slowed. She had no way of knowing how far down she had come. Ran started to swim, catching a glimpse of a green-blue light a long way below, a point to aim for.

There was pain as she swam, unlocalised but sharp. She had little air left in her lungs and her chest hurt from the pressure of the water.

She swam down and down. It was harder than she had expected as the water closed in around her, a tangible force struggling to repel her, back to the surface, to eject her from depths where she had no place. Her ears ached from the pressure, and her arms began to cramp; her lungs felt starved of air.

She reached the point where she knew she could go no further. With a final thrust of her arms, she fumbled one-handed for the horn, with no more breath or strength to keep herself under. She brought the horn to her lips and blew into it with all the will and strength and the little breath she had left.

She thought how odd it was that she should hear no sound, then wondered if there was any sound to hear; then there was no more breath in her. A piercing pain engulfed her chest and Ran inhaled water.

Affer.

Then there was only darkness.

Chapter Fifteen

Dark Fall – Night, Day Fourteen

Ninian pulled herself across the ledge to where Ran had dived and looked down with a wave of lurching sickness; it was so very far down.

The depths were dark; there was no sign remaining of Ran's entry, no ripples. Ninian swallowed, stricken with guilt and relief, feeling weak and useless. Her arms trembled as she sat up to feel the wind cool against her hot face.

Down below, the waters of the deeps began to boil.

At first she thought it only a fever-dream. Ninian sat, numb, watching as bubbles began to erupt from the deep water in a mass of white foam. Moonlight caught the pale colour, and soon it seemed to Ninian that the whole of the caldera was outlined in froth and bubbles.

From its centre rose a blue-green light very like the one that shone on the island, except that this was brighter, more brilliant, no memory but presence.

'Ran,' Ninian breathed. The name caught in her throat; she could see no sign of her cousin. Pain stabbed at Ninian, a sense of bitter loss, and she bit her lip. It should have been her life, not Ran's; the duty had been hers.

She continued to watch. The deeps boiled.

Water spouts erupted from the surface like hot springs. The whole lake seemed to shiver, as if waking from sleep. Ninian thought the cliff shook, too, and she slipped a little closer to the edge. She reached out to grasp the grass with both hands, terrified anew of falling.

The blue-green light rose to the surface of the water, and Ninian could now see it was not only one light but many, although most of the brightness came from a single point much larger than the rest. As the light came up towards air, so the sound of the eruptions in the water came up to Ninian in a roar, breaking the stillness of the night.

The tip of something bright shattered the surface of the lake.

Ninian forgot her fear, recoiling as a giant head broke the water. It was followed by a massive bulk of enormous length, balanced by a pair of immense wings to either side and what looked like long, thin threads, dappled by specks of light, which streamed out from the main body. A short pair of forelegs ending in jagged claws stopped the creature appearing serpentine, and as the hindquarters appeared Ninian saw its rear legs were long and powerful.

'The Avar,' she murmured. What was it? A water serpent? Some survivor from a past so ancient its physical appearance had been long forgotten? She stared at the awesome creature, suddenly thinking it was like the fish on her thumb ring.

Huge head raised, the eyes caught the moonlight in pupils which were as gold as the sun. With wings spread and filaments fanned out around its body, the beast was ablaze with colour as it exploded from the waters of the lake, head, body and wings alight with dazzling blue-green fire.

Ninian sat back, half-blinded, as the Avar's head rose up the blank face of the cliff, until it was on a level with her own. The head alone was twice her size, the jaw long and narrow, beak-shaped, opened to display an evil array of teeth. The eyes were the size of her head, fully gold in colour. A pair of short, oddly stumpy ears marked the broad brow, the creature's skin, or scales, or whatever, a dark green; but it was hard to be sure because at the centre of the brow glowed a circle of blue-green stone, the most brilliant stone Ninian had ever seen. Light shone from it, spreading across the lake like twilight.

'The Tearstone,' Ninian whispered aloud, then realised she was wrong, for that had been destroyed long before she was born. This, then, must be the first stone, its other half.

'The gift,' she said in sudden understanding. 'That must have been Arkata's gift.'

The creature flew skywards, but Ninian thought that as it passed her ledge the great head came down and golden eyes opened wide to peer suspiciously at her before moving on and up, higher into the night, the wide wings creating a powerful backdraught and a sound like the north wind. She caught a whiff of the beast's breath, which smelled of the lake before the weed had come, a cold, muddy, reedy scent.

The creature rose still higher. Ninian followed its progress with amazement. At what seemed to be its zenith, the beast raised its head and let out a dreadful cry, a howl of fury and triumph, of loneliness and sorrow. Ninian knew it; she had heard it before, in her mind. In response came a roll of thunder and a flash of lightning directly over the huge head.

'*Ran!*' A tear dropped onto Ninian's nose.

In the depths, the waters were calm again. Ninian swallowed her misery, getting to her feet with immense effort. She turned west to Wellwater, suddenly remembering the boats.

The three were some distance from the island, all overturned; she could see figures clinging to their sides. Evidently the eruptions from the deeps had caught them in their wake.

Below, on the main part of the island, to her surprise the light was still flickering and threatening to go out. Ninian frowned, new fear gnawing at the pit of her stomach. If the light went out, then it would go out forever; she had said it, and it was therefore true.

Something else made her stop breathing for a moment; there was a figure down by the shore, lying half in and half out of the water. Ninian did not hesitate. Fear and fever had hindered her ascent, but she was heedless of both as she climbed down the cliff, fingers and toes finding holds without conscious effort, impatient of any impediment.

Her feet were bare as she ran on down to the shore, where gentle waves rocked the body lying in the water. How it had got there, Ninian did not know, for there was no current, and Ran had dived into the deeps on the other side of the island. It was a night for miracles. Ninian took Ran under the arms, for she was lying on her back, and pulled her to land.

'Ran,' she asked softly. 'Ran, can you hear me?'

But Ran did not move, and Ninian breathed in sharply as moonlight showed her a pale, still face. In terror that she was dead, Ninian put her ear to her cousin's mouth, rewarded by the sound of a rasping breath. Blood trickled from Ran's nose, perhaps the result of pressure from her dive, but she did not seem aware of Ninian's presence. She lay with her eyes closed, her body cold and lax.

'This should have been me, not her,' Ninian whispered in anguish. 'It should have been me.'

She knelt and lifted Ran's head onto her lap. The horn was gone, lost in the deep water; the Stewards of Arcady had summoned the Guardian of the lake for the last time.

Ninian looked up at the creature hovering above the lake, defying gravity with sweeps of its powerful wings. Something must have happened, for it reached its head west, towards Wellwater. A lightning bolt flickered near the stone in its brow. The Avar folded its wings briefly in a wild dive as it descended with another of its terrible cries.

A single figure stood outlined on Wellwater's pier in the distance, a speck of dark against the light.

On the island, the light flickered dangerously, casting only a very faint glow. Ninian stroked the wet hair away from Ran's face and watched, stony-faced, wondering what would happen if, or when, the light went out.

Quest rattled the bars of the cell, shouting all the while for a guard.

'Get over here and let me out! Unlock this door, you fools! Can't you see what's happening?'

He was sweating, cursing himself. Where was Ran, and where was Ninian? He glanced up at the giant creature hovering in the brilliance of the skies, a galaxy of stars all unto itself.

'Get back from the door and I'll unlock it!'

To Quest's surprise, a thin, dark-skinned guard materialised by his cell, wielding a large key, which he proceeded to insert into the lock. Quest obligingly stood back. The door swung outwards, and the guard beckoned.

'You can come out. I don't know what's happening, but I think it must be the end of the world; a man deserves to face that with his freedom, not shut in a box until the walls fall on him.'

The man was dark-skinned with golden eyes, a sandman, Quest realised. He made a hasty exit.

'My thanks.' He stood staring up, unable to believe his eyes. '*Avardale*,' he breathed. 'This must be the Avar!'

'What?'

Quest turned to the anxious guard. 'I'm sorry; did you say something?'

The man pointed skywards. 'What is it, and what does it mean? You're a priest; you should know.'

'Know?' Quest shook his head. 'I can only hazard a guess. We *akhal* tell stories to our children about the creature that lives in the lake, but I never believed them until now.'

'All that light – all that brightness – ' The guard's face filled with an expression of awed reverence. 'It can't be bad, can it? Not when it's so bright?'

'In any case, what is there left for it to harm?' Quest asked bitterly. 'My people are dying, and the lake, too. Perhaps this beast has been forced from its home in the deep water by the filth and weed.'

'If it's the end, then I'm glad I've seen this,' the guard said softly. 'I never thought to see anything so glorious.'

'Perhaps, after all, it has come to fight the dark,' Quest

answered, his attention caught by a long shape moving down on the pier by the water. The creature in the skies let out another howling cry, then lowered its head and wings and dived, apparently straight for Wellwater.

'Gods preserve us!' breathed the guard, ducking down.

'There are no gods.' But, as he watched, Quest suddenly wavered in his new certainty. The Lords of Light might not be deities worthy of worship, but this creature of legend was as far beyond his understanding as any god.

'It's coming here.'

Quest recoiled instinctively as the creature dived lower, the fantail of filaments spread about its immense body, each thread speckled along its length with blue-green light. 'This is the source of the evening lights,' he murmured. 'It must be. But how?'

'Who's that on the pier?' The guard paled. 'The creature's going to attack.'

A dreadful screeching came from the flying Avar, and its splendour suddenly dimmed; Quest froze, not knowing why he should suddenly be afraid.

On the end of the pier, the tall figure raised its arms and spread them wide in apparent defiance of the creature hovering overhead, and despite the disparity of size between the opponents, did not look foolish.

All at once the Avar's lights paled, no longer bright stars but only embers, and the skies darkened, and the thunder roared.

The part of his mind which was still Kerron could see a light somewhere in the distance. It was not a very bright light, but it was so much better than the absolute dark surrounding him that he wanted to reach it, no matter how hard the way. He yearned for it, ached for it.

Somewhere outside in the night was the other Kerron, the voice-Kerron who had cast him out, taking possession of what had once been his.

There was a disruption in the pool of obscurity into which he had been cast. Kerron had no body with which to feel, yet he did, in some fashion, sense the waves of upset which spread through the dark, letting in more of the precious gleams of light. He felt suddenly stronger and less helpless. Where was the other Kerron?

'No! This cannot be! This should not have been possible.'

It was odd, but he could hear the words of the voice-Kerron again in his mind, the link between them not entirely severed. Kerron strained his will, trying to force a way back to his body, to his own self, using the light as his focus as if it would show him the way.

'The light will fade into darkness, as it must. Just as those other lights, too, will be put out forever, and there will be no more.'

He was closer. Kerron felt he had reached the place where he had been split in two, his real self and the voice-Kerron; he stretched out with his will and pulled himself painfully back, despite the instant furious protest from the voice. He was close enough now to see what was happening to his other self, even if he could do nothing to influence its actions.

Then the lights dimmed.

He clung to his place, unable to progress any further. He was frightened again, afraid of being cast out once more into the endless dark, and he dared not let go his will by even the smallest amount. He was once again only a spectator, not a player.

The voice-Kerron stood on the end of the pier at Wellwater, robe plastered against its body by the force of the wind and the draught from the powerful wings of the creature that hovered high overhead, screeching down its angry and despairing cries. Even from below, it was possible to see that every part of the creature was composed of light, even the claws and the web of filaments fanned out around the immense body. The eyes glowed gold, giving the Avar's face an implacable directness which had nothing to do with the narrow jaw and jagged teeth. The blue-green stone at the centre of its brow was a circle of perfection, melded to the beast as part of itself, its shape and brightness repeated on a smaller scale throughout the immense body and wings.

Yet as Kerron watched, the stone's light faded, and the beast glowed less strongly, and he was afraid.

The voice-Kerron was angry, terrifyingly angry, with the impatient fury of ravening hunger, as if the creature of light was an enemy preventing it feeding on its chosen prey. Kerron was aware of an utterly inhuman quality of the voice-Kerron, something quite unfamiliar, a force which dwarfed his own puny emotions. His own hates had been as a speck of dust, his own anger a drop of water to this mountain of hate, to this ocean of anger.

As he watched, he thought the voice-Kerron changed, not so much in content as in form. It flung out its arms to ward off the hovering beast of light, a small, incongruous figure that somehow did not look at all ridiculous. Force flowed between the pair, invisible but tangible; the voice-Kerron struggled to absorb the light and destroy it, using its power to feed its own hunger, dispensing in return only utter darkness.

The creature faded further.

'No,' the real Kerron said in his mind. He ached to see the light dim, aware at some intuitive level that his own existence was bound up in the same light. He wondered if there was anything he could do to aid the great beast; but he had only his will, and he needed all of it to cling to his other self, to save him from the ultimate dark.

'*The light will die, and then all things will die,*' cried the voice-Kerron, screaming its determination to the creature. The beast roared back. The two seemed drawn to one another, unable to break apart, locked in a private war.

Kerron caught glimpses of lightning, but they did not seem to be in the sky overhead but came from somewhere else, much further distant, within the same unearthly otherness into which he had been cast. The flashes of light were inflicting damage on the darkness, raising more waves of disruption. Kerron clung to his place.

In the skies overhead, Omigon, the Dark Star, pulsed brightly, shadowing Pharus and Annoin.

'No,' Kerron said in his thoughts. 'No, this is wrong!' He knew it as surely as he had known that the lights in the lake were a force for good, not evil.

For a moment, the creature seemed to glow more strongly, but the voice-Kerron countered instantly with whatever power it possessed, and the light faded once more, becoming all the time weaker than before. Kerron felt his will weaken with it and clung, more tenaciously still, to his precarious perch on the borders of the land of the dark.

There were no gods, he had always known that; but what the voice was, the Avar, he did not begin to understand. Kerron was suddenly overwhelmed by his own insignificance, his existence ephemeral, irrelevant; except that through him this voice-Kerron had entered the world and grown strong, strong enough perhaps to defeat the creature of brightness. His will had become the other's weapon.

'Was that why I was born? To be the means of death? A gateway for evil?' he asked himself.

How had he done it? How had he managed to create so powerful a monster of the darkness as the voice-Kerron? What was it the creature had said to him as it cast him out – that his own hate and anger had fed it, watered it.

What if he gave up that hate? A piercing thought.

His life had been centred on hate. It had been his reason for existing, his reason for entering the Order and rising high within its ranks, his reason for ignoring the plague when it first came to the *akhal* in the north. Hate and anger had given him energy and ambition, something against which to strive and with which to disguise, even from himself, the knowledge that he was alone and that the one person he hated above all was himself. Bellene had disliked him, Ninian had pitied him; Ran alone had accepted him as he was – anger, hate and all the rest.

She had turned on him and betrayed him when he proved himself worse than even she could stomach. In return he had been willing to destroy her, and watch the destruction of all her people. And for what?

For injured pride which would not be healed.

For the hurts of being abandoned; unwanted; alone; different.

For the nature which would not permit him to be satisfied with anything less than coming first, whether in affection, or status, or value: which made his life among the *akhal* intolerable, so that he would rather they ceased to exist than that he should suffer the least humiliation.

For knowing him, as Ran and Affer and Ninian and Quest had known him, as he truly was, not as he wished to believe himself, with all his confusion and loneliness and jealousies. That knowledge alone had been a reason to hate them, far safer than despising himself. Hate was stronger than any soft emotion.

'Your light fades further, creature of the deep water. Soon it will go out and you will die.'

Could he help? Was there anything he could do to aid the creature, more positively than his long refusal to obey the voice's demand to discover and destroy the source of the evening lights? He knew the answer, realised he had known it from the start.

He must let go, not just loosen his will and allow himself to drift back into the land of the dark, but he must loosen his anger and hate, too. Which were the greater part of himself.

The light flickered again, so close to dying that he knew there was no more time.

Kerron felt no more anger; he let loose his hate at will, setting it free to dissolve into nothing in the light.

'Stop! I cast you out! Go back, back into the dark –'

Kerron released his hold on his other self and let himself drift away, back from where he had come, weightless and mindless. The dark was waiting to enfold him, and he was afraid, but he did not resist it; he had given his will to the creature of light and had none left to spare for himself.

For a moment, a series of faces flashed in front of his mind, none familiar to him, the faces of many women and men and children, some dark-skinned, others fair, some *akhal*, all sharp defined flickers of an instant before they were gone. He wondered who they had been, or were, and if they were all, like him, creatures of the light or the dark, engaged in the same battle. But he did not know.

The dark was waiting.

It took him in once more, closing around him in a shroud, and he was afraid, afraid for himself but also that he had been too late, that the creature of light was already dying.

Then the dark exploded, taking him with it, and as he was sent spinning he caught sight once more of the distant lake and the two combatants in a sudden flash of light; and he saw the voice-Kerron fall, and then the flying creature was once more ablaze with blue-green brilliance, and he was content.

He allowed himself to drift in the nothingness.

Whatever the price, it was worth it; it had been enough.

Ninian knelt with Ran's head in her lap.

As the light began to die, so her hope, too, faded, but she did not move, just knelt with a hand on Ran's head, although Ran did not seem aware of her. The light on the island was so faint she could barely see it, only a pale memory of brightness against the dark.

'Oh, Kerron; how did this happen?'

She watched waves of force flowing between the two combatants, the outcome to be the end of a new beginning for her people. She knew it was Kerron who fought for the dark, because she recognised he was a fitting vehicle for destruction, of himself as well as others, for he had always followed his darkest impulses.

The Kerron figure seemed to grow as the light faded, and Ninian knew it was powerful, existing only to swallow the light. She sat, frozen, wondering if it were in any sense her doing that Kerron had become this thing, this creature of destruction, if any word or action of hers could have prevented it. Or was it only arrogance, because she had taken no part in the battle, she had even failed in her duty to perform Arkata's dive, that made her wonder? Was she assuming an importance not rightly hers?

The creature of light was weak, hardly managing to stay aloft. Ninian felt hope dying.

Ran stirred.

'Stay still,' Ninian whispered.

'Why is it so dark?' Ran broke off, coughing.

'Just stay still.'

Ran fell silent again. The light was so faint it was only a patch of pale shadow.

'Please,' Ninian whispered, not knowing quite what she was asking for; 'Please, don't go out. Kerron – '

A flash of lightning made her jump. There came another spark of brilliance, and suddenly the Kerron creature on the pier crumpled and fell, and the flying creature rebounded, powerful wings drawing it upwards, the Avar outlined against the stars with a luminosity to match their own. It gave out a high, triumphant, keening cry and beat its broad wings, blue-green light shining over Lake Avardale. As its brilliance covered the lake, so it seemed to Ninian that a shower of coloured dust, or perhaps specks of light, fell to the waters of the lake, a rain of sparks which briefly touched the surface.

'It's raining light,' Ninian said aloud, lifting a hand to receive the insubstantial shower. Nothing touched her skin, but she was aware of warmth.

The Avar trumpeted again, then wheeled in the air, beating its wings as it flew north. Overhead came another roll of thunder that went on and on. 'Look.' Ran lifted her head slightly. 'Look up, Ninian; the skies are alight with colour, blue-green and red and white and amber and other shades, too. It's a whole rainbow.'

'The Imperial Lights.' Ninian's eyes were suddenly wet with tears.

The Avar was flying high over the far end of the lake. Overhead, Ninian could make out Annoin, Arkata's star, shining brightly, Pharus with a matching brilliance, but Omigon had faded.

'I saw them,' Ran murmured. 'At least I saw them.'

Inland, the image light strengthened, growing in intensity until it seemed to match its partner on the Avar's brow. As the light glowed more brightly still, Ninian began to think she really could make out the cast of a tall woman, holding in the palm of her open hand the dome shape of the lightstone which had been the Tearstone of the *akhal*.

The light from the image Tearstone expanded and rose skywards to join other shafts of colour, and somehow the pattern unfolded to take in the island, with both herself and Ran, so that they were all completely bathed in light.

Ninian at last allowed herself to hope.

Ran had been cold, but the light was warm.

'Kerron,' she whispered, experiencing the ache of loss, but relief, too, that he would suffer no more torment. She could forgive him everything, because the Kerron she cared for was not

316

the one who was guilty of bringing death; that had been the other, the one who lived inside him.

Ran thought perhaps the whole world had changed, or had passed and was no more. It was very still.

The light was so warm, so comforting to her chilled limbs, frozen by her dive to the cold and the pressure of the depths. She remembered the instant of flight from the cliff, the exhilaration as her body shifted from element to element and the physical satisfaction of perfection.

'I was afraid,' she breathed. 'I never understood before how it felt.'

Overhead the lights were fading and separating into their component colours, but Ran was still warmed by the memory of brightness.

'Ninian?'

'Ran?'

'It's all right, let me sit up.'

'Ran?'

There was joy in Ninian's voice, and Ran was touched to the heart, shamed at how little she deserved such affection, feeling oddly new and fragile, as if she had been granted a second life.

The moon was still visible, shining down on the peaceful waters of the lake. Ran bathed in the warm night air, wondering if any of it had happened, or if it had all been a dream.

What she saw told her it had been quite real.

'Ninian,' she whispered. 'Ninian, look. Look at the lake.'

Chapter Sixteen

Dark Fall – Day Twenty-four

The sun, which had long been invisible, first by reason of the fog and subsequently due to a period of incessant rainfall, rose to blue skies; its mere appearance was enough to restore heart to the most pessimistic spirit.

A warm breeze traversed the tower room at Arcady, blowing from the south, bringing with it scents of grass and meadow flowers. A fisher bird let out a cry as it swooped down to the water, its passage marked by the fluttering of wings and the bright blue head denoting its male sex; its mate owned a more sober shade, having no need for display.

Ran turned from an east-facing window, sighing loudly with pleasure and relief, remarking: 'Not everything died, after all.'

'Enough.' Quest stared broodingly to the north, to Sheer Island and its cliff. 'But we can begin again.'

Ninian, seated in Bellene's old place at the table, accounts and lists spread all about in organised disorder, thought that while everything had changed, it was also still very much the same. In Ran's newly sensitive face she could nonetheless read the old yearning to explore the boundaries of her own physical limits. Her cousin was looking moodily towards the mountains and beyond, to Ammon, no matter that she might pretend to observation of the lake. And Quest: he strove, too, with a need to discover something to take the place of the faith he had lost, to fill the spaces in his mind and heart.

'We can begin again, but it will be hard work,' she opined at last. 'None of the estates escaped unscathed. We'll all be short handed, and it'll be a struggle to get enough supplies in before the winter. We've nothing left in our stores here at Arcady.'

'Is that all you can think about?' Ran turned back to her distant view with an impatient gesture. 'Just work? What about everything that happened, that might happen?'

'But we don't know, or can't foresee, such things,' Ninian said quietly, curbing her annoyance at the unjust criticism. 'It's my duty to care for the people left at Arcady. I have to think of food and drink and wood and fuel and candles.'

'I suppose so.' But the restless movement of her hands betrayed a lack of interest in such concerns.

'I think Ran's right,' Sarai put in from her perch, a high stool beside her mother. Her face was pale and strained, and she looked uncomfortably older, not so much a child any more. Ninian was sad at the alteration, but no one had passed unscathed through the plague.

'Do you?' she asked quizzically. 'So you think me very boring to sit here and try to form a plan to feed us over the next year. But someone has to do it, Sarai.'

'But why you? You were *there* when it happened,' she said importantly. 'You saw it all.'

'Did I?' Ninian shook her head. 'No, I don't think so. I think what happened here, over the lake, was only our small part of the battle. I think somewhere else in the Empire there are other peoples who have won or lost, and sit counting the cost.' A catch came into her voice as she thought of all the dead of Arcady.

'I should like to go and see,' Sarai said, scowling, perhaps recalling those of her friends she would never see again. 'Like Ran.'

'Would you? Then I think I had better tell you all something I've decided.' Ninian looked across to Quest, hoping he would support her. 'I have to name my heir; you may think it premature, but it's foolish to let these matters slip until it's too late. I've decided to name Amori as my successor; she's shown herself strong and dependable in these past weeks.' She put a hand on Sarai's head. 'You're too young, Sarai, and I don't think at the moment you feel that unquestioning bond of duty to Arcady you must to be its Steward.'

Her daughter's face took on a look of bitter rejection. 'Because you don't trust me.'

'No; not because I don't trust you, but because I don't want you to have the burden of Arcady on you as you grow up,' Ninian answered, keeping her tone even. 'You said you'd like to go and see something of the Empire, like Ran; I don't see why you shouldn't. But if you were my heir you'd have to stay here and learn how the estate is run, and all the other tasks which are the duty of the Steward. Perhaps, when you're older, if you change your mind, then we can think again; but for now I have made my decision.'

Sarai's expression was set in angry lines, but Quest intervened before she could make any suitable, or unsuitable, observation.

'Then perhaps you'll have time to help me, Sarai; I want to explore the island, and learn everything I can about it, and about the temple which once stood there.' His eyes lit with enthusiasm. 'Now Bellene is dead and her memories with her, we know so little about that period of the past; but you've records here, and we've some at Kandria, too. There's so much I'd like to know about the time before the Order came.'

'Why do you want me to help?' Sarai sounded suspicious.

'To stop me making any more mistakes.' The smile was a mirror of Sarai's own, wary, fearful of rejection. 'If you want to, of course?'

Ninian breathed more easily, seeing the beginnings of a new and happier relationship between the pair. 'What about the guard and priests left at Wellwater?' she asked. 'What will they do now?'

Quest shrugged. 'Who knows? With Kerron dead, there's no one in command. I think they'll wait for orders from the capital, and they may wait some time if what the Plainsman Carrol says is right. I imagine Lord Quorden has more to think about than the Wetlands, with a full-scale revolt on his hands.'

'Will you go across and give them some direction?'

'I don't think anyone will stir unless they have to; when I left they were busy locking the gates behind me, and finding they didn't close properly!'

'So you think the time of the Order at Wellwater has come to a close.' Ninian nodded, thinking. 'I hope you're right.'

'I don't think anything will stay the same.'

'So we should be left in peace to begin again. That's what it is, isn't it? A new beginning.' Ninian looked down at the table, knowing how much work awaited her, how much organisation of essential labour was required to restore Arcady to anything like its customary condition: 'It's hard to believe.' She lifted her head and smiled at Ran, looking past her to the waters of the lake beyond the window. 'It all seems impossible to believe,' she added softly.

White clouds skittered across the sky, momentarily obscuring the sun, playing games with its shadow. Sunlight gleamed on the surface of the lake, which rippled gently in flashes of gold above the deeper blue-green of the water, no longer weed-bound but clear and pure. How had it happened? Ninian thought they might never know, or never understand, what quality of the light had purified water which had been so rank and defiled. It looked much as it always had, except that its usual denizens were in short supply. It would be years before fish and reed stocks could be built up again.

'That was our last chance, wasn't it?' Ran asked from her place, not turning round, but Ninian guessed from the tremor in her voice that she was remembering her dive. 'Arkata's horn is gone, and we've nothing else.'

'I think we need to put something there, not rely on a miracle to save us a second – or is it a third? – time.' Ninian glanced at the place on the wall where the plain horn had hung, struggling to express her certainty. 'We let this happen, all of us, and not just because we failed to keep our side of the bargain that Arkata made, that all our ancestors made in the long-ago past – if it was all true. We let the weed in, and we let ourselves be separated by distance from other *akhal*, and the rest of the Empire, leaving external communication and politics to the priests. It's too easy to blame the Order alone, or Kerron, and forget we all did our share, paying too much heed close to home and not enough beyond our immediate bounds.'

'Not you, Ninian.' Quest gave her a rueful smile.

'Me as well as the rest of you,' she disagreed, shaking her head. 'I was too engrossed in my own problems to see further than my nose.'

'I want to see if there's something on the island, if we should rebuild the old temple.' Quest looked at Sarai encouragingly. He had abandoned his soutane and reclaimed his *akhal* clothing. 'I saw so much that night that I don't understand, but which must have come from the past. I don't want to make another mistake, but it may be we can find something there, on the island, which we can trust. Some form of power, perhaps. We need to reclaim the truth in our history, not ignore it as only legend.'

'In the old days there were no priests,' Ninian observed, an edge to her voice as she saw the old enthusiasm come into his face. 'Remember that, Quest. There was only a temple; no sacrifices, no sermons, no rituals, but only a place and a stone.'

'I won't forget, Ninian; I don't intend to try to set myself up as leader in a creed of my own making.' He gave an unhappy laugh. 'I've learned enough about myself to know how false that would be. No, if the lights we saw were objects of power, and if there are forces behind the lights which are creatures we could call gods, I think they have a better idea of divinity than I. They're not men, to make fools of themselves with questions of power and hierarchy and gender, to invent terrors and threats of punishment for those who dare have minds of their own. They wouldn't demand I give up my love for my daughter – ' He broke off. Ninian wondered for how long he would continue to reproach himself for past mistakes, and the cynical part of her nature questioned how long it would be before he came to be regarded by the *akhal* as a priest of this new, impossible power.

'And you, Ran? Do you really want to leave us so soon?' she asked, changing the subject before her thoughts could depress her.

Ran left the window and came across to the table. She was thin, but the old fire burned in her eyes, and behind the new overt fragility lay a will of iron.

'I learned something that night; that life is only a moment, and if I don't take hold of it, it will pass me by and leave me mourning.' Ran smiled at Sarai. 'Take heart, little cousin. If you want to come with me when you're older, I'll take you travelling. But now I want to go to the city of Ammon with the Plainsman Carrol and discover what's happening there, and then go east, and on to the ocean to see it for myself.'

'Will you send us word? If you can?' Ninian asked, her brow creasing. 'There may be pedlars coming this way.'

'I wish I was going,' Sarai mumbled under her breath; but the glance she shot her mother suggested it was only an assay.

'And if you reach the ocean in the east, what then?' Ninian wanted to know, experiencing an odd lurch of envy. 'Will you come back?'

Ran gave her a quizzical smile. 'How can I know, Ninian? Who can say what will call to me, what place or mountain? And don't begrudge me this, as you may well do, but think there was a time that night when I believed I was going to die. This is all I've ever wanted. Perhaps I shall get tired of it and want to come home and help you, but I know your generous heart; you won't try to keep me here, as Bellene did.'

'No, I won't,' Ninian agreed, forcing a smile. 'Even if I wanted to, without Affer I've no means.'

Ran hesitated, then looked away. 'You could ask me.'

The offer was so unexpected it brought tears to Ninian's eyes; embarrassed by her rapid change of mood, she gave a laugh. 'I shan't.' She knew she would never ask.

'Then wish me well.'

'I do. Quest?' Ninian asked dryly. 'Will you, too, desert us?'

He shook his head, his attention still partially absorbed by the island. 'There's so much I need to understand. About Kerron and what happened to him, how all this evil came to us, and why we came so close to destruction,' he said intently.'And I should like to know more about the first drought and the Order and its foundation, and the truth about the Barren Lands, and so much more I shall have enough to keep me occupied if I stayed here several lifetimes.'

'Then at least I shall have company.' But Ninian was aware she was speaking essentially to herself, that none of the others would understand.

'I think I want to go for a last swim, before I leave the Wetlands and find there's no water,' Ran remarked generally. 'Sarai, do you want to come with me?'

The girl looked to Ninian for permission, and at her nod slipped from her stool to join Ran. There was a shadow hanging over her, so Ninian thought, the shadow of uncertainty, because her whole life had been a process of being torn between opposing forces. Now, although those forces seemed to have joined, she was still wary and mistrustful, and who could blame her?

None of the children of the *akhal* would be the same now. There were none who had not lost a friend or close kin to the plague. Nor did the miracle of Avar make it easier to bear such loss. There would always be doubts as to why it had not happened sooner, why there had to be so much lost before the cure.

Was it her fault? Had she delayed too long? Ninian would not speculate; she would never know.

'I might come with you.' Quest looked at Ran and Sarai, waiting for their invitation, beaming when it was forthcoming. 'I haven't swum for more than ten years,' he mused. 'Sarai, you had better stay close to me and rescue me if I show signs of drowning.'

Sarai giggled, not quite certain if it was a joke, and Quest made a face at her; reassured, she let him take her hand.

'Go on, all of you; I've a lot to do this morning, better without distractions.' Ninian waved them away, keeping the smile on her face. It was an effort that required a surprising amount of will.

As soon as she was alone, Ninian sank her face in her hands, no longer trying to hide the ache in her heart she knew must remain her secret, and hers alone.

Ran would go to Ammon, and to the eastern ocean, and would see the Empire and its people and be happy. She deserved it, for her dive and for her long patience. Ninian thought she would always remember her cousin's offer to stay at Arcady; although she would miss Ran dreadfully, she was equally glad she had the courage to let her go.

Sarai, too, would leave her, in time. Even now she had lost a small part of her to Quest, and must learn not to resent it, for she had no cause. Sarai had been hers, and hers alone, for a time; but even that was not true, for she did not own her daughter, any more than Quest did.

No, nothing would ever be the same again.

Quest would stay at Avardale, engrossing himself in his studies, for he was the kind of man who must always have a puzzle to absorb his energies, who would rather think than act, but the *akhal* needed him as well as herself. Someone must have time to dream, to write the songs. And if for the moment he was more parasite than labourer, it was only for the moment, and she must conquer all such ungenerous thoughts. All such envious thoughts. They would need an *akhal* like Quest in the hard days ahead to cheer their spirits.

'But what about me?' she asked the empty room, lifting her face from her hands in despair. 'What about me, and what I want?'

She was the centre, the foundation of their dreams. While she performed her duties at Arcady, Ran could travel; Sarai could be free; Quest could occupy himself with the enigma of the stones and the Imperial Lights. That was the bargain she had made, but it seemed that only she understood the true nature of the arrangement; the others took it for granted, just as they believed all she wanted was to stay at Arcady and rebuild it for the next generation, even if she could not in honesty leave it in Steward-ship to her own daughter.

Not one of them had asked her what she wanted.

'And I – I'd like to be free, too, to go with Ran, and see the ocean, and the cities,' she said bitterly. 'And I never shall; not now. When Bellene died, she ended my choice. No – when she chose me, and I agreed to be her heir. I left Arcady once, on that evil pilgrimage, but now I must stay here for the rest of my life.'

She would allow herself this one outburst, this one complaint, and then she would be silent and make herself content with what she had, which was, after all, enough for which to be grateful.

'It was only that once, just once, the cage opened, and showed me what lay beyond the bars, and now there will always be a part of me which cannot be satisfied by the bounds which must be mine.'

The pilgrimage to the Barren Lands had left its mark on them all: on Affer and Kerron who were dead; on Quest; and Ran; and herself and Sarai, who was born because of that pilgrimage. Ninian thought the blighted lands were a place accursed, a part of the darkness which had come to the Wetlands, which had entered Kerron's heart and had fought with first him, then the creature of light, the Avar of Arkata's legend.

Because she had visited the Barren Lands her life had been changed, a barrier which was Sarai set in place between herself and Quest for ten long years, a barrier she doubted would ever fully be brought down.

What was it that had seized them all, in that dark place? What had looked into their hearts and chosen them for the parts they were to play? What demon had taken hold of Kerron, twisting his confusion and loneliness into something more, something malign? What had played on Quest's fears to persuade him to imagine he could cheat death through sublimation with his gods? What had transformed Affer's sensibility into a gaping wound which drew all meaning from his existence?

The temptation she herself had found there was with her still, tantalising her, luring her to forget her duty, to choose her wishes above her commitments. The siren voice spoke to her in tones filled with seductive understanding and compassion.

Ninian slammed her fists down on the table in a sudden revulsion of feeling, furious with herself, refusing to submit to any whisper of the dark.

'But perhaps the Empire will come to me, and even here, at Arcady, we shall see other peoples, and hear the tales of the cities,' she heard herself say, in a voice of pure astonishment, knowing she spoke the truth. 'And perhaps I shall find myself free to go when I hear a call, like Arkata, but to me it won't be the Avar but some other duty that summons. Why should I be so willing to believe the worst, after a night when I saw so much that was better than the best?'

Her depression lifted, and the shadows in her mind took flight, so that she could bend her head once more to the papers, to the lists of stores and necessities, of trading goods and medicinal herbs required, and take heart from her ability to deal with the duties of a Steward.

When at last she raised her head, adding a final stroke of the pen and melting the precious wax for her seal, Ninian let herself gaze out through the unshuttered windows to the north, where the sun shone dazzlingly down from its midday high over the island.

Although the distance was too far for her really to have seen it, in her mind's eye Ninian thought she caught the image of a dome of blue-green light, held out on the open palm of the tall figure of a woman, a woman of the *akhal*, who might have been Arkata, and whose strong features reminded Ninian of Ran. And, still in her mind's eyes, she thought the stone woman became aware of scrutiny, and slowly turned her head to Ninian and bowed gravely to her.

Ninian got to her feet and moved across to the window; feeling not at all foolish, she stood and returned the bow.

There was no foolishness, but only courtesy, one Steward returning the salute of another.